THE
RACE

MICHELE G. CHARRIER

TotalRecall Publications, Inc.
1103 Middlecreek
Friendswood, Texas 77546
281-992-3131 TEL
www.totalrecallpress.com

ISBN: 978-1-59095-388-4
UPC: 6-43977-63886-1

Printed in the United States of America with simultaneous printings in Australia, Canada, and United Kingdom.

FIRST EDITION
1   2   3   4   5   6   7   8   9   10

To Betty Crawford. She invited me into her kitchen for a perfect cup of tea. We chatted about good books, detective stories and English history. In my mind I never left that kitchen.

About the Author

Michele Charrier, former radio broadcaster and communications professional, launched her career as a women's fiction writer while still managing a career, fitness training, and supporting her family. She is an alumnus from Ryerson University and graduated with a degree in Radio and Television Arts. Michele began writing in her late teens and pursued creative writing projects for several years until marriage and family became the priority. A few years ago, she was presented with the ideal opportunity to resume her craft, and The Race is the outcome.

Michele is married to a man who makes her laugh every day, and together they have raised three outgoing girls, who are currently scattered all over the globe. Michele is an avid swimmer, runner, cyclist and xc country skier. Travel is a major interest in her life, and she uses these solo travel adventures to observe and absorb different cultures and landscapes which are woven artfully into her novels. Though a Quebecer by birth, Michele and her husband live in Ottawa, Ontario Canada.

Acknowledgements

I could not, in good conscience, allow this book to be published without acknowledging and thanking the people who supported me through this process.

To my husband, Peter, for being patient and understanding when I shut my office door and refused to talk to him for hours; to my daughters Jacqueline, Elyse, Justine and partner Diana who didn't laugh when I revealed my plans to write a book; to my sister Louise who became my biggest fan and confidence booster; to my friend Carlyn Matz who agreed to travel with me (with some risk) while I immersed myself in the Northern Irish landscape and to Sian Jones for her brilliant suggestions and support.

I would also like to thank Sigrid Macdonald for her consummate editing skills and story-telling insight that allowed me to complete the manuscript and Jenny Dempsey in Bantry for volunteering to be my Irish reader.

Finally, I would like to thank my Clonakilty friends (yes, this community does exist) who introduced me to the West Cork culture, language, and traditional music.

In particular, I would like to acknowledge Maura, David, Mark, Roisin, Michelle and Martin for including me in your circle and daily life in Clona! I was never lonely.

Thank you all.

00:00:01 Transition Zone

The downtown bus sputtered along Avenue du Parc, overflowing with commuters anxious to get home for the long Easter weekend. Maddie St-Laurent stood holding on to the upper handle, looking around for a seat, but all were taken. She hated standing in a crowded bus. It was tiring and uncomfortable. Every time the bus started and stopped, her large body twisted and rocked as she tried to keep her balance, one hand on the rail and the other holding her heavy knapsack.

It was impossible to do anything but stand, sway, and think. Maddie was wearing earplugs, but the music was turned off. Music was too distracting and interfered with her concentration, as she mentally prepared a list of all the things she needed to do for the upcoming Easter dinner. Maddie's staunch Roman Catholic mother Julia would be disappointed with her daughter if she skimped on this annual tradition.

As Maddie concentrated on her to-do list, the bus accelerated through a busy intersection, trying to cross before the light turned red. Suddenly, the bus braked hard, pitching Maddie forward violently, throwing her 180-pound body into the lap of a small, elderly man. The man groaned loudly and his face looked pained, as though he had just been crushed by a cement block. For an instant Maddie sat awkwardly on his skinny legs, unable to move. She tried pulling herself off, but there was nothing to grab onto. Two teenagers standing a few feet away moved in quickly, lifting Maddie up and off the man's lap. Everyone on the bus seemed to be staring, as if to blame her for the incident. Her face turned several shades of deep pink.

'Je m'excuse' Maddie said regretfully, and then switched to English, a habit she had picked up after a lifetime spent in Montreal. 'I am so sorry.' The man smiled meekly and said, looking up and down at Maddie's body, 'Maybe you should sit down.' Now more embarrassed than ever, she responded to the offer by smiling and replying, 'No, I'm perfectly fine standing. But thanks anyway.' She turned away and quickly squeezed herself to the very back of the bus, feeling self-conscious and uncomfortable.

The bus windows were dirty, wet, and smudged with finger prints. In the distorted glass, Maddie could see her reflection well enough: the slightly damp hair pulled back in an attempt at a fashionably messy up-do, the long, wrinkled overcoat covering her wide hips, the flat shoes that had seen better days. She hardly recognized the middle-aged face starring back at her. That morning, she had flown out of her Outremont home to arrive just in time for the early staff meeting, forgetting to apply makeup or comb her hair.

For the next few minutes, Maddie stood, getting increasingly hot and sticky in her long overcoat and trying to avoid the frumpy, overweight and haggard woman staring back at her. *Enough,* she thought, and got off the bus to walk home.

The air felt cool and refreshing on her face. She opened her coat, threw the knapsack on her back, and started walking toward Rue McEachran, where she, her husband Dominique, and their two boys had lived for twenty years. The big, classic home was quiet now, except for the middle-aged couple. The eldest son, Jean-Luc, had left home at 17 to attend military college in St-Jean. He was now working somewhere in western Canada with the Canadian Armed Forces, though Maddie was not sure exactly where, as he constantly moved around. The youngest son, Xavier, was working for an Environmental Engineering company in Alberta.

Maddie walked briskly down Avenue du Parc, trying not to be invisible to the oncoming pedestrians, her mind reviewing the numerous subtle and not-so-subtle reminders that her once lovely face and youthful body were lost in the folds and pudginess of a soon-to-be 50-year-old woman. The half century mark was fast approaching and she was dreading it. Incidents like the one she had just experienced were happening with more regularity, each one cutting a little deeper into her fragile self-confidence. Did she look old enough to require help carrying her groceries? Why did the handsome young office clerk ask her for advice on buying his grandmother a birthday gift? Why did the pharmacist mention the Tuesdays' senior discount? …And what about that guy who had asked her for a cigarette outside the Provi Soir? She never smoked!

When symptoms of the 'change of life' appeared, Maddie worked hard to accept the inevitable and not allow the uncomfortable physical characteristics to rule her life. She approached the change as pragmatically as she did most things: she became knowledgeable about the subject and prepared herself for the side effects. She considered herself luckier than most women, because she had fewer emotional outbursts, the physical symptoms were manageable, and the transition from fertile to barren was mercilessly quick.

But when her monthly cycles finally ended, the transformative effect of menopause had been swift and cruel for Maddie, as it was for many women. She gained 30 lbs seemingly in a matter of weeks, her once shiny dark red hair became dry and brittle, and her youthful and rosy complexion was more red then rosy, amplified by facial lines too numerous to count and a wrinkled forehead. Time and aging had accelerated aggressively, like a time lapse video of a new pair of leather shoes left outdoors for a few days: the shine eroded, the leather cracked and dried out, and the sole inflated with moisture.

In spite of her diligent research and acceptance of the natural aging process, Maddie was not prepared for the impact menopause had on her body. Though she didn't feel any different than she had twenty years earlier, people seemed to be treating her differently, including her husband of twenty-five years.

In her mind, she was still sharp and clever, outgoing, optimistic, and interested in the world around her. She was very good at her job as a French to English translator, and the office authority on complicated medical translations. She embraced new technology, new music, and the modern language. As far as she was concerned, she was still a vibrant, intelligent, and 'youthful' woman who was forever 30 years old - on the inside.

The conflict between the external and internal weighed heavily in her thoughts as she approached the house. The walk had not really helped her mental and emotional state, and it had given her a huge blister.

00:00:45 Swim

At 5:30 pm Saturday night, Maddie was expecting her guests to arrive for Easter dinner. On cue, the doorbell rang and Julia, Maddie's mother, made her entrance. She kissed her daughter curtly on one cheek, and handed her a bottle of sherry.

'You know I like to bring my own drink,' Julia said, as she handed Maddie her coat and the package, then proceeded into the living room and sat down in her usual chair, next to the fireplace. Maddie went to the side board of the dining room, and put the unopened bottle of Spanish Premium Sherry next to six other unopened bottles. She poured a glass of Sherry from a bottle opened a year earlier and handed her mother the petite glass.

'Thank you, dear.' Julia glanced around the big room and noticed the dining room table, festively set for five people. 'The flowers are lovely Madeline; the fresh tulips must have cost a small fortune.'

Maddie nodded to her mother. 'Yes.' She wanted to add, any amount of money to make you happy this evening, Julia.

The doorbell chimed again, and Maddie opened the front door to greet her best friend Sofia, escorted by her mother Camelia.

'You look beautiful as usual, Camelia,' remarked Maddie. At 80 years Old, Camelia was an older version of Sofia, a little shorter than her daughter, and fuller in the hips and breasts, but with the same dark, sultry Latin looks and sensual smile.

'You are too kind to this old lady,' Camelia remarked in her broken English.

'My mother doesn't age,' added Sofia. 'Come Mama, let's have a drink, shall we?'

They walked into the living room to see Julia, sitting in her high-backed chair, sipping her sherry. 'Hello, Camelia. It's been a few years since we've since each other,' Julia added coolly. All three women began exchanging pleasantries, while Maddie sat in the club chair, drinking a glass of red wine and watching.

Maddie was envious of Sofia's relationship with her mother. Camelia knew everything about Sofia's life, including the intimate details of her romantic escapades. Sofia never held anything back from her mother. They were best friends and it had been this way since Sofia was twelve, when her father died. Mother and daughter shared everything, and over the years, their relationship seemed to have gotten stronger – *if that was even possible*, Maddie thought.

She looked at her own mother and wished Julia was the type of mother with whom she could share her innermost secrets and doubts, especially lately. But Julia was not anything like Camelia. She protected herself from any emotional risk by maintaining an invisible metal cage that was securely wrapped around her. Nothing got out and certainly nothing came in. That's the way it had been for the last thirty-eight years, and it was unlikely to ever change. Maddie could never have an intimate conversation with Julia about her troubled marriage or her fear of turning 50.

Dominique eventually made his usual gracious entrance, about twenty minutes later, greeting both Sofia and Camelia with a warm hug and Julia with a cool handshake. Dominique did not hide his disdain for his mother–in-law, and the feeling was quite mutual. Once, in a heated encounter, Julia called her son-in-law an overly attractive dandy who never got his hands dirty. Dominique, in turn, called Julia a sad excuse for a mother. After that exchange, they tolerated each other, but just barely.

Dominique was a striking man, and on that account Julia was not wrong. Tall, over 6 feet, with very dark hair, almost black, large azure eyes, a broad nose, and the whitest teeth possible, Maddie had been smitten the moment she'd spotted him, thirty years before, at a McGill University pub night. She thought he was Quebec's version of Al Pacino, but taller. From that moment, Maddie only had eyes for the charming and seductive francophone, and chased him for months until Dominique finally relented. They had been together ever since, first living together in a tiny walk-up apartment and then, when Dominique finally graduated from medicine at McGill, they moved into their spacious, classic three storey home within walking distance of the Parc Mont-Royal.

At 6:30, everyone sat down for a lavish and well-prepared four-course dinner. Maddie had worked the entire weekend to prepare this French feast, and it showed. The dinner table was impeccably set with her little-used wedding china (a gift from Julia), crisp white table cloth and multiple wine glasses, the larger ones topped with neatly-folded fabric napkins. Maddie served various courses, and all were delicious. Sofia and Camelia praised Maddie for her skills in the kitchen. Julia nodded in agreement, but ate sparingly, enough to say that she was full, but not enough to indicate she really enjoyed the meal.

The guests chatted non-stop throughout dinner. Sofia, in particular, was a natural storyteller, and recounted her latest adventure in South America.

'I'm going back to Brazil in a few weeks to start a new contract. I leave right after your big birthday, Maddie.' Sofia replied, winking at Dominique.

Sofia and Dominique were planning a surprise 50th birthday party for her, and they had invited seventy-five people to celebrate this milestone, at their home, on the day of her birthday. While Maddie had insisted that she wanted to celebrate the mid-century mark with her family and only a few close friends, neither Sofia or Dominique had paid any attention to Maddie's wishes. While it was supposed to be a surprise, Maddie had found out about the party anyway, and reluctantly went along with the ruse.

'And you, Maddie, what have you been up too lately?' asked Camelia.

'Not much. Now that Xavier finally sorted himself out and finished his degree, I've gone back to work more or less regularly. I'm working four days a week now, and it's keeping my translation skills sharp,' Maddie replied.

'And where are Jean-Luc and Xavier these days?'

'As you know, Jean-Luc is in the Army. I'm not sure where he is right now, to be honest. He moves around quite a bit. Deployment to parts unknown is a consequence of military life. He calls home often, though. As far as Xavier is concerned, he moved to Calgary and is working for a big company doing investments and acquisition, I believe. I call him but he's always busy…or with his girlfriend.'

'I'm glad to hear that Xavier is more settled. You must miss your boys Maddie,' Camelia responded, 'but I am sure you are keeping yourself busy with other things?'

'Oh yes. I'm on this year's organizing committee for our annual

'Women of the Hospital' Fundraiser, which is just before my birthday.'

'What are you raising money for this year?' Sofia asked.

'The Brain Injury Association.'

'That's an interesting choice,' Camelia replied.

'It's the first time they received money from us. Well, every year, the local non-profit organizations that work hand in hand with the hospital submit a proposal for financial support. We have to pick a new one every year, based on the strength of their proposal. The BIA's proposal was the most compelling of the bunch!' Maddie smiled, thinking about the hours she spent reading each proposal carefully and thoroughly. She was looking forward to reading the paper on the Association's research into PTSD.

'...and what are you wearing to this event, Maddie? I'm sure you could wear any old dress and it would still look amazing on you,' Camelia added thoughtfully in her accented English.

'That's sweet, Camelia. I don't know what I'm wearing yet, I'll have to go shopping soon to find an outfit,' Maddie replied.

'I'll come with you,' Sofia piped in, adding, 'you know how I love to shop!'

Maddie appreciated Sofia's offer to go shopping, and she enjoyed spending time with her best friend, but she preferred to go shopping alone. Sofia's taste in clothes suited her race-horse physique: body-hugging dresses with plunging necklines and high slits. Maddie was much too self-conscious about her weight to be shopping with friends, especially a skinny one.

'I'm not sure when I'm going, but I will let you know,' Maddie answered diplomatically. 'How about some dessert now.... I've made your favorite. Julia, lemon meringue pie. Not French, I know, but it works with Easter!'

Maddie struggled with baking, especially pie crust, but she knew from her childhood memories that this was one indulgence her mother truly liked to eat. It had taken Maddie two tries and a full pound of butter before she finally got the pie crusts just right. She returned from the kitchen with a perfect pie, the crust flaky and tender and the meringue the color of toasted almonds.

'It's very good, Maddie, but you know, it's full of calories,' Julia commented, taking a small bite of the wedge.

'Oh, come on, a few calories won't hurt once in a while…' Maddie replied.

'I wasn't talking about myself,' Julia responded, without thinking.

Maddie put her fork down and sat very still. She was too embarrassed to look up from the plate and just stared at her pie wedge, her face flushed from Julia's stinging comment. Sofia looked at Maddie from across the table and could sense every painful fiber coming from her best friend, the humiliation of being publicly shamed by her own mother incomprehensible.

'Julia, for heaven's sakes…' Dominique started to say, but stopped mid-sentence. He was not interested in getting into a confrontation with his miserable mother-in-law and used Julia's jab as an excuse to leave the table. 'I have an early morning. Goodnight, Sofia and Camelia.'

Sofia was visibly angry at Dominique's swift departure from the dinner table. Maddie's humiliation by her mother was bad enough, but Dominique's refusal to stand by his wife only made it worse. Sofia wanted to say something nasty to Julia, but Maddie shook her head as if to say, *Don't, it's not worth it.* Instead, Sofia got up from the table and hugged her friend tightly, whispering, 'We'll talk soon.'

Julia was the last to leave the house. She stood in the foyer, waiting for the taxi to arrive and take her to her home in Westmount. Julia never learned to drive and relied heavily on Maddie to act as her part-time chauffeur. Tonight though, Maddie declined to drive her mother home. She had had too much to drink, she said. Julia would have to take a cab.

The lights of the taxi cab lit up the dark foyer. Julia opened the door to leave, but hesitated. She looked up at her daughter, who towered above her small frame, and opened her mouth to say something. For a brief moment, Maddie thought that Julia was going to apologize for her earlier comment, the comment that put a swift end to the dinner party. Julia simply said, 'Call me tomorrow. I need groceries.'

*****

Later that evening, Maddie was ready to crawl into the thick cotton sheets of her bed. She was emotionally drained from the last few hours and wanted nothing more than to fall into a deep, unconscious sleep. She was pleasantly surprised to see Dominique sitting up in bed reading when she walked into the master bedroom.

'I was not expecting you to be awake...don't you have an early morning?' Maddie asked as she undressed in the privacy of the walk-in closet.

'Yes, but not that early,' replied Dominique. His voice sounded hopeful, Maddie thought; maybe she could salvage something from the evening. Perhaps he was feeling remorseful about not defending his wife at dinner.

It had been a very long time since she and Dominique had been intimate.

The had once enjoyed an active sex life. Regular and satisfying sex was an important part of their marriage. After the kids were born, sex was less frequent but more intense – short and impassioned sexual interludes in the middle of the day while the boys were out and Dominique had a few hours in between surgical procedures. Maddie lived for these spontaneous moments. It reminded her of when they were both at university and on-demand sex was a foundation of their relationship.

When menopause took over Maddie's body, it also took control of her sex life. She was dry as chalk and her lustful sex drive all but disappeared. When Maddie did feel an urge to have intercourse, the dryness made it painful. Maddie also became self-conscious about her body, hiding under the sheets and undressing in the dark, so Dominique would not notice the weight gain and the slackness of her skin. She refused to be naked in front of the man she had known intimately for decades. After a few months of unpleasant and self-conscious sex, Maddie stopped offering and Dominique stopped asking. This became the new normal in the marriage.

At first, Maddie was optimistic about the future of her marriage, assuring herself this lapse in their sex life was a temporary consequence of menopause. *We'll get it back, and I'll start feeling better about myself,* Maddie thought, *once the boys move out.* When the boys did finally move out, the couple's sex life did not show any signs of returning to normal. In fact, the relationship took a downward spin. Dominique was rarely home, spending seventy hours a week at the hospital. When he did show up late in the evening, he either went straight to bed or fell asleep on the couch watching the news and completely ignoring his wife. Maddie tried to get his attention, but he continued to ignore her. Her self-esteem eroded with every small gesture of rejection.

'Did you enjoy the dinner…' Maddie asked Dominique, trying to get a sense of his mood.

'It was great. You've always been an amazing cook,' he replied.

Maddie snuggled into bed next to Dominique and looked at him longingly. Instead of stroking her full breasts as he usually did when something was about to start, Dominique leaned over, kissed Maddie on the forehead, patted her red head like he would an obedient dog, and promptly rolled over and went to sleep.

00:01:30

Unable to put off the dreaded shopping trip any longer, Maddie wandered into the Carrefour Laval Shopping Mall a few days before the Hospital Fundraiser, looking for a suitable outfit to wear for her upcoming social events. Maddie loathed clothes shopping, and she rarely attended big parties, but given her social obligations, she had no choice but to be suitably dressed. She did not call Sofia to join her on this unpleasant chore. Sofia would likely have suggested they go downtown and stroll along busy St-Catherine Street and visit some hip new stores, or spend time at La Maison Simard, the famous Montreal department store that was a magnet for the Montreal socialite. The Mall was considerably safer. It was out of reach of Maddie's work and social circle and it was highly unlikely she would run into Sofia or anyone else she knew.

Maddie walked through the Mall for over two hours, searching for an outfit that was fashionable, age appropriate, and would fit her generous frame. It was busy for a week night. The weather was unseasonably warm for mid-April and shoppers were anxious to exchange their heavy clothes for a new summer wardrobe.

As Maddie had anticipated, the shopping trip was a waste of time. There were dozens of retail clothing stores in the Mall, each showcasing a slew of beautiful, sexy outfits. This was Montreal after all, and the young city women had a global reputation for being impeccably dressed, no matter what the occasion. There were lots of outfits and dresses to choose from in the Mall--if you were thin and young. None of the clothes displayed in the store windows would be appropriate for an overweight, middle-aged woman with big breasts and thick arms.

*****

Maddie sat down on a bench to rest her aching feet and to reconsider her options. She was tired and extremely discouraged with outcome of her shopping experience.

It didn't help that the retail stores were disproportionately geared toward the youth market, Maddie noted, but the Mall was filled mostly with women over 50. They all seemed to share similar characteristics:

overweight, enormous breasts, dull haircuts, and thick ankles. Maddie glanced over to the crowded coffee bar. A scattering of middle-aged women were sitting at the small café tables, sipping their herbal tea and eating muffins. They blended so perfectly into the non-descript furniture that they were almost invisible. Maddie looked down at her swollen feet. *Is this where I am heading,* she thought, *spending the next chapter of my life drinking tea alone?*

Maddie watched a very old, diminutive woman with a cane shuffle into a book store at the speed of a snail. As tiny as she was, she caught the attention of several people who graciously offered to help her with her purchases. She was the cutest little thing, clutching a square black purse and smiling to everyone with sparkling eyes, enjoying the attention. When you're that old, Maddie thought, people treat you like an endangered species.

There was no such luck for women over 50. Neither cute, vulnerable or desirable, middle age women are caught between two polarized generations - the hot and sexy years when the body is firm and husbands lust after their wives, and the very old years when the body is worn out and sitting in a chair looking out of a window is a perfectly fine way to spend an afternoon. Between menopause and 80 are the invisible years when women lose the youthful glow and the toned body, yet they still want to be noticed, appreciated, and desired. This was cruel and unusual punishment for a woman who had spent twenty-five years diligently looking after her family.

Maddie glanced at her reflection in the store window and winced again at the woman staring back her. She looked just like all the rest of the middle-aged women in the Mall. She was wearing leggings and a long baggy shirt that was long enough to cover her hips and wide enough to minimize the E-cup breasts. Her hair was tied back in a tight ponytail, and she was wearing boring flat shoes. This was the uniform that was thrust upon her aging body. Any resemblance to the formerly curvy and youthful Madeline St-Laurent was buried under rolls of fat. Her face was puffy from lack of sleep, eating and drinking heavily, and ignoring her body's need to exercise. Her once slim and curvy hips were wide and thick. There was fat in places she didn't think were possible, along her upper back and neck. Her once extraordinarily slim ankles, toned calves, and thigh muscles had all but disappeared under a layer of tapioca pudding. Why had she been so blind to this change?

The transformation had been rapid, Maddie was reminded. After the boys left the family home, she fell into a progressively dangerous daily routine of self-neglect. Once an early bird, Maddie started getting up later in the morning. She didn't bother getting dressed or wearing make-up during the day, as there was no one around the house to notice. Maddie was a 'big girl', as her mother liked to say, with broad shoulders, full breasts and curvy hips. She had always carried her above-average size well, paying close attention to her daily food consumption and being careful not to gain more than 5 pounds at any time. Now, her new stay-at-home work habits meant she ate sporadically, often relying on easy fast food that was less than nutritious. She drank too much coffee, and in the evenings, she sat alone drinking wine, something she rarely did when she was a busy mom. Maddie never thought about exercising, though she had been physically active until her early 40s. She intentionally avoided the full-length mirror and the bathroom scale. She both ignored and dismissed the signs that a series of events were conspiring to work against her as she slipped into a pattern of personal neglect.

The physiological consequences of menopause were out of her control, but everything else that happened in the last few years was her own fault, including Dominique's neglect. Maddie could easily list twenty-five reasons why she was too busy to look after herself, but the facts were glaringly obvious. Sitting on the hard bench at the Mall, resting her tired body and starring at her fat ankles, Maddie came to the unpleasant realization that she and she alone was the master of her own unhappiness.

'*I deserve it*,' she said, getting up from the bench and heading home. Enough shopping for the day. She would have to make do with something in her limited wardrobe.

00:02:45

The Hospital Fundraiser luncheon was held in the Oval Ballroom of the iconic Ritz Carleton Hotel in downtown Montreal. The fundraiser was a popular annual event, raising thousands of dollars for a charity or needy organization. The organizing committee members rotated every year to give all the women affiliated with the hospital an equal chance to volunteer their time. It was a privilege to be asked to work on the event, and people signed up every year to volunteer. This year, it was Maddie's turn, and she was happy to use her exceptional organizational skills for a greater good. She was appointed as member of the Executive Committee and responsible for ticket sales. Like almost everything else she did, Maddie worked diligently to ensure a sellout crowd. She was so good at this task, she volunteered to help in other areas. Maddie was genuinely liked by all the volunteers and she got along well with most of them, with the exception of Jasmine LaPointe, wife of Dr. E. LaPointe from Thoracic Medicine.

The petite, attractive blonde with the perfectly-proportioned figure irked Maddie to no end. She and her small entourage of snickering friends would walk into a Committee meeting deliberately late, dressed identically in either white or black, carrying their Chanel and Louis V. bags. Instead of working and contributing to the enormous work load, they would sit shoulder to perfect shoulder and exchange the latest gossip. Jasmine represented everything Maddie disliked about society's fixation on youthful perfection. Her unmovable facial muscles never betrayed an inch of emotion; her lips were a perfectly exaggerated pout, her forehead as smooth as a baby bottom. She was more of a living statue than a human being, thanks to copious amounts of Botox and cosmetic surgery.

In spite of her discomfort with the woman, Maddie was cordial toward Jasmine until the woman's hypocritical attitude started having a negative impact on some of the volunteers and the committee as a whole. Jasmine was haughty and condescending toward the women whom she deemed beneath her. She made other women feel uncomfortable, especially those who did not measure up to her perfect standards of beauty, and she did so deliberately. Several times, Maddie heard Jasmine make a nasty slur behind the back of an unsuspecting victim.

Jasmine, for her part, tried to stay clear of Maddie. She was deeply intimidated by the big, strong woman who was easily twice her size, whom everyone else on the Committee not only liked, but respected. Compared to Jasmine, Maddie was well-liked by all, resourceful, hardworking, the perfect volunteer who could always be counted on to get the job done.

The Executive Committee members were expected to sit together at the banquet table during the fundraiser event. Maddie sat next to Debra, a sweet and very plump woman in her sixties who had retired from nursing five years earlier. Across from Maddie sat Jasmine and her gossip partner, Lenora. Jasmine, as usual, was dressed in an expensive white silk dress that hugged her perky breasts and trim waist. *Only skinny women can wear white*, Maddie thought, looking down at her sensible black suit and white shirt. Her feet were killing her, but she avoided the temptation to kick off her plain black pumps.

The luncheon preamble dragged on far too long. The speeches were long and numerous, but finally, a cheque for $50,000 was awarded to the Brain Injury Association to support long-term research into mental health issues associated with traumatic brain injuries.

Finally, the speeches ended and the waiters began circulating the food. Everyone stopped talking and started eating, except for Jasmine. Lenora made the mistake of commenting on Jasmine's lack of appetite. If the woman had kept her mouth shut, none of the events that followed would have happened, Maddie recalled later that evening.

'Jasmine, you're not eating?' asked Lenora.

'No, I'm not really hungry,' replied Jasmine.

'It's really good,' Debra said, stuffing a big piece of steak into her mouth.

'I don't care much for fat,' replied Jasmine, picking up a piece of red meat and grimacing at it with disgust. 'I have to watch my weight.'

Maddie was irritated by Jasmine's insipid comments, which were clearly directed toward her overweight friend Debra. 'She is only saying this so that everyone at this table will tell her how amazingly slim she is, and compliment her excessively,' Maddie muttered quietly to Debra under her breath, trying to take the sting out of Jasmine's snippy remark.

'Maddie, did you say something?' Jasmine asked, having overheard a word or two of Maddie's comment.

The tall redhead could feel the heat rising in her cheeks, as everyone at the table looked at her anxiously to see how she would react.

She hesitated a moment before saying anything. She could feel the slow simmer inside her stomach and knew that pursuing any further discussion with Jasmine would lead to an unpleasant confrontation. Maddie was known to explode from time to time, a consequence of being a redhead, or so she had been told. While she could simmer for hours with loathing and anger, once an invisible line was crossed, there was no turning back. She stared at Jasmine with sharp amber eyes.

'Yes, well, maybe you should spend more time 'watching' what you say, instead of watching what you eat?' Maddie replied in a clear voice.

An uncomfortable silence permeated the banquet table. Maddie had thrown the first punch and everyone was waiting for a response from the diminutive blonde.

'What does that mean?' asked Jasmine, her turned up nose looking a little sharper, her voice sounding shrill.

'Let me explain this to you with words you can understand…not everyone at this table is obsessed with being unnaturally thin,' replied Maddie with some satisfaction.

'Well, I think,' Jasmine continued nervously, staring at Maddie and knowing that the entire table was riveted to her words, 'if more women paid attention to what they put in their mouths, their husbands would not be fooling around on them.'

A collected gasp was heard around the table. Jasmine had delivered a hurtful blow about Maddie's weight with the strategic precision of an aerial bomb.

'Maddie, just leave it alone…she's not worth fighting with,' whispered Debra, pulling at Maddie's arm, afraid of what the redhead would do next.

Maddie did not hear a word Debra had said. Her anger and frustration from the past several weeks funnelled into one sharp point. The internal simmer was now a raging boil. Jasmine made the unfortunate mistake of crossing Maddie's invisible line of tolerance.

Without thinking, Maddie stood up from the table and walked slowly around to the other side, a glass of red wine in her hand. Jasmine stood up to confront Maddie, her wrinkle-free mask was tinged with a smug grin. Maddie's large and overpowering presence dwarfed the diminutive blonde.

Jasmine starred at Maddie with the same condescending smirk as she had had all afternoon. 'Lost for words, Maddie?' Jasmine asked sarcastically.

'Sometimes, Jasmine, actions speak louder than words,' Maddie replied coolly. She took her glass of red wine and dumped it over Jasmine's blond head, the trickle of red liquid flowing down her platinum hair and onto her pure white silk dress. Jasmine, for once, was speechless, her arm raised in suspended animation.

'Send Dominique the dry-cleaning bill.... I'll make sure he pays it,' Maddie said as she put the empty glass back on the table, turned around and walked out of the ballroom, tall, proud, and shaking. She muttered to no one in particular, 'I'm sure there are a few people in this room who won't be attending my birthday party, after all.'

Maddie left the hotel quickly and took a taxi home. Curiously, she was not upset or embarrassed about what had just transpired, but rather, she felt a sense of relief that she had acted according to her true instincts. It was a bold act and it took confidence to pull it off. The very public display of retribution may have been impetuous and ill-advised, considering the audience, but she was delighted in the fact that she got the last word.

Maddie was sitting in the living room, reading the news on her laptop, when Dominique arrived home later in the evening, visibly upset. 'Why did you do it?' Dominique asked, trying to control his anger.

'Hi Dominique, how was your day?' Maddie replied sarcastically.

Dominique shook his head in disgust.

'What is wrong with you these days, Maddie... someone makes a stupid, shallow, and completely false comment, and you react by having a temper tantrum? You know you have a bad temper!'

'I don't have a bad temper Dominique, I have an explosive temper...and the little witch deserved it. She's been trying to provoke me for months,' Maddie replied, calmly.

'This type of behaviour could cost you a law suit, and maybe my job. Did you think about that as you poured red wine on the woman's head?' Dominique added angrily.

'Oh please, Dominique. She wouldn't dare. There were plenty of witnesses who would come to my defence and attest that she provoked me...'

Dominique shook his head and walked away.

'Dominique, come on. Let's talk about this...'

Dominique left the room, unwilling to take the conversation any further.

00:04:15

A brief but noisy thunderstorm, followed by a downpour, sent everyone running to the giant tent set up in the backyard, but otherwise, Maddie's 50th birthday party was a success. Seventy people showed up with funny birthday gifts aimed at embarrassing the birthday girl. There were humorous speeches and stories about Maddie's life and her particular idiosyncrasies, including her penchant for red wine, in a glass or on someone's head. Debra was at the party and amused the guests with her descriptive account of what actually happened during that infamous afternoon at the Ritz, calling it an episode out of "Real Housewives of Montreal". Maddie's bold and impulsive move was hotly discussed, lauded by some and criticised by others. Regardless of their point of view, the guests were treated to a lively and memorable birthday party.

Shortly after midnight, the last guest left the house. Only Maddie and Sofia remained to clean up the mess. Dominique had already slipped off to bed, pleading early morning surgery. Maddie began cleaning up while Sofia plopped herself down on the couch, kicked off her stilettos, and poured herself a tall glass of wine.

'Maddie, come on, you can do that in the morning. Come sit with me and have a glass of wine.'

Sofia poured another glass of wine and handed it to Maddie.

'That was quite the stunt you pulled off the other day, at the luncheon. It was *the* topic of conversation this evening. It reminds me of something you would have done when we were students,' Sofia remarked.

Maddie could only laugh. 'Well, you know my temper...and besides, someone had to shut her up.'

'I do know your temper, Maddie, and it can be explosive, but only if and when you've been seriously provoked. That incident was not about the blonde loud-mouth, I suspect, it was about something much deeper. Yes?' Sofia asked, getting straight to the point.

Maddie could feel the emotional tension rising to her throat. If she started talking about her sadness, she would start crying uncontrollably. Instead, she took a deep breath and tried to compose herself. Sofia was her very best friend and they were as close as twin sisters. They shared almost everything from the time they could sit upright, and were inseparable through childhood and university.

'It's hard to hide anything from you…' Maddie replied, waving her hands in the air to gain some composure.

'What's going on, Maddie? You haven't been yourself for some time,' Sofia asked.

'The short version? My marriage is crumbling. I hate turning 50. I feel like my life is over. I am so confused right now…' Maddie took another deep breath before continuing to stream her feelings of inadequacy.

'You are right about my temper. I did that because a small part of me was jealous, jealous of that woman's tiny little figure and perfectly turned-up nose. She made me and everyone else at that table feel fat and unattractive. The sad truth is, she's right. Look at me! Every time I look in the mirror, I cringe. I don't recognize the person starring back at me. God, Sofia, I used to be hot and sexy like that woman, now…now I'm the furthest thing from sexy. There's not a shred of sexiness to admire on this body.'

'You are far from unattractive. You are still a beautiful woman, Maddie,' Sofia replied tenderly.

'Yes, well, Dominique doesn't think so.'

'Do you still love Dominique?

'Yes, I do, very much, and I still want to be married to him. When I was younger and raising my active boys, I would dream about this time in our lives…kids gone, the freedom to do what we wanted to do and the money to do it. It certainly has not turned out that way. This is far from my ideal of middle-aged life'.

'Do you think Dominique is having an affair, as that woman suggested?'

Dominique's rumored infidelity was a subject Maddie had tirelessly pushed out of her mind. It was too painful to contemplate. Now, sitting here with Sofia, Maddie could not ignore the question or the obvious signs: he was never home, he ignored her when he was home, and the rumors were rife that he was carrying on with another woman, mostly likely someone many years younger and many pounds lighter.

'Yes, I think he is having an affair. Or something sexual, casual or intense, I don't know. He's not with me, either physically or emotionally.'

'I'm so sorry, Maddie.'

'It really shouldn't have come as a complete surprise, especially to me,' Maddie continued, a few big tears trickling down her cheeks. 'We went through a period of time when I couldn't really have intercourse; it was painful. You know how sex was a big part our relationship. Maybe it took too much of a dominant place, because now that it's gone, so is our relationship. I can't believe I've only just realized this…'

'What do you want, Maddie? Do you want to try and save your marriage?' Sofia asked thoughtfully.

'Yes, I think so. I'm willing to try. I don't know if Dominique is, though.'

'What if the relationship can't be saved? What if Dominique stubbornly refuses to make an effort?'

'I honestly don't know. I don't know if I can or want to start over on my own…you know, I've never seen myself as a risk taker. I may have the occasional spontaneous moment, but as a general rule I like stability, routine, and familiarization. It's scary to think about moving out, starting over, changing my lifestyle. I am pretty sure I could live in a comfortable rut for years.'

'Well, I think you are more adventurous then you realize or give yourself credit for. In any event, stop thinking about a life without Dominique. Start thinking about a new and adventurous life for yourself.'

''I'm not sure I follow you…?' Maddie asked, unsure of where Sofia was going.

Sofia stopped talking for a moment and sipped her wine. Maddie's head was down, looking at the carpet, uncomfortable and yet relieved that she could finally admit the unpleasant truths about her sad life.

'Maddie, we are both 50 years old. Realistically, we have maybe thirty good years left before our bodies and maybe our minds really start to decay. We should make the most of the next thirty years, because we can't see into the future. We could end up with a life-threatening illness next week, or we could fall in love with a mysterious stranger next year.'

Sofia took Maddie's hand.

'Do you remember the first time we watched the *Wizard of Oz*? We were what, six, seven years old? There is one scene in that movie that has always stuck with me. The wicked witch turns over this enormous hourglass and tells Dorothy she only has a short time to give up her red shoes, otherwise she will die. The sand in the hourglass is falling so fast, and Dorothy is paralyzed with fear. The hourglass analogy may be a bit of a cliché, Maddie, but time is not. Time is real, and your life today is just like the sand in that huge hourglass. Listen to me carefully. You're only fifty, not eighty. Your life may be half over, but you're not half-dead. You need to take control and shape your future while your health is good. Figure out what you want that will bring back the confident and self-assured person that I knew years ago. I don't know what you should do or what that looks like - maybe a fitness program, a personal trainer - but find a new passion, inspiration, and motivation, and get going. It's that simple. You need to rediscover who you are. In the process, you may save your marriage, but what's really important is saving yourself…'

*****

Early the next morning, Maddie's restless mind was moving in every direction; sleep was out of the question. She replayed the emotional conversation with Sofia over and over again.

Maddie reluctantly accepted ownership of her problems. Her present situation may not have been entirely her own fault, but only she could turn things around before the hourglass was empty and it was too late to recover. Sofia had wisely suggested that Maddie focus exclusively on herself and let the marriage issue resolve itself over time. This was about her and only her.

She quietly got out of bed so as not to disturb Dominique and started cleaning the house, spending the entire time thinking about where to start her journey. She remembered translating a research paper about Stream of Consciousness journaling, a style of writing that is uninterrupted, unedited, and unstructured. The article claimed it was a useful tool in problem-solving. The research paper was complicated and Maddie couldn't remember the theory attached to it, but she did recall that the process was simple and often worked to help people sort through their innermost challenges and internal conflicts.

Once Maddie was satisfied that the house was in good shape, she sat down in the kitchen with a cup of coffee, a thick notepad, and a pen, and started writing down words, phrases, and places, without paying any attention to grammar, spelling, or format. Whatever popped into her head, she wrote down. She did this exercise for ten furious minutes straight, without trying to make sense of her unconnected and disjointed thought processes. There were hundreds of random thoughts that found their way to the paper.

Afterwards, Maddie reviewed the gibberish and unconnected ideas and, to her surprise, found a very distinct pattern about what was going on in her mind. On a second piece of paper, Maddie connected the words and seemingly random thoughts into specific goals. The first goal was to lose weight. This was obvious from the words that jumped off the page, and she knew, in her heart, that there was no point in going any further if she didn't lose weight. She really didn't need this psychological exercise to tell her that - the rolls of fat on her stomach were a daily reminder. Nonetheless, she persevered with the exercise.

The second item on her list of goals was to get fit. Many of the dozens of words and sentences were connected to sports and fitness, such as *cycling, soccer, weights, swimming, body,* and *muscle.* This was not out of character for her either, though it had been many years since she had played soccer or gone to the gym regularly. Maddie wasn't convinced playing soccer was a good idea at her age, but swimming had some possibilities, and she had been an avid cyclist at one time, cycling through parts of France and Switzerland in her early twenties. She knew going to the gym as a 'fat' person was going to be challenging, but then she remembered that some gyms were 'women only'.

As she continued to read the results of the journaling exercise, several words relating to intimacy jumped off the page: *libido, lust, intimacy, mouth, kiss, pleasure,* and *hand.* Maddie laughed when she saw more words related to intimacy than she did about weight loss. She concluded, with a smile, that that sex would only happen if she lost the weight. She relegated this to goal three. Curiously, she did not included Dominique, and his name never came up in the exercise. She simply wrote out *Resume intimate relations,* and in brackets, she wrote, *Lots of great sex!.*

Maddie interpreted the fourth goal as language-related. Words such as *challenge, Arabic, eastern, spiritual, Farsi, reasoning,* and *educated* seemed to indicate a need to step up her skills. Maddie could speak four languages fluently and she was an excellent French to English translator. Years before, the experienced translator had started to learn Arabic, but gave it up because of the time commitment. Arabic was a challenging language to learn, especially in North America. She put this on her list: *Learn to speak another language.*

The fifth goal was a surprise and could only be interpreted as relating to some type of volunteering activity. Words like *repay, give back, humble* indicated a need to do something altruistic and unselfish. She would fill out the specifics at a later time. For now, it was a reminder that her middle-aged years were also time to give back to society.

The remaining words were a curious mixture of thoughts related to adventure, risk, and spontaneity. It was clearly directed at doing some type of activity out of her comfort zone. Words like *jump, dark, murky, dangerous, unknown, move, try, adventure,* and *scary* indicated a strong desire to try something new. In the last two decades, Maddie's personality shifted from that of a high-spirited and adventurous woman to one who carefully avoided surprises, preferring to plan every aspect of her life and that of her family. This change was thrust upon her as a consequence of being married to a medical student with little to no money, raising two boys and looking after the family home. Risk was simply not an option, nor was making a drastic change to the family's lifestyle. Maddie confidently added 'adventure' as her fifth and final goal, but she was unsure if taking a risk meant a daredevil activity, like skydiving, or dancing naked in the streets of Rio during Carnival. She was confident she would know what to do when the time came.

Once done, Maddie reviewed her list carefully. It was overwhelming and intimidating to read her new goals for the next year out loud. There was so much to do. Maddie considered tearing up the notepad without ever having taken one solid step in a new direction. No, she thought, she had to at least give it a try. She could always attempt the stream of consciousness exercise again in a few months to see if her subconscious mind was moving in another direction.

Maddie started a new page from her notepad, this one entitled 'Action Plan'. This type of planning was typical of Maddie's organization skills, and she jumped into with ease. She approached the Action Plan using the same systematic process as she did with most of her personal, as well as business, projects: she created a checklist of important components that were necessary to start and reach the project goals. She also included a goal date: 12 months hence, so she could plot her progress month to month. She would need to buy a few important items to get started, such as a bicycle, and find out where the closest 'women's only' gym was to her house.

By mid-morning, Maddie's lists were complete, just as Dominique finally got out of bed. Maddie had no immediate plans to share this with Dominique or the boys, but she was going to thank Sofia for her help and tell her to stay tuned. By noon, Dominique had left the house for the hospital. Maddie wasted no time in starting on the first item in her Action Plan: throw out the junk food. She went through every cupboard, every drawer, and the refrigerator, filling three large garbage bags with food that was not lean, low calorie, and healthy. All the leftover party food got thrown into the garbage bag.

Next, Maddie raided her wardrobe. She had three different types of wardrobes: a selection of older 'vintage' outfits, twenty-five years old, that she kept for sentimental reasons; a 'normal' wardrobe that was sized forty pounds lighter then she was at present; and finally her 'oversized' wardrobe, the clothes she was forced to wear due to her large size. She threw everything in the 'oversized' category in a big green bag, with the exception of a few outfits she would need to wear until she lost a sufficient amount of weight to buy a new 'normal' wardrobe. Maddie was now firmly committed to moving forward, and she was already feeling better about her future.

The next item on the list was buying a new bicycle. She had always enjoyed riding a bicycle. Quebec was cycling friendly, and the province boasted thousands of paved bike trails within an hour's drive of Montreal. Cycling was also great introduction to getting fit. Anyone could ride a bicycle, including an overweight middle-aged woman who had not been on a bike saddle for decades.

Maddie spent an hour on the internet looking over the specifications of various bike models. It had been twenty or more years since she'd owned a decent bike, and the technology had changed significantly. Back then, she had been quite knowledgeable about bicycles, and her maintenance skills were the envy of the neighborhood. Today's bike was far more complicated, and the sport specifications were mind numbing. After a lengthy search, Maddie settled on a road bike. She went to the online *Cyclist Buyer's Guide* and thoroughly reviewed the variety of makes and models in line with her experience and goals. She chose three different bike manufacturers. There was a bike shop not far from her house, on St-Denis Street, and they sold two of the three bike manufacturers that looked promising for her needs. Maddie took a quick shower, chose something to wear from her 'oversized' clothes, combed her long dark red hair, and headed to the bike shop to check off one more item on her list.

The young sales clerk who greeted her when she walked into the bike shop was knowledgeable, friendly, well-built, and much too good looking. He spoke English with a strong French accent, even though Maddie made it clear she spoke and understood French very well. Maddie's French was nearly flawless, but most people assumed Maddie was unilingual, based on her Anglo-Celtic coloring. The young man asked Maddie a few questions about her cycling experience and why she wanted a bike, and then proceeded to recommend a few models. He pointed to a few hybrid-recreational models designed for the recreational cyclist or commuter. Maddie politely but firmly told the clerk she wanted a carbon fiber road bike, with a crank size that was designed for hills, electronic shifting, Speed play pedals, Power Meter, and a GPS computer. She also told the young man that her budget was around $6,000. He looked at Maddie, smiled and said, 'You know what you want. I'm impressed.' He switched his sales tactics and got serious.

They spent two hours together reviewing the pros and cons of various reputable bike models. Maddie found his good looks distracting, and she was mortified when he took out a measuring tape for the bike fitting. She was happy he did not ask to her to get on a scale. They agreed on a bike manufacturer and model that was ideally suited for Maddie's' budget and cycling goals. Next, the young man brought out cycling shoes and clothing. Maddie stepped out of the change room to look at herself in the full-length mirror. She thought she looked ridiculous in the tight-fitting spandex shorts that overly accentuated her wide, child-bearing hips, and the matching jersey was glued to her large breasts, but the young sales clerk held a different opinion. He smiled reassuringly and said, 'The fit is perfect, and the color suits you well, Madame.' Maddie turned the same shade of pink as her bike saddle. It had been many years since any man, regardless of age, had flirted with her so openly, even if he was doing it as part of his job.

While Maddie waited for the bike to be adjusted and the special equipment installed, she glanced at the store bulletin board. There were lots of posters and announcements about cycling clubs, cycling tours, and running groups, but one black and white poster caught her eye immediately. The poster was advertising a beginner Triathlon Training Program, for adults only. The summer before, Maddie had watched hundreds of ultra-fit athletes competing at a triathlon event in Mont-Tremblant. She was fascinated by their athleticism, stamina, and endurance. There were also hundreds of participants who didn't look much different than her. She had mused about the possibility of doing a triathlon someday—she had once been a good swimming and cyclist – but dismissed the idea. As she stood staring at the invitation to join the group, waiting for her new bike and armed with a new purpose, she thought, *Why not?* Maddie snapped a photo of the poster with her phone. She would look up the details on their website later, to find out more about the program.

Finally, the bike was ready. The young man rolled the shiny, new, bright green and white bike with the hot pink saddle out to Maddie's car and said warmly, 'Free servicing is included on all our bikes, so please come back in a few months to have this bike adjusted. If you have any questions, ask for me personally. My name is Frederic!'

Maddie thanked the handsome young man with a bright smile and got into her car, thinking she might want to return to the bike shop sooner rather than later.

Around 8 pm that evening, Dominique arrived home. Maddie was sitting at the kitchen counter, reading an article on nutrition.

'There is a green and white bike sitting in the garage that I've never seen before. Who does it belong to?' Dominique asked, without saying hello to his wife.

'Hi Dominique, did you have nice day?' Maddie asked sarcastically, glancing up at her husband of twenty-eight years. His looks never failed to take her breath away even after all this time. Blessed with a lean frame, a robust metabolism, and good skin, Dominique's arresting good looks had only improved over time. The laugh lines and crow's feet added a worldliness to his face. While he was a little heavier now, it suited his tall frame. He still played tennis regularly. He ate whatever he wanted and it never seemed to do any damage.

'The bike is new and it's mine. I bought it today.'

'You bought a bike? You haven't biked in over twenty years.'

'You know what they say, Dominique: you never forget how to ride a bicycle!'

'Why did you buy a bike today?' Dominique asked, seemingly interested in this new acquisition.

Maddie closed her laptop and turned to Dominique. 'Because I want to get back into a regular exercise program, and I've always liked cycling. I am going to commute to the office when I need to, and try and ride at least three times a week.'

'Commute to downtown Montreal? Maddie, that's ridiculous. Montreal drivers are the worst. It's too dangerous.'

'Only if you cycle in traffic,' she answered, refusing to fall into a negative discussion with her husband. The first day of her journey had gone very well, and she didn't want Dominique to spoil her mood. 'There are lots of cycling paths and lanes around Montreal that are safe and well-maintained.'

'Okay, well, it's your life. I just hope I don't find you lying on gurney in the hospital waiting for brain surgery because you've just suffered a horrific accident.' Dominique replied as he opened and closed the kitchen cupboards.

'I'm also going to train for a triathlon,' announced Maddie.

Dominique stopped looking through the cupboards and faced his wife.

'What? Doesn't triathlon involve swimming in open water? I don't understand. You hate the water.'

'I don't hate the water. I like swimming in a pool and, well, there's more to triathlon than swimming.'

'You are full of surprises,' Dominique said, as he continued to search for something to eat.

'…And by the way, what are you looking for?' Maddie asked her husband.

'The leftover party food…I'm starving. Where has all the food gone? The fridge is almost empty.'

'Oh…I threw it out,' Maddie replied, waiting to see Dominique's reaction.

Dominique stared at Maddie in disbelief. 'What? What am I going to eat now?'

Maddie just shrugged her shoulders.

'I'm going to watch the news.' He found an apple and left the kitchen.

So much for spousal support, Maddie remarked to herself.

She opened her notepad with the list of action items. She ticked off five items and smiled. 'Five down and forty-five more to go,' she said out loud. The first day of the second half of her life had gone pretty well. She hoped tomorrow would be as good as today. She turned to her cell phone and sent Sofia a quick text. 'Thanks for the push. I needed it. Got a plan now and will keep you posted.' Within a few seconds, Sofia replied, 'No push – just a gently shove to get you started…I can't wait to hear about your plans, and of course, the results!'

Maddie responded 'K, take care. I love my best friend and I'm looking forward to the next 30 yrs.!'.

00:05:17

Maddie woke up at 5 am. with no compelling reason to be up so early on a swim-free Sunday morning, except that she was wide awake and excessively annoyed. The sumptuous romantic master bedroom was irritating; the clock LED light cast a sickly green glow in the room. The neighbor's cat was whining incessantly outside. Dominique was snoring loudly, oblivious to his wife's discomfort. He had the uncanny ability to fall asleep as soon as his head touched the pillow, and he usually didn't move an inch all night, a skill Maddie both grudgingly admired and resented.

Maddie's journey to turn her life around was one-year old today, the day after her 51st birthday. In the past twelve months, Maddie had not only reached some of her initial goals, she had surpassed them beyond her own high expectations. The weight loss came soon after she started swimming and cycling. Within six months, she'd lost thirty pounds. Maddie joined a triathlon club and signed up to do a long-distance triathlon in Mont-Tremblant, and the race date was only six weeks away. She trained regularly with a group of men and women, mostly younger than herself, and embraced the new sport with energy, enthusiasm, and dedication. The triathlon group was social as well, and they met regularly for a light beer and nutritious pizza after a particularly long day of training. Her schedule was gruelling in the beginning. She was often tired and sore from hours of cycling and running long distances. Over time, though, Maddie improved enough that she was able to keep up reasonably well with the experienced athletes. Her confidence improved with her fitness level, and she delighted in accomplishing an activity purely for her own enjoyment and self-satisfaction. She felt sexy again and thought often about sex regularly, a sure sign that her libido had returned after a long absence.

Maddie got of bed and walked downstairs to the living room, lit only by the amber haze of the outside street lights. She would lie on the couch and wait for the morning sun. She made herself comfortable on the sofa, propping up a few cushions and grabbing a throw. As she lay there, lonely and dejected, Maddie reviewed the evening's events that had ended in crushing disappointment.

She went over every detail carefully in her head. She had thoughtfully planned the evening for weeks. It was going to be her reward for twelve months of the intense, and at times painful, sacrifice to transform her body and her attitude back to the early version of Maddie St-Laurent, the one Dominique had fallen in love with. She was certain that she had made it obvious to Dominique that she was looking forward to celebrating her birthday. She chose her outfit carefully, selecting fitted short black pants, strappy sandals and a body-hugging crisp white shirt that showed off her new toned body. Maddie styled her long, dark red hair for Dominique's benefit. Even though it was her 51st birthday, Maddie insisted that she prepare her own birthday dinner instead of going out to an expensive restaurant and prepared one of Dominique's favorite meals: filet mignon, asparagus, and salad. On the recommendation of the SAQs' in-house sommelier, Maddie bought three bottles of expensive French wine to drink with their meal.

As the evening progressed, Maddie's' desires increased in anticipation of what was to come. They were enjoying themselves. It had been a long time since she heard Dominique laugh and share the latest gossip about the surgical unit he worked in. Maddie listened attentively to his stories; she sat close to him, flirted incessantly, and invited him to touch her as she had done when they first started dating. She could not have been more obvious about her intentions that evening. Maddie did not need to pretend to want her husband. She still found him extremely attractive, with his slightly greying hair and deeper laugh lines. He was as beautiful to her that evening as he had been when they first met. She longed for him to wrap his arms around her like he used to and bury his face in her full breasts.

While Maddie was busy cleaning up the dishes, moving quickly through the process, Dominique slipped away quietly to the basement and promptly fell asleep on the couch. Maddie was devastated. She walked around the house aimlessly for twenty minutes, getting angrier by the second, trying to decide whether to wake Dominique up or put a pillow over his face and smother him to death. Instead of murdering her husband, she took solace in the good wine she had bought for her birthday, drank the entire bottle, and then stumbled into their big, cold bed, very drunk. She thought about self-satisfaction, and tried sexual imagery to induce desire, but her body wanted the real thing, and as hard as she tried, it would not respond to any touching of her own. It had been a lifetime since she'd felt Dominique's slow hand and gentle sensual touches, and the joy of exploring each other's bodies. She craved intimacy, and the lustful abandonment that can only be experienced when you are truly in love and trust your partner implicitly.

The last time they'd had sex, Maddie recalled, was five months previously, a brief and dispassionate interlude in the shower that was less than satisfying.

The lack of intimacy in their marriage was compounded by their deteriorating day-to-day interaction. They passed each other in the kitchen every day, and the only physical contact the couple had was the occasional brush of their shoulders. They acted more like roommates in their big traditional home than a couple married for over two decades. They went to bed at different times, and lately, Dominique preferred to sleep at the hospital when he was working a double or triple shift. Their conversations were usually superficial and short, focusing mostly on mundane subjects and their two boys. Dominique hardly every spoke to Maddie in a meaningful way, and used his heavy work load at the hospital as an excuse to be away from the house. When Dominque was home, he spent most of his time watching the news or working on his laptop. If Dominique was disenchanted with their marriage and wanted a way out, he was not talking about it directly, preferring action over words.

It did not help that Dominique was not overly supportive of Maddie's new interest in training for an endurance race. On the few occasions when Dominique spoke up, he expressed his concern, as a doctor, that pushing the body to physical extremes was harmful to Maddie's health and wellbeing. Maddie vehemently disagreed. The training was helping not hurting her. She looked at least ten years younger. She glowed with self-confidence and purpose and was enormously proud of what she had accomplished. It had been an epic and transformative journey for Maddie. Dominique did remark once or twice that she looked 'good', but added that obsessing about calorie counting and nutrition was just as unhealthy as being fat.

Maddie had embarked on her personal journey primarily to save herself, but secretly she clung to the hope that this physical transformation would also save her crumbling marriage. She knew, or strongly suspected, that Dominique was having an affair, and her efforts to revitalize their relationship and compete with the 'woman' were not working, regardless of how many hours she spent at the gym. The immutable fact was that Dominique no longer loved her and that their marriage of twenty-nine years was beyond salvation. Maddie was, for all intents and purposes, leading a lonely and single life.

00:06:19

'Sorry I'm late. Have you been here awhile?' asked Sofia.

'About twenty minutes. I should know better. You are never on time. You'll be late for your own funeral!!'

Sofia laughed. 'So true! My flight was delayed. I only just arrived in Montreal two hours ago.'

The friends had arranged to meet for drinks and a late-night dinner to celebrate Maddie's 51st birthday, before Sofia flew off to Brazil to meet another new client. Sofia chose Tara's, of course, a very cool retro bar on Laurier avenue with plush cozy seats, a menu featuring old fashioned cocktails, and waiters wearing black aprons and stiff white shirts. The bar was very popular with men and women under 35.

'You look amazing, by the way. That dress really shows how fit you are now!' remarked Sofia.

Maddie smiled. Sofia had followed her best friend's progress over the last twelve months via phone calls, email, texts and the occasional brief chat over coffee. Sofia was aware that Maddie had reached her first two goals, though she had not seen her friend in several weeks and was stunned by her transformation. Maddie's wide hips had slimmed down significantly, and the above-the-knee little black dress she bought specifically for tonight showed off one of her best assets – her slim ankles and calves. Maddie had let her dark red hair grow since the beginning of her journey, often tying it back in a ponytail. Today she'd visited her hairdresser, and the result was a new style that made her wavy hair look shiny and luscious.

Maddie looked rested and relaxed, sitting in the overstuffed divan in the bar. Her face had lost its puffiness and her amber eyes sparkled. Maddie was not skinny like Sofia. At 14 years old she had blossomed into a voluptuous woman with ample curves and large breasts, something she complained about every time she needed a new sports bra. She'd resigned herself to always being 'big', though her height, almost 5'9, distributed her fullness proportionately. During their university days, Maddie's wholesome looks could turn heads walking into a crowded room. Even though she was 40 pounds lighter, Maddie still considered herself 'big' compared to her svelte friend, but she was leaner and fitter.

'You look as good tonight as you did when we were students! I am so proud of you, Maddie, for sticking with the program. When I think about the hundreds of hours you spend in the gym, in the pool, scrutinizing every calorie you put in her mouth. Well, tonight we are going to break your strict routine, and celebrate by indulging in our favorite cocktails, gourmet food, and lots of really good French wine.'

'I will drink to that!' Maddie replied, grinning.

'Let's order,' suggested Sofia. The waiter came by and both women ordered a Cosmopolitan, their favorite 'bar indulgence'. The waiter returned a few minutes later. 'For you, Madame,' he said, as put the drink on the table and then looked straight at Maddie. 'Compliments of the young man at the bar.' Both women looked over. A man was leaning against the bar, clad in tight black pants that accentuated his long legs and an immaculately pressed grey shirt. His long hair was combed back, showing a fresh and youthful   face. He raised his glass and nodded to the women.

'What gives, Maddie?' Sofia asked, as Maddie got up from the table and walked over to the bar to thank Frederic, the young sales clerk who sold her the bike twelve months earlier.

'Thank you for the drink, Fréderic.'

'You remember me? This makes me very happy to hear,' Fréderic replied in broken English as he moved closer to Maddie. 'Are you still cycling?'

'Yes of course I remember you, Fréderic! And yes, I am still cycling. In fact, I am registered for my first triathlon in a few weeks, in Mont-Tremblant.'

'I am not surprised. I can see that you are in good shape now. Good luck Madeline, I am sure you will be successful!'

'Thanks! I hope I succeed too!' Maddie smiled demurely and returned to the table.

'What was that all about?' asked Sofia again.

'He's the sale clerk that sold me the bike last year,' Maddie answered nonchalantly, trying to hide her surprise of being remembered by the attractive man from the cycling store.

'It's good to know the art of buying a drink for an attractive woman has not died completely! And by the way, he's really striking. He resembles… Francois? I can't remember his last name…the French actor?'

'Francois Lamont.'

'That's him…lucky you. Maybe I should go and buy a bike?' Sofia said, laughing. 'Based on his body language and the way he looked at you sashaying toward the bar, he certainly has your number!' Sofia laughed louder, unable to contain herself. 'I could leave now and you two could go off somewhere for the night? I will gladly vouch for you if Dominique notices the empty bed tomorrow morning.'

'What? You're funny, Sofia, and please keep it down. He might hear you. Don't be ridiculous. He's young enough to be my son. I do admit he is easy on the eyes, and well, his build matches his handsome face, but I am not you. I am not free to do what I want!

'It's that Catholic sense of propriety creeping in… besides, I wouldn't use your marriage as an excuse not to hook up with him, or anyone else for that matter. What's his name?'

'Frederic.'

'I think 'Fred' is in his thirties, by the way, if that's all the encouragement you need.'

'I think not, Sofia. Can we please change the subject?'

Sofia and Maddie's mismatched personalities and lifestyle choices were so glaringly opposite it was hard to understand why their friendship had endured for almost four decades.

Sofia was brilliant, as far as Maddie was concerned, and the most accomplished and versatile woman she had ever known. Sofia could master any task or subject, from complex math problems to oil painting. She once saw an Alex Colville painting at an exhibit in Montreal and decided she needed it for her home. She painted an exact copy and had it framed. To the untrained eye, it looked original.

While attending university, Sofia could have selected any number of promising career choices, but she chose commerce and business. Sofia's fluency in Spanish, English and French, served her very well when she became a junior finance consultant with an international consulting firm located in Montreal, after completing her MBA at McGill. It wasn't long before Sofia's language skills, combined with her business acumen, were being rewarded with short term international assignments, mostly in Europe. Her career took off rapidly, and for many years, while Maddie was raising her boys, she was hardly ever in Montreal. Sofia travelled the world, living in Europe, the Caribbean, and in South America.

Sofia's outspoken personality often got her into trouble with friends and co-workers. Quick tempered, sharp, and shrewd, Sofia never minced her words and usually said exactly what was on her mind, regardless of whether she embarrassed herself or anyone else. Maddie admired Sofia's' supreme confidence and directness, but many people found it unsettling and at times intimidating, especially if you were sitting across from her in a business meeting. While Maddie had always wanted to get married and have children, Sofia never wanted a family. She had made that decision the day after her father died. The prospect of marriage or any long-term committed relationship was also, by association, eliminated from her life. She was often in love, but the relationships always ended when the would-be husband could not persuade Sofia to have a child.

Sofia's decision to remain childless gave her an enormous amount of freedom to build a career without constraints and to do whatever she wanted, whenever she wanted. She took assignments that suited her and travelled to places that looked interesting. Sophia's sultry Latin look, sensuous mouth, and untamed long hair guaranteed that she could pick up lovers anywhere she dropped her suitcase. She shared many of her strange and weird sexual escapades whenever she and Maddie were together. Maddie loved hearing these stories, living vicariously through her best friend's exploits.

'I guess it's no wonder young men find you attractive, my dear friend. I can't say it enough times. You look fabulous, Maddie, and I am so very happy for you,' Sofia said as they sipped their drinks.

'I feel great physically, but more importantly, I feel as though I found something in me that was doomed to be buried and lost for ever. I have you to thank you for that!' Maddie said, raising her cocktail to salute her best friend.

'How's the training going? When is your marathon again?'

'Sofia, it's not a marathon…it's a TRIATHLON,' Maddie replied, articulating the word slowly.

'Yes of course. What is that again? It sounds horribly long and hard.'

'Indeed, it is: 2 kilometers swimming, 90 kilometers biking, and a 21-kilometer run, one after the other, on the same day.'

'That's incredible. I get tired just thinking about it! So, when is this race, exactly, and where?'

'It's coming up quick in six weeks, and it's in Mont-Tremblant.'

'I can hardly believe you're doing this. Of all the things you could have picked, and you chose a sport that involves swimming in open water, which petrifies you, or used to anyway. What an amazing accomplishment, to overcome a fear of water. Has your mother noticed the change in you? Does she know about your plans to do this triathlon?'

'Well, you know Julia. She's never been one to compliment, and I don't think she would understand my motivation. It's too extreme for her sensibilities. I have not told her about the endurance race because I don't think it would go over too well.'

By all rights, Maddie and Sofia's' close friendship should have ended the day their fathers died. Julia and Camelia, Sofia's mother, had never been very close friends. They accepted each other because of their husbands' friendship, but when both men passed away in a boating accident, the women's relationship was more of polite tolerance than deep-rooted friendship. Julia bought a small townhouse in Westmount a year after the men died, and mother and daughter moved out of their predominantly French neighborhood into an strong Anglo neighborhood full of lawyers and doctors. Maddie never forgave her mother for pulling her away from friends, school, and especially her best friend Sofia.

Julia, a stern and reserved woman, rarely talked about herself. Maddie suspected that Julia's childhood had been troublesome, but since she never talked about her own family, or her childhood, in any detail, Maddie could only speculate why Julia was so cheerless. For years, Maddie tried to understand why her fun-loving, caring, magnanimous father, the antithesis of Julia, had married a cold, stern rigid woman. Maddie had many memories of her dad, and she could not recall if he ever made an unpleasant or nasty remark to Julia. Their marriage was a mystery to her, until one evening at dinner, while Julia was lecturing Maddie about her lifestyle decisions, Julia let slip that she got married because she was pregnant. Maddie loved her father fiercely, holding on to her faded memories of him year after year. After hearing about his commitment to duty, she loved him even more. He was an honorable man who did the right thing, even though he probably never loved Julia. It must have felt like a prison sentence to be married to the woman. Maddie never asked any more questions.

'Do you really care what your mother thinks, anyway?' Sofia asked.

'No, not really. She's never going to change and I've accepted that. I do my duty, look after her needs as required, and I don't expect anything in return.' Maddie paused looking at her best friend sitting across from her. They knew each other so well they could anticipate each other's next move. The next question to pop out of Sofia's mouth would be about Dominique.

'Has Dominique said anything to you about your weight loss? What about all the training you're doing? Is he going with you to Mont-Tremblant?'

'Sadly, no,' replied Maddie. 'It conflicts with his annual golf weekend. He never misses it—attends it every year without fail. I didn't insist he come to the race because he thinks it's dangerous. As soon as I told him I registered for the triathlon, he arrived home that evening with a list of medical reports about the dangers of endurance sports, especially for a middle aged, unfit athlete like myself. Truthfully, Sofia, I would find his presence at the race distracting. I would be worried all weekend that he was bored out of his mind!'

'There you go defending him again.'

'I know. You're right. But he's my husband and I'm trying to make it work. You know me, Sofia, I don't give up easily. I'm stubborn that way. When I set my mind on something, I rarely give up.'

'And that's why I love you. If I was ever in trouble and needed help, I know I could count on you to save me!'

Both women laughed.

'You didn't have to marry Dominique, you know,' Sofia continued, trying to stay on the subject of Maddie's troubled marriage.

'No, we didn't HAVE get to married – we wanted to get married, we planned on getting married anyway – we just adjusted the date forward. We were in love, remember? We were glued at the hip, never far from one another. That's usually what happens when you're in love.'

'What about now, today, this moment? Are you in love with Dominique, and does Dominique love you? Has your relationship improved since you began your journey?'

Maddie paused, taking a small sip of her chilled cocktail, the sting of disappoint from her birthday celebration this past week still lingering in her mind.

'I don't think Dominique loves me. I think he loves someone else, or at the very least, he's lusting after someone else. But it's not me.'

'I'm am truly sorry to hear that. You had hoped that this transformation would help salvage your marriage?'

'Yes, my hope was that if I lost weight and got into shape, turned myself around physically and mentally, our relationship would get back on track. But it's not working. We barely see each other.'

'How depressing is that! As far as I'm concerned, you are a single woman in all but title. Maddie, there is no point in staying home and waiting for Dominique to have an epiphany. You'll squander the last good years of your life if you do that.' Sofia stood up and adjusted her tight-fitting dress. 'Time…time is ticking away my dear friend, like the infamous hourglass. I'm going to the bathroom. I'm so mad at Dominique right now, this conversation makes me want to pee. Order another drink for us, will you? We still have lots to talk about.'

Sofia may have been angry, but she took the long way around to the bathroom, so she could be seen by the attractive men at the bar. The club scene was very different these days compared to when she and Maddie were in their 20s, long before smart phones and dating apps. Most of the men at the bar hardly looked up from their cell phones to see a gorgeous, tall Latin beauty waltz by in a body-hugging dress, her hair a mass of flowing dark curls. Sofia was the sexiest woman in the bar, and the only man who actually noticed was the bartender, who followed her circuitous path to the bathroom without blinking an eye.

Maddie was not comfortable with the direction of their conversation. She wanted this evening to be fun and frivolous, with lots of laughter, listening to Sofia's hilarious stories about the people she met or the adventures she had during her latest round of business trips. Instead, the topic of her failing marriage was turning her birthday celebration into a gloomy reminder that she had to face a tough decision about her future. She felt lonelier than ever.

Maddie couldn't help but notice the bar filling up with a slew of men in all shapes, sizes, and skin tones, wearing a uniform of sorts: expensive grey shirts and snug black pants. Some of the men were ridiculously fit, their massive upper arms bulging out of crisp, tailored shirts. A sea of seriously attractive men, so young and so perfect, Maddie thought, and all beyond her reach. Maddie looked around nervously for Frederic, wondering if he was still in the bar, but he had either left with some beautiful young thing or he was hidden from her view. Just as well, Maddie thought. The more she drank, the more emboldened she would become, and likely would embarrass herself by making unwanted advances to the good-looking sales clerk.

Maddie felt out of place in this crowd. It was not helping her mood either. Instead of feeling attractive and slim as she should, she felt too old and large for this crowd of perfection. The DJ arrived and replaced the soft jazzy background music with electronic rhythms– loud and pulsating, no doubt trying to shake the patrons away from their cell phones. Maddie reluctantly ordered two more drinks, but she was anxious to leave this bar and go somewhere more suited to her age and melancholy mood.

Sofia returned from her walk about, looking miffed. 'So much for getting anyone's attention,' Sofia said sitting down.

'I'm so sorry to have brought up the subject of your marriage,' Sofia said, reading Maddie's thoughts. 'This is supposed to be a fun and carefree evening, and it wasn't fair to spoil it by talking about the challenges in your marriage. Let's finish our drinks and get some dinner…I'm starving!'

00:07:00

Maddie and Sofia sat in a quiet corner of a lovely little French restaurant a few blocks from Tara's bar. They ordered a bottle of red wine from Maddie's favourite French wine region, St-Estaphe, and perused the simple but enticing menu. The atmosphere in the restaurant was elegant and subdued. The waiters were quietly shuffling from table to table, serving the patrons. There was a hint of piano music playing in the background. The place suited Maddie perfectly. She and Sofia leisurely drank the exquisite wine and exchanged a bit of gossip about their mutual group of friends. Sofia recounted her recent trip to the Middle East, which was full of amusing stories and mishaps. Maddie relaxed more as the evening progressed, letting the wine move languidly through her system, trying to quell the sadness about her failed marriage and uncertain future.

'How are you feeling?' Sofia asked, though she knew that her best friend was putting on a happy 'Maddie face' for her sake.

'Fabulous – the food and wine are exquisite. What's really been the best for me tonight though is spending a few hours with you. I always enjoy listening to your stories. You are so bold! I can't believe you haven't been arrested yet!'

'Yes, well, I am confident the company would bail me out if that happened.' Sofia wanted to continue their conversation from earlier in the evening, so she eased gently into the delicate topic of Maddie's failing marriage.

'As I recall, you had a bit of the devil in you when we were roommates: that innocent face, those big amber eyes, the wholesome demeanour. You got away with murder. Underneath the soft and virtuous exterior was a woman who went after exactly what she wanted, much like you have done these past twelve months. The old Maddie has emerged!'

'Yes, well, the old Maddie was always there, just buried under the weight of family responsibilities and 40 pounds of excess weight.'

'Now that we are on this subject of your life today, I want to make a suggestion,' Sofia continued, choosing her words carefully.

'Oh, what are you going to suggest? Divorce Dominique?' Maddie shot back, the wine loosening her tongue.

'No, I am not going to suggest divorce. You're a big girl, and if you want to stay married because it's comfortable and predictable, who am I to question your wisdom? No, I was going to suggest you start dating again.'

'Sofia, come on... I don't think dating is an option when you're married.'

'Of course, it is, and it's not called dating. It's called having an affair, getting it on, having quasi-anonymous sex. Lots of married people carry on extra-marital activities. It's a popular hobby.' Sofia smiled at her own joke. 'Listen, all this goal-setting stuff has been hugely beneficial to you. I can see that. But there's still something missing. You need validation, a reward of some sort, and you are certainly not getting that from Dominique. You need someone – preferably a young gorgeous man – to rip your clothes off and bury his chiselled face in your full breasts. It's called lust.'

Maddie laughed at Sofia's outrageous statement. 'Honestly, it's not always about sex.'

'Oh, yes, it is. I want to have sex until my long legs are fused together. You've forgotten about all our wild adventures. We had fun in those days.'

'That was then – this is now. I can't even picture myself doing something as outrageous as carrying on with someone other than Dominque.'

'But Dominique is not there for you. My suggestion is that you step outside your comfort zone, outside the marriage bedroom that has not seen any real action in years.'

'And how am I supposed to do that? I haven't been with anyone but Dominique in almost three decades. I wouldn't know where to start.'

'Have you ever heard of Tinder? Discreet? Plenty of Fish?' Sofia asked.

'You mean swipe 'n sex? Yes, of course I know about dating apps, but these services are for young single women and men. I honestly do not think I am a good candidate.'

''Swipe 'n sex'? That's so funny, but true,' Sofia replied, laughing.

'And besides, Sofia, there's nothing more pathetic than seeing an old jaguar trolling for a young buck at a bar. I can just image what that looks like online,' Maddie added.

'That really depends on your interpretation of old jaguar! Anyway,' Sofia continued sipping her wine, 'listen to me carefully. These are hook-up sites, pure and simple. It doesn't matter if you are married, single, lesbian, gay, or a Buddhist monk. It's just about sex. Understand?'

Maddie nodded reluctantly. She was not comfortable discussing this or another other suggestion that involved testing the boundaries of her marriage.

'Come on, let's look at today's inventory.'

'Inventory? …now I've heard it all,' responded Maddie.

'It's just like shopping for a dress online, but more fun!'

Sofia took out her phone and opened the app. She began to swipe through the 'hits', men who had indicated an interest in meeting her. Sofia did not waste any time reading their profiles, unless a particular man captured her attention for more than a second or two.

'No. No. No. Oh god, no. Look at this one, like I really want to see your erection before I see your face. Honestly, what was he thinking?' Sofia continued to swipe through dozens of responses while Maddie watched with interest.

'Wow, Sofia, you have a lot of followers. What did you post to get so many responses?' Maddie asked innocently.

'I posted a sexy picture of myself.'

'Let me see it,' Maddie asked anxious to see what her friend had done to attract so many followers. Sofia opened her profile and handed the phone to Maddie.

'I can certainly see why you are getting so many responses. It's pretty obvious from your clothing, or lack thereof, what you're looking for!'

'That's the point, Maddie. I make no apologies. I am not looking for romance or a long-term commitment. I think this picture is exactly what I am trying to convey, no? Okay, let's keep looking.' Sofia quickly swiped the various hits on her phone.

'And you wonder why guys are sending you photos of themselves stark naked and ready for action. Seriously, Sofia.'

'Whatever, I'm getting lots of hits, and sometimes I get lucky and they're really good. Oh, he looks promising. More your type than mine.'

She handed the phone to Maddie. She carefully examined the photo of a man, perhaps 45 or 50, who was reasonably attractive and professional looking. There was scant information about on him, but he had a kind, benevolent face, and he was fully clothed.

'How many men are lying, do you think?' Maddie asked, showing a little more interest about the last profile. .'Is this real or is it photoshopped?'

'You can be reasonably assured that many, many men lie about their looks, their age, and their profession. I've met men who don't even come close to looking like their photos. They scan a photo of a model and cut and paste it into their profile. As if! They are total idiots!'

Sofia got the waiter's attention and ordered two cognacs, which the waiter brought immediately.

'So this is what it comes down to, Maddie. I am not about to waste what little time I have on nonsense. I've developed a strategy to cut through the BS and vet out all photo-shopped wannabe models, the charlatans, the imposters, and the nefarious and creepy types who don't even come close to being who they say they are. It's very simple strategy and highly effective. You'll like my plan – it suits your risk-adverse personality.' Sofia eyed the amber liquid in the cognac glass and then took a sip, before continuing to explain to Maddie her safety procedures.

'When I'm in town, I contact whomever looks to be a reasonably good candidate for an evening of fun, and I arrange to meet them at the Maisonneuve Public Library.'

'The library? Are you kidding? And they go along with this?'

'Yes, they do. They'll do anything for a quick hookup. For me, it's a perfect place to meet the date: safe, quiet, and secure. First, I invite the man to meet at the library. I give him specific instructions about where to sit. I did some recon at the library and found the ideal spot, which is usually empty, to set up the 'meet'. Next, I go to the library earlier than our agreed upon time, wearing a big scarf wrapped around my head and face and dark glasses. I position myself where I have an excellent view of the designated rendezvous point, so I can observe the man when he walks in.'

'Usually, the man will arrive after me, in which case I can size him up and decide if I want to pursue or not. Is he the same guy who posted a response or is he a fake? If he's a fake, I send him a text message telling him that I've cancelled and not to respond again. This can get really funny. I watch them get the text and they immediately look around, sheepish and embarrassed, like they've just realized they are being watched by a hidden camera. They don't hang around the library after that. They usually bolt out faster than you can say 'sex anyone'!'

'Occasionally, a man will arrive before me – it's rare, but it does happen. I guess he's thinking the same thing in case I don't meet his standard of sexual perfection. Since I'm covered up, they don't take notice. Either way, I have the upper hand. I control the situation. I make the decision- is this a red night or a green night?'

'Sofia, I am so impressed with your unique strategy. This is surprising coming from you. As a general rule, you're adventurous and tend to throw caution out the door. And does it work?'

'It works like a charm. I knew you would be impressed! I think you should try it. Just for fun, and see where it leads you. What have you got to lose?'

00:08:10

All the lights were off, even the porch light, when Maddie finally arrived at her home around 2 am. She and Sofia had consumed at least two bottles of wine at the restaurant, in addition to the cocktails and cognac. She was very drunk. She fumbled with her purse, trying to locate the buried house keys, made even more difficult by the falling rain trickling down her black dress. Eventually, she found her keys, and with some dexterity unlocked the front door as quietly as possible.

Maddie was not sure whether Dominique was home – she couldn't remember exactly what he had said that morning about his evening plans. Was he working in Emergency? She hoped he was not there. She wanted to be alone. She wasn't in the mood for a lecture about late nights and drinking heavily.

'Water, I need lots of cold water, or otherwise I'm going to feel like shit tomorrow,' Maddie mumbled to herself, walking into the kitchen. She filled a tall glass with ice and cold water from the fridge and sat down by the kitchen counter to steady her dizziness. The room was dark except for the water dispenser in the fridge. A streak of white light flashed across her eyes, signalling to her that a headache was imminent. She quickly popped three headache pills and drank more water.

Maddie was regretting having drunk so much wine. This was not how to behave weeks before her first major long-distance triathlon. Even though she was exhausted and wanted nothing more than to crawl into bed, the morning would be unbearable if she went to bed drunk. Maddie decided to stay awake until the drugs eased her headache. If she could manage six hours of sleep, her plans to go for a training ride in Mont-Tremblant with her group would not be affected by a hangover and adversely impact her ability to finish the upcoming race.

Maddie opened her laptop computer and casually checked the weather forecast for Sunday afternoon: sunny, hot, and humid, with a chance of a thunderstorm. She then checked her email account to see if there were any new or urgent messages. It was late, and there were no messages that either required an immediate reply or were particularly interesting. Maddie was deliberately stalling, and she knew, full well, that all this mindless and casual web surfing was a pretense to where she wanted to go and what had been on her mind the better part of two hours.

She finally found the courage to type 'Discreet', the name of the hook-up service that Sofia had mentioned catering to married people. Instantly, the website popped up on her screen. She opened the link nervously, worried that someone was tracking her every click. Maddie was alert and focused now, the heavy, drunk feeling all but erased from her mind. She read what little information there was on the website. She had not done anything, and yet, it felt like she was cheating on her husband. *This is silly*, she reminded herself, *who cares if I visit this or any other adult website? I'm not doing anything wrong.*

This uncomfortable feeling was familiar. Many months earlier, curious to see what online porn looked like, Maddie tried exploring the porn universe by typing the word PORNOGRAPHY in the web browser. Instantly, a hundred graphic images and short videos of naked men and women actively engaged in the sex act flooded her computer screen. She panicked, paranoid that her IP address was permanently tagged with these unwanted images and could potentially pop up anytime she was working, perhaps in the downtown office of the company she worked for. She immediately took the necessary measures to erase the history and cookies from her laptop and went as far as completely re-imaging her computer to avoid any potential embarrassing problems.

Maddie carefully read the instructions on how to register as a member of Discreet. She was not able to scroll through any of the candidate's profiles because she was not yet a 'registered, paid member'. Before she proceeded with creating a profile of herself, she first created a new email address, one that was not linked to all her electronic devices and that only she could open. Maddie set up a new email account using an encryption service that provided several layers of protection, including authenticity management. Only Maddie could open, read, and compose emails, using a complicated and layered password system. It seemed a bit extreme, even for the risk-adverse translator from Montreal, but Maddie got an immediate thrill from this covert activity. It felt empowering to be the master of her own choices and desires. It was thrilling to have a secret, a part of her mundane and routine daily life that no one knew about. She had never thought of herself as mysterious, and this foray into the clandestine world of marriage dating was out of sync with her personality. Yet, Maddie thought, the risk was minimal. She wasn't breaking the law and she certainly wasn't hurting anyone.

The profile requirements for Discreet were sparse, which made the entire process very quick, though she could add more detail later. Maddie guessed that this was intentional and in keeping with the type of service the website offered: ask few questions, hook up instantly, move on quickly.

One question that Maddie did need to consider more thoughtfully was where she wanted to meet someone. It would be more practical and convenient to meet in Montreal, but there were numerous risks. Someone may recognize her as Dr. Trembley's wife. The truth was, Dominique, the anesthesiologist at the Montreal General Hospital, had no public profile. Most patients never saw his face, or even knew his name. He hid behind a surgical mask for almost every surgical procedure. As a married couple, they rarely went out to social functions, and Maddie had not attended a medical conference with Dominique in several years. Nonetheless, discretion was important to Maddie, so she chose to have a rendezvous in Toronto, not Montreal. She could easily find an excuse to fly to T.O. for a night or a weekend, if she found someone compelling enough to meet intimately.

Next, the service suggested posting a photo or several photos of yourself in the profile. Unlike Sofia, Maddie was not comfortable posting a full, head-to-toe, semi-nude photo. She wanted her profile to be attractive and engaging, while also being demure, with a touch of mystery. The more she revealed in a photo, the more likely she would get responses from naked men with less clothes on then her. She was not interested in meeting men who were overly sexual, crass, and predatory. Maddie thought about Frederic, the bike sales clerk. He was tall, well-built, and engaging. He smiled and laughed easily. He was attentive, complimentary, subtle, and had a sensuous quality about him. If this type of man responded to her profile, she would be thrilled.

Maddie scrolled through her phone photos. She hadn't realized it, or was too drunk to remember, but Sofia had taken several photos of her that evening in various natural poses. Maddie agonized over the choice of the perfect profile photo to submit. The photo would either make him stop, read, and respond, or simply swipe past to move on to the next captivating candidate. The photo had to deliver the right combination of sexy, age-appropriate, and attractiveness. The photo had to compel the viewer to act immediately and take it to the next level. Maddie could always add more photos later, but the profile photo was key to finding the ideal candidate. There were many good photos to choose from in the phone album, as Maddie was naturally photogenic, her classic good looks blossoming under the camera lens. She chose an attractive head shot, where she was smiling nicely to the camera, her eyes bright and sparkling. Maddie thought she looked approachable and pretty. The room lighting softened her skin and camouflaged her real age. In this photo, she could be between 30 and 45 years old.

Maddie reviewed the details of her profile carefully before hitting the submit button. She was anxious but excited about the prospect of getting a hit and secretly hoped she had many to choose from. 'I can't believe I'm doing this,' Maddie said out loud in the empty kitchen. At 3 am, the unlikely adulterer closed the tab in her browser and made sure to delete all the cookies and history before going to bed. The room had stopped spinning and the headache had never surfaced. She walked upstairs to the master bedroom, stripped off the dress and stockings, and fell into the large empty bed, falling asleep almost instantly. Maddie did not give her newly registered profile on Discreet a negative thought.

*****

At 8:30, a little over five and half hours since she went to bed, Maddie was fully awake.

She made herself a strong cup of coffee. She knew what she wanted to do, but decided that it was much too early in the day to check for a response on her Discreet profile. No married man in his right mind would be responding to her profile on a Sunday morning. Maddie reminded herself that the day ahead was packed with activity, enough to keep body and mind busy and distracted from email.

Sofia called for an update and asked how Maddie was feeling. Was she hung over? Did she have fun? They chatted for about ten minutes about the evening, keeping it light and irrelevant. Sofia did not ask Maddie what she thought about their conversation regarding her marriage, and Maddie, in turn, said nothing to Sofia about signing up for Discreet.

'Let's wait to see what happens,' Maddie said to herself after she hung up the phone. 'I may get nothing out of this – I'll wait until I have something significant to report to Sofia.'

Around 10:30 am, just as Maddie was about to load her bike into the truck to meet her training partners, curiosity overcame her will to wait until later in the day, and she checked the new email account.

Maddie was dumfounded. There were no less than fifteen requests in new email account, all originating from Discreet. She reluctantly signed out of her account and headed out the door for the rest of the day.

*****

The cycling group met at the foot of the Station Mont-Tremblant for a 90 kilometer bike ride that would familiarize the group for the upcoming triathlon race. There were thirty-five riders, broken up into smaller groups depending on speed and fitness level. The strongest and fastest boys were out front by several minutes. Maddie was in a slower group, but not the slowest. The ride required all her focus and concentration to keep up with the lead rider. She was acutely aware not to fall behind the pack and lose the benefits of the draft. This was the fourth long ride in as many weeks, and this time, she was able to maintain a consistent speed and stay with the group. The long ride was a blessing in disguise. She temporarily forgot about all the emails waiting for her in her new inbox.

The bike course had several undulating hills and valleys, and a few were very steep climbs. The head wind was fierce travelling along the 117 Highway heading toward Labelle, and the air was hot and sticky. It was early June, and forecasters were predicting more of the same all summer long. This type of weather usually brought severe and unexpected thunderstorms, always a danger for cyclists on the open road.

At the end of the three and half hour ride, a small group of triathletes, including Maddie, continued their training by doing a short thirty-minute run off the bike. The warm and sticky conditions continued on the run, but the wind had stopped and dark grey clouds were moving toward them.

Maddie soon found herself alone on the run as the younger and faster runners took off quickly. Maddie's legs were tired from the bike; she was sleep deprived and was beginning to wane from the lack of sleep and too much wine the night before.

Halfway through the slow, easy run, a cyclist pulled up beside her. 'Bonjour, Madeline, how are you today?' Maddie pulled out her earphones and stopped running. Next to her stood the charming young sales clerk, resplendent in a bright yellow cycling kit.

'My goodness, Frederic, what a nice surprise to see you here!' Maddie blurted out breathlessly. 'What brings you here? I don't remember seeing you with this group before.' Maddie was genuinely curious to find out why the young Francophone was here, only hours after she had seen him at Tara's. Frederic explained that he recently changed cycling teams and was now cycling with this group.

They had an animated conversation for the rest of Maddie's run – Frederic matching her run speed on his bike and talking to her about cycling and racing. He asked her questions about training, and he seemed empathetic when she recounted her challenges and feelings of anxiety about the upcoming triathlon in the very area they were running through. Throughout the twenty-minute run, Frederic never asked Maddie about the night before at the bar, keeping their conversation topical and friendly.

By the time they arrived back at the parking lot, the rain was falling heavily. Maddie was soaked in perspiration and rainfall. Her hair was greasy and sticking to her head, her face was gritty, and she was worried that she smelled like an old pair of sneakers. She hardly felt attractive and would have liked nothing more than to go home, get out her wet clothes, take a long hot shower, and then read her emails.

Frederic either didn't notice Maddie's dishevelled and exhausted appearance or didn't care. Instead of letting her go home, as she wanted, he insisted she join the tri-team for food and drinks at a nearby restaurant in St-Jovite. Maddie reluctantly followed Frederic and the group to the restaurant.

Once at the restaurant, Frederic made sure to sit next to Maddie, and he paid close attention to her. He gave her a dry towel and a long-sleeved shirt to wear so she would be comfortable. He suggested a couple of menu items that she would like.

No longer self-conscious about her attire, and now a bit drier, Maddie relaxed around this captivating young man. Instead of shying away from his face and looking at the floor, as she normally would do, she looked straight into his eyes. She smiled freely at his comments. She became more receptive to his body language, leaning into him when they laughed. She was flirting with him, and he responded willingly, gently pushing her wet hair away from her face, and stroking her arms so she would be warmer. Maddie was attracted to Fred and considered, for a brief moment, that she may want to have an affair with him, instead of total stranger 450 kilometers away in Toronto.

The single act of signing up to have an affair gave Maddie the confidence she needed to be more receptive to the idea that romance was still within her reach. She felt enormously liberated for the first time in years, free to explore whatever and with whomever was out there. Sofia would approve and applaud Maddie's bold new attitude.

Around 8 pm, Maddie arrived home exhausted and intensely curious. The last twenty-four hours have been nothing less than extraordinary. She was beaming and energized in spite of a long day of training. She was getting anxious to know who had responded to her profile on Discreet. While driving home from cycling, she was tempted to log in into her email, but threw her phone in the back seat. 'A distracted driver is a dangerous driver,' she told herself with conviction.

Dominique was not home, presumably working in emergency medicine, though Maddie suspected he was out on personal business. Maddie had the quiet house to herself. Her patience almost done, Maddie sat on the couch, in her warm pyjamas, and powered through the twenty-five requests from Discreet.

00:10:10

The Porter shuttle from Montreal to Toronto arrived at Billy Bishop Airport a half-hour later than planned but still plenty of time to check into the downtown Sheraton Hotel, change into a suitable dress and freshen up before Maddie met her date in the Hotel's lounge.

Maddie told Dominique she was attending a conference for the weekend. This was not entirely a lie. There was a translator's conference being held in the west end of Toronto, but she did not register for it, as many of her associates had. Instead, Maddie had followed through with Sofia's suggestion about going on a 'date'.

She hated using that word. This wasn't dating at all, but out and out adultery, infidelity, hooking up, on-demand sex. Dating had nothing to do with it, but Sofia insisted on using the verb with her conventional and reluctant friend. It sounded less indifferent and more personal. Sofia's choice wasn't fooling anyone, but since there wasn't a proper term for what Maddie was doing, it stuck.

At 6:30, Maddie made her way to the lounge to meet Jamie, one of the twenty-seven men who had responded to her profile photo on Discreet. In the beginning, Maddie was overwhelmed with the attention and responses. Soon, though, she realized that many of the hits were bordering on fraudulent, pasted photos of male models and even one of Richard Gere as a young man. She laughed, swiping through many false and misguided attempts to hook up. Maddie was a stickler for detail and inconsistencies. If she liked a profile photo, she would immediately cross-check the candidate's viability, a task that was time-consuming but effective in painting a truer version of the potential candidate. Sitting in her office, late at night, she would shake her head in disbelief at people's stupidity about the internet. Tracking people was not difficult, as most left a trail of their interests and lifestyle as obvious as an eight-lane highway.

There were only two men Maddie wanted to meet: Jamie and Daniel. Their profiles were consistent, and both prospects appeared reasonably safe, attractive, and fit, but not outrageously handsome. Maddie contacted Jamie first. After a few back and forth messages, they agreed to meet at the lounge in the Sheraton. Maddie also contacted Daniel, in case Jamie fell through and she needed a backup plan.

Up until she arrived at the hotel, Maddie considered the steps she had taken for this rendezvous as a fun game that toyed with the idea of sleeping with stranger. Now that she was actually walking into the busy cocktail lounge on a Friday night, she wondered whether she had the courage to sleep with a married man she had chosen from a digital display case. It was impersonal and out contrary to her character.

She recognized Jamie immediately from his photo, sitting at the bar with a drink. When he stood up, Maddie's heart sank. He had lied about his height, and she was instantly put off by this false representation. Wearing two-inch heels, Maddie towered above him. His profile said he was over six feet tall, but he was barely 5'7. They both sat down at the bar, and Jamie nattered on about the weather and Toronto, though Maddie was too preoccupied with his disingenuous profile details to pay attention. After a few uncomfortable minutes, Maddie excused herself and headed to the washroom.

She sat on the toilet seat, thinking about what she should do next. She had come to Toronto to have a quick affair, and at this point, her meticulous planning was not going very well. She wasn't the least bit interested in carrying on with a man who couldn't be honest about his height. More importantly, she was not attracted to him.

Maddie's phone vibrated, and she opened her message inbox. As luck would have it, there was a message from Daniel, asking if she was still interested in meeting him for a drink.

'Yes,' Maddie answered and suggested they meet at the Royal York Lounge in twenty minutes. He replied with a thumbs up.

Instead of slipping out of the lobby discreetly, and avoiding a confrontation, Maddie walked confidently to the bar and placed herself inches from Jamie.

'Hey, you're back,' Jamie said nervously, looking at the tall red head.

'How tall do you think I am, Jamie?' Maddie asked in a strong voice as she kicked off her shoes.

'I don't know, 5'4...5'6?' he replied.

'Really? Stand up, Jamie,' Maddie said loudly, so everyone could hear.

Jamie sheepishly stood up, his forehead only reaching below Maddie's nose. The bar tender stopped working, and the people sitting around the tables became very quiet.

'The truth is, Jamie, I'm almost 5'9 and you're are maybe 5'6. Your profile says you're over 6 feet tall.' Maddie paused before continuing. He wouldn't make eye contact with her and did not say a word. It was tempting to dump the drink over his head, as she had done once before, but she decided against it. This public humiliation was enough penance.

'I am not attracted to men who misrepresent themselves because they lack the confidence to be who they are,' Maddie continue loudly, 'and like most women, I detest being duped. Here's ten dollars for the drink. Goodnight!'

Maddie put her heels back on and headed outside, toward the Royal York Hotel on Front Street, walking quickly and looking over her shoulder to make sure Jamie wasn't chasing her. She was beaming with delight. It had been a very long time since she spoke up for herself, saying exactly what was on her mind. It felt good to be assertive and in control. Maddie couldn't wait to tell Sofia.

Daniel arrived at the Royal York Hotel moments before Maddie. She was pleased to see that he had not lied about his height. In fact, he was as genuine as his profile indicated. Her mood changed. The chatted for the next hour over cocktails. Daniel spoke quietly and intelligently about living in Toronto, his job in investment management, and his fitness routine. He did not touch on any specific details about his personal or married life. Maddie tried not to analyze him too closely, but she was sure he had had several casual relationships in the world of quick hookups. He spoke in a soft, seductive voice, and touched Maddie's arm gently as he spoke. His clothing was casual, but tailored, and designed to accentuate his fitness. Daniel was supremely confident, perfectly scripted, and deliberate. Every move, every word was aimed at getting to the point of the clandestine rendezvous. He was the ideal candidate for Maddie's purposes, a man who knew what he was doing and why.

The couple left the Royal York to head back to Maddie's room at the Sheraton. Daniel put his arms around her as they walked through the quiet business section of downtown Toronto. His body language and his intentions were obvious. They took a detour and stopped to watch the fountain in Nathan Phillips Square. He told her in a quiet voice about how he lusted after her photo and couldn't wait to meet her. Hearing these flattering comments after an eternity of silence was the validation she needed after a full year of sacrifice and hard work. This was the perfect opportunity to let herself go and enjoy the moment, without hurting anyone, without feeling guilty. It sounded convincing enough. Maddie said nothing but smiled modestly.

Daniel took her smile as invitation for intimacy. He pulled her close to his chest and kissed her smoothly on the lips. Instead of reeling with pleasure, Maddie's body reacted to Daniel's touch with a cool detachment. It was like being kissed by a cousin or best friend: friendly but lacking any real passion or desire. There was not enough chemistry to explore the man any further.

*****

Once they arrived back at the Sheraton Hotel Lobby, she turned to Daniel, put out her hand, and said goodnight. She told him that she wasn't ready to sleep with him, or any other man from Discreet, and then took the elevator to her room, alone and discouraged.

She sat in the hotel suite with an opened bottle of red wine and munched on pretzels.

She knew that Sofia would be disappointed with her for walking away from the attractive stranger, but Maddie had no interest in inviting Daniel to her room.

The next morning, Maddie took a taxi to the Conference and spent the rest of the weekend listening to speakers and attending workshops relevant to her job as a translator. As soon as she arrived back home on Sunday night, Maddie closed her Discreet account, but not before she checked the new crop of potential candidates. She was curious to see the latest requests. Nothing had really changed in two days– same type, different faces. They were all a carbon copy of one another, a bunch of chiseled faces looking impersonal and smug.

Later in the week, Maddie recounted her experiences with Sofia on the phone. She thanked her for suggesting the 'dating' scene, but told Sofia that the experience with Discreet taught her a vital lesson: she was not looking for instant gratification. There had to be something more than 'going through the motions of having sex'. This type of hooking up was too calculating and detached for Maddie's sensibilities. She told Sofia that she wanted the spontaneity and instant chemistry to be genuine and not manufactured because of forced circumstances. Maddie admitted to Sofia that her attitude toward hook-ups was not very modern, or adventurous, but that she was happy to go back to her uneventful and tame life. Besides, she told Sofia, she had something more important to focus on these days, and it had nothing to do with finding someone to sleep with.

00:14:39

They arrived early on Wednesday morning in Mont-Tremblant, four days before Maddie's long-awaited premiere triathlon race. Maddie was feeling a bewildering combination of impatience and dread. She was anxious and ready to start the race, and the next four days seemed an interminably long time to wait, yet she was dreading the thought of diving into the water at the start gun.

The last few weeks of training had tested her physical and mental readiness. She'd thought about nothing else for weeks. She pushed away all negative thoughts, including the state of her troubled marriage.

Caitlyn was Maddie's race roommate for the weekend. She was younger than Maddie by fifteen years. In spite of the age difference, they were equal in terms of cycling and running abilities. They were on the same triathlon team and had established a good relationship that inevitably drifted toward training and nutrition whenever they were together. It was pleasant, uncomplicated, and perfect for weekend roommates.

Maddie had visited Mont-Tremblant many times before, both in the winter for skiing and in the summer for golf. Now, just a few days before the event, the transformation from a seasonal resort area to international race venue was impressive and boldly colorful. The area in and around Mont-Tremblant was humming with activity. The race set-up crews were actively installing bike racks, special carpeting, and the athletes' village, and raising the huge finishing arch that all the athletes would run through at the end of their epic journey on Sunday.

As soon as they arrived in Mont-Tremblant, Maddie and Caitlyn headed to the beach for a swim, to get acclimatized to the cool water and to familiarize themselves with the swim course.

A large white sign greeted them as they strolled into the swim reception building: *Welcome Athletes!* A color map of the swim course was prominently displayed, along with the current water temperature. Today it was a brisk 17.5 degrees Celsius. Although the air was warm and humid, the lake was still quite cool. The race organizers were predicting that the water temperature would warm up to a more comfortable, 19 degrees by race day.

There were only a handful of athletes in and around the swim building. It was still early in the week. The majority of the experienced athletes would not start to arrive until Friday. There were no lifeguards or kayakers at the beach for the women's test swim. Another big sign was posted at the entrance to the beach: 'Swim at your own risk'. Maddie was nervous about swimming in open water without supervision, so she chose to use a rescue belt, in case she had a panic attack or got a cramp in the water.

The two women began the laborious process of putting on their neoprene wetsuits. The suits were extremely tight, and putting them on, one foot and leg at a time, was time-consuming and challenging. The wearer had to be careful not to poke a finger through the thin fabric.

Caitlyn was aware of her training partner's anxiety about open water swimming, as she had witnessed her trepidation when the team had their weekly practices at a lake just outside of Montreal. The decision to head early to the race site and try the course before the crowds arrived was Maddie's idea.

Caitlyn dove into the water first. Maddie took her time, walking slowly through the calm water until it was up to her chest, pushing the rescue float behind her. She splashed water on her face a few times while carrying on an internal dialogue about the need to relax. By the time Maddie was ready to start swimming, Caitlyn was at least 250 meters ahead and her anxiety was more acute than ever. She dove into the water and started swimming very slowly. At around the 400-meter mark, Maddie made the mistake of stopping to look for her partner. She could not see Caitlyn, which led to instant panic. Maddie felt the wetsuit tighten around her throat, constricting her breathing. She started coughing, almost choking, unable to control the fear. She could not swim any further. She turned back and paddled to the shore, using the breast instead of the freestyle stroke, the fear dissipating as she swam closer to the beach.

The women said nothing to each other while they changed into their cycling clothes. Caitlyn witnessed Maddie's struggles in the water and was not able to offer her training partner any words of wisdom that could help overcome her anxiety. The swim portion of the race on Sunday was almost 2000 meters, and it had to be completed in under

70 minutes. Based on this brief swim trial, Caitlyn seriously doubted that Maddie was adequately prepared to swim that distance, let alone finish the race.

This was an inauspicious start to Maddie's' first endurance race. She was quiet as they walked back to the hotel to exchange swim gear for cycling gear. Maddie knew this was going to be tough, but until that morning, she had not fully grasped how challenging it would be. She now faced the realistic possibility that she would be unable to find the courage to swim on race morning. Almost a full year of training would be lost if she was forced to abandon the race due to fear.

*****

Caitlyn had arranged to meet her coach for a pre-race briefing in the early afternoon, so the roommates agreed to meet later for a short bike ride along a paved trail that served as the run course.

Maddie spent the next a few hours killing time by strolling around the race site. She enjoyed people-watching, and this was an ideal place to sit in an outdoor cafe, drink a cappuccino, and watch the hundreds of tourists and athletes mingle about.

After drinking a coffee and checking out a few of the interesting and unique retail shops along the cobblestone promenade that ran the length of the Station Mont-Tremblant, Maddie strolled to a wooden bench near the tented athlete's village to wait for Caitlyn, quietly watching the traffic of people and bikes.

There were more men than women at this event, she noted, and it was easy to spot the experienced, hard core, ultra-fit athlete who took racing and results seriously

She watched with interest as they strutted about the race site, their egos as wide as their expensive bikes. There was no shortage of money spent by the experienced competitor: $1500 wetsuits, the very best in race wheels, and $800 timing devices, not to mention the quality of their triathlon bikes. Some of the bikes were over $15,000, a huge sum to pay for a machine that would only go as fast as the person peddling it. Sleek, fully integrated, and usually colorful, triathlon bikes were not only designed to impress, they were built to move very fast.

The male athletes were just as colorful as their expensive bikes, and they were easy to spot due their similar physical characteristics: very lean, clean shaven, short to average height, short-cropped hair with bold tattooed arms and calves. Tight spandex shorts, tank tops, and neon-colored compression socks were the uniform of choice as they strutted about like peacocks at a zoo, occasionally stopping to check their phones or their oversized watches. The women were no less colorful: supremely fit, ultra-lean, and tightly bound in body-accentuating clothing. *I wish I had their confidence,* Maddie said to herself wistfully, unable to shake off the disappointment of her morning swim.

In the sea of black and neon spandex, a tall, large man drifted through the crowd of athletes and walked towards her. Maddie was not sure if the man was in Mont-Tremblant for the triathlon race or a passing cyclist stopping by to check out the action.

Walking confidently along the cobble stone promenade, the striking cyclist appeared as fit and athletic as any around the athlete's village, yet he was not outfitted like the rest of the men. His older model bike was heavily scratched, his bike helmet had a few dings, and his cycling shoes were secured to his big feet with a flimsy and tattered Velcro strap that hung meekly from the shoes. He had long, messy, curly hair, a fair amount of stubble, and no visible tattoos. He was not wearing a watch of any kind, and a lonely water bottle was sitting empty in a cage on the bike frame. The only piece of equipment that stood out was his green, white, and orange striped cycling jersey.

There was no shortage of attractive men in triathlon racing, firm, fit, and a touch conceited, yet this towering man, with his outdated equipment and modest clothing, stood out. He had a commanding presence, an aura that rose above the crowd of inflated egos and high tech-cycling gear. Maddie was fascinated and watched him closely until he turned his face and looked at her, nodded, and broke into a warm smile that invited her to smile back. She should have acknowledged him in some way but instead, she cast her eyes downward on the pretense of looking at her bike gears to avoid meeting his gaze. She watched his tattered shoes walk by slowly, then he jumped on his bike and cycled away.

Maddie put on her bright pink helmet and went looking for Caitlyn, glancing nonchalantly up to the overcast sky. It had darkened in the last few minutes, and the air had that distinct smell of a looming rain shower. Maddie was anxious to get on her bike and do a quick test ride before the inevitable downpour.

00:16:15

About twenty minutes into the late afternoon bike ride, Caitlyn slowed down in front of Maddie and then stopped, turned around to face her training partner, and said 'I think we should turn back – look at those low grey clouds, I think we're in for a huge downpour.'

Maddie looked up at the sky, and sure enough, a mass of grey billowing clouds was approaching rapidly. She was annoyed with Caitlyn because she didn't want to stop cycling, regardless of the weather. She had suffered through periods of anxiety and dread all day, the swim weighing heavily on her mind, and cycling was a good way to purge the doubt. The enormous sacrifice of time and hours she devoted to training would be wasted if she could not regain her confidence before race day.

'Why don't you go back to the hotel?' Maddie suggested. 'I'll meet up with you later – I won't be long. I'm going to try and beat the storm.'

'Okay, it's up to you,' replied Caitlyn, a bit mystified, 'just be extra careful. The roads will get slippery and treacherous if it rains, and you don't want to get injured four days before your wave starts…okay, see you!' and off she went, peddling quickly back towards the hotel.

Maddie continued to ride along the paved trail. It was quiet now, the calm before the storm, she guessed; not even a bit of wind was blowing into her bike helmet. She could see the Montee-Ryan intersection in the distance, about one kilometer away, and a lone cyclist was coming towards her. When they passed each other they both nodded and Maddie thought the cyclist yelled 'nice bike' but she was not sure. She realized, too late, that this was the man she had admired earlier in the afternoon, with the striped jersey and the older bike.

As she glanced back at the man, she saw a streak of lightning in the distance, immediately followed by a low grumbling noise. There was no chance Maddie could outrun the storm, and it was too dangerous to cycle in lightning. She made the decision to cut her ride short and cycle back to the hotel as quickly as possible. She turned around and headed back into town along the same paved trail.

The lightning streaks intensified, illuminating the grey sky every few seconds, followed by more rumbling and loud cracks. Maddie could feel a slight drizzle on her face, and the air was thick with humidity. She increased her speed as the gun metal sky closed in. She was gaining ground on the lone cyclist in front of her, now only 50 meters away.

Suddenly, an enormous shock of lightning tore across the sky, followed seconds later by an ear-deafening explosion of thunder.

The cyclist and Maddie both looked up. Neither one of them saw the agitated deer emerge from the woods, running frantically at full speed, and bolt across the bike path directly in front of the cyclist. The cyclist reacted quickly and attempted to brake, but it was too late. He nailed the deer in the flank and somersaulted over the startled animal, bike and body as one. The cyclists' feet disengaged from the pedals, and he landed at the edge of the bike path, sliding headfirst into a tree, the bike careening into the bushes, a random and spontaneous event that would profoundly disrupt the delicate equilibrium of Maddie's middle-aged life.

Maddie reacted instantly to the chaos in front of her. She slid to a complete stop, frantically trying to get her feet unclipped out of the pedals. She almost ended up on her knees, but managed to clip her foot out just in time to regain her balance.

At that exact moment, the clouds burst open, and the rain fell so hard Maddie could barely make out the crumpled cyclist lying on the ground under a tree. She ran to towards the man, bent down on her knees, and examined him closely, trying to remember all the first aid steps she had learned years before.

The cyclist was lying on his back, his face turned slightly away from her. Maddie was shaking so badly she wondered if she might be in shock, but the cyclists' pathetic condition forced her to focus on him instead of herself.

Maddie made sure the man was breathing by putting her hand over his mouth and the other hand on his wrist, searching for a pulse. She was relieved to see that he was alive and breathing on his own. Next, she examined his head gently. There was blood on his face, seeping from under the helmet. She thought it best not to move his head or take his helmet off, for fear he may have suffered a head injury, or worse, a spinal fracture. Instead, she leaned into the man on the ground and spoke to him, not knowing if he was unconscious or not.

'Hey, I'm here to help you. My name is Maddie,' she said, her voice barely audible in the falling rain. There was no response. She tried again. 'Hey, are you okay? Is there anything broken? Are you hurt anywhere?' This time, she raised her voice so she could be heard. She was about to start tickling the inside of his hand to wake him, but he turned his helmeted head toward her, and said, in a slow and groggy voice. 'How's the deer?'

Maddie almost burst out laughing. At the very least, he is a good sport, she thought.

'She did not stick around long enough for me to ask her!' Maddie shot back.

With difficulty, the cyclist tried to sit up. Maddie steadily put her arm under his and lifted him carefully so he was propped up against the tree he had hit moments before. He was a big man, but Maddie was strong, and she managed well enough. The cyclist tried to remove his helmet, but his hands were shaking, and he was unable to unclip the strap. She slipped her fingers under the strap, squeezed the buckle, and cautiously removed his helmet. A mass of wet, bloody, thick, wavy hair fell to his face.

'Let me see where the blood is coming from,' she said to the cyclist. Her fingers pushed his hair aside and probed his head, looking for contusions. The cyclist's head was sticky, and it was difficult to see much, but Maddie was quite certain that the blood oozing down his face was from a cut above his left eye, around the hair line. 'I think you have a cut on your head, but I can't tell if you need stitches or not,' Maddie said. The man did not respond, but simply stared at her with light green eyes. Maddie attributed his lack of response to mild shock.

'If you don't mind, I'm going to check for any broken bones,' she continued with some authority. After all, she was married to a doctor and hence should be comfortable around the sick and injured. Maddie put both hands around and under his face, and then down his neck and shoulders, looking for fractures, exactly as she was instructed to do so at the first aid course she took a few years before. She looked closely at his legs, running her wet hands along his knees and ankles, checking for broken bones.

The injured cyclist sat silently on the wet ground in the pouring rain while Maddie examined him head to foot. Her hands were warm and gentle on his bruised body. He closed his eyes and forgot about the accident, his throbbing head and stinging underside. He made no effort to move or speak and seemed to drift off into sleep.

'I don't think anything is broken,' Maddie said, noting that he was nodding off. Drowsiness could be a symptom of a head injury, she remembered from the course. She pinched his arm and said loudly, 'Stay with me. Don't fall asleep.'

'Damn deer. I've never been hit by a deer before,' he finally said with a pronounced accent, trying to sit up straight.

'Yes, well, we have a serious deer problem in this part of the country,' Maddie replied, 'but usually deer collisions happen on the highway and with cars, not on bike trails with cyclists.'

'My name is Aidan...Aidan O'Callaghan,' the cyclist said above the noise of the wind and the roar of thunder in the distance. They both looked up at the sky. The rain continued to fall around them, though they were partially protected by the canopy of tall trees that surrounded them.

'I'm Madeline St-Laurent, or Maddie for short. What do you want me to do? Are you far from home?'

'Well, I'm quite far from home, as you can probably tell from my accent,' Aidan continued, stretching his neck and moving his torso, 'but I don't think I am far from my accommodations. I have a flat on the Cap Mont-Tremblant, I think it's called, a few miles up the road. I've a rental parked in the garage,' Aidan replied.

'I'm not sure if your bike was damaged or not,' Maddie said, looking over at the bike lying in the bushes, 'but you have a few cuts, and your head is still bleeding, as far as I can tell. I do not think it's wise for you to try and cycle back to your...flat.' She paused, thinking about how to proceed with the injured man. 'I know exactly where the Cap is. Can I suggest I cycle to your accommodations and drive back here with the rental to pick you up?'

Aidan closed his eyes and took a deep breath. 'Yes, I think that's a good idea. I could not manage biking up that big hill!'

'You may have a concussion,' Maddie continued, looking around for another cyclist, or even a vehicle on the road, which was about 100 meters from the trail. 'I don't want to leave you alone, but I don't think we have a choice. There is no one around to help us and the rain is really coming down hard. I should go right now.'

'I'll be fine. I will be here when you to come back,' Aidan said in a half smile.

With some difficulty, Aidan gave Maddie the address to his condo, and she retrieved the keys from the back of his torn cycling jersey. She immediately jumped on her bike and headed toward the Old Village as quickly as her legs would take her, using the highway instead of the bike path to save time.

Once on the open road, the rain began its assault again and stung Maddie's bare forearms. Her cycling glasses could not protect her eyes from the rain, which was falling almost sideways against her, pushed by a fierce wind. Her helmet was no match either for the miserable conditions.

Cap Tremblant overlooked several lakes and the Old Village. This area of the Mont-Tremblant region was charming, quaint and only partially developed. It was a difficult climb up the hill to the condo. Maddie's heart was beating at maximum rate, more from stress than physical exertion, as she finally located the last unit sitting on the edge of a row of similar units, high on top of the hill.

It was quiet when she entered the unit. She wondered whether Aidan had a wife or girlfriend with him, but all signs indicated that he was alone. There were two grocery bags on the counter, two empty cans of beer, two wine bottles, and one piece of beat-up luggage in the foyer. Maddie found a towel in the laundry room and then jumped into the white rented SUV and drove back down the road.

Aidan was exactly where she had left him on the bike trail, but he was standing rim rod straight, examining his bike. Maddie was relieved to see him upright, but it was clear he had suffered more than a head injury in the accident. His cycling shorts were ripped on one side, exposing his scraped and bloodied thick thigh and partial left butt. One of the back pockets of his cycling jersey was hanging loosely, and the jersey sleeve was torn at the shoulder. His unique cycling kit was ruined, and he was covered in dirt. In spite of the obvious physical damage to his clothes and body, Maddie was struck by how elegantly he stood, an impressively built man with the broad square shoulders of a swimmer, narrow hips, and long legs.

Maddie immediately took charge of the situation. Without asking, she grabbed Aidan's bike and loaded it into the vehicle. She gave him a towel to put on his forehead. Aidan smiled and appeared amused by Maddie's earnestness. He followed her slowly to the SUV, holding his cycling shoes in one hand and his helmet in the other. Maddie helped the injured cyclist into the front seat of the SUV, though he did not need any assistance.

00:17:01

The five-minute drive back up to the Cap was quiet. The only sound inside the vehicle were the wiper blades moving at full speed and the rain lashing the sun roof. Maddie could see Aidan occasionally wincing in pain, shifting in the seat to get comfortable. She had left the garage door open, and parked the SUV in the driveway to give Aidan room to maneuver himself out of the truck. Maddie jumped out, ran to the passenger side, and opened the door. The injured cyclist waited for Maddie to help him out and into the unit.

'How are you doing'? Maddie asked, as she gathered some meager items to clean up his wounds.

'I feel okay. T'is the dirt and blood that makes me look worse. I'm a wee bit wet and sticky and cold!' Aidan replied, sounding normal but shivering slightly from the cool, air-conditioned temperature inside.

'You've had a nasty accident, Aidan. You went flying through the air and you landed quite hard. You may need stitches on your head, but it's hard to tell.' Maddie paused, collecting her thoughts about what to do next. She doubted that stitches would be necessary, but it was better to proceed cautiously. She couldn't just leave him to tend to himself until she was sure that his injuries were manageable. Common sense and some meager training told her it was important to clean him up first and make sure he was warm.

'Can I suggest you take a shower if you are up to it, and then we can access the damage better? Or would you prefer to go to the hospital and let a doctor assess you properly? It's really up to you and how you are feeling,' Maddie said.

'I dunna need to go a hospital, but I could use a good hot shower. That'll do the trick,' he replied quickly in a strong-accented voice; it sounded familiar, but Maddie couldn't identify its origins.

*****

'I can help you with your jersey, but …you may need to do the rest on your own. Do you think you can manage it? If not, I'll find a blanket or something…'

'Och, I can manage just fine, thanks,' Aidan said.

Maddie carefully walked with the cyclist to the master bedroom off the living area. It was an enormous room with an oversized ensuite bathroom. The shower stall was large enough for four people, and it even had a bench.

'Well, there you go,' Maddie said, pointing to the seat. 'If you're feeling weak, just sit down!'

'I certainly will do that...' he replied, smiling.

Aidan was standing inches away from Maddie, and he could see she was shivering slightly.

'You are cold too.' He peered behind the bathroom door and grabbed a white bathrobe. 'Here, this will do for now until I can find yeh some proper clothes to wear. The other toilet is just down the hall.'

'Thanks. Now let's get you organized.'

After she helped Aidan remove his torn jersey, trying not to blush at the awkwardness of undressing a stranger, she turned on the shower, gave him fresh towels, and left the bathroom. She kept the door partially open in case he needed something or, god forbid, he fainted. She was not entirely sure what she would do if he called for her, or how she would handle it if he passed out.

Maddie went into the powder room and examined herself in the mirror. Her wet cycling clothes clung to her like a second skin, stretched across her ample chest, the fabric almost translucent, showing every flaw in her middle-aged body. Her face was deeply flushed and speckled with mud splatter, and her long red hair was plastered to head. Her arms and legs were also covered in mud splatter, which had hardened in the last few minutes. The bathroom had little in the way of accessories to fix herself up. All she could do was wet a facecloth and wipe down her dirty body, removing as much of the mud as she could without taking a shower. She looked for a comb, but there was nothing in the drawers. Maddie tousled her hair with a towel and put on the big fluffy white bathrobe Aidan had given her, wrapped it tightly around her torso and instantly welcomed the warmth and comfort of the cozy, thick material.

This was a wholly unusual situation, she thought, and though she did not feel vulnerable or frightened about being in an isolated condo with a total stranger -after all, he was injured and couldn't move very fast- the circumstances did force her to pause and think. She decided she would leave as soon as she was confident that Aidan did not need any further attention. She grabbed her wet cycling clothes and headed to the laundry room while Aidan showered.

Aidan's was still showering when Maddie returned to the large bedroom. She sat on the edge of the bed, waiting patiently for Aidan to finish his shower and for her clothes to dry. She heard him yell out 'Woooo!'

'Sorry...are you alright?'

'It stings a bit, but I feel better already! Thanks, Madeline,' Aidan said her name with the emphasis on the 'line'.

Maddie, bemused by his pronunciation, called back 'Call me Maddie. Everyone does.'

'Indeed I will. And what's the story for you? I mean to say, are you from here?' Aidan asked over the noise of the shower.

'Close enough. I live in Montreal.'

'Montreal! Such a beautiful city. I worked in Montreal for a few months, many years ago. Lots of really good food and bars, as I recall.'

'I wouldn't know. I never go out,' Maddie murmured to herself.

'What did yeh say, I didn't hear that?' Aidan asked.

'Where are you from? I can't quite place your accent. Is it Irish?' Maddie asked

'I'm a bit of everything, you know. A bit of the English,' and he said this with a haughty English accent. 'And then I have a bit of the Highlander in me,' as his accent changed to a pronounced Scottish lilt, followed by a sentence could not understand, and finally Aidan settled on a more familiar accent. 'Just kidding,' he continued laughing. 'You are correct. I am Irish, through and through. I arrived this mornin' from Dublin. I'm here for the race on Sunday.'

'How are you doing now with getting the dirt off those scratches? Maddie asked, just as the shower turned off.

It was quiet now in the bathroom. Maddie waited and listened for the sound of someone falling, or moaning. All she could hear was a rustling and a scraping noise, and the water faucet running. 'You need to really scrub the dirt off. I know it's painful, but you don't want to risk getting an infection...'

Aidan opened the door and stood leaning on the frame, his slightly damp body wrapped in a towel, the smell of fresh laundry trickling into the master bedroom. The man standing before Maddie bore little resemblance to the crumpled lump that had been lying on the trail just forty-five minutes previous. The transformation was arresting. His hair was pushed back of his clean-shaven face, and he stared at her with wide expressive green eyes, framed by a slightly darker skin, as though nature had decided to enhance his eye color with a smudge of makeup. Aidan's long face was tanned and weather-beaten, the face of someone who spent most of their time outdoors. His pronounced cheeks were flushed by the hot shower, and his narrow, aristocratic nose was slightly off center. He was a solid man, with a broad chest and massive square shoulders. He stood confidently, radiating a playful mischievous personality.

Maddie visceral reaction forced her to look away from him. He was absurdly sexy standing in the bathroom doorway, with nothing on but a towel, grinning broadly. She felt the heat rising to her face and hoped he would not notice she was blushing like a silly schoolgirl.

'That was quick…and you shaved?' Maddie said, trying to sound casual, as though this scenario was as normal as the sunrise.

'Well, I couldn't take any more hot water, and my attempt at growin' a beard was only temporary. It was time…the hairy legs are next!!!' he said with a wink, lifting his leg just high enough for the towel to hide what was underneath. 'I feel much better now. Maybe I just needed a hot shower after hours of travellin'. My injuries don't seem as bad now,' Aidan said smoothly.

'Where are you from, exactly, in Ireland?' Maddie asked.

'I live in West Cork, a beautiful area of Ireland. Have you ever been?'

Maddie nodded no and smiled at him. In spite of his arresting good looks, Aidan's easygoing nature and charming voice made her feel comfortable. His sense of humour was infectious, and he clearly liked to laugh, given the deep lines around his eyes. 'Will you sit down?' Maddie asked, as a small trickle of blood made its way down the side of Aidan's head. 'Let me take a good look at your head. It's bleeding again.'

Aidan dutifully sat on the padded bench at the end of the bed. Maddie tugged at her robe to make sure it was tight and moved closer to the bench, parting Aidan's hair back to see a small cut high up around his forehead.

'I don't think you need stitches,' Maddie said nervously, 'although I am not a doctor. Let me fix this up with a sturdy bandage.' She applied a mild disinfectant and placed her fingers on the wound, putting a bit of pressure to stop the bleeding, tugging often at the white robe to ensure it would not come apart.

Aidan said nothing, but kept his gaze fixed on Maddie's face as she attended to his wound.

'What do you do in West Cork?' Maddie asked as she applied a butterfly bandage.

'I work in construction. I'm a heavy equipment operator,' he replied, flinching slightly while Maddie worked on this head. 'So, in your medical opinion, Dr. Maddie, how does it look? Has my cycling career come to an end?'

'Not unless you are planning on cycling on your head!' Maddie shot back.

Aidan laughed loudly. 'You are a fine woman, Maddie, and you make me laugh!"

'The cut looks innocuous enough,' Maddie continued, trying to be serious. 'It's not what I see, it's what I can't see that has me a bit concerned. How's your vision? Are you seeing double? Do you have a headache?'

Aidan shook his head no and added, in a soft voice, 'I feel fine. In fact, I've never felt better in my life.'

'Are you sure? I'm worried about a concussion,' Maddie took a step back, looking at him closely. She was not convinced he was telling the truth.

'No need to worry, we Irish are far too thick and stubborn to be traumatized by a little knock on the head. I'm feelin' just fine, and you're doing an excellent job of patchin' me up,' he said, as he carefully reached up and put his hands on her waist.

'Thank you for taking care of me,' he continued quietly, looking up at the uncertain expression on Maddie's face. 'T'is very nice to be looked after by such a gentle and fetching woman.'

Maddie froze. His spontaneous gesture of affection was so surprising, and so unexpected, she wasn't quite sure what to do next. She knew, though, that if she removed his hands from her waist and walked away, he would let her go.

Instead, her body remained perfectly still. She didn't want to walk away. His hands felt like they belonged there. She was attracted to Aidan and had been the instant she saw him on the Promenade.

Aidan waited for Maddie to push him away, but she made no effort.

He moved his hands to the bathrobe ties and slowly untied the knot. Maddie let him. Her heart was beating so loudly, she thought for sure Aidan could hear it too. He slipped his hand inside the bathrobe and softly caressed her breasts and stroked her nipples. She felt lightheaded, almost dizzy. Her insides were fluttering like the delicate wings of a hundred hummingbirds.

Aidan opened the bathrobe a little more and kissed her tummy delicately. The intimacy of what he was doing was both exhilarating and terrifying at the same time. His hands lingered down her hips and between her damp legs. His touch was exquisite. Maddie closed her eyes, and the swirling dizzy sensation only increased. This was all happening too fast, she thought for a split second. Instead of pushing him away, though, she dug her fingers in his shoulders, encouraging him to journey further.

Maddie kissed the top of his wet head gently, his face and then his mouth. His dark, full lips were chapped but inviting. He was a good kisser, sensuously using his mouth and tongue to explore hers.

Aidan pulled the white robe away from Maddie's shoulders and admired her full breasts, strong shoulders, and wide hips. He stood up and peeled away his towel, pressing his firm erection and full body against her, his hands grabbing her voluptuous buttocks, kissing and stroking her breasts. She could have stood for hours with him pressed hard against her. He whispered something in her ear that she did not understand.

One moment they were standing clutching each other, and the next they were lying on the bed, Aidan consuming every inch of her ample body, teasing her relentlessly with his lips and fingers.

'Aidan,' Maddie said breathlessly, 'your head? Your injuries?'

'T'is gone,' was all he could say, as the fire in his blood surged through his veins, obliterating the headache and the pain from the accident.

His large, calloused hands were surprisingly gentle on her skin. The throbbing between her legs was so overpowering, it was almost painful. She pulled him up and he laid on top and penetrated her, his hands on her hands, his pelvis pushing into her as she locked her legs around him. Maddie tried to silence her voice, but the groans escaped. He stayed with her, his fingers coaxing her wet cleft while their bodies stayed in rhythm. Aidan felt Maddie shudder, releasing a million tiny cells of absolute pleasure.

It had been a lifetime since she felt this wave of bliss and pure surge of joy, the pulsating feeling lingering. He was so unselfish, she realized; it was all about her pleasure, her enjoyment. In one swift movement, Maddie gently rolled Aidan over on his back and straddled him, moving up and down in a steady, sensuous motion. They stared at each other intently, smiling and enjoying the feeling of their wet and sweaty bodies glued to one another. They kissed feverishly, and he grabbed both her arms, closing his eyes tightly, and she watched as he released himself, panting quietly.

They lay perfectly still for a long time, drunk with pleasure and locked together like vines on a fence.

Eventually Maddie released herself from Aidan's grip and lay next to him. He closed his eyes and took a deep breath. She put her head on his chest, and he placed an arm around her shoulder. They listened to the wind lashing the windows. They hadn't realized that during their intense intimacy, the power had gone out, and the entire Mont-Tremblant ski hill was blanketed in almost complete darkness, with the exception of a tiny emergency light that shone meekly in the distance. Maddie tried rolling over to give Aidan some room, but he tugged her close to him. 'We'll have none of that right now,' he said in a tired voice. This man's thoughtfulness was undeniable.

Maddie closed her eyes, too. Her body and mind quietly drifted toward a peaceful sleep in the arms of a complete stranger. She had never felt better.

00:18:30

Maddie might have slept for an hour or two when she snapped awake, suddenly remembering Aidan's injuries and the possibility of a concussion. She glanced at his face and thought about waking him, but he looked well enough. He had only just arrived in Mont-Tremblant from Dublin, and he was likely exhausted from his long trip, not to mention the stress of the deer accident.

Maddie stared at the man she had met but a few hours earlier. She had been so transfixed earlier by his physique and spontaneous sensuality, she had failed to notice much else about him. Lying inches from his tanned face, she could see that he was young. While his hair was tinged with grey streaks, giving the appearance of an older man, his soft, sleepy face told a different story. Maddie was quite sure she had just slept with a man that was at least ten years younger than herself.

If he only knew how old I am, Maddie told herself, her mind shifting into the real world with more clarity, casting doubt on her impetuousness. *If he only knew how old I am*, she muttered to herself, *.and what in god's name is a man like that doing with me?*

It was a relief that the room was dark, too dark, she hoped, for Aidan to see the flaws of her middle-aged body. The somber shadows in the bedroom camouflaged her numerous imperfections: the saggy breasts, the lose skin of her upper arms, the slackness of her thighs, and the bumps and bruises from training fifteen hours a week. The ecstasy and pure joy she'd felt two hours previously were quickly replaced by overwhelming regret. This was not the body of a young woman, and the morning light would surely unveil the ugly truth. *This was a mistake. What was I thinking. I just had sex with a complete stranger. What am I doing here*, she mumbled to herself. Her body shuddered, and she buried her head in the sheets to escape the embarrassment and shame of being such a foolish woman.

Maddie's only thought was to leave quickly before Aidan woke up, and thus avoid the awkward face-to-face the next morning. All she could think about was getting out of that room, jumping on her bicycle, and finding shelter and comfort in her hotel room a few kilometers away, the events of the last few hours to remain a pleasant memory. She doubted she would ever see him again. This was, after all, equivalent to a one -night stand, a coincidental meeting of two sexually needy adults and not too dissimilar to her unsuccessful rendezvous a few weeks prior.

Maddie quietly slid her legs off the bed, but a hand reached out to grab her arm. 'Where are you going?' He asked, in a half-hearted attempt at sounding menacing. Aidan sat up and propped a pillow under his head. 'I could hear you talkin' to yourself…something about leavin'?'

Maddie had no choice but to sit back down on the bed. 'I thought I should go now,' she said, a touch embarrassed.

'Nonsense,' Aidan said confidently 'There's no need. As you can plainly see, t'is dark inside and out. T'is not safe for you to venture out now. Come, sit here.' Aidan propped another two pillows against the headboard. Maddie reluctantly sat next to him, pulling the bed sheet up to her chest to cover her naked body. Aidan pulled her closer, seemingly reading her thoughts.

'I remember you from earlier in the day. In the Promenade. You walked by me? I think you saw me too?'

Maddie nodded, starring at her feet at the end of the bed.

'If the truth be told …god strike me down if I am not, I lusted for yeh the minute I set my eyes upon your pretty face.'

Maddie shook her head, dismissing what he was saying.

'Indeed I did! I first noticed your bike – I've soft spot, yeh see, for green and white, with a little orange added in for good measure.' He smiled more broadly and, sitting this close, she noticed his slightly crooked front tooth. 'And then I noticed the tall, voluptuous beauty attached to the bike, wearing a cycling jersey and shorts that fit tight and accentuated those wholesome curves. I couldn't help but notice a robust woman in a forest of bamboo trees,' he said, laughing.

'What didn't you notice?' Maddie asked, smitten by his amusing if not accurate description of her assets compared to other women, or shortcomings, as she would have said.

'You seemed a wee bit lost in the crowd, too, clutching your bright pink helmet. When I saw you again on the trail, I slowed down, hoping you would follow me. I would likely have never seen yeh again, though I would have tried looking for yeh all weekend, if the weather had not intervened on my behalf. T'was fate. We were meant to cross paths, Maddie, even if it was a wee bit painful,' he said, laughing again at his own joke, in a heavily accented soothing and hypnotic voice.

'It's quite the tale, isn't it?' he asked, staring at the woman next to him, who looked bemused but sceptical.

'It is quite the tall tale, and it sounds nice,' Maddie answered, 'but I think I should leave, Aidan. I have a roommate back at the hotel and she's probably wondering what happened to me.'

'I don't want you leave. Please stay,' Aidan replied, with some urgency. 'Och, we'll deal with the roommate tomorrow,' Aidan replied, stroking her face with his rough hand.

Maddie was having second thoughts about making a hasty exit. She suspected that Aidan's charming Irish accent was interfering with her judgement, and she was willing to overlook the possibility that he might be telling her exactly what she needed to hear.

Maddie could hear Sofia's voice in her head, telling her not to squander a rare opportunity that, quite literally, fell into her lap. Remember the hourglass, she would say. Sofia was right, of course; she was always right about these types of things.

'I can see you're thinking rationally about what I just told you and wondering if it all makes sense?' Aidan said.

'That's right,' she answered honestly.

'Sometimes, Maddie, you just have to seize the moment and not think too hard about the consequences. Stay. Please.'

'What you've just described is called a 'coup de foudre' in French,' Maddie said. 'It means a sudden, unforeseen event.' She didn't tell him it also meant 'love at first sight' in some cultures.

'I don't know if there is a comparable word in Gaelic, but it sounds much better in French anyway...coup de food!'

Maddie laughed at his poor French pronunciation. 'Coup de foudre,', she said slowly and clearly.

They fell into each other's arms, laughing hysterically.

Aidan knew full well what coup de foudre meant, but kept that to himself.

00:19:45

A pulsating light woke Maddie from a deep sleep. In her semi-conscious state, she couldn't tell whether the light was coming from outside the large picture window or somewhere in the room. She closed her eyes and tried to return to a cocoon of drowsiness. Minutes later, she was interrupted again by the pulsating light; this time it was blinking with more urgency, or so it seemed. Maddie's phone was partially buried under a heap of damp towels. She picked it up and looked at the dark screen. She tapped the button and several separate text messages from her weekend roommate, Caitlyn, appeared, each one more frantic than the last: 'where are you?' 'are you okay?'; 'I'm concerned?'' 'we have no power here at the hotel'' 'it's really dark everywhere.' 'please answer me'.

Without a second thought, Maddie replied swiftly: 'fine. safe. see you later in the morn.' She turned off her phone and tossed it to the floor. Fully awake now, she stood, covered herself in the white robe, and walked to the picture window.

The night sky was beginning to break. A fine, thin line of soft pink was visible in the distance. She opened the window to feel the air temperature, and it was cool. It was going to be a nice day, Maddie thought, disappointed. She hoped for rain, ceaseless rain, so she would have an excuse to stay in this room all day.

Maddie could hear sounds coming from somewhere next door. It sounded familiar. Someone was playing music, she realized and it was the unmistakable sound of Lhasa, singing one of her most hypnotizing songs, 'De Cara a la Pared'. *How fitting*, Maddie thought. If lovemaking had its own distinct musical sound, it would be the soft drumming of falling rain, accentuated by the erotic strings of the violin and Lhasa's unique, sensual, and passionate singing voice, rising and falling. Every time she heard Lhasa's voice, she thought of uninhibited passion.

She turned to look at Aidan. His nude body was sprawled on the edge of the bed, one thick leg hanging slightly over the edge of the mattress, one arm curled under his head. He was breathing deeply, and his face had the serenity of a sleeping child.

Maddie watched him for a long time. The early morning sky produced a dreamy glow in the bedroom. Aidan's long, muscular legs were dotted with many deep, old scars, scratches, and a few dark bruises from the bike accident. His long face had two deep laugh lines perfectly placed on either side of his mouth, and his wavy, dark hair was peppered with more grey than she had originally thought. Aidan had the weathered face of a man who embraced hard work, not hard living. Though his body had seen some wear and tear over the years, he was raw, masculine, and utterly beautiful while he slept peacefully.

Aidan, still half asleep, sat up momentarily and turned his back. Maddie was immediately struck by his resemblance to an exquisite nude male painting she had seen at the Musee D'Orsay in Paris a few years before. She and Dominique had attended a highly unusual and provocative exhibit focused exclusively on the masculine nude form. Dominique was visibly uncomfortable with deluge of the nude male paintings, some graphic and sexually explicit, especially the images of endowed gay men in the throes of aggressive lovemaking. Maddie was completely mesmerized by the art. Her favorite painting was the 'Academy Drawing of a Man', by Jacques-Louis David. The nude man was thought to be his interpretation of Patroclus, Achilles' warrior friend and perhaps lover, from Greek mythology. The original painting captured the essence of the male physique in all his hard beauty. She'd stood looking at that painting for fifteen minutes before Dominique's uneasiness with the art forced her to leave. She had bought a print of the Patroclus painting and hung it in her own bathroom, so she could admire it every day.

As the dawn broke, and the room grew lighter, the remnants of the last several hours were fading with the darkness. Maddie grew melancholy. Aidan had taken her to a dreamy place, and she didn't want to leave. She closed her eyes and tried to capture this unique feeling, immortalize this place and time so she would always remember it when she needed to escape. The room did not feel real, nor did her body, which was strangely diaphanous and weightless. It struck her again, the improbability of meeting the charming Irishman, and letting things develop as quickly as they did.

She heard the sheets rustling and turned around. Aidan was awake, lying on his side and watching her. He was always smiling, it seemed, and in the morning light, his high cheek bones glowed a rosy hue. He opened the sheets and beckoned her to join him. She slid under the sheets and wrapped her thighs around his pelvis as they continued where they had left off only hours before, smothering her with his lips and tongue, circling her nipples, soft belly, moving down her body and between her legs. He did not know how or when to stop. She tried to pull him up, but he resisted and said quietly, 'Shh.' She laid back with eyes closed, her fingers in his thick hair. It was pure pleasure as he expertly explored the most intimate part of herself. Another wave of pure bliss, this one more powerful than the last, made her breathless. She could hardly move; she was paralyzed with pleasure. She opened her eyes to see him staring, and she kissed his wet face hungrily, their bodies pressed together so tightly his broad chest was almost suffocating her.

He rolled onto his back, pulling her on him. Quietly and rhythmically they rocked together, slowly at first. The intensity quickly reached a feverish tempo. Aidan threw Maddie onto her back. He was big and strong, but not rough, the perfect foil to Maddie's equally sturdy frame. 'Oh god, I cannot get enough of yeh,' he whispered, barely audible, as his body contracted, then released.

There was a moment of quiet as he laid on top of her, both out of breath and damp, before they collapsed, laughing wildly like a pair of randy teenagers.

The sun was shining brightly and the outside air was already hot and humid when the couple finally got out of bed several hours later. The electricity had returned. Aidan got busy making coffee, and Maddie texted Caitlyn to reassure her she was fine, then jumped into the shower. Five minutes later, she walked into the kitchen to find a full Irish breakfast of sausages, fried potatoes, eggs, tomatoes, toast, and strong coffee laid out on the kitchen table.

'Oh my goodness, what a feast! You can cook?'

'I do indeed!' Aidan replied proudly.

'I'm really impressed...a man who cooks. You are way too perfect!' Maddie replied, and kissed him soundly on the lips.

Maddie ate her breakfast with enthusiasm. She didn't care about the calories, or the nutritional value of eating eggs and fried potatoes so close to her race. She was too hungry to care.

'This is delicious!' Maddie said, enjoying every bite.

'I like to cook for a woman with a big appetite!' Aidan replied, grinning proudly.

After eating, Aidan immediately started clearing the dishes from the table.

'I'll do that,' Maddie said, 'you cook, I clean; it's only fair.' She stood and took the hand towel away from him.

'Before yeh do that, can we sit for a moment an' chat? I have something to ask yeh,' Aidan said.

They moved to the sectional sofa that occupied most of the space in the living area. The view from the oversized condo window was spectacular –the Mont-Tremblant ski resort was easy to spot even from a distance of 5 kilometers. Colorful race banners and flags dotted the road leading in and out of the race site. To the left was Lake Mont-Tremblant, the venue for the swim portion of the race. It sparkled a deep green in the morning sun. It was dead calm and enticing, even to Maddie, who loathed open-water swimming.

Aidan took Maddie's' hand and held it. He was pensive, his bandaged forehead wrinkled in a frown. Maddie wondered if he was about to tell her that he was married and his wife was expected any second. She was waiting for the inevitable bomb to drop and was mentally planning her exit strategy in case a woman walked in, though Aidan seemed more contemplative than nervous.

'I want yeh to stay here with me until after the race,' Aidan blurted out.

Maddie was dumbfounded. This was not what she was expecting. This request was sudden and seriously impulsive. They hardly knew each other, but he was asking her to move into together for a few days.

'I know what you're thinking, my fine lady. It's impulsive. We hardly know each other and what is the point, being that yeh'r married?'

'How did you know I was married?'

'I really wasn't sure until this moment, though I doubt your marriage is going too well these days – otherwise he would be sitting next to yeh instead of me.'

'That's true enough, Aidan. I am married, but it will soon be over,' Maddie replied honestly. 'Are you married?'

'I am not married, and I am here alone,' Aidan replied, leaning back. 'I must return to Ireland on Monday, after the race. I've been away for many months. Yeh see, I've been working in Nepal, toiling away in the mountains. I only decided a few weeks ago to come here for this race. Rash decision at the time, but I am glad I made it,' he added, grinning.

'Where you working in construction? Maddie asked

'I was in Nepal for another reason.' Aidan reached for Maddie's hand. 'I was doing a rescue and recovery operation, though I must say, it was more recovery. I work as a volunteer for a humanitarian organization. I am a member of the rapid response team. Whenever there's an earthquake or some type of natural disaster, we get called in to help the local community with rescue, recovery, shelter, medical treatment, water- whatever they need. We usually arrive within hours. After the earthquake struck the Gorhka District in Nepal, I stayed for several weeks, workin' long days without any real contact with the outside world, other than the crew, other NGOs, and the old Nepalese ladies that fed and took care of me. They hugged me often to thank me. T'was very sad at times.'

'I'm so sorry to hear this Aidan,' Maddie replied. She could never imagine herself running off to some remote part of the world, working day and night under extreme and difficult conditions, sacrificing her comfort to help others. Aidan was an exceptional person.

'When I first saw you on the promenade, I couldn't keep me eyes off yeh. I was having thoughts of seeing you naked too,' Aidan said, winking. 'And then the deer struck and my head went spinnin'. The moment yeh put your hands on me, I could almost feel your heartbeat surging through me. Perhaps it was the consequence of being alone for so long, but I would not have touched yeh so brazenly if I had not felt that way, or if yeh had pulled away.'

'I know you would have,' Maddie replied.

'Maddie, I believe we have a special connection, and we don't have a lot of time. Only a few days, really.' He shook his head, as if in denial of the truth. 'I can't tell you what will happen tomorrow, next week, or the next month, but I do know that we have a unique opportunity, and we should make the most of it whilst we can... call me a fatalist, but in my experience, you have to snatch those rare moments in life that make you deliriously happy, and hang on to them for as long as you can. Once they're gone, you can never get them back. Do you understand?'

She did understand exactly what he was saying, and he was right about seizing the moment. The chance encounter with the Irishman and the wildly spontaneous aftermath could not be ignored. She was having an amazing time, after all, why not make it last just a few days longer? She wasn't hurting anyone. As far as Dominque was concerned, she gave little thought to his feelings. He was looking after himself these days, and if he truly cared about their marriage, as Aidan pointed out, he would have come to Mont-Tremblant. For once, Maddie was making a decision that was all about her.

The only doubt that crept into Maddie's organized mind was about the man himself. Aidan was not acting like a man indulging in a sex-filled fantasy weekend. He was attentive and affectionate, even emotional, acting more like a man in love than someone carrying on a short lustful affair. Perhaps, Maddie mused, this was the Irish version of a casual affair.

'Okay, Aidan. Much against my better judgement, I am giving in to your considerable charms.'

'That's music to my fat ears! Although, the truth be told, my Granny once lectured me to stay away from redheads. She said t'is unlucky to meet a woman with red hair first thing in the morning when going on a journey, 'for her presence will bring ill-luck and certain evil',' he added, raising one eyebrow.

'Really? Well, I sure hope for your sake that she's wrong about that!'

'Och, I don't believe any superstitious nonsense anyway,' and they both laughed.

*****

Maddie conducted a thorough check of Aidan's bike. The front wheel was completely bent and unusable. The pedals turned well, the chain was moving smoothly, and the back wheel was spinning without rubbing, but both the front and back gears needed adjustments. The handlebars had shifted to the right on impact, and so had the seat.

Maddie took out her tools from her small bike pouch and started adjusting the gears on Aidan's older model Quintana Roo bike.

'Hey, what are you doing with my bike?' Aidan asked as he walked into the garage, wearing a short sleeved green t-shirt and a pair of men's capris. Until that moment, Maddie had seen him only in torn cycling clothes or naked. This was the first time she had seen Aidan in casual street clothes, and she was immediately distracted by his imposing height and arresting good looks.

'Ah…well, your bike needs a bit of work- minor adjustments really. But…' she paused to choose her words carefully, 'Your front wheel is totally bent. It has to be replaced. The good news is, a wheel can be replaced easily. The bad news is, your wheel is a 650c, and I don't know where we will find a bike dealer around here who still carries this type of wheel.'

'Go on outta that...you can fix a bike?' Aidan

'What a funny expression, Aidan. Anyway, in answer to your question, yes, I can fix bikes, among other things!' Maddie continued to poke around Aidan's 20-year-old bike. '…in my University days, my nickname was Maddie MacGyver…'

'C'mere!'

'No, it's true. I could and still can fix a lot of stuff,' Maddie replied emphatically, 'I grew up without a Dad, so I had to fend for myself when it came to mechanics and… well… I have a talent for being resourceful. When my husband was going through medical school and we didn't have much money, I learned how to do minor repairs in our little apartment because we were always broke, and we couldn't afford to buy anything new.'

'Maddie MacGyver…Maddie MacGyver…it has nice ring to it. You are full of surprises – not only are you fine looking and intelligent women, you can repair stuff, too!'

Aidan grabbed Maddie's waist, pulled her close, and kissed her, leaving her breathless. 'We should leave now and look for a bike dealer…otherwise we will never leave this condo,' Maddie said as she reluctantly pulled herself away from him.

'Och, you're so serious!' Aidan said.

They drove to the race site to retrieve Maddie's belongings and to find a bike dealer that stocked Aidan's unusually sized wheel. Their first stop was the bike service tent up in the Athletes' Village. In flawless French, Maddie explained to the bike technician what they are looking for, and he shook his head – no, he didn't carry this product. He suggested they try a bike dealer in Ste-Agathe, 35 kilometers away. 'We should go now, in case we have to drive all over eastern Quebec looking for a 650 c wheel. What do you think?' Maddie suggested, hoping that a delay to the hotel would give her enough time to come up with a plausible excuse to her roommate Caitlyn about her change of plans for the rest of the week.

'I say we pick your stuff first-unless you've changed your mind?' Aidan asked, looking at Maddie for signs she was uncomfortable with their arrangement.

'No, no…it's just that it's a bit awkward. I don't know her very well and I'm not sure how she will react.'

'She'll be fine as soon as she meets me,' Aidan replied confidently.

Maddie didn't take this bold statement as conceit or an inflated view of oneself. Aidan was self-assured, but not cocky. She had no doubt he could charm a rabid bear, if required.

They made their way to the hotel, which sat conveniently at the corner of the Promenade and the main thoroughfare. Maddie texted Caitlyn to tell her she was on her way back to the room and that she was not alone.

As soon as they walked into the hotel room, Aidan immediately reached out to Caitlyn, and introduced himself as Maddie's high school friend. In spite of the thick Irish accent that Aidan tried hard to diminish, and the fact that he was clearly younger than Maddie, Aidan's engaging and effervescent personality won Caitlyn over instantly. The awkward issue of 'moving' out was smoothed over with the implausible explanation that the pair wanted to get caught up on the past twenty years. Caitlyn was much too astute to be fooled by Aidan's charm, and the story was utterly inconceivable, but she willingly went along with it as she saw how smitten Maddie was with the athletic and handsome man.

On the way out the door, Caitlyn whispered 'Lucky you,' and put her thumbs up and then to her lips, indicating to Maddie that she was in on this ruse, and not to worry.

Once in the car, Maddie could not help herself and said to Aidan, smiling, 'You're incorrigible.'

'Indeed I am…I encourage people to go along with my wishes!'

'Don't TINK for a minute that she believed a word you said,' Maddie replied, making fun of Aidan's thick, sing-song accent.

'Did I not get what I wanted – to have you all to myself for the next few days? A man will do whatever it takes to have a woman by his side,' Aidan added laughing.

The couple spent the rest of the day driving around the area, looking for the elusive 650c wheel. They ended up in St-Jerome, about 90 kilometers away, at a bike dealer that stocked the wheel. While the mechanic was busy installing the tube and wheel to the bike, Aidan and Maddie walked around, looking at the immense variety of new, colourful road and triathlon bikes. The entire day had been relaxing and effortless, as though they had known each other for years, not hours.

'Oh my, I've never seen such a display in me life. The last time I visited a bike shop was years ago. Things have really changed. I think it's time I give up my old beast of bike. It has served me well these past fifteen and some years,' Aidan said with a touch of sadness, as he stopped and examined a sleek green and black triathlon bike with the latest electronic gadgets. The price was over $12,000.

'Once you get the new wheel, you will be fine to ride your bike.

There is nothing wrong with it, except that it's a bit out of date and rather heavy for endurance racing — but if it works for you, then why change it?' Maddie replied, not wanting to embarrass Aidan any further. The haughty bike mechanic made it very clear what he thought of Aidan's old-style bike, handling it with extreme caution, as though it had a contagious disease. Triathlon racing could be a showy sport, and the pressure to purchase the latest and best equipment bordered on fanatical. Maddie was not sure about Aidan's financial situation and whether a new $12,000 bike was within his means.

'My old Quintana has been with me everywhere. I've taken her to all my races, and I've done so many I can hardly keep count. I do love her, but... this will be her last race...' Aidan paused for moment, thinking about what to do next.

"Will you do me a favour, Maddie? Will you take the bike with yeh to Montreal and donate it to a bike shop for me? Maybe they can hang it in a bike museum or display it as vintage art?'

'Why get rid of it?' Maddie asked.

'It's time I made a few changes in my life. She represents the past. I want to move forward.' Aidan said nothing more, but stared at the sleek black and green machine.

'That is one of the top-selling bikes and it's also very expensive,' Maddie added.

'Och, it's just money...'

Maddie woke up suddenly and violently from a dream. Once or twice a month for the past six months, Maddie had had the same unsettling and disturbing dream. She knew, full well, why she was having this dream.

The dream begins with Maddie standing on the shore of an unfamiliar lake. The sun is shining and the air is warm. Maddie is wearing her swim gear: a full wetsuit, goggles and cap. Someone, whose face is obscured by a big hat, is sitting in a dark blue kayak holding a paddle. Maddie plunges into the water and starts swimming, the hidden kayaker paddling at the speed at which she is swimming. The water feels comfortable. Maddie continues to swim, occasionally glancing to her right to ensure the kayak is still within sight. Maddie falls into a rhythmic stroke pattern. Time elapses a quickly, she thinks, because suddenly Maddie in the dream stops swimming and looks around. The kayaker is gone, the water is still and the sky is a deep dark blue, almost black. Maddie is in the middle of a dusky lake, at night, by herself. No whistle to call for help; no floatation device to rest on and no one in sight. In the dream, Maddie starts to feel the panic rising to her throat, and she wakes up, soaked in sweat.

'Maddie – what's wrong?' Aidan asked, a look of panic on his face as he reached for her arm.

'Nothing, I just had a dream. I will be okay,' she replied in an unsteady voice.

Aidan was not easily convinced. 'It looked more like a nightmare than a dream. Perhaps you'd best tell me about it?'

The both sat up. It was a beautiful, cloudless night. Through the bedroom window, tiny iridescent lights dotted the Mont-Tremblant ski hill several kilometres away. It was not late by Quebec standards, around midnight, and all the bars and restaurants were still open and busy. The race was in forty-eight hours, and most of the competitors had arrived by this time to settle in and enjoy the festive atmosphere.

Maddie recounted her dream to Aidan in detail. She held nothing back. Since spending time with her over the last two days, Aidan had learned a great deal about the lovely Canadian, including her fear of open water swimming. She had not explained, though, the reasons for her anxiety. 'I told you my dad died when I was twelve... but I didn't tell you how he died...'

'Go on, then...'

'He drowned. He and his best friend. I was 12 years Old, and we were at our rented cottage on Lake Massawippi. The Eastern Townships of Quebec are glorious, and we rented a cottage every summer there. Anyway, my dad Peter and his best friend Frank went fishing, as they often did during our annual summer holiday. The men were gone all day. By 5 pm, the weather turned nasty. A sudden, fierce storm descended on the lake, and the wind presumably overturned the moving boat. The pair were not wearing lifejackets. They found the boat first, driving in circles, the throttle in full gear and locked, without anyone on board. Later, they found their lifeless bodies floating near the shoreline. I guess they were trying to outrun the storm and took some chances.' Maddie stopped talking. The emotion of recounting the loss of her dad was utterly exhausting. It's been a while, years in fact, since Maddie told the story of the boating accident. This was not something she shared with friends, let alone strangers. 'You don't have to be a psychoanalyst to connect my fear of swimming with my father's untimely death in water.'

'I'm so very sorry, Maddie. Such a terrible loss for a young vulnerable girl.' Aidan pulled Maddie close to him and instinctively hugged her for protection.

'My father died when I was sixteen.' Aidan said, clutching the redhead close to his body. 'Believe me, I know this pain.' He understood more than most the heart wrenching loss of watching a parent die.

'You love the water, don't you, Aidan? Maddie asked, wiping her wet face with the back of her hand.

'I do indeed. Unlike you, the water has always been a safe haven for me. It muffles the sounds, blocks out the world. It's always been a good friend to me in times of need. Reliable, predictable, constant. When I swim, it's just me and the water. Nothing else seems to matter.'

*****

Twenty-four hours before the big race and Aidan woke up very early. Maddie lay next to him, snoring softly. He wanted to take her as she slept, her warm nude body was so luscious in the early morning, but he chose to get up and watch the sun rise in the living room. In spite of his obvious sexual desires, he was not feeling particularly good this morning. His headache had returned, his temples were throbbing, and his stomach was nauseous. *There was time enough this morning to take her,* he said to himself quietly, so he let her sleep.

Since they had met only three days before, Aidan and Maddie had been in a timeless universe. They locked themselves away, existing for no one else but each other. The intimacy he shared with the lovely Canadian was the closest thing to an honest and loving relationship that Aidan had experienced in twenty years.

The big race was now a mere twenty-four hours away, and the reality that their time together was coming to an end weighed heavily on his mind.

Aidan heard Maddie's voice in the other room, calling his name.

00:27:37

Race morning. In spite of Aidan' enthusiastic and selfless efforts to relax his partner the night before, Maddie had not slept well. She could not stop thinking about the race, her mind replaying over and over again the sequence of events that would lead her to the finish line. Finally, the day had arrived, and she could no longer put off facing the task ahead of her.

This was the reason she was in Mont-Tremblant; this was why she had spent the last fourteen months working tirelessly to accomplish her goals. She knew her body could get through 6.5 hours of the endurance race and propel her to the finish line. She was not nearly so confident about her mental condition. Her mind was working against her, filling her with doubt, especially the dreaded swim. The thought of swimming in open water for two kilometers made her stomach heave. Maddie felt like throwing up and worried that she did not even have the courage to start the race. Aidan was aware of her anxiety. They had spoken about it, and he had suggested, more than once, that they go swimming together. He could help her, he said, but she stubbornly refused.

Maddie was anxious not to forget an important piece of gear on race day. She reviewed, packed and repacked her gear the day before, placing all her stuff in a nice neat row on the floor: swim, bike, and run gear, all lined up and in perfect order. She had visited and re-visited that pile at least a dozen times to ensure she was not forgetting something critical. As a precaution, she wore her timing chip to bed, something Aidan found very amusing.

In spite of a minor headache, Aidan had woken with his usual eagerness. Lying next to Maddie, he gently pressed his body against her back. and put his hands between her legs. She flinched ever so lightly. Her shoulders tensed up and her back muscles contracted. He pulled his hand away, and instead comforted her by stroking her hips.

Maddie could feel Aidan pressed against her, his warm hands caressing her intimately. For the first time since they met, Maddie did not respond to his touch. She was in Mont-Tremblant for a reason, and it had nothing to do with meeting Aidan, though she reminded herself he had been the unexpected reward for the sacrifices she had made in the last year.

The alarm clock went off loudly. Quietly, the couple got up from the bed and moved about the condo, packing up their race gear in the semi-darkness, drinking coffee and eating bagels with peanut butter. The night sky was slowly dissipating. It was going to be a clear, cool morning. The weather forecast indicated a high of 22 degrees for the day, with low humidity and no wind, the absolute ideal conditions for a long-distance triathlon race. The couple loaded up the truck in complete silence and drove to the race site.

When they arrived at Le Station Mont-Tremblant, the site was humming with activity. Hundreds of volunteers were already working, giving directions and orchestrating traffic in and out of the Transition Zone that held an individual spot for all 2200 athletes. Maddie found her rack number and proceeded to lay out all her equipment: bike shoes, helmet, gloves, socks, running shoes, visor, sunglasses, energy gels, and water bottles. There was so much to think about on race morning that Maddie was feeling overwhelmed. After finally checking and re-checking her stuff, Maddie racked her bike. Aidan was not far away, one row over from hers. He had thrown everything he needed in a bag that morning, and quickly set out his gear in just a few minutes. He waited patiently, watching Maddie talking to herself.

Aidan was relaxed. He had done these types of races dozens of times. His only anxiety that morning had nothing to do with the race, but after it was over…

Maddie stopped what she was doing and looked at Aidan, panic written all over her face. 'Oh no, I've forgotten my timing chip…damn. Jeez, what the…'

Aidan broke out in a roaring laugh and pointed to her ankle.

'Oh,' was all Maddie could say, her ears turning a bright pink.

After securing their race gear, Maddie and Aidan walked to the athlete marking area so that their individual race numbers were clearly visible on the upper arm. Aidan waited while Maddie got marked.

'Aren't you getting marked?' Maddie asked as a volunteer carefully wrote on her arm.

'I never do…it doesn't wash off.'

Once that small task was complete, they walked to the swim start, about a half kilometer away from the transition area. All 1500 men and 700 women were walking along the road, carrying or wearing their wetsuits, talking and laughing. Music was blaring from the loudspeakers dotted along the route.

At the swim start, spectators and participants were treated to a festive scene. Colorful balloons hung along the water pontoon, a large inflated blue arch was secured in the sand designating the swim start entrance, and blue carpeting covered the sandy area. All participants were wearing brightly colored swim caps according to their age and swim wave. There was more music blaring on the beach, and the announcer was talking over the music, reviewing the swim course. Small boats, kayaks, and paddlers were getting ready to head out on the swim course to offer assistance during the race, should a participant need help. The scuba divers, whose job was to look for anyone sinking to the bottom of the lake, were lined up on the beach, checking their masks and fiddling with their tank gauges. Massive orange water pylons dotted the swim course every 100 meters. The atmosphere at the swim start was more of a giant beach party than a major international competitive sporting event.

Maddie and Aidan went into the water to warm up before the start. The water was cold, but not nearly cold enough to cancel the swim. Maddie had secretly hoped that the water temperature would fall below the acceptable minimum standard of 14 degrees, and the organizers would be forced to cancel the swim. The water temperature was a balmy 19 degrees, and the swim would start on time. After a short warmup, Maddie and Aidan stood on the crowded beach, waiting for the race to finally begin.

'You should have something to eat,' he suggested, trying to break the tension he could see on her freckled face. 'Here, I brought you a banana.'

'Thanks, but I don't think I could eat anything right now. My stomach is not cooperating,' Maddie replied. Her heart was palpitating wildly and her throat felt dry as baby powder. She was shivering from fear, not from the cold. Why on earth did she think she could swim 2000 meters in open water?

'You look so sexy in that wet suit I'd do you here if I could get that thing off without anyone noticing,' Aidan said, pulling Maddie momentarily away from her morbid thoughts of drowning. She laughed at his comment, the first heartfelt laugh all morning.

'Is that all you think about? No one is sexy in a wetsuit!'

'Well, yeh'r to me…Maddie mhuirnín,' Aidan said in Gaelic 'I know how terrified you are – it's written over your beautiful face.' Aidan took Maddie's face in his hands and spoke to her gently but firmly, oblivious to all the other athletes standing inches from the couple.

'Listen carefully to me and do exactly as I say. At the sound of the horn, start swimming slowly, from the back of the pack. Forget about all the other women flailin' and panickin' around you. Focus only your stroke, one arm over the other. Breathe in – breathe out. Don't get ahead of yourself. I want you to swim to the 2nd orange pylon, at 200 meters. Do yeh see that?' Aidan pointed toward the lake and the bright orange markers dotting the swim course. Maddie nodded. 'Good…stop when yeh get to that pylon, and I will meet you there, and we can swim together to the finish.'

'What are you saying? You are going to sacrifice your race to look after me? No, no, don't be mad. You have your own race to win. I'll be fine.' Maddie's reply was tentative and not the least bit convincing.

'I don't need to win today. I've won plenty of races over the years. You are more important to me than a stupid $5 medal.'

'You didn't come all the way from Ireland to come in last place,' Maddie snapped back.

'I came all the way from Ireland for the sole purpose of meeting you. Go now, you are up. See you in a couple of minutes. No arguments.' Aidan kissed her on the cheek and then pushed her toward the group of women standing at the swim entrance. Maddie looked back to see Aidan smiling and gesturing at her emphatically. She was so caught up in the enormous task before her, she didn't give Aidan's comments a second thought.

She moved to the start line but placed herself at the very back. She looked around and saw that all the women standing next to her were just as terrified as she was. The announcer counted down, one minute to go. Maddie put her goggles on. There was another shout at 30 seconds, and then 10 seconds. Maddie wanted to throw up at that moment. She dared not look back at Aidan. The horn blasted, and immediately all the women at the front plunged into the pristine lake. A mass of rubber clad women began fighting for position in the water. Maddie held back until the faster, more competitive swimmers took the lead, then she slowly dove in the water and began to swim, counting each stroke as instructed by Aidan.

Maddie could feel the fear gripping in her throat. Her wet suit was closing in on her, too tight around her upper body, neck and shoulders. Another swimmer was swimming too close to Maddie, and kicked her a few times before she finally broke away. Maddie's' punctuated stroke started to break down as she swallowed a mouthful of water. Get to the second buoy, she told herself. It's only 150 meters. Maddie kept going, one arm in front of the other, calming herself as she approached the rendezvous point. She wanted desperately to stop, to end this torture, but she also did not want to disappoint Aidan, the gallant man who was going to sacrifice his race for her. She had reason to persevere.

Aidan watched Maddie at the start and followed her progression along the swim course. Even at that distance, he could spot Maddie's unmistakeable swim style, slow and deliberate. He could also tell she was struggling but she didn't stop. *Good girl… she'll be just fine*, he said to himself.

It was almost time for his wave start. Aidan bent down on one knee and discreetly pulled the Velcro strap of his timing chip to loosen it. The ankle bracelet would disappear into the deep lake as soon as he started to swim. Aidan then moved quickly to the front of the line so he would be first in the water. Getting to Maddie quickly was paramount to his plan. …5, 4, 3, 2…. The horn blasted again, and the men dove into the water. There was a mass of water spray and waves, and in the huge melee, Aidan' long arms pulled ahead of the group. Aidan was a superb swimmer. He easily swam ahead of all the men in the 40+ age category, with the exception of one or two whom he knew from other triathlons. Aidan reached the 200-meter buoy, and Maddie, in two and a half minutes.

Maddie was breathless when she arrived at the buoy, but Aidan was hardly breathing when he arrived seconds later. 'How do you do that so easily – so quickly?' Maddie asked, bobbing in the water.

'I am very motivated.' Aidan replied. 'Listen, we need to go now, love. Let's stay on this side of the buoy to avoid the men coming up. I'm right next to you. I will stay the whole way.'

'Aidan, you don't have to do this…I will manage.'

'I do not have to do anythin', but I want to! Maddie, the sooner we get to shore, the sooner we finish this race, the sooner I get you in my arms.'

She nodded yes, and started swimming, following the orange buoys as instructed by her new swim coach. Aidan stayed close to her for the entire swim, making sure no other swimmer disturbed their rhythm and pace. It was a slow swim, very slow, but Aidan did not care. He was enjoying being the protector and watching Maddie improve her pace and confidence at each

100-meter mark. Most of the strongest men in his age group were passing him, but Aidan only cared about the woman swimming beside him and making sure she not only finished the swim, but finished the race.

They both emerged from the water together. Maddie was dizzy but joyful. 'I did it! I did it,' she yelled out.

Aidan was smiling, too. 'One down, two more to go,' he said to Maddie. They ran along the blue carpet into the Transition area together. There, they quickly stripped off the wet suits, put on socks and cycling shoes, snapped on their helmets, and headed toward the bike exit.

'Maddie,' Aidan yelled to get her attention, above the noise and loud music, 'start cycling. I will either be behind yeh or in front of yeh. Don't look around to find me. I will be there.'

Maddie again nodded no and yelled out, 'Why don't you try and catch up to your age-group now? I will be fine now.'

'No, I want to stay with yeh. Don't argue with me now… let's go.'

Aidan was perfectly content to stay close to Maddie. Under normal conditions, he was an exceedingly competitive athlete. He raced to win, and he won many of the races he competed in. He could win his age category even when he trained for only a few short weeks.

Maddie was the main reason he was taking this race slowly. He was so smitten by the redhead, it made him giddy. He was acting like a love-struck schoolboy whose only ambition in life was to please his new girlfriend. This was perfectly fine with him. The most important person at that moment was Maddie, and he was going to put every effort to see her through to the end of the race. Aidan had another reason for treating this race more as a training effort than a race. Since the bike accident, he was in some physical pain. He was still sore and bruised, and the low throbbing headache would not abate, regardless of how many pills he popped.

Maddie and Aidan took turns leading on the bike course. They travelled at a good speed and were careful not to stay too close to one another, for fear of being penalized for 'drafting' off each other in order to conserve energy and improve speed, a practice that was highly illegal in these races and could lead to disqualification.

Towards the end of the bike course, around the 75-kilometer marker, they reached the toughest part, the dreaded Cole Duplessis. It was a short climb, only 4 kilometers long, but very steep, with a gradient percentage of 11% in some places. Many inexperienced tri-athletes would either fall off their bikes trying to climb the steep hill, or get off and walk this portion of the course. It was hard, intimidating, and tiring and it was at the end, when the leg muscles were depleted of energy. Maddie had climbed the Cole Duplessis on several occasions during training rides. In spite of her best efforts, climbing hills, either on the bike or on the run, was not her strength. She dreaded climbing hills, almost as much as she dreaded open water swimming. Maddie blamed her above-average size for her inability to scoot up a hill quickly. Nonetheless, she was a reasonable good cyclist for her age, and she attacked the Cole Duplessis with a vengeance. Her confidence had soared after the swim, so there was no reason she couldn't tackle this hill with the same veracity. She also wanted to prove to Aidan that she could do this on her own steam.

As they climbed, Maddie could feel every laboured pedal stroke in her tired muscles. Her heart rate was at threshold and pounding in her chest, and her breathing was loud and noisy. Aidan and Maddie arrived together at the summit in reasonably good time, both panting and wheezing from the effort. Aidan smiled and yelled out to Maddie, 'That was a wee bit of an effort on the legs…'

Wasting no time, Maddie responded 'Let's see who can get to the bottom first!' She took off back down the Cole Duplessis. Aidan could only stare at her, smiling.

Maddie's belief in herself had increased with every minute of the race.

Maddie attacked the downhill portion of the Cole Duplessis with the conviction and assuredness of a professional cyclist. She stayed in a deep tuck position, legs glued to the frame, squeezing her shoulders and body as tight as possible. While her large frame made climbing hills particularly arduous, it was well suited to downhill cycling. Maddie's weight propelled her forward. She weaved in and out of the bike course, passing numerous cyclists on the descent, attempting to make up the lost time from the ascent. Maddie was fearless. *Why not go faster and increase the risk factor*, she thought, acutely aware now that the Mont-Tremblant experience was more than just a race – it was all about risk and stretching the boundaries of her physical and emotional comfort zone.

Aidan followed Maddie, and she impressed him with her bike handling skills down the technically challenging course. He was worried, though, that she was going too fast and taking too many chances. A crash at these speeds would cause serious damage, or could be fatal.

Maddie gained ground and was 200 meters ahead of Aidan. He lost site of the pink helmet around a sharp corner. He pushed harder and faster on the peddles to catch up with her. As he turned the corner, he could see the green and white bike in the distance, and the bright pink helmet glistening in the morning sun. He could also see a group of other riders just ahead of her. His heart stopped when one of those cyclists, unaware or ignorant of cycling protocol, pulled out ahead of Maddie without looking back, causing her to swerve quickly to the left to avoid a nasty collision. Aidan could hear Maddie swearing loudly in French at the cyclist for his stupidity, but she neither slowed down nor pulled back on the downhill attack.

Aidan kept his eyes and his bike on her back wheel until they reached the flat section, and then he relaxed. They both survived the downhill at speeds in excess of 65 kilometers an hour and were about to enter the Transition Zone to start the run, the final leg of the race.

*****

Her face flushed with perspiration from the hard climb up the Cole Duplessis, Maddie was jubilant as she made her way to the bike rack to switch from cycling to running. *Now the real test of my fitness begins,* Maddie thought. Aidan had advised her not to think too far ahead during the race and to focus on each skill separately. The prospect of running 21 kilometers was now unavoidable and almost impossible to imagine. While she was feeling emotionally elated, her body was beginning to show signs of fatigue.

'Are you okay?' Aidan yelled out, pulling on his running shoes.

'Yes, just a little tired,' Maddie replied, 'but I'm okay.'

'Have a gel. We will grab some coke at the first aid station. It will help with low energy.'

As she had done since the start of the race, her fate rested in Aidan's capable and experienced hands. He told her to trust him, and so far, the race had gone beyond her expectations. *If I can still walk tonight, I am going to generously reward this man,* Maddie thought trying not to smile.

'Maddie, let's go.' Aidan grabbed her hand, and they ran through the Transition Zone to start the 21-kilometer run to the finish line.

The first 5 kilometers of the run course was nothing short of brutal. It was mostly up and down short hills. With each hill they climbed, Maddie legs were screaming to stop, rest, and walk. Aidan did not let her walk an inch. He coaxed her along until they reached the first aid station. There, he handed her a coke and another energy gel, and they slowed down for a brief walk.

'Take these,' he said.

'Another gel?' I don't think I could eat another...'

'Trust me. Your body needs it. Go, come on.'

Reluctantly, Maddie took another gel and a shot of coke, and they resumed running. After only a few short minutes, Maddie got a burst of energy, and she felt better. The short hills eased off, and they entered the flatter, easier section of the run course.

The run course meandered through the tiny quaint section of Mont-Tremblant affectionately called the 'Old Village', not far from Aidan's' condo. There were hundreds of people lined up along the route, cheering wildly and calling their names. The couple continued to run at a steady pace, Aidan talking to Maddie the entire time. Maddie could hardly breathe comfortably running, let alone talk, so she let Aidan speak for both of them. He commented on just about anything he found funny and unusual. He constantly yelled out encouragements to those runners they passed or who were running towards them, on the return leg of the run course. His comments were especially humorous regarding the various triathlon outfits people wore, their color schemes and embellishments. One man in particular stood out. He was wearing a neon green tiny speedo bathing suit, a short vest that just barely covered his hairy torso, bright green socks, and a visor.

'Nice outfit. Maybe I should wear the same thing…what do yeh think, love? Can yeh see me wearing a bright micro speedo?' Aidan yelled out.

Maddie burst out laughing. 'Oh, please. No man, regardless of his age or physical attributes, should ever wear such an outfit. You are a great looking guy, Aidan, but I don't think even you should run in a speedo bathing suit. Ever.'

They ran without stopping. Maddie was curious to learn more about Aidan's personal life, his background, and his family.

'Aidan, tell me about the work you do for that humanitarian organization you mentioned a few days ago?' Maddie asked breathlessly, trying to keep up with Aidan's boundless energy.

'I'm on the rapid response team. As soon as we are called to action, we get deployed, usually within forty-eight hours, and start a search and rescue operation, working closely with the impacted community, looking for survivors, that is, if we get there in time. Time is critical – every hour counts, and it can mean the difference between rescue and recovery, life versus death. Sadly, mostly of the work is recovery. It is painstakingly slow and hard work. Progress is measured by inches, not feet, and it's mostly done by hand, though my skills as a heavy equipment operator are put to good use. It's a very delicate operation to move debris whilst trying to recover a loved one.'

Aidan loved the work, he told Maddie. Over the last twenty years, he had volunteered at several humanitarian and relief operations: the earthquakes in Haiti, China and Pakistan; the tsunamis in the Indian Ocean and off the coast of Japan. The construction company that he worked for gave him the latitude to take on these special assignments, when they came. He usually travelled two to three months of the year.

'It sounds very nomadic and unconventional. Do you go alone? How and when do you train, if you are gone so much?' Maddie asked.

'I do indeed go alone. As far as my triathlon training methods, they are unusual but highly effective, consisting of heavy lifting, walking and running up steep mountains or trails, navigating boulders and demolished buildings, and swimming occasionally in polluted, feces-filled rivers.' Aidan said with a smirk.

'That's not fair! I train for months, religiously sticking to my grueling schedule of fifteen hours a week of progressive activity and you…you just show up, get dressed and race,' Maddie responded, shaking her head in disbelief.

They ran past the spot where Aidan had had the bike accident. For a few seconds, neither one said anything. Maddie was not sure if Aidan remembered where the accident had occurred. This spot, along with all the events that followed, were permanently etched in her mind.

They continued to run along the paved trail. Maddie was not a naturally gifted runner. She had to concentrate on her form and movements to avoid making many of the novice runner mistakes, like swinging the arms to the middle and over-striding. Aidan, on the other hand, was a marvel to watch. He had a smooth, effortless running style that was surprising for such a big man. Most big men tend to power their way through the run, pounding hard on the pavement, breathing heavily, and leaning forward in an attempt to lower their centre of gravity. Aidan was graceful and elegant. He touched down on every step with his forefoot, springing back lightly. He had balance, rhythm, timing, and strength. He was just as smooth on the bike as he was running. No rolling or swaying from side to side, his legs tucked in nicely and close to the bike frame, his hands on the handlebars looking comfortable and in control of his every movement.

At Montee Ryan, the turn-around point for the run course, Maddie was growing weary. The pace and effort were gruelling, as Aidan was pushing at a pace that was significantly faster than what Maddie was used to. It was still another 10 kilometers to the finish, and Maddie's legs felt like boat anchors; her arms were swinging wildly, and her shoulders had dropped. She was losing her running form, and her whole body was screaming to stop, walk, and maybe lie down for a nap.

While Maddie was struggling just to stay upright, Aidan's running was as smooth and controlled as it has been from the beginning. He glanced over to Maddie and could see that she was laboring with the brisk pace. He slowed down momentarily.

'Are you getting tired, Maddie?' Aidan asked.

'Yes, a bit,' but she added, without thinking, 'I'm too fat to run. I need to lose more weight.'

Aidan stopped running, grabbed Maddie's elbow, and abruptly pulled her to the side of the running trail.

'Did I just hear yeh say yeh are too fat?' Without waiting for an answer, he lashed into her as dozens of athletes ran by.

'Listen, I never want to hear you say that yeh're too fat for this or that. That's complete and utter nonsense. You're built the way the good lord intended women to be built. These women here are unhealthy looking—too skinny. It's not right.' He stopped, then added, 'I'd never go near a woman like that; it would be like making love to a bag of antlers.' He was smiling, the seriousness gone from his voice. 'We'll have no more of this talk, do you understand?'

Maddie replied, shaking her head, 'Making love to a bag of antlers? Really? Where do you come up with this stuff?'

'I was an Irish poet in my past life! No more negative talk. Let's go.'

They resumed running at a slightly slower pace.

Talking was a good distraction for Maddie, and Aidan described, in more detail, his mission in Nepal. Aidan was passionate about his work. He lived for call-ups. He was modest about his role in these humanitarian efforts, and spoke with compassion about the people he had come to know during the last twenty years of volunteering. He called them his 'other' family, and they were generous, hard working and selfless. Listening to Aidan' stories of loss and devastation, and the human capacity to rebuild, forced Maddie to re-think her present situation. Suddenly she did not feel as tired and overwhelmed with the prospect of running another 8 kilometers to the end. Her job was easy and self-inflicted. She chose to test her will, yet those people Aidan spoke about and helped had no choice. Instead of thinking about her weary body, Maddie's thoughts shifted to his work: moving debris, looking for survivors and coping with tragedy. Maddie had never met anyone whose life was as spontaneous and unpredictable as Aidan's. On the surface, he was not complicated – he lived life by only a few simple rules. She admired him. She wished she could be more like him, unencumbered by responsibility, free to offer her skills and services wherever they were needed. She wished at the moment that she could fly off somewhere exotic and be helpful to those who needed it most.

They arrived back at the Old Village, with only 5 kilometers left until the finish line at the foot of the ski hill. Maddie looked around at the other participants, many of whom were walking or running very slowly. Some of the athletes were in serious pain, rubbing their tight calves or stopping to massage their cramping thighs. The facial expressions of these non-elite athletes were serious and sombre, oblivious to the hundreds of spectators parked along the run route, yelling out their names with words of encouragement. At this stage of the race, proper running form all but disappeared, as most were just going through the automatic motions of putting one foot in front of the other, willing themselves to the finish line. Maddie considered herself extremely fortunate to have a pacing partner for the entire race.

At the final 2-kilometer mark, the celebratory atmosphere was in high gear. Thousands of spectators were now lined up along the cobble stone promenade that meandered through the station. The high energy atmosphere was contagious, and Maddie's pain and fatigue evaporated. She took in every second of the final kilometer, up the big steep hill, around the ski lift, back down again and into the final blue chute, the finish arch only 50 meters ahead of them.

Aidan was holding himself back behind Maddie so she could cross the timing mat first. It was unthinkable for Maddie to cross the finish without Aidan. She grabbed his hand and pulled him forward so they could cross at exactly the same time.

Once over the timing mat, they stopped, and Aidan wrapped his sweaty arms around her wet torso, dipped her backwards and kissed her smack on the lips; the crowd of spectators and supporters applauding enthusiastically.

'Aidan, thank you is not enough...' Maddie said breathlessly. 'I would not have found the courage to finish this race if you had not been there to support me, encourage me...help me every step of the way.'

'Och, nonsense, yeh did it all by yourself. But thank yeh anyway. T'was an enormous pleasure to see yeh cross the finish line so triumphant like!' Aidan took a deep bow in front her.

After retrieving their medal and finisher hats, the couple walked arm in arm to the food tent. Maddie was euphoric, smiling and laughing, chatting non-stop about the race from beginning to end. She ran into Caitlyn, and the two women discussed in animated detail every aspect of the grueling race.

Aidan was quietly holding on to Maddie's waist so she would not wander off without him. He was truly and sincerely happy for her, and shared in her joy. He willingly let her take centre stage, to enjoy a rare moment of euphoria. The physical pain would surely follow later that day, but for now, it was only about being happy and proud.

Aidan was in pain and he was hiding it behind a pleasant smile. His head throbbed, and his minor cuts and scrapes were burning from the salty perspiration. He could tolerate the physical pain well enough, but the pain in his chest was almost unbearable. His heart was aching with every minute that slipped by, knowing that by this time tomorrow, he would be on a plane, flying back to Ireland alone.

He watched Maddie with profound tenderness and longing. She was so lovely, flushed and beaming from her big moment. He wanted to reach out to her, hold her very tight, cry on her shoulder, tell her that he loved her fiercely, and never let her go.

00:32:49

Aidan eventually persuaded Maddie to leave the race site and drive back to the condo. The fatigue of racing for over six hours did catch up with Maddie, and she wisely decided to forgo celebrating their success in a restaurant. Instead, they picked up a pizza and bottle of wine in the Old Village and settled in for the rest of the day, to enjoy the precious time remaining before they parted ways.

Maddie sat comfortably on the sofa, happily eating her pizza, reliving the race over and over again. Soon, the wine had the desired effect, and she lay down on the big sofa, gazing at the view of Mont-Tremblant in the distance, the euphoria of the race still lingering in spite of her exhaustion.

Aidan, though, was unsettled. Instead of relaxing on the sofa and enjoying the moment with Maddie, he walked around the big room, looking for something to do. He tinkered with his iPad and turned off the Irish music that was always playing, and began looking for music that was calming and relaxing. He'd hardly touched the pizza, and his wine glass remained full. He moved about the space like a caged animal.

After several minutes of watching Aidan move about the space restlessly, Maddie decided it was time to ask him directly if anything was wrong, though she suspected his intense mood might have to do with saying goodbye to each other in less than twenty-four hours. While she had tried to ignore the inevitable conclusion to their brief affair, it had crossed her mind during the race that the end was in sight. They would be, literally, crossing the finish line of their brief but intense relationship and going their separate ways.

'Aidan, what's wrong? You seem upset. Is there something you want to talk about?'

Aidan finally sat down next to her and took a deep breath. He was serious, and, looking straight into her tired amber eyes, blurting out without a hint of warning, 'Will you marry me?'

Aidan said exactly what had been firmly wedged on his mind for the last four days. Stunned into silence, Maddie just stared at him, unable to fully grasp the implications of what he just asked her.

'Now, yeh see I should have started at the beginnin' and not at the end, to give you some context about that very important question. The truth is, I'm fiercely in love with yeh and want to spend the rest of my life with you, until we're both old and decrepit.' Aidan picked up her hands, and kissed the inside of her palms gently. 'You rock my very soul Maddie.' He starred at her, his green eyes beseeching her to feel the same as he did.

Maddie could only stare back at the man that had brought her four days of absolute and unrepentant joy. She said nothing for a few moments, but finally blurted out, to her own surprise, 'I love you too, Aidan.'

'I thought maybe yeh'd need a bit of persuasion,' he said, smiling, though a bit surprised the hear Maddie's affirmation that she loved him too. She had been guarded with her emotions for the entire week, treating him with controlled yet sincere affection. He did not know, until this point, how she felt about him.

'Aidan, you've been doing nothing but that since the moment we met,' Maddie added.

'Indeed, I have, from the moment you stepped into this place,' he said, waving his long arms. 'Well, you know, I've not been celibate all these years as a single man, and I've had my share of lovely women...but I've never left my heart open long enough to settle down. Until now, that is. Will you have me, then? Will you have an impetuous and flawed Irishman? Will you have me, warts and all?'

Maddie laughed at Aidan's choice of expression. 'Indeed, I will, but first we need to get serious and discuss a few important realities of life. Are you with me?'

'Yeh're so complicated...'

'Not complicated, but sometimes conflicted...in any event, you know I'm older than you?' Maddie hesitated, afraid about revealing her age, a subject that they had yet to broach. 'I'm fifty-one...and you are?'

'Fifty.'

Maddie shook her head, smirking.

'Bullshit. Be honest, now.'

'I'm forty-four. As long as you're younger than me Mammy, than

I'm just fine with the age difference.'

'Okay. Now, let me ask you another question. Do you want to have children? You are still young enough and, shall I say, virile enough, to have children at your age. My child bearing years, though, are well behind me, and I would not want to hold you back if you want to be a father.'

Aidan's expression changed at the mention of children and being a father. This was a chapter in his tumultuous life that he had meant to share with her, over time, but since the subject was now in the open, he chose not to withhold this vital piece of his information from his past.

'I'm already a father...' Aidan replied.

'You told me you weren't married,' Maddie asked, without letting Aidan finish his sentence.

'I'm not, Maddie. I've never been married. But I do have one son, that I am aware... there may be more weans, but so far only one woman has come forward,' Aidan replied, grinning, but then added, 'I was eighteen, and I got my girlfriend pregnant. This is Roman Catholic Ireland after all, and abortion was and is still illegal. I offered to marry her, but she refused. She and the young lad moved away to Australia when he was four, to live with her sister I see the lad once in a while, but we aren't exactly close, I'm sad to say.'

'How did your family react to this?'

Aidan hesitated before he replied.

'I'm not terribly close with some members of my family...t'is the reason why. When I was eighteen, I was a really good swimmer, good enough to be invited to swim with Ireland's national swim development program. My family was elated to have a one of their own being groomed for the Irish national swim team, and potentially making the Olympic Games. I come from a modest background, yeh see, and this was an opportunity to break out and accomplish something that no one in the family had done. My two brothers were the brains, while I had the athletic talent...which isn't to say that I'm stupid, but I certainly excelled in sports most of my life.'

'It's hard not to notice your athleticism. I wondered about your effortless swim skills,' Maddie added.

'In any event, off I went to train in Dublin, barely eighteen years old. I met Katie there, and we were young, lonely, and not very experienced in matters of love and sex. We were not careful, and Katie got pregnant. It was a terribly unwelcome incident that both our families had difficulty dealing with. We both quit swimming and stayed together, but we were young and we fought endlessly. By the time the lad was four, she told she didn't love me and that was that. Off she went to Australia. By this time, I was twenty-three, and it was far too late to resume my swimming ambitions.'

'I'm so sorry to hear this,' Maddie replied, understanding Aidan's terrible loss at not only losing the affections of his son, but his youth. 'I think you would be an amazing dad,' Maddie added. 'You sometimes remind me of my own father. He was big and burly like you, with a mischievous smile and an attitude toward life's challenges that was always positive and heartfelt. Like you, he didn't hide his emotions under the guise of masculinity, and he was refreshingly honest...'

'I'm glad to hear, because I have one more secret to tell you.'

'Oh? What would that be?'

'I have a sort of a girlfriend at home. She'll likely be waiting for me when I arrive at the airport.'

''Sort of '? Are you living together?' For a brief moment, Maddie's internal alarm system reacted with this news. He had not been honest with her about this important fact, but she quickly checked herself. How could she criticize Aidan about having a girlfriend, when she was still married?

'No, no,' Aidan replied, shaking his head emphatically. 'We've been together as a couple for a bit of time. We spoke before I left for Canada, and she asked me to move in with her, wanted an answer about our future. T'was a fair question. I told her I would give her an answer when I returned from my trip, but I had planned on saying no, anyway, and breaking it off.' As if reading her mind, he added, 'that's why I didn't tell you sooner. I knew it was over anyway.'

'And now...what will you say to her?'

'I will tell her the truth. I will tell her I met someone else and have fallen in love. I have to be honest. I can't lie to her, I can't invent a wild story just to placate the woman. I'm not that type of person.' Aidan paused.

'She will hurt by this, Aidan.'

'I know. She loves me and has patiently stood by, hoping that I would eventually come around. It will never happen.'

The sticky matter of Maddie's marriage needed to be discussed openly. Aidan knew that Maddie's marriage was in serious trouble long before they met, but he asked her the pointed question. 'And you, love, what about your husband? What will you do now?'

'My relationship with Dominique has been deteriorating for a long time,' Maddie answered truthfully. 'I kept working at it, hoping that it would somehow repair itself. The truth is, I've been comfortably miserable for a long time. My husband is not interested in salvaging twenty-nine years together. He has apparently found someone else to share his life with. I was going to leave Dominique eventually, even if I had not met you,' she added.

'He sounds like a fool. Anyway, it's a fine thing that I found you before someone else claimed yeh!' Aidan added. He reached out to pull her close. 'Maddie, yeh need to understand what you're getting yourself into. There's lots about me you don't know. For example, I'm not content to stay safely at home, tending to my garden and such. Are yeh prepared to have a wee bit of adventure? Are yeh prepared to embrace an uncertain and unpredictable future?'

'Adventure and excitement sounds good, Aidan. I've been longing for more adventure in my life. I'd like to join you on your humanitarian missions, working side by side. Maybe we could travel to some destination races, like you've been doing all these years, or maybe just travel with our bikes and backpacks?' Maddie could easily picture herself travelling to exotic places with Aidan, doing good work and making a difference in someone's life.

Leaving her husband and spending the second half of her life with a man who embraced life with boundless enthusiasm seemed like the most natural decision she had ever made. Her relationship with Aidan was easy and uncomplicated. He didn't play relationship games, and he said whatever was percolating in this head. He had an was honest and heartfelt view of the world, and at times, it was a little disarming. His spontaneity was infectious, and she wanted to be part of his unique world.

'Do you have more secrets to share, Aidan?' Maddie asked teasingly.

'I think not...maybe a few unwelcome skeletons will appear later, but by then, I'll have yeh all to myself and it won't matter a wit...' he said with an easy smile.

'Yes, well, I'm sure that I will find out a great deal more about you, and vice versa, over the next little while.'

They sat huddled together for a long while, in the big room, both caught up in the new the reality of their lives. Maddie was thinking about what she would tell Sofia and Julia. Sofia would not endorse this impulsive decision to run way with the Irishman. She would certainly try to talk her out it. As far as Julia was concerned, Maddie had to live her life as she always had and push aside Julia's negativity. *She'll just have to adjust, regardless of where I am,* she thought.

'So here's what I'm thinking we should do,' Aidan finally said. 'I'll go back to Ireland tomorrow as planned and get a few things sorted out that will not impede our plans. Yeh do the same… you will have to seek a lawyer and all that, and I'll have to figure out how to get us married in Ireland sometime in the future. I don't know the rules of marrying a foreigner...do you happen to know if you have any recent Irish ancestors?' Aidan asked.

Maddie had not considered moving to Ireland, but this made more sense to her than Aidan moving to Canada. There was nothing for Aidan here. As far as she knew, his work and his entire family were all in Cork City. Maddie, though, could find work in translation, no matter where she lived, as the bulk of her projects were managed online.

'I'm sure I have Irish blood somewhere, but how recent, I wouldn't know. My mother's mother died quite young. I think she was part Irish. My mother never talks about her past, so I will have to find out.'

'I believe you have some Irish, given your lovely red hair and fiery passion!' Aidan replied. 'If your Granny was born in Ireland, yeh can apply for Irish citizenship and a passport.'

Maddie leaned into Aidan arms and put her head on his chest. Her life was about to move into an entirely new and unplanned direction. Instead of feeling overwhelmed at the prospect of moving to a new country in a new relationship with a man she barely knew, she felt completely safe and secure that this big, larger than life man would take care of her, and she him. They would look after each other, she felt certain.

Maddie thought about how organized and judicious she was about planning every aspect of her life. How could she possibly have planned to fall into the arms of a complete stranger within an hour of meeting him, and spend the next five joyful days making love, losing herself completely, and now moving to Ireland to spend the rest of her life in a perfect relationship?

The effects of the red wine, combined with their emotional conversation about the future, not to mention the exhaustion from the race, caused Maddie and Aidan to fall into bed and sleep soundly, their tired bodies locked together.

Maddie's last thought before drifting off was how impossible this all seemed.

00:35:19

Maddie opened one eye to look out the window. Today would be a long, hard day, she thought. She rolled over on her back and tried stretching. She felt fine – not an ache or pain from the previous day. This was a good sign, though she suspected that the pain and discomfort of racing were camouflaged by the new reality in her life and the man lying next her. She was going to miss him terribly, especially his inexhaustible appetite for making love.

Maddie turned toward the sleeping giant, his back to her, and she gently circled his broad shoulders with her fingers lightly. She moved her hands and stroked his firm stomach, grazing the soft hairs, kissing his taut back. She moved closer and pressed her breasts against his body, her hand taking hold of him. He was already firm, wet, and waiting patiently, she realized. Maddie could hear him breathing deeply and rapidly as she continued to fondle him. He stirred with her exquisite touch, kissing her palms and sucking her fingers with more urgency. He couldn't hold himself any longer and turned, pinning her down, kissing and almost biting her mouth, hard and fast, as if to eat her alive. His need for her was urgent, almost desperate. She guided him and instantly he released his warm flow, quivering and panting, his full weight bearing down on her. Aidan buried his wet face in her shoulder, and Maddie realized he was weeping softly. She tenderly enveloped the big but vulnerable man in her arms, softly stroking his back, speaking to him in a low whisper. 'I love you, Aidan, please don't be sad. It won't be long, and I'll come to Ireland. I promise you that I will follow you soon.' Aidan could not utter a word.

They drove for two hours toward Montreal in silence, each caught up in their own sadness.

Aidan parked in front of Maddie's house in Outremont, preferring to say their goodbyes in the solitude of her garage over the busy airport parking lot. Dominique was still away at his golf tournament. They retrieved Maddie's gear and Aidan's old bike from the trunk of the SUV.

'Are you going to donate my bike, for me, as you promised?'

'Of course. I'll find a good home for her...' Maddie replied.

'Here, I have something for you...' Aidan put his hands in his pocket and pulled out an envelope. In it was a small bracelet, made of human hair. It was crudely made, the dark brown salt and pepper hair braided around a simple piece of kitchen string and thread. 'T'is pretty corny, I know, but my Granny believed in ancient Irish spells, charms, and the like. She told me it was customary in old Ireland for a man to braid a bracelet from his hair and give it to the woman he loved – a gift of trust, she called it. Human hair has supposedly magical properties, a love bond, and it wilna' work unless you accept and agree to the spell. Do yeh accept?'

'You mean, this bracelet will ensure we stay in love only if I accept and agree to the spell?'

'Indeed, it does...or so my Granny said. I've never actually tried it before...'

'Is this the same Granny who told you to be wary of red heads in the morning?' Maddie asked.

'No, that was my Granny on my father's side. She believed in evil, superstitious stuff. My Granny on my mother's side believed in positive spells!'

'Okay, then, I willingly accept this beautiful bracelet and I agree to the spell...whatever that may be.'

Aidan tied the delicate bracelet around Maddie's wrist.

'T'is not very secure, so I wouldn't wear it too often!' Aidan said with a soft, sheepish smile.

'I will keep it close...' Maddie responded, wondering when Aidan slipped away from her long enough to make this touching gift of himself.

'I have to go now. I can hardly stand it another minute,' Aidan said sadly, not willing to touch her for fear he would not have the courage to drive away.

'Me too...will you send me an email as soon as you land so I know you have arrived safely? Otherwise I will be worried sick about you,' Maddie said bravely.

'Och, don't worry, as soon as I land in Ireland, I will send you all you need to know.' He tried to smile, and her heart ached just looking at him, as she too struggled with being brave and not crying.

Aidan got back in the truck and drove away, leaving Maddie watching him until she could longer spot the big white SUV on the road. She slumped on the floor of the garage and started crying and sobbing, shoulders and head shaking uncontrollably. The pain was relentless, a thousand tiny pointed daggers piercing her skin. Maddie had not cried that hard in many years. After a few minutes, she got up and walked into her quiet house. The crying episode left her spent and empty. Thankfully, Dominique would not be back from his golf trip until the next day; plenty of time for Maddie to dwell on the last few days with Aidan and plan their future together.

She would not discuss a divorce with Dominique immediately. There was no rush to involve Dominique as this point, as she would be leaving him regardless. The marriage was over. She would, in the meantime, wait for Aidan to settle back into his normal life and make whatever arrangements were required to welcome his new fiancée into his community. There were a few lingering questions in her mind. In the solitude of her home, she thought about the last few days and tried analysing a man she hardly knew. Aidan had not elaborated on his specific plans to break off with his girlfriend, nor did he say much about his family in Ireland, except that they were not close. They had little time to discuss how or when Maddie would move to Ireland and what she would do there, besides being his wife.

An hour later, Maddie's phone vibrated indicating incoming mail. It was a brief email from Aidan, and the last one she would receive from him.

'*Mhuirnin* arrived at the airport, safe but very sad. Miss you terribly. I will not be able to think about anything else flying home... I love you so much I can hardly breathe.'

00:39:12 Transition 1

Aidan sat in the airport lounge at Pierre Elliot Trudeau Airport, waiting to board his plane home. He turned on his phone and sent his best friend and business partner Michael a quick text message. He followed up with another message to Meghan with the details of his arrival in Dublin. Finally, he wrote Maddie one last email before boarding the plane:

'Maddie. I love you! I wish I were a poet so I could tell you in so many different ways what has happened to me the last 5 days, but sadly, I am not a poet, not even a good writer. I know this is a bit corny and old-fashioned thing to say, but I've searched my life to find a woman that I could love and trust enough to share my complex and sordid family story. Until I met you, I did not think it would ever happen. You are the love of my life. I want to share everything with and spend the rest of my days making you (us) happy. A coup de foudre? – Indeed it was. I couldn't be happier! Love you forever Aidan.'

Aidan was about to push the send button on his phone when his name was called over the lounge intercom, and he was asked to report to the boarding area immediately. The email promptly moved into the draft inbox, safe and secure until he opened it again. By the time the seat assignment confusion was sorted out and Aidan was on the plane, the battery of his cell phone had completely died. Frustrated and annoyed, Aidan tried to locate a plug for his phone, but the flight attendant closed the doors of the plane, and the passengers were instructed to put away their hand-held devices away until they were airborne.

Within minutes of taking off, Aidan fell into a deep sleep, and did not wake up until thirty minutes before the plane landed in Dublin.

00:40:00 Bike

Before their separation, Aidan and Maddie agreed to communicate only through their respective private email addresses. Maddie did not want Dominique to stumble upon her private life by accidently leaving her phone open. Email was safe and locked in her private account that could be opened only with a password. Maddie received Aidan's last, brief email around 8 pm, the night he left for Ireland.

The post-race fatigue finally caught up with Maddie, and she went to bed early. She was looking forward to getting an email from Aidan as soon as he landed, sometime around 3 am. She kept her phone on so she wouldn't miss that familiar ping and the light flash as soon as an email showed up in her account. At the very least, she would be greeted the next morning with a heartfelt message just in case she slept through the ping.

At 5 am the next morning, Maddie woke up from a deep sleep and immediately checked her email. There was no message from Aidan. She checked again twenty minutes later, worried that her notification system wasn't working properly. Still no message from Aidan. Maddie continued to check her private message system every twenty minutes for the entire day. The waiting was excruciating, and the longer she waited, the more uncomfortable she felt. The only message she received that first day was a short text message that read 'I', and it came from a private number. Maddie dismissed it as a wrong number.

Dominique finally showed up from his weekend golf tournament late that afternoon and asked her how the race went. Maddie replied with a long-winded answer that made little sense to her, and probably to Dominique. By this hour of the day, Maddie was distracted and anxiously waiting for news. She had no patience for Dominique and wished he would to stop pretending to be interested in her race experience and leave her alone.

Maddie glanced at her watch for the sixty-fifth time that day. It was nearly twenty-four hours since she and Aidan had last spoken. Maddie rationalized his silence by assuming his flight had been delayed, and his phone was probably dead. This happened frequently, she reasoned, as most people forget to turn off their phone and the battery drains rapidly in flight. If Maddie had known what airline and flight number he was travelling on, she would have checked herself, but since Aidan had not provided any details about his return leg to Ireland, she had no idea when or with whom he was flying to Ireland. There were so many travel variables, and it would be impossible to check his whereabouts. The airlines were loathe to provide passenger information, even under the guise of an emergency. Her only choice was to wait, be patient, and push any nagging negative thoughts to the back of her mind. Still, she had an uneasy feeling that something was wrong.

By early morning of the second day of silence, Maddie's concern was mounting. She feared that something terrible had happened to her would-be fiancé. She surfed the online Irish news services, looking for information about a possible downed, damaged, or even hijacked plane. As morbid as it was to search for a tragedy, it was better to know there was a legitimate reason for Aidan's silence then no reason at all.

There were many breaking news stories coming out of Ireland, but nothing that related to an airline or downed plane. The only piece of news that made reference to an airport was about a traffic fatality that occurred on the busy Dublin Old Airport Road, involving a lorry and an SUV. The driver of the sedan, a woman, died instantly, while the passenger and lorry driver, both male, were in critical condition with life threatening injuries. Maddie saw the disturbing image of the crumpled SUV resting on its roof and the smashed lorry, but no other details were not provided. An investigation was under way due to the suspicious nature of the accident. Maddie dismissed the accident and moved on to other stories. It was at this point in Maddie's intense search that she realized she did not know or could not recall Aidan's last name. *He told me, but I've just forgotten it,* Maddie thought to herself trying to be rational. *I'll find it on the results page of the race.*

Maddie went directly to the Mont-Tremblant Race website and looked up the final results and rankings for 'Males, 40-45 years'. To her shock, there was no listing for 'Aidan', either first or last name, under this age group or any other. She tried an assortment of spelling options for the name 'Aidan', but nothing even remotely familiar came up in the men's category. Registrants were all required to list their nationality, but she could not find any entrant, male or female, from Ireland. All participants had to wear a paper bib number, but Maddie couldn't remember Aidan's specific number. She remembered he wore his bib turned toward the back. She had asked him about this unusual practice, and he told her the paper chafed his thighs while running.

Later that evening the dream-like quality of spending five days with the charming Irishman began to fade, and she started to think with more clarity. The rational side of her personality took control, as did the first seed of doubt regarding Aidan's sincerity and legitimacy.

Maddie turned to social media for assistance, but without Aidan's last name, it was nearly impossible to find his profile and check his status on Facebook or any other social media feed. Nonetheless Maddie patiently scrolled through hundreds of Aidans around the globe, using different search filters and spellings. She did not believe that he had a Facebook or other social media profile, so the entire exercise was pointless. Nonetheless, she persevered for hours, finally giving up in frustration at 5 am on the third day of his silence.

Searching for the elusive Aidan was becoming a dangerous obsession, and the more she searched, the more her sensibilities pointed to a string of evidence and the immutable facts that she had been duped into believing that he really cared for her. The entire experience in Mont-Tremblant was looking more like an elaborate charade to bed a lonely and vulnerable middle-aged woman.

Anger is a copious motivator, and if Aidan had indeed deceived Maddie so callously, then she wanted to find out if other women had also been taken by the charming lover.

Maddie had watched a documentary a few months before about a group of women, scattered across North America, who were all married to the same scam artist. The handsome and enigmatic man had seduced each malleable woman with his fabricated stories about life as an undercover agent, an outdoor adventure guide, a rock climber; the list of his invented profiles was endless. He eventually stole their hearts, along with their money. Maddie remembered thinking that something like this would never happen to her, as she was far too analytical and shrewd to let a strange man sweep her off her feet. Evidently, she was not immune to a clever deception.

Blogs and online chat groups about women falling victim to

unscrupulous men were prolific. Maddie's search in the blog and chat rooms for specific information about a charming but nefarious Irishman seducing vulnerable women around the globe produced nothing tangible. Maddie read the descriptions and true-life stories written by innocent victims and though they were depressing, they were also comforting in a small way, as none of the men described in these romantic scams resembled Aidan. He was, thankfully not on an international list of male scam artists.

Maddie shifted her search strategy and focused on the various humanitarian and relief organizations in the UK and Ireland. Perhaps he was called away unexpectedly for urgent business? Aidan had described in detail his humanitarian work, but failed to mention the name of the organization that he volunteered with. Most of the websites Maddie located did not contain specific information about individual volunteers. The photo galleries, if they existed, focused mainly on local people affected by a natural disaster, lining up to get clean water and food packages courtesy of the respective NGOs.

Maddie then turned her attention to the tried and true White and Yellow Pages, and other business directories in and around Cork City, looking for a familiar name. She couldn't recall if Aidan had told her the name of the company he worked for. She found nothing useful. She did locate a number of businesses in excavation and heavy equipment, but the links to these websites had minimal information and very poor websites.

Maddie tried to recall exactly what Aidan had said about his family. She could only remember that he had two brothers, a son, and a girlfriend whom he didn't name. They had talked endlessly for five days; why couldn't she remember more about him? Maddie chastised herself for her poor memory and for not paying more attention to the details of Aidan's personal life, but soon realized that the fault did not reside with her. Aidan had learned a great deal about the lovely redhead during this time, as he asked her a lot of questions, yet he intentionally withheld important details about himself and his family. Maddie recalled that whenever the conversation turned to his personal life, he would skillfully change the subject by focusing his attentions on her. It worked every time. Maddie was so caught up in the physical and emotional attentions of the charming man that she realized, to her horror, that she knew nothing about the elusive Irishman. How could she have been so stupid, she asked herself more than once.

By the fourth day, frantic with doubt about Aidan's sincerity and questioning whether she had been callously deceived, Maddie sent the first of three emails to Aidan. The first email was short and to the point, asking him if everything was alright in Ireland.

The second email sent a day later, besieging him to contact her immediately, as she was worried sick. Still, she received no reply.

The third and final email, sent six days after he left Canada, simply read 'I'm fine if you've changed your mind about us. I just wish you would let me know instead of stringing me along.'

Shortly after Maddie sent the third and final email, she received an email, not from Aidan as she had hoped, but from the professional photographer who had taken photos from the race in Mont-Tremblant. She anxiously opened the link and there, before her wide eyes, was a photo of the couple crossing the finish line together, smiling and holding hands, looking deliriously happy in spite of their fatigue from six hours of racing.

Maddie's physical reaction to seeing the photo was immediate; her heart began to beat widely and she could hardly catch her breath. It was the only photo she had of him, and he looked as handsome and captivating as she remembered. Her anger and frustration toward him temporarily evaporated. He was as real in the photo as he had been in her life.

Maddie looked at the photo carefully. Her race number was clearly visible in the photo, but Aidan's was turned around, and his upper arm did not bear the black race number, as hers did. This was more than just coincidental. In the deep recesses of her mind, Maddie knew this was deliberate. It was obvious now that Aidan had purposely avoided being body marked, and he had hidden his race number from the camera lens and bystanders. But why?

Maddie continued to stare at the photo, zooming in on his face and body, looking for more clues, however slight, as to why he would intentionally misrepresent himself. Maddie kept thinking back to their brief time together. It did not seem possible that he could have kept up the ruse for so many days. She thought carefully about the long hours they spent together, looking for a crack in his story, a misstep, an inconsistency that she may have overlooked. Absolutely nothing came to mind. He seemed so natural and comfortable with himself, so spontaneous and genuine, it was hard to believe that this was the same man whose actions and charismatic voice were deliberately programmed to sweep Maddie off her feet for his own selfish purposes.

Maddie shook her head in disbelief. Aside from the missing race numbers, the photo on the computer screen captured the face of an honest, kind, somewhat weary man that she still loved dearly. *'I don't understand,'* she repeated to herself, again and again, tears trickling down her cheeks, *'this is not the face of a calculating and cruel man. This makes no sense at all,'* yet the evidence seemed was irrefutable. She had been duped to falling in love with the elusive Irishman for reasons that she simply could not understand. He didn't ask her for money, property, or shelter. He seemed to have gone to extremes just to sleep with her. Maddie felt stupid, the ultimate foolishness of a lonely, desperate, and sexually deprived middle-aged woman.

Much against her better judgement, though, Maddie bought a copy of the photo, uploaded it to her phone, and placed it in a folder buried deep in the photo albums.

After two weeks of endless searching, sleepless nights, too much caffeine, and way too much wine at 2 am, Maddie decided to stop actively looking for him.

She had done everything in her power to find Aidan, and there was no point in continuing to search for someone who did not want to be found. All evidence indicated that he had chosen not to tell the lovely Canadian too much about his personal life or leave any clue as to his real identity. The only information she had was his first name, what he did for a living, and where he lived, somewhere around Cork City, and Maddie was not sure if any of this information was actually true. In spite of modern, sophisticated online search engines, Aidan could not be tracked down, at least from Canada. She reluctantly accepted the fact that she been completely had by a very charming, romantic, but duplicitous Irishman.

Before going to bed that night, Maddie sent her two boys an email. It was long overdue. They had been asking for details about her experience in Mont-Tremblant, and she kept putting it off, distracted by her search for Aidan and embarrassed that her first triathlon race was more about being seduced and then discarded than about the race itself. For an hour, Maddie wrote a lengthy race report about the experience in Mont-Tremblant, alluding vaguely to Aidan as 'a supportive' athlete who helped her overcome her fear of water.

00:44:00

Life returned to something that resembled normal. Maddie returned to work and buried herself in complicated projects that required long hours of concentration. Dominque's attitude toward his wife and his marriage didn't change, though he took the time to tell Maddie that he was proud of everything she had accomplished and encouraged her to continue with her fitness routine. Maddie took Dominique's advice and resumed running and cycling.

One morning, three weeks after Mont-Tremblant, Maddie's phone rang. Every time this happened, her heart would skip a beat, her mind willing the phone to be Aidan, but the screen only showed a call or text from someone at work, Sofia, or her prickly mother.

This call was no different. It was Julia, asking her daughter to come over to the house right away, as she had something important to discuss. Reluctantly, Maddie jumped on her bike and cycled to Julia's townhome, located in Westmount, one of the most exclusive areas of Montreal. Julia had been living in Westmount for thirty-eight years, and while most of her neighbors were professionals and very well off, Julia had been living off her husband's small death benefit, combined with her senior's pension. For that reason, Julia was frugal, and managed her meagre monthly living allowance to the penny.

Since the beginning of June, the weather in Montreal and surrounding areas was the hottest on record, each day another muggy and uncomfortable assault on the body. There had been several thunderstorms that brought short bursts of much-needed rain and a brief respite from the uncomfortable hot weather, but the humidity persisted. Maddie suspected that Julia wanted to vent about the weather and her upcoming summer hydro bill. She could be difficult and cranky when it came to paying bills, and lately, the much-dreaded hydro bill was causing Julia sleepless nights. She was nearly impossible to deal with, even though Maddie offered to pay her electricity every month.

'Julia, it's me, your daughter,' Maddie yelled out as she opened the front door to her mother's townhome, a blast of cold air hitting her in the face. 'Geez, Julia, it's colder than Nunavut in here...no wonder your hydro bill is high,' she yelled again, waiting for Julia to respond. Other than the hum of the air conditioner, the house was silent. Julia detested any kind of noise, even music. She said it gave her a headache.

Maddie put her bike in the down stairs foyer and walked up to the living room on the second floor, to find her mother sitting in her usual spot by the window with several boxes strewn around her.

'Julia, what's going on here... what are all these boxes doing here?' Julia's home bordered on sterility; not a cushion or cup was ever out of place.

'I brought them up from the basement. I need to sort through them as soon as possible. There may be important documents in here that you should have,' Julia replied, sitting in her big flowered chair looking especially tired and un-kept, sounding more than usual weary.

'Is that why you asked me to come over...to go through these with you?' Maddie asked.

'Not exactly, Madeline,' Julia answered, using Madeline's full name instead of her nickname, something she stubbornly refused to use. 'There is time later for you and me to review the most important documents together, though I wanted to get a head start and spare you the tedium of reviewing each and every file.'

'What's the rush? Are you finally moving out of here and into a proper senior's apartment?'

'No, dear. I'm not moving,' Julia answered, and then stopped her file search. She looked at the pretty, freckled face of her daughter and immediately thought of her own mother, whom she could only remember through a few grainy photos. Maddie's resemblance to her was uncanny.

Julia took a deep breath and resumed their conversation. 'I'm dying, Maddie. And quickly. If the young doctor is correct in his estimation, I could be dead in three to four weeks. Time is quickly running out for me. I need to make sure everything is in order so you are not left with a big, tangled mess,' Julia answered.

'What? What are you talking about?' Maddie was naturally skeptical when she heard her mother talk of death and dying. The woman had a tendency to exaggerate her frequent illnesses, and she spent long days worrying about every ache and pain that was bothering her.

'Come sit down, please,' Julia said, gesturing for Maddie to sit on the sofa. 'I know you think I'm a bit of a hypochondriac, and in this case, I wish it were in my head, but sadly, I'm not making this up, Madeline. I saw the doctor yesterday, one of many visits to the clinic that I have had to endure the last few months. After numerous tests, the doctor finally confirmed that I have a very aggressive form of cancer, one that probably started months, maybe years ago. It has now spread to my brain, among other places. I won't suffer too much, the doctor assures me; drugs will help with the pain, but I will waste away very quickly. This is why I asked you here...to help me plan and organize my demise and ease my way into whatever awaits a dead person. Heaven, I hope, but I lost faith in that belief a long time ago.'

While she did not have a close relationship with her mother, Maddie did care about Julia, even though the woman was contrary and hard to love. She had always been a dutiful daughter and gave her mother as much support and comfort as her mother would allow. Julia was independent, though, and rarely asked Maddie for anything, except to take her grocery shopping and listen to her vent. Today, though, was different.

'Julia, I'm...I'm so sorry. I wish you had told me about your health issues sooner. I would have taken you to your appointments,' Maddie replied.

'That's fine, dear. You seem distracted lately. I didn't want to burden you with my numerous health issues until I knew for sure what was wrong,' Julia said, with no hint of sarcasm. 'We all have to go sometime, and the good Lord has decided that my time is sooner than I expected.'

Julia stopped the paper-shuffling and looked at her daughter. She often wondered how she could have produced such a warm and kind person, when she herself was anything but. Maddie may have inherited some of Julia's family's physical traits, but her personality and disposition were pure St-Laurent.

'It would mean a lot to me, Maddie, if we could deal with this together,' Julia added quietly.

'Of course. We will do this together,' Maddie responded reassuringly to her sick mother. This was an unknown territory. Julia had never reached out to Maddie for any meaningful help, especially emotional support. Even after Peter died, Julia moved through the following weeks and months in total control and as though nothing significant had happened. This was a new side to Julia, and Maddie would have to put aside her own biases, built over a lifetime, to help her mother during the next few difficult weeks.

Wasting no more time with sentimentalities, Julia got down to the business of dying. 'I have a list of things I want you to do for me. Do you have the time?'

'Of course. I'll make the arrangements with my boss and hand off my current projects. It should not be a problem...I will give you all the help you need, Julia.'

'Good. That's a relief. I was worried you might be too busy,' Julia added, as she opened another old and faded folder from the blue box.

In spite of Julia's stinging remark, Maddie smiled and shook her head. As sick as she was, Julia would never stop saying exactly what she was thinking.

'I will let Dominique and the boys know. Do you want me to move in with you during this period?'

'Yes, I think so, but not today. Maybe later in the week?'.

For the next hour, mother and daughter reviewed an itemized list of errands to run and phone calls to make, to Julia's satisfaction. They discussed her estate, some specific details regarding her will, and Julia's preferences for her funeral arrangements. Within an hour, the two women created a list of the next steps in preparation for her death. Exhausted, Julia was too tired to continue, so Maddie said goodbye, but promised to return the next day.

Later that evening, when she returned home, Dominique was in the kitchen, eating a bowl of leftover soup. As soon as Maddie walked in, she burst into tears, unable to maintain the stoic composure that Julia always expected in times of emotional difficulty.

'Maddie, why are you crying?' Dominique asked, getting up from the counter stool and gently pulling his wife closer to him. 'Are the boys okay...did you have a scare on the bike?' Dominique's expression of genuine concern toward his distraught wife was touching, and she took comfort in his arms.

'Julia is drying of cancer,' Maddie said through a flood of tears. 'I know you don't like her much, but she is my mother, and she's all I have now.'

'I'm so sorry to hear this Maddie. Really, I am. How pervasive is the cancer?'

'It spread to her brain. The Doctor told her to get her things in order, as she doesn't have a lot of time'.

'That is extremely aggressive. She must have been sick for some time. Is there anything I can do to help? Do you want me to see about getting a second opinion?' Dominique asked.

Maddie was sincerely touched by Dominique's offer to help. This was the first time in months Dominique showed any interest in Maddie's problems. Though their relationship was not caustic, like many unhappy marriages, it hovered in limbo, as neither partner wanted to make the first move toward ending their relationship.

'No, I don't think so, Dominique. But I really appreciate the offer to help. I won't be home much for the next few weeks, though. I will be with Julia sorting out what's left of her short life.'

*****

Maddie moved into her old bedroom in the townhouse and stayed until Julia was ready for the hospice. The room was sparsely furnished, with a single bed, a chest of drawers, and a mirror. There were few mementos or personal items in the room, except a series of photos of Maddie as a young girl, a teenage shortly after her sixteenth birthday, and her university graduation picture.

Maddie spent every day following Julia's specific instructions. She spoke to the lawyer about the management of her estate, the funeral director, and the doctor. A local real estate agent was interviewed and then hired to sell the townhouse in Westmount, on the understanding that the house was to be put on the market and sold as quickly as possible. Julia purposely asked the real estate agent for a low listing price, well below the market valuation, so she could unload the house in a short time. The truth was that Julia was no fool when it came to her investments, and had managed her estate, after Peter died, with the same business acumen of an MBA grad. She managed to live off the life insurance policy and her seniors' pension quite comfortably for thirty-nine years. Within two days of the initial real estate listing in the highly desirable and toney neighborhood of Westmount, the agent received an offer which was significantly above the asking price. Julia accepted it without hesitation.

Maddie purged the townhouse of old and uncomfortable furniture and packed up boxes to donate to the local thrift shops. Julia had generally kept a simple and uncluttered home, so the task of purging took little time. Maddie asked for a few of Julia's smaller china pieces; a series of black and white photos of an old but stylish car that her grandfather, Julia's father, had apparently loved, as well as trinkets that once belonged to her grandmother and great-grandmother.

After three weeks, Julia was ready to move into the hospice. The cancer had taken a firm hold of her once-strong body, and now she slept most of the day. She was experiencing more discomfort, her vision had deteriorated, and she would soon require a stronger pain medication.

The night before Julia was scheduled to move into the Hospice wing at the Montreal Cancer Centre to spend her last days in relative comfort, she and Maddie were having a glass of sherry in the almost-bare living room of the townhouse. The only two pieces of furniture left in the room were Julia's favorite sitting chair, which she was bringing with her to the hospice, and a love seat, which was being picked up by a charitable organization in the morning, along with the remainder of the townhouse furniture.

Julia was surprisingly alert this evening. She had slept all day and seemed to be saving her energy for the last night in her home.

'Maddie, I want you to have the documents in that blue box,' Julia said, her veined hand pointing to a large blue cardboard box. 'They are important because they contain all the information about me, my mother, and her family. There are also some interesting documents about my dad's business that are worth looking over, when you have the time. He was a pretty interesting man.' Julia took a tiny sip of her sherry and closed her eyes. She always enjoyed her nightly glass or two of sherry.

There are birth and marriage certificates,' Julia continued, 'old photos, letters, and several other papers related to your genealogy. Some of these papers will useful if you plan on becoming an Irish citizen.'

Maddie could hardly believe what she is hearing. How could Julia possibly know about her recent dalliance with the seductive Irishman?

'Julia, why would I want to get my Irish citizenship?'

'Well, I thought you might be interested in making a change in your life. I don't think I ever shared this with you, but my mother was born in Ireland, which gives you the legal right to apply for Irish citizenship and, more importantly, obtain an E.U passport.' Julia took another tiny sip of her sherry, her frail hands delicately holding a paper cup, the only thing left in the kitchen to drink from.

'There's no harm in having dual citizenship, you know,' Julia continued. 'I thought about doing it myself at one point, but since I was no longer employable, and I didn't plan on getting reacquainted with my Irish roots, what would be the point? You, on the other hand, could move to Ireland, or perhaps other parts of Europe, and work in translation. As far as I'm concerned, there is no reason for you to spend the rest of your life in Montreal. Your kids are gone now, and Dominique, well, I don't know what's going on in your marriage, but I suspect that it has run its course. The point is, dear, you have so many choices. You are still young enough to start over again and beautiful enough to find someone who will love you.'

Julia's compliment to her one and only child not only surprised her daughter, it opened an emotional barricade that had been there for most of Maddie's life.

'I know I failed as a mother, and maybe it's too late to say this, but I do love you, and I admire you for turning your life around. You have the strength and tenacity that I never had to realize your goals. Look what you've done to turn your life around. After your father died, I settled for comfortable and predictable. I was determined that his death would be the last time I was going to have to deal with emotional chaos. I regret it now. I should have done more with my life than watch it pass me by.'

Julia's voice was heavy and slow. She was growing weary from talking about a painful subject and the effects of the painkillers.

'Listen to me carefully, my dear daughter. If I can give you any advice it's this: leave here while you are still young and healthy. Explore the world. Take a leap of faith and start over again somewhere else. I know you will succeed at whatever you do.'

Maddie was unable to utter a word, for fear she would start crying and never stop.

'Soon you will have a bit of money,' Julia continued slowly 'at least enough money to get you started with a new life. The townhome is under your name and has been for two years. The money from the sale of the real estate, plus my investments, will help you financially. If you are careful, as I have been, you will be comfortably well off, no matter where you live.'

00:54:16

On cue, and as Julia predicted, Maddie buried her mother the following week, three and half weeks to the day after she first revealed her terminal illness.

There were only a few people at the funeral service, as Julia had, over time, either alienated most of her friends, or they moved to warmer climates. The boys came for the service, as did Sofia and her mother Camelia.

Julia spent the last week of her life in relative comfort, thanks to a medication pump and the company of her daughter. In spite of vision loss, nausea, and a host of other symptoms of imminent death, Julia shared many details of her life growing up. She told Maddie about her own mother, whom she knew only through letters and anecdotal stories, since the woman had died shortly after giving birth. Julia's father, inconsolable after his wife's death, found excuses not to be around his only daughter, as she was a constant reminder about his loss. Maddie's grandfather had several businesses abroad, mostly in France and Italy, and spent much of his time travelling. Julia, left behind, grew up lonely and unwanted and in the care of family and friends. It was a sad life, but Maddie was thankful that her mother had finally shared some of her past, which explained, to a large extent, why she was so cold and unhappy most of her adult life. It was exciting to learn a tiny bit of history about a woman who had guarded her emotions and rarely shared any insight into her life.

While mother and daughter did not entirely reconcile their differences, they did gain a respectful understanding toward each other. Maddie was surprised to find out that her mother paid more attention than she realized. Julia had watched Maddie make positive and significant changes in her life in the last year, but she knew her daughter was struggling lately with a problem and was searching for a solution. Without directly telling her what to do, and without knowing the details of Maddie's unhappiness, Julia told her daughter to forget her marital obligations and follow her instincts, wherever they may lead. She told her that she had made mistakes as a single parent, and could not go back and fix all the damage, but she could encourage her daughter to explore her potential by breaking free of Dominique and setting out on her own. Julia told her in no uncertain terms that it was time to get on with her life as a single woman.

Taking care of her mother over the final weeks of her life had been immensely fulfilling for Maddie. She was able to say goodbye to her mother without feeling guilt or regret. They had said what they needed to say without sentimentality.

During the day, Maddie was too preoccupied with Julia to dwell on Aidan, though she thought about him often at night. Unable to fall asleep after a taxing day of helping her mother, Maddie would sometimes replay the hours she had spent with the enigmatic Irishman, trying to remember everything he said, looking for a pattern of behaviour or a clue that confirmed their affair was nothing more than a brilliant ruse by Aidan to bed her. It was seemed to elaborate an undertaking just to have sex; it made little sense, and neither did his sudden silence.

Maddie did not return to work after her mother died. Instead, she took time for herself, patiently waiting for an epiphany, an inspiration that would give her a reason to move forward with her life. Her resolve to leave Dominique and start over again by herself had waned. While Julia's advice about striking out on her own resonated in her head, such a bold move was too much change at once. While she was unhappy with the state of her marriage, and didn't love Dominique anymore, she was comfortably miserable, as she had once told Aidan, and secure in a daily and predictable routine. She was content for now to stay put, and not make any hasty decisions. The last impetuous decision she made a few months earlier had broken her heart.

On her mother's advice, Maddie applied for Irish citizenship, though she did not have any plans of travelling or moving to that country. Her mother had been right about obtaining dual citizenship; an E.U. passport was a hugely beneficial if she ever found the courage to pack her bags and move to Europe. The application process was relatively easy, and her new passport and citizenship papers arrived quickly.

Maddie did not resume any serious triathlon training. She was not motivated to train for another race, and besides, anything to do with racing was just another painful reminder about a love affair gone terribly wrong.

*****

On a whim, late one hot and sunny afternoon, and out of sheer boredom, Maddie cycled to the bike shop on St-Denis Street, ostensibly to look at new wheels for her bike, but in reality, she was curious about the young and attractive cyclist who seemed so infatuated with her a few months ago. She had not seen Frederic since before the race in Mont-Tremblant.

Frederic greeted Maddie with an ardent smile and a warm hug. 'Bonjour, Maddie, it's so nice to see you again! I've missed you!'

'Yes, it's been a while…it's good to see you, Fred.'

'How did the race in Mont-Tremblant go for you?' Fred asked, in slightly broken English.

'It went really well. I finished it in just over six and a half hours' Maddie replied, standing very close to the strapping young man and thankful that she had washed her hair that morning before venturing outside.

'I have not seen you at the Sunday rides in a while…are you still training?' Fred asked.

'I took a break from training to take care of my dying mother. She passed away a few weeks ago.'

'Desolee. I'm very sorry to hear this.' Unprompted, Frederic put his arms around Maddie and hugged her affectionately.

They stayed like this for a moment or two, before Maddie pulled away, her ears turning a deep rosy pink. 'Thank you. She did not suffer too much. It was quick.'

They chatted for a few minutes about wheels and new tires, walking around the store on a quiet week day afternoon, Frederic's amiable personality putting the tall redhead at ease.

'Maddie,' Fred started to say, visibly nervous. 'I am getting off work in a few minutes. Will you join me for a glass of wine?'

Without hesitation, Maddie said yes. She knew exactly what would happen with Frederic in less than an hour. His warm embrace was more than a simple hug for a grieving friend. He desired her, that was obvious. The anticipation of being with this attentive and robust young man lifted Maddie's spirits, both physically and mentally. Finally, she would have a worthy replace-ment for Aidan and put to rest, once and for all, the lingering notion that he would miraculously re-appear into her life.

01:01:04

Frederic invited her to stay the night, insisting it was too dark and dangerous to bike home, but Maddie waved him off with an excuse about an early morning meeting. She was anxious to leave the confines of his suffocating, hot apartment.

They had spent a few hours in Fred's tiny and messy walk-up filled with bikes, trophies, and cycling memorabilia. They drank cheap wine, talked, and kissed frequently and passionately. Frederic was a sensuous and skilled kisser and Maddie had no doubt that he would make love to her as wonderfully as Aidan had.

Fred declared his infatuation with the attractive redhead, in charming broken English, telling Maddie how he wanted to be with her since she first walked into the store last summer. He said he adored her and did not care that she was married and older than him. Fred was everything a fifty-one-year-old. woman could ask for in a lover, yet Maddie's conflicted emotions were working against her. Instead of feeling exuberant and elated that a man half her age desired and worshipped her, she felt uncomfortable with his declaration of love, and she was ashamed of herself for wanting to take advantage of the young man's vulnerability for her own personal enjoyment. Maddie stroked Fred's face reassuringly as they talked, but she was not interested in falling in love with Frederic; she was only interested in pure physical exploitation.

The 10-kilometer bike ride home along the dark streets of downtown Montreal was treacherous and, for any reasonable cyclist, foolhardy. Maddie was not wearing any reflective gear, nor did she have a bike light. She squeezed herself between the parked cars and the busy road to find space to avoid being hit by moving vehicles. The parked cars, in particular, were a constant threat, as many cyclists have gone down hard by being 'doored' -hit by a driver opening their car door without looking.

Maddie should have been focused on cycling. Instead, all she could think about was how uncomfortable she felt about the last few hours. Sofia, the woman who spent most of her free time chasing after men like Frederic, would laugh at Maddie's predicament and remind her best friend that men have sex with women all the time for their own personal pleasure and never feel an ounce of regret or remorse. Maddie's thoughts moved to Aidan, as she painfully recalled this exact scenario with him.

In the end Maddie, could not bring herself to sleep with the young and energetic Franco. She knew her reasons were not particularly modern, nor where they based on any moral dilemma about being married. She wasn't feeling self-conscious about her age or her looks, as Fred had made it crystal clear how much he desired her.

The reasons were simple and uncomplicated; Maddie was still very much in love with the phantom Irishman, and sleeping with another man, no matter how desirable he might be, was not going to fix her aching heart.

01:15:06

Maddie sat at her desk in the front room of her house. It was mid-September, and she still had not returned to work. Her smart phone was close by, and she glanced at the blinking light. It was another text message from Frederic, one of several he had sent her in the last few weeks, asking to meet for drinks and dinner. He was persistent and would not give up on her, even though Maddie told him emphatically that their relationship could go no further. She ignored the message by deleting it, as she had done all the others.

The daytime air was pleasant and refreshing, a welcome change from the last two months of intensely hot and uncomfortable humid weather. The large oak and maple trees that dotted Maddie's quiet residential street in Outremont were slowly turning various shades of brilliant orange and red. It was typical Montreal fall weather, and perfect for the cycling and running enthusiasts. Maddie pondered going for a ride or a run on this brilliant Tuesday morning, but instead, she sat staring at the computer screen.

Since Julia's death, Maddie was no further ahead in sorting out a labyrinth of complicated emotions. One moment she felt a crushing sadness and heartache, thinking about her unhappiness, while the next moment she was frustrated and impatient to leave the comforts of her home and loveless marriage and start a new life by herself. Julia's advice and encouragement played in her head like a musical worm. She thought about Julia often, more than she had ever thought about her mother. She wished Julia had not waited until the last weeks of her life to be the mother that Maddie had always wished for; a mother full of good advice, encouraging words, and support. In spite of their short time together, Maddie had grown close to Julia, and was thankful that they had reached an understanding of each other.

Maddie was languishing in a sea of indecision, fearful of making the wrong move, yet Julia's sudden death was a grim reminder that time is a precious commodity that should not be squandered. If Julia and her best friend Sofia were sitting in this very room at this very moment, they would both tell her, in very direct terms, to move on with her life by setting some new goals. Today was Tuesday, September 15th. Maddie starred at her computer screen and said, out loud 'That's it…by Friday I will make a decision about my future.' She gave herself three days to come up with a plan, even though she was hopelessly out of ideas.

Mixed in with the emotional soup was a nagging feeling that a significant event was about to present itself, yet nothing happened. Every day was a continuation of the same mundane routine. Maddie got up, did some exercise and household chores, read the news, and watched movies. It was a lonely and unfulfilling existence. Though she tried to supress thoughts of Aidan, a tiny part of her emotional brain would not allow her to abandon all hope of ever seeing him again. Sometimes she read the Irish news or listened to traditional Irish music, though this only added to her loneliness and deep sense of loss.

She casually glanced at the white parchment envelope resting on a book of French grammar. She stared at that the envelope, which held her most valued possession, Aidan's crude bracelet. She willed it to speak, to fly, to explode, to do something other than be a sad reminder of her vulnerability.

She turned to look at her computer screen. The answer to her struggles to make sense of the last few months was surely out there somewhere, and not in this room. As Maddie carried on an internal dialogue with herself, a new email alert popped up in the lower corner of the computer screen. It was another notification from the Mont-Tremblant Race Organizers, reminding athletes to visit the Photo Gallery before the site was closed permanently.

Maddie hesitated before clicking the link. While she was curious to see if there were any new photos of her and Aidan, the photographic evidence was a reminder about her middle-aged foolishness.

Maddie's curiosity was stronger than her resolve to fully erase Aidan from her life. She opened the link. Sipping her tepid coffee, she mindlessly and quickly scrolled through hundreds of photos that she had already scanned several times before. With the exception of two photos, which only showed her struggling through the last kilometer to the finish line, there were no new photos of Aidan. The only photo of Aidan that existed was the one of the couple crossing the finish line. She was struck, again, by how Aidan had eluded so many cameras along the race course.

Maddie was just about to give up and close the website for good when a flicker of an image registered in her brain. She stopped for a moment and looked at the screen. She zoomed in on the image. It was yet another image of a random athlete running toward the finish line, identical to almost all the other thousand-plus photos in the database from the race. Maddie slowly scrolled back, looking carefully at the previous images, one at a time, to ensure she hadn't missed an important detail buried somewhere in an image. She stopped at photo '1078 of 1095' and scrutinized it with care.

This photo was unlike the others. The photographer had pointed the lens at the cheering crowd along the barriers. On the left side and in the background, walking away from the spectators, was a man towering above the rest. Though the image was fuzzy, Maddie recognized the athlete with his back to the photographer. The muscular frame, long legs, and wavy hair was a mirror image of Aidan on race day. She looked closely at the race bib tied around his waist, and while the image was in a low resolution and she couldn't read the fuzzy pixelated numbers, they were visibly there. Maddie nervously checked off the photo, paid for the high download with her PayPal account, and waited.

The process of purchasing and downloading the photo to her email account would take about an hour, an excruciatingly long time to sit in front of her laptop. Maddie instead laced up her runners and headed outdoors for a therapeutic run.

When she returned fifty minutes later, an new email was waiting in the inbox. Like a child on Christmas morning, Maddie frantically clicked through it and opened the attachment.

The high definition digital photo was infinitely clearer. She switched to 'zoom mode' on her computer and scanned Aidan's body carefully to ensure it was really him. There was no doubt at all about it; the green tri-suit was a dead give-away. Next, Maddie scanned his race number: it read 190600. She wrote down the number and then went to the Race Results web site. It took only a few seconds to load. Maddie typed the number in the search field and a name popped up: *A. O'Callaghan*. The name triggered a faint memory of their awkward introduction shortly after the bike accident. Aidan introduced himself, but his voice was muffled by the falling rain and thunder. All she remembered hearing was his first name. No wonder she couldn't remember his last name.

There was limited information attached to his name, not even a city of residence or nationality was listed. The only piece of information that corresponded to the Aidan she knew was the gender and age categories: Male/40-45 yrs. Curiously, there was no recorded final race time. Aidan's results were located in the DNF category – Did Not Finish.

Maddie sat back in her chair and shook her head in disbelief. This explained why she could not find him in earlier searches, in spite of cross-checking every possible configuration. But why she thought, did he end up in the DNF database? Maddie scrupulously examined both digital photos again, and realized that Aidan's timing ankle bracelet was missing from both photos; he had evidently crossed the line without this vital piece of history. She had not even considered searching the DNF list, located in a separate database, because they had both finished together. It all made sense now, from a search perspective. Since Aidan was not wearing his timing chip, he would not have a finish time, and therefore his name did not show up in the race results.

Finally, Maddie had found something that was worth pursuing, a bona fide link to a man who had kidnapped her soul and then disappeared. Though faint, Maddie allowed herself to feel a tiny crumb of optimism, that perhaps Aidan's silence and presumed disappearance could be explained if she looked further.

The discovery, though significant, prompted more questions about the elusive Aidan O'Callaghan. Why didn't he include his nationality in the profile? What happened to the timing chip? Did it fall off or did he deliberately remove it? Why was he so careful about his personal information? Why didn't he share more about his life? Maddie hoped these questions would get answered in time, but for now, she resumed her laborious search for the missing man starting with the name O'Callaghan.

O'Callaghan was a fairly common name in Ireland, and there were thousands and thousands of references to the name O'Callaghan in Google search. Maddie came across a plethora of historical and ancestral information in both the Republic of Ireland and Northern Ireland. There were a few news articles and references about the notorious O'Callaghan criminal family in Belfast, but there was no obvious link to Aidan O'Callaghan. She dismissed this connection outright and continued the search.

Maddie tried Facebook and spent an hour scrolling through hundreds of members, but nothing came up. This did not surprise her, since she had already concluded that Aidan did not subscribe to any social media apps. Next, Maddie tried narrowing the search perimeters to only excavation companies with the name O'Callaghan in Cork City, but nothing significant came up either. It was a frustrating and tiring morning. The internet, with all its infinite search capabilities and power to literally zoom in to people's backyards, was not helping her find the one thing she wanted more than anything in the world: to locate Aidan O'Callaghan.

A one o'clock, Maddie was hungry and in desperate need of a strong cup of tea. She quickly made herself a salmon salad and a large pot of tea, and resumed her detective work, eating while scrolling.

Annoyed with her progress, and frustrated with the plethora of useless results, Maddie switched to Google Images and tried different search parameters, which sometimes yielded better results than a typical web search. She typed in Cork City Excavation and, predictably, hundreds of unrelated and unconnected images loaded on to her screen. Dutifully she scrolled through them until she came upon a grainy image of the Cork City Excavation Football Team photo. She clicked on the photo and studied it carefully. There, in the back row, was a very tall man, with long wavy hair and a sheepish smile. The man was a young and lean version of Aidan. The caption under the photo listed the members of the Cork City Excavation Company's 2003 Football Team, and A. O'Callaghan was among the team members. It was not possible to zoom into the scanned photo. When she tried, the image became severely pixilated and un-viewable. Nonetheless, she felt confident that the man in the photo was a younger version of the elusive Irishman, proof that he was from Cork City and that he did work for an excavation company, at least in 2003.

Maddie allowed herself a few minutes to enjoy this small but significant victory. So far, everything he told her, though limited, was true. She looked at the grainy photo again and smiled. Aidan was younger and slimmer in the photo, and his hair was much darker, but his youthful good looks only increased her longing for him. Maddie wrote down the name of the company in her notebook, along with the rest of the members of the football team, and then typed the name of the company in Google search. Curiously, she could not find the Cork City Excavation Company, either in a global Google search or the Cork City online business directory. The closest affiliation was the Clonakilty Construction Company. Maddie clicked the link to their website. As expected, Aidan was not listed anywhere on the site, but a Michael Bennett was listed as President, and he was also sitting in the front row of the football team photo from 2003. Now she not only had a clue, she had a connection to a real person and a phone number.

The next important step was to call the company directly and first ask for Aidan by name. Perhaps he still worked for this company, and if he didn't, they might know where he was. Maddie dreamed up an excuse about the reasons for her long-distance call – she would tell them she found his camera at the race site and was finally able to trace it back to him. It was a plausible story, and she would need to sound convincing on the phone.

Nervously, she dialed the international exchange number, then the local phone number for the Clonakilty Construction Company. After four long rings, an automated female voice message came on with instructions on reaching specific individual employees. Maddie typed in Aidan's name, but the message replied in a pleasant Irish accent 'no one by that name is listed in the company directory'. She hung up the phone. *Now what?* she thought. Perhaps she spelled his name incorrectly? She needed to speak with someone directly who could answer her question about Aidan's whereabouts. Maddie took a deep, relaxing breath and called the number again. As soon as she heard the automated instructions, she hit the zero button and waited as the phone rang. The same pleasant Irish voice answered, this time a real person.

'Good afternoon, Clonakilty Construction, what can I help yeh' with today?'

'Good afternoon... I...I ...I would like to speak to Aidan O'Callaghan, please" Maddie blurted out nervously.

'Aidan is...aw,' the distinctive Irish accented voice at the other end stopped in mid-sentence. 'Excuse me, we do not have such a person employed here,' she replied more professionally. 'Can I direct your call to someone else, or perhaps yeh would like to speak to Michael

Bennett, the president?'

'Sure...' Maddie answered, not knowing what she was going to say to the president, sitting in her home office 6,000 km away.

The Irish woman returned to the phone thirty seconds later 'He's away from the office at present. Can I take a message, then?'

'No... No thank you. I will call back later.' Maddie hung up the phone. She was both relieved and disappointed.

Maddie stared out the window, reviewing the brief interaction with the receptionist. The telephone conversation had taken less than a minute. Did she hear the woman correctly? It sounded like she was about to say something about Aidan, but stopped. The woman seemed to recognize his name, Maddie was sure of it, but why say otherwise? There was something about the sound of the woman's voice that was not natural. During that brief conversation, the woman in Clonakilty sounded almost fearful at the mention of his name.

Maddie considered calling back the next day to speak to the president. Her instincts, though, were telling her that speaking on the phone with a complete stranger about someone she barely knew did not seem like a productive way to gain vital information about the now-missing Aiden O'Callaghan. She doubted that the president would tell her anything on the phone. He could easily lie, or fabricate any story, and Maddie would not be able to challenge his word, sitting at a desk across the Atlantic Ocean. Maddie wanted to speak to Michael Bennett in person, read his facial expressions, watch his body language and other subtleties of human interaction, to know if he was telling her the truth. If Maddie wanted to discover the secret of Aidan's disappearance, she would have to present herself in person to Michael Bennett.

Her next decision was swift and decisive. The middle aged French translator from Montreal, armed with only a name, a photo, and one precious lock of hair as clues, was going to Ireland to find out exactly where Aidan was and why he had remained silent all these months. Maddie looked at the calendar on her desk. It had only taken a few hours to make a decision about her future. In less than a month, she reasoned, she would be on a plane bound for Clonakilty, Ireland, wherever that was, to confront the enigmatic Irishman and resolve, once and for all, the mystery of his silence.

01:35:10

'Madeline, are you sure you don't want more of the family patrimony? As your lawyer, I highly recommend that you seek at least fifty percent of the value of the marital assets, and I also strongly suggest we could argue for more. You are entitled to it.'

'No thanks, Pierre,' Maddie replied to Pierre Lalonde, one of her long-time friends from University. 'I have my own money - plenty in fact- and I don't want to embark on a long and nasty fight with Dominique. I want this legal separation and divorce to be done as quickly as possible.'

'I respect your decision, Maddie. We can back-date the legal separation to eighteen months ago – the last time you and Dominique were intimate?' Pierre asked, reading from his notes from an earlier conversation they had had about the details of Maddie's failed marriage. 'I am confident that with a bit of tweaking of the facts, we can get the divorce completed in less than six months… as long as Dominique is agreeable.'

'I don't think Dominique would dare refuse me,' Maddie replied confidently. 'He wants out of this marriage as much as I do, and besides, he's been carrying on with someone for a long time. I'm quite sure he and his girlfriend will agree to all the terms you and I have laid out.'

'There are no terms Maddie,' Pierre replied, with disappointment, 'you are being very gracious and much too generous. Dominique is getting most of the assets…at least for now. It's your decision, of course, but as your lawyer, my job is to advise you. As a friend, though, I am curious to know about your immediate plans. Do you care to share them with me?'

'Not at all. I am going to go on an extended trip to Europe. I may live there for a while, as I have an EU Passport, so I can work if I need to. I am really looking forward to getting on with my new life as a single woman, but I have much to do before I leave. Thank you for this, Pierre. I will be speaking with Dominique this evening, so you are likely to hear from his lawyer any time after tomorrow.'

On her way out of Pierre's office, Maddie texted Dominique and told him, not asked him, to be home by 7 pm. She urgently needed to speak with him.

At 6:52 pm, Dominique walked in the door of their house in Outremont. He was surprised to see that Maddie had made dinner for the two of them. The dining room table was nicely set, with their rarely-used wedding china, candles, a fresh green salad, and homemade dressing. In an ice bucket rested an opened bottle of crisp St-Estaphe wine. The smell of coq-au-vin floated throughout the downstairs rooms.

Maddie was dressed in tight black pants, sling back shoes, and a body-hugging, low-cut, soft pink sweater, which flattered her athletic body. Maddie's long, dark red hair was loosely tied back with a messy ponytail. She looked relaxed and content, standing by the stove stirring the French stew with one hand, a Martini in the other.

'Hello Dominique…glad you could make it tonight. I haven't seen you in such a long time,' Maddie said sarcastically. 'How about a Martini? No, that's right; you don't drink Martinis. How about some wine?'

'Oui, merci,' Dominique replied. He wasn't sure what Maddie was up to this evening. She looked happy and a bit drunk, a far cry from the restless and sad woman who had kept to herself over the last three months, leaving the house only to train and run errands.

Maddie poured Dominique a glass of wine, and they both walked into the living room and sat on the couch.

'This is nice, Maddie. You haven't cooked in months,' Dominique said truthfully.

Maddie wanted to respond with 'And you haven't been home long enough for me to make dinner,' but she decided it was pointless to get into an argument with the man she was divorcing.

'What's the occasion?' Dominique asked.

'Well, tonight is a celebration of sorts for us, Dominique,' Maddie answered.

'Oh? What are WE celebrating?' Dominique asked curiously.

'Our legal separation and divorce,' Maddie replied, handing Dominique an envelope with the legal forms. 'It's all in there, Dominique. The documents for our legal separation, back-dated eighteen months ago. I'm sure you won't mind if we get this over with as quickly as possible? Once you sign these papers, then we can proceed with the actual divorce. In a matter of months, you will be free to spend as much time with your girlfriend as you like!'

'Is this a joke, Maddie?' Dominique asked, opening the legal-size envelope and peering in.

'It's not a joke, Dominique. It's time we did this. I've thought about it for months, as I know you have. I need to move on with my life, and I want to do it as quickly as the legal process will allow. We are not going to fight about this. The divorce conditions are all clearly spelled out in the documents. I am quite sure you will like the terms. You don't even have to move out of this house; you can stay here as long as you want. I, however, will be leaving in twenty-one days. Over that period of time, I will pack up my personal belongings, sell what we don't want to keep, and basically, close this chapter on our marriage.'

'This seems very sudden. What are you going to do? Ou vas-tu?' asked Dominique, using both English and French in the same sentence, as was his habit when speaking to her.

'You've known me for a long time, Dominique, and you know that once I make up my mind about something, I do it swiftly, but without a lot of fanfare. As far as my future, I'm leaving, going to Ireland. I am not sure how long I will stay there. It depends on the availability of work and other factors,' Maddie replied truthfully.

At this early stage in the divorce process, Maddie thought it wise to withhold the real reason for her journey to Ireland with her husband and her sons, until she had some answers regarding Aidan. She was not sure if she would find Aidan, and if she did, what would come of it.

Dominique did not know what to say. He just stared at the envelope for a few moments and sighed.

'You're always doing the unexpected, Maddie. This is what I found exciting about you early in our relationship, and why I fell in love with you decades ago. It's good to see the former Maddie St-Laurent in action, full of optimism about the future, embracing life's adventures with enthusiasm. I'm relieved that we can both move on with our lives, but I'm also a bit envious. Going to Ireland? That's bold and rather exciting! But I won't stand in your way. Whatever is in this envelope is fine with me.'

This was the perfect time for Maddie to finally lay into her unsupportive and unfaithful husband. She was tempted to say that Julia had been right about him all along, but held herself back. What would be the point in getting into a slugging match with the man she was anxious to leave? Though the boys were adults now, she worried, too, that an acrimonious divorce would have a lasting impact on her relationship with them. They were close to their dad, and she didn't want to find herself out of their lives.

Instead, Maddie replied, laughing 'Well, you'd better read the terms and conditions first, before you commit! But let's eat now, before this Martini goes straight to my head!'

01:46:56

Maddie sat, cramped but comfortable, in a seat in the front section of the Air Canada Boeing 747, gazing out the window as the giant plane taxied towards the runway. *This is what it feels like to run away to the circus*, Maddie thought, watching the movement of the planes lining up, nose to tail, in preparation for take-off. The early October weather was a complete contrast to the past few months, unseasonably cold, with bitter winds blowing a mixture of rain and sleet on the tarmac. It was a miserable day for travelling. Most of the outbound flights had been delayed by thirty minutes, due to the un-forecasted freezing rain. The pilot had personally informed all the passengers that the take-off would be a bumpy one, but once they reached altitude, the remainder of the flight would be comfortable and quiet. They were expected to land in Dublin around 7 am, local time.

Maddie imagined Aidan sitting in this exact seat, wondering what he had been thinking for seven hours. The discovery of Aidan's full name and his association with an excavation company was a meager lead, but it was enough to convince Maddie that Aidan's silence since June was not intentional. In broad terms, he had told her the truth, though his deliberate actions to withhold vital personal information was troubling and mysterious. Something must have happened in Ireland, an unforeseen event that prevented Aidan from communicating with her, Maddie hoped. There was a rational explanation for his prolonged silence, and she was determined to uncover the truth.

Maddie had planned this moment with meticulous detail, in spite of the fact that her best friend Sofia was not overly supportive of her plans. Sofia had expressed her concerns many times, advising Maddie that this journey to Ireland would likely end in disappointment. She had no use for the calculating charlatan, as she called him, and told Maddie she could do much better by moving to Brazil and living with her. Sofia added that there were plenty of attractive and available men in Rio. Maddie reminded Sofia that she had been unhappy and trapped in a sad marriage long before she met Aidan. While this pursuit gave her the impetus she needed to start a new life, she told Sofia that the future remained unpredictable and uncertain, yet she was prepared to manage the consequences, good or bad.

Maddie was acutely aware that she also setting herself for disappointment if Sofia was correct in her opinion of Aidan. There was strong evidence to support his duplicitous behaviour, at least according to Sofia. His intentions may have been wholly self-serving, but by travelling to Ireland and facing the unpleasant truth, Maddie could move on with her life, however painful that might be. It all sounded so simple and straightforward.

*****

At 6:59 am, the Air Canada plane landed safely at the Dublin Airport. Though tired from lack of sleep, Maddie disembarked from the half-full plane practically skipping, and quickly made her way through Customs. From there, she waited at the giant baggage handling area for her lone suitcase. It, too, arrived quickly, but soaking wet. The glass and steel modern terminal was well laid out, and she had no trouble finding the car for hire area, to pick up the rental for the drive to Clonakilty in West Cork.

Driving on the left side of the road was going to be a challenge, Maddie thought, as she stood in line waiting for service. She had driven in England and Scotland a few times, but that was a long time ago. Maddie was nervous about navigating the rental car out of the busy Dublin Airport during rush hour traffic. She had heard the Irish drive very fast and there were many roundabouts to manoeuvre through. The rental company suggested renting an automatic and buying the extended insurance coverage and road side insurance, just in case she got into an accident or needed help.

Before driving away from the airport parking garage, Maddie reviewed the driving route to Clonakilty. It seemed straightforward enough on paper, but just in case, she programmed the GPS on her smart phone to provide additional verbal instructions. Annoying as this was, the prompts would ensure she didn't end up in the centre of Dublin, instead of on her way to West Cork.

Remembering to keep left at all times, Maddie carefully navigated out of the Dublin Airport and onto the Old Airport Road. It was busy, but the traffic moved quickly. She was overtaken by most of the cars and trucks, all going faster than the posted speed limit. On the side of the busy airport road, she saw a white wreath hanging from a post, evidence that a car accident had occurred at this spot. It was a grim reminder to keep below the speed limit.

Maddie followed the prompts attentively to the M50. Once on the M7, she stopped at a petrol station in Rathcole to buy a coffee and something to eat. She took the opportunity to relax for a few minutes and compose herself. Maddie's hands and arms ached from holding on too tightly to the steering wheel, and she had a throbbing tension headache. She was looking forward to arriving in Clonakilty to enjoy a nice lunch and perhaps an afternoon glass of wine.

The rest of her trip was uneventful. The radio was turned off, and the only sound Maddie could hear was the wind pushing against the closed windows. Maddie allowed herself the occasional glimpse of the beautiful lush and green landscape of Ireland. In Cork, Maddie drove through the city without incident, following the prompts at every turn and roundabout. It was pretty, and she hoped that she would have time to return to the quaint area and visit at some point in the near future.

Finally, four and half hours later, Maddie pulled into the Quality Hotel and Leisure Club in Clonakilty. She specifically chose this hotel because it had a pool, a steam bath, and a sauna, something she was looking forward to using later in the day. The large, sprawling complex was in an industrial park, surrounded by a few other businesses. If she got bored, she could always take in a movie at the theatre next door.

After checking into her room, Maddie headed into the town centre to buy some lunch. The town was tiny, and most of the restaurants, pubs, and shops were located along the two main streets.

Her first stop was at the Visitors Centre, to pick up some information and a few maps. The brightly lit retail shop was jammed with free information. The woman working that day was talkative and friendly. She told Maddie that Clonakilty, meaning 'Castle of the Woods', was rich in history and over four hundred years old, but there was evidence that the tiny community could trace it origins to the Bronze Age.

Following the woman's advice, Maddie walked up McCurtain Hill to the original site of the first 'castle', eventually replaced by the Church of Ireland. She strolled around the gravesites to read the ancient tombstones. From there, she headed to Asna Square to see the 'Kilty Stone', the only remaining piece of an original castle. She continued to wander around, peeking into the big Catholic church with the bright red doors, walking through Spinners Lane courtyard and the original stonework from the 18th century. The facades of the buildings on the main streets were painted in bright colors of orange, yellow and green. The effect was warm and inviting. There were a fair number of people walking about, carrying on with their daily activities. There were few tourists about, as the high season was long over.

The town centre had all types of stores, from butchers to bakeries, clothing stores, sport shorts, pharmacies, and so many pubs that Maddie lost count. After walking up and down Pearse Street a few times, Maddie chose to eat a late lunch at Mac's Pub, as the street billboard lunch menu looked promising.

She ordered homemade soup with soda bread, followed by tea and pie. While she waited, Maddie ordered a glass of wine and watched the regular patrons seated at the antique oak bar, drinking dark beer and engaged in a soccer game on the large screen TV. There was animated shouting and loud swearing, as the patrons grew more vocal as the game progressed.

The food arrived quickly, hot, delicious and filling. Afterwards, Maddie strolled around the area, before heading back to the hotel and an hour-long swim and a relaxing steam bath. Though she was fatigued after a busy day, it was still too early to go to bed. She forced herself to stay awake until 9 pm, and then fell asleep with her reading glasses still propped on her head and the lights on.

The Clonakilty Construction Company was four kilometers from the town centre, along a narrow and twisting country road, flanked on both sides by an ancient stone fencing partially covered by lush vegetation. Maddie realized, too late, that she should have walked to the office instead of drive, and enjoyed the picture-perfect country landscape and pretty heritage homes dotted along the meandering route. A walk would have been a good idea. While she had no trouble falling asleep in the comfy confines of the hotel room, she woke up frequently during the night and had trouble getting back to sleep, plagued with nervous tension about meeting Michael Bennett. She worried that he would dismiss her, or worse, she would find out that she had made the journey for nothing.

Maddie turned into the laneway of the Clonakilty Construction Company. There were several buildings on the vast property, presumably housing large pieces of equipment for construction and excavation projects.

The general office of the company was located in a two-story painted farm house sitting on the property closest to the road. There were a few trees and large bushes surrounding the impressive heritage house and a low stone fence that bordered the front with a lovely garden inside still showing signs of life, though it was now early October. At the turn of the 20th century, this property had once been a large and prosperous working farm.

Maddie walked along the stone path to the front door and looked for the doorbell. Instead, she read a small brass sign placed over the mail slot that read: 'Please walk in'. Maddie opened one half of the narrow black double door and stepped into the foyer, as a musical chime echoed throughout the first floor. Within seconds, a pretty, dark-haired woman wearing rectangle-shaped glasses greeted her.

'Good mornin'. What may I help yeh' with today?' the woman asked. Maddie recognized the clear and distinct Irish accented voice from the company's automated answering service.

'I am here to see Michael Bennett,' she replied nervously.

'I see. Is he expecting yeh?' the woman asked, looking up at the tall, middle aged woman, who appeared nervous and slightly uncomfortable standing in the foyer of the office.

'No. I don't have an appointment. My name is Maddie St-Laurent. I am from Canada. I am here to see Mr. Bennett on a personal matter.'

'I'll see if he is free. Please, take a seat in the sittin' room. I won't be long,' the woman replied, pointing to the company's official sitting room.

The room was neat but sparsely furnished, with two leather loveseats and a coffee table, a modern contrast to the dark wood-panelled walls and floor. One full wall of the space was covered with black-and-white and color photos. Maddie recognized a few of the places from the news headlines– the aftermath of the earthquake in Haiti and Nepal, and helmeted volunteers moving enormous chunks of fallen concrete with bulldozers. There were photos of children and women as well, carrying their meagre supplies in the harsh and destroyed environment. The photos were both beautiful and unsettling.

There were other photos hanging in the space, more typical of the company's daily business and a demonstration of the scope of their projects. There were photos of the company employees working at various sites and participating in events in and around West Cork. Maddie scanned all the photos carefully, looking for Aidan

She almost missed the partially hidden man with long hair, dark glasses, and a white constructions helmet sitting in the glassed cab of a Hitachi front-end loader, his bare arms maneuvering the gears of a big machine. She knew instantly the man in the photo was Aidan. If she had any lingering doubts about Aidan's connections with the Clonakilty Construction Company, they vanished as soon as she saw the photo. She had not made a mistake in showing up unannounced.

Michael Bennett had walked in to the sitting room quietly while Maddie was looking intently at the photos. He watched her for a few seconds before announcing himself.

'Hello, I'm Michael Bennett,' he said in a deep voice.

Startled, Maddie turned around, to see the president of the company standing behind her with his hand extended. He was shorter than Aidan by at least half a foot, and stocky, with massive forearms, a barrel chest, and heavyset legs, exactly the physical characteristics of someone who worked in construction all day. Michael had bright red hair, blue eyes, and his face and arms were covered in freckles. Maddie extended her hand to shake Michael's enormous and rough hand.

'My name is Maddie St-Laurent.' Without hesitation, not giving Michael a chance to speak, she continued, 'And I am looking for this man,' pointing her finger directly at the photo of Aidan on the wall.

Michael did not acknowledge the photo, but kept his eyes on the Canadian. 'Why don't we talk about this in me office?' Without waiting for an answer, he gently guided Maddie up the well-worn farmhouse stairs to the second-floor office and shut the door.

'Can I see your passport?' Michael asked. 'We have a company security policy to check everyone's identification when they come into our offices.'

Though surprised at this unusual request, Maddie dutifully opened her knapsack and retrieved her passport and the photo of Aidan and her crossing the finishing line in Mont-Tremblant. She handed her Canadian passport and the photo to Michael. He examined both briefly and gave them back to her in silence.

'What can I do for yeh, Ms. St-Laurent?' Michael asked cautiously.

'Please, call me Maddie. I have travelled a long way to find Aidan O'Callaghan. I met him in Mont-Tremblant in June, at a triathlon race. He was supposed to contact me when he got back to Ireland, but he never did. I am anxious to speak with him. Can you please tell me where I can find him?' She handed Michael the only photo she had of them together.

Michael looked at the photo for a few seconds, without giving her any sign that he either knew or recognized the man in the photo.

'I dunna have the time to talk to yeh right now about one of our former employees. You've unfortunately come at an awkward time, as I am headin' out to one of our current projects, and I'll be busy all day,' Michael responded in a matter-of-fact tone.

'Oh. I see,' Maddie answered, the disappointment clear in her voice.

Maddie waited as Michael Bennett continued to scrutinize the photo. She hoped that seeing this photo would give him second thoughts about talking to her. To her relief, Michael spoke up.

'Can I suggest we meet later in the day, 5:30 like?'

'Okay. I can do that...where should I meet you?'

'There's a pub in the Town Centre called Mulligan's. Do yeh know where that is?'

'No, but I will find it. Thank you. I really appreciate it.'

Michael walked Maddie to the front door, and she left without saying another word.

'What did she want?' Michael's wife and business partner, Colleen, asked, as they stood looking at Maddie walking along the cobblestone path to her car.

'She's lookin' for Aidan,' answered Michael.

'That's curious. Do yeh remember the long-distance call I received, about three weeks ago, from a woman lookin' for Aidan?'

'I remember yeh tellin' me about the call.'

'Do you think t'is the same woman?'

'I do believe so. Indeed, I do.'

'Oh dear, why is she lookin' for Aidan?'

Michael pulled out his smart phone and scrolled through his text messages. He then handed Colleen his phone.

Colleen read aloud the text message from Aidan, sent to Michael the night he boarded the plane back to Dublin from Canada.

'I have exciting news for you and Colleen. ♡ I've never been happier. C U soon.'

'I don't understand,' Colleen asked. 'What does this text message have to do with that woman?'

'I don't know all the details yet, but apparently she met Aidan in Mont-Tremblant. Now it's all startin' to makes sense. I received this message just before Aidan came home. At the time, it did not seem particularly relevant because I thought he was referrin' to his girlfriend Meghan in his text message. Yeh remember, Colleen? He was talkin' about finally gettin' married, settlin' down, maybe havin' a couple of weans? Based on the text message, I thought he was going to announce his engagement to Meghan. But I got that very wrong. 'T'was not Meghan he was referrin' to. I am quite sure now that Aidan was writin' about this woman, Maddie St-Laurent.'

'Lord have mercy. Aidan's situation has suddenly gotten more complicated. Can she be trusted, do you think?'

'As far as I can tell. Her passport checks out, and she seems honest enough, and quite determined to find him. I tought she was going to burst into tears when I told her I didn't have time to talk. She's quite smitten with him, to be sure.'

'And are yeh going to tell her wha' happened to Aidan?

'She's come a long way to find him. I don't think I have a choice in the matter.'

01:53:37

When Maddie arrived at Mulligan's Pub at exactly 5:30 pm, Michael was already seated in a semi-secluded booth, surrounded by a dark-panelled wall and a small window. It was still early by Irish pub standards, and there were only a few patrons in the pub, who were watching a soccer game on the television monitors hanging on the walls.

When Michael saw Maddie, he stood up, smiled, and shook her hand. Maddie was attractively dressed in a pair of black leggings, high black rubber boots, a casual dark grey long-sleeved knit top, a grey scarf, and a dark blue raincoat. When she walked into Casey's, the few patrons sitting at the bar looked up at the tall redhead striding with purpose toward the back booth.

Michael was much more relaxed than he had been earlier in the day. Gone were the work clothes and work boots. He was wearing a pair of fitted and faded jeans, a blue sweater which matched his eyes perfectly, a black leather jacket, and running shoes.

'Hello... Maddie, is it? Michael asked. 'Thanks for meeting here. I am sorry I could not speak to yeh at the office, but I was havin' a challenging day and your unannounced visit took me by surprise. We don't get too many strangers wanderin' into our office. Call me overly protective, but I am not keen to share information about our former employees with strangers…yeh' understand?'

'I understand,' Maddie replied in a confident voice, though she was feeling anything but. In spite of an hour-long run along a quiet country road and a vigorous swim at the hotel's 20-meter pool, Maddie was nervous about the outcome of her meeting with Michael. After they sat down and ordered a couple of pints of Guinness Stout, Michael asked Maddie to see the photograph again.

Maddie opened her knapsack and pulled out the same photo she had shown Michael earlier in the day.

'He must be very important to yeh, to come all this way from Canada,' Michael said, looking at the colorful image. Maddie nodded in agreement, her expressive amber eyes revealing the depth of her feelings for the man in the photo.

Michael was not mistaken about her. It was obvious that the Canadian woman was in love with the man in the photo.

'I can see that yeh'r most anxious to have news about Aidan's health and whereabouts, so I won't delay a second longer. Aidan is, as far as I know, alive and safe, but he is not here in Clonakilty.'

'It's a relief to know that he's safe, though I didn't think he would be here,' replied Maddie softly.

'I wish he were here. I do miss him terribly. I have not spoken to him directly since June, just before he went off to Canada to race.'

Michael took a sip of his cold pint, looking at the photograph of his deliriously happy friend, clutching the woman sitting in front of him. 'T'is where you met Aidan I take it? In Mont-Tremblant?' he asked.

'Yes.' Maddie sensed that it was important to gain Michael's trust. He had been aloof and careful during their brief conversation at the construction office. He asked for her passport, which was in itself an unusual request for anyone not in the travel business. He had not been overly friendly, and he initially referred to Aidan as a 'former employee'. It was obvious that he was reluctant to share what he knew about Aidan to a total stranger. If Maddie was going to learn the facts about his prolonged silence, then Michael needed to know the whole story about what happened in Canada and why she was in Ireland.

'Let me explain the circumstances of our chance meeting, Michael. Aidan and I met during a ferocious thunderstorm,' Maddie continued. 'We were both out on a practice ride, you know, getting ready for the triathlon race, when a huge storm moved in. Aidan was alone and cycling in front of me when suddenly a deer bolted out of the bushes and hit him...'

'A deer? Go on outta that!'

Maddie smiled, thinking about how Aidan had used that same expression several times. 'As improbable as that sounds, it did happen. I can't say this is an everyday occurrence in Canada, but yes, he and the deer collided violently, the animal likely startled by the thunder and lightning.' Maddie took a tiny sip of her beer, though she didn't really enjoy the taste, and eased into the improbable story of their romance.

'Aidan was hurt, but not badly; he was alone and his bicycle was damaged. By this time, it was pouring rain, so I helped him back to the rented condo. From that point...things developed very quickly between us, and we spent the next five days together. You see, Michael, Mont-Tremblant was my first ever triathlon, and I would not have been able to get through it without Aidan's support. More importantly, we fell crazy in love, like a couple of teenage kids. I know it's hard to image falling in love when you're well past your prime, but it's true. It did happen. At least, I thought it did. Before saying goodbye, we promised to settle our personal affairs– I was going to finally walk away from my sad and unhappy marriage, and he was going to 'take care of things', he said. The last message I got from him was this one, shortly after we parted in Montreal.' Maddie opened her purse to retrieve her phone. She handed it to Michael so he could read Aidan's last email.

'M, arrived at the airport, safe but very sad. Miss you terribly. I will not be able to think about anything else flying home. I love you so much it hurts. Aidan.'

'When Aidan loves, he loves fiercely, to be sure.' Michael said, his face breaking out into a huge smile, trying to camouflage the sadness he felt regarding Aidan's wretched situation.

Maddie opened her knapsack again and took out the crude hair bracelet that was tucked in an envelope and placed it on the table, next to her phone and the photo. She looked squarely at Michael.

'Michael, I've been honest with you about why I am here, and I've travelled thousands of kilometers to learn the truth, good or bad. You have to trust me and tell me what's going on. Where is Aidan? What happened to him?'

Michael hesitated before speaking. He picked up the crude hand-made bracelet, examining it more closely, then reached for his cell phone from inside his jacket pocket, made a few swipes, and then placed it on the table next to Maddie's phone.

'I am not Aidan's employer, Maddie. We are business partners and he's also my best friend. I care very deeply for him.' He turned the phone toward Maddie so she could see the image on the screen.

There, in full color, was a horrific image of a mangled SUV lying on its roof, next to a crushed tractor trailer.

'This is what happened to Aidan,' Michael replied, pointing to the photo.

Maddie starred at the graphic image of the crumbled heap of metal, flinching at the thought that Aidan was in that vehicle. 'But you said he was alive…it doesn't look like anybody could survive that?' she blurted out.

'He miraculously survived, but just barely,' Michael took another sip of his beer. 'Let me explain. Aidan did arrive back in Ireland, as he planned. He was picked up at the airport by his… girlfriend, Meghan.'

'Yes, I know about his …friend. He was planning on breaking it off as soon as he landed in Ireland. That's what I thought he meant about 'taking care of things'. He was concerned about hurting her, and I know it weighed heavily on his mind,' Maddie replied.

'Meghan was driving the SUV back to Clonakilty from the Dublin Airport. I guess Aidan was too tired to drive, so Meghan was behind the wheel. About ten minutes into their journey, the front section of the vehicle exploded. Meghan lost control when the hood blew off, and it shattered the windshield. They hit an oncomin' lorry almost straight on. Stupidly, Meghan wasn't wearin' her seat belt, and she died instantly on impact. Aidan was sittin' in the front, but fortunately, he was wearin' his seat belt. He was pulled from the wreckage seconds before the vehicle was engulfed in flames. He survived the crash, but he suffered numerous serious injuries.'

Maddie was horrified at the thought of Aidan lying in the wreckage and felt instantly sick to her stomach.

'I drove immediately to Dublin, as soon as I heard the news,' Michael continued, 'I was frantic to see him, but when I got to the hospital, it was a very difficult and complicated situation. Aidan was in a medically induced coma, I think they called it, and the doctors and his family were not allowin' any visitors. I never spoke to him at the hospital. I only talked to Annie, his sister.'

'I didn't know Aidan had a sister.'

'Annie is not only his sister – she is his twin.'

'Why didn't he tell me about that?' Maddie mumbled to herself, shaking her head.

'Sorry? What did you say?'

'Nothing important. Please go on.'

'By the time Aidan recovered enough to sit up and talk, about three weeks later, he was whisked away from the hospital'.

'Whisked away where, and by whom?' Maddie asked.

'To Belfast, in Northern Ireland. His brothers and sister took him back to their home.'

'Belfast? I didn't know his family was from Belfast...and you haven't seen or spoken to him?'

'Sadly, no,' replied Michael.

Maddie was confused and it showed on her face. 'But why, Michael? Didn't you just say you are his best friend and business...?' she asked impatiently.

'Indeed, I am,' Michael answered curtly.

'Michael, what is going on? I do not understand any of this. Aidan gets into a serious car accident, his girlfriend dies, he survives but suffers life-threatening injuries, and then he disappears? Is there something wrong with him? Did he suffer extensive brain damage, or memory loss, can he walk, talk...why haven't you reached out to him?' Maddie's questions came out in rapid fire. She was trying hard not to lose her patience, but this news was not making any sense at all.

'Oh, I've reached out to him, Maddie, indeed I have, but the problem does not reside with him.' Michael sighed, wishing that he did not have to take this conversation any further with the Canadian woman, but it was unavoidable. He could not, in good conscious, invent a story to placate the woman. She had come to Ireland for the sole purpose of finding Aidan.

Michael knew that his best friend would never misrepresent himself when it came to love. Aidan was not the sort of man to take advantage of an opportunity, nor was he the type to declare his love if it was not true. Michael was quite confident that Aidan had fallen in love with the lovely redhead sitting in front of him. He had no choice now but to reveal the truth, however disturbing the details.

'Maddie, I am prepared to tell yeh what I know, so please be patient with me. I can see that yeh are honest and sincere about your feelins' toward Aidan, but before I tell yeh anythin' more, I need to ask you few questions. Would that be okay?' Michael asked, in a calm and reassuring voice.

'Yes, of course.'

'Did Aidan share any specific details regarding his family?'

'He never spoke about his family, not that I can recall anyway. It's a curious thing, Michael, something I did not notice at the time, but

Aidan asked a lot more questions than he answered. The only details I can recall were that he has two brothers and that his father died when he was sixteen.'

''T'is all true. Yeh didn't know that Aidan's home country is Northern Ireland, and not the Republic of Ireland?'

'I had no idea. To be fair to him, though, he told me he lived in West Cork, but he never said he was from West Cork'

'What else do yeh recall about his life?'

'I know he has a twenty-five-year-old son from a previous relationship, but the young man lives in Australia. He told me about Nepal and other missions in rescue and recovery operations. He said he worked for a construction company most of the time and operated heavy equipment. He was vague on everything else, though. I feel so foolish. I know virtually nothing about a man I have been obsessing about for the better part of four months.'

'Don't feel foolish. Aidan is a great friend, and a good man, and I love him dearly as a brother, but it's taken me over two decades to find out about the real Aidan O'Callaghan.'

'The real Aidan O'Callaghan? You make it sound like he is some kind of fugitive,' Maddie replied with a half-smile. Michael smiled too.

'In a way, he is a fugitive, Maddie' Michael continued, the smile gone from his serious face, 'a fugitive not of the law, but of his past. Aidan's story is so out there, so far-fetched, so removed from your life and mine. Yeh have no idea who he is and wha' he's been through. Clearly, he did not share the intimate details of a sad and violent early life that has come back to haunt him in the most egregious way, a true story that may force yeh to reconsider your search for him.'

Maddie could not fathom what troubles the good-natured Irishman had endured. He seemed so well-adjusted and happy, so perfect in every way, one of the few people Maddie had met in her life that didn't carry any excess emotional baggage. For a brief moment, Maddie contemplated leaving the pub, closing her ears and her mind to any further revelations about the enigmatic man, keeping the precious memory of their brief romance pristine and unsullied.

'I was wonderin' how much yeh know about recent Irish history, particularly in Northern Ireland?' Michael asked Maddie, coaxing her back to their conversation.

'I don't know much about Northern Ireland,' Maddie replied honestly. 'Like most Canadians, my knowledge is limited to the news headlines. Aidan only talked about his homeland in broad and glowing terms, its breathtaking beauty, but he never spoke about specific areas of the island. We never discussed politics, or religion, unless it had something to do with his humanitarian work.'

Michael shook his head. 'Like I said, Aidan's story is so complicated and wild, I don't think yeh will even believe me when I tell you. But this is Ireland, after all, a country with a long, violent and bloody history of religious and political clashes. Yeh will have to do some readin' about Irish history to get caught up, but for now, I will tell you what I know about Aidan and why you may not have heard from him.'

Maddie sat back in her seat, took off her scarf, and readied herself as best she could to hear the intriguing details about the Irishman's past life.

'I first met Aidan in London in 1994,' Michael continued. 'We was both working for the same construction company in East London. I was new to the big city and somewhat naïve. I had just arrived from Cork City. Aidan impressed me the minute I met him. He was a hard worker, pleasant, smilin', and utterly charmin'. Everyone on the site liked Aidan. He was big, strong, and so likeable. He had a real knack for drawing people out, too, makin' them feel comfortable like. T'was easy to get to know him – or at least, that's what I thought. But over time, I realized I knew nothin' about the man. He kept his personal life to himself. When people did ask him personal questions, he would change the subject with such skill and finesse, you forgot about the question entirely!'

Maddie nodded in agreement. This was a character trait she now recognized. He had done exactly the same thing to her. This realization, that he held back most of his life story from the woman he purportedly loved, stung ever so slightly.

'One night, Aidan and I got very drunk. I remember it clearly, because he had a letter tucked into his shirt pocket and kept openin' and readin' it. He said nothin' about the contents, only he kept drinkin' and drinkin', which was in itself unusual. Aidan liked to go to our local pub after a long day of work, but he limited his pints to one or two. T'was the first time I saw him drink heavily, and I also saw the emotional pain he was going through. He did not share much that night, but he did reveal enough that I understood about of his past life in Ireland. It was far from pleasant. He told me he grew up in North Belfast, a Catholic, in the middle of the Troubles, one of the worst and most violent periods in Irish history, I would say. His father died when he was sixteen, shot I tink.'

'Shot? Oh my god...'

'His two older brothers had quit school early and joined the Provisional I.R.A., doing a lot of truly nasty, dirty work that no one else had the stomach for. His brother Thomas, the eldest, had a mean streak well-suited to paramilitary work. When he got onto the subject of Thomas O'Callaghan, Aidan's mood changed. I'd never seen him like that, seethin' with anger. He said that if he had a choice between fighting a Komodo dragon and Thomas, he'd choose the dragon. I tried to avoid the subject of his brother from then on, as it seemed to really set him off.'

'I had no idea,' Maddie responded. 'Aidan only mentioned his brothers briefly. He said they were smart. He said he was the athlete in the family and they were the brains.'

'The athlete part is true. Aidan was, and still ism an outstanding athlete, but he is also very smart. His brothers, though, are not just smart; they are cunnin', controllin', and dangerous.' Michael paused to take a sip of his beer and looked around the Pub before he continued, his eyes darting about, looking for faces he did not recognize.

'Unfortunately, Aidan's bright future was cut short when...'

'...when he met Katie and she got pregnant?'

'Indeed, so you know about the facts surrounding Aidan's son?' to which Maddie answered 'Yes, but I take it there is more to the story than mother and child moving to Australia without him?'

'Probably, but he never shared more than that with me. By the time I met Aidan, he was livid' alone and workin' in London.'

'What about the letter he had been carrying?'

'T'was from Katie, telling him that she was gettin' married to an Australian bloke because she wanted their son to have a full-time father. It was tough for him. I think he had aspirations of movin' to Australia someday to reunite with her and the baby. That, sadly, never happened, after he received the news that she was gettin' married.'

'He didn't explain their relationship quite the same way,' Maddie replied. 'He told me they were not getting along and she left for Australia. What you are telling me is that he still loved her when she moved away? That's so sad. Poor Aidan. I wonder why she moved to Australia when he was still in love with her? Aidan doesn't strike me as the type of person who gives up easily.'

'I don't know, Maddie. He didn't talk about it, though I suspect that his family had a lot to do with her movin' away.'

The Pub was getting noisier as the local patrons started streaming in. Everyone seemed to know each other, and conversations were lively around the bar. Dinner service had just started, and the aroma from the kitchen was making Maddie hungry.

'It was shortly after receiving the letter that Aidan took an interest in many other activities, includin' triathlon racing,' Michael continue. 'He moved on with his life, I guess. We raced together for a time, but I could not compete with the likes of Aidan O'Callaghan. He started travellin' around the world, racin', and then discovered his passion: working as a volunteer for the Global Humanitarian Relief Organization. He found a way to soothe the pain of losin' his family with the joy of helpin' others, I think. He loved the work. Every mission was a race against the rescue clock. This suits his fierce, competitive nature.'

The waiter came by to offer Michael another pint, which he took.

'For meself, I met a girl from Cork City while workin' in London; we feel in love and we moved back to Ireland as soon as we could afford it. Yeh met my wife Colleen; she was the woman who greeted yeh at the office? In any event, I started my own excavation business and invited Aidan to join me. It took a bit of persuasion, but eventually he agreed to move to the Republic. Though not his home country, at least it was familiar to him in some way. He insisted that his role in the company be kept at a very low profile. He never wanted to be photographed or listed in any company documents. He never wanted to call attention to himself.'

'Why?' Maddie asked.

'For fear that his notorious, militant brothers would start to implicate themselves in his new life. He was short on details and never explained to me the history of his brothers and the family. I only found out about this later. In any event, t' was one of his firm stipulations, and I didn't question it, not one bit. I respected his wishes. Aidan wanted to work as the other men did, on the job. He left the management of the company to me. You could say he truly was a silent partner. We started the business in Cork City, but a few years later, we moved here to Clonakilty, and if yeh stay here long enough, yeh will understand why.'

'And what about the strained relations with his brothers? What happened to them?' Maddie asked.

'As far as I know, the O'Callaghan brothers continued their involvement in the IRA, each one movin' up the chain of command in the organization. They became quite powerful, or so I've heard. When thirty years of civil conflict finally ended in '98 and the paramilitary groups associated with the violence supposedly disbanded, I thought for sure Aidan would reunite with his mother and twin sister, at the very least, and resume a more normal familial relationship, but no. Nothin' really changed. He spoke to his mother and sister on the phone occasionally and via email. Sheila, his mother, visited Clonakilty a few times, but Aidan never ventured up north. He kept a safe distance away from his brothers. That was the extent of his family relationship. He never talked about his brothers, saw or spoke to either one of them…at least not directly.'

'But the Troubles were over, and life, presumably, went back to normal. I don't understand,' Maddie asked, feeling a bit nauseous from the strong dark stout, while listening to the facts about Aidan's unusual life story.

Michael stopped talking and looked around the pub again. No one was sitting near them, or could possibly hear their conversation, but Michael wanted to make sure that the information he was about to tell her could not be overhead. He leaned in closer to Maddie and spoke, almost whispering.

'Well yeh see, t'is like this. Thomas O'Callaghan is one of the most feared and ruthless persons living on the island today, not because of what he can do himself, which is pretty bad, but what he is capable of gettin' others to do. Yeh don't cross Thomas O'Callaghan for any reason. Just being in the same room with him incites absolute terror. He has many sworn enemies from his past life as a commander with the IRA. People in that business dunna forget the likes of Thomas O'Callaghan, and he hasn't done much to dispel his reputation. Aidan has stayed away from Belfast and his brothers for good reason.'

Michael glanced at the photo of the happy couple. There was no reason not to tell Maddie everything. Perhaps revealing the real dangers of being associated with the O'Callaghans would be enough incentive to send the Canadian home, far away from danger, as Aidan would want.

'Maddie, you should know that while I don't claim to have first-hand knowledge of the O'Callaghan family dynamics and their business organization, t'is common knowledge that the family is involved in criminal activity. Now, you see, after the Peace Agreement, a lot of former militants, on both sides on the political fence, ended up without real jobs. I guess they had nowhere else to apply their unique skills. From what I've heard, Patrick O'Callaghan, the middle brother, is the financial brains of the family's empire. He and Thomas have apparently built an enormous business, founded on criminal and illegal activities—drugs, mostly. And the drug world is nasty. Apparently the O'Callaghans are supremely powerful and a target for retribution among other criminal gangs.'

'Are you saying that Aidan is involved in this criminal gang stuff?' Maddie asked, incredulous that Aidan would willingly be associated with the underworld.

'Absolutely not!' Michael answered emphatically. 'He has kept well away from his family all these years. But Aidan is an O'Callaghan, and therefore a target by association.' Michael took a sip of his beer and lowered his voice again to a whisper. 'I spoke to Annie shortly after I arrived at the hospital. She told me unequivocally that the car accident was no accident. It was deliberate. Someone planted a bomb under the front hood. T'is is one deadly extermination method, by whom and why I do not know, but it was clearly intended to kill Aidan, not Meghan. If Aidan was the target for retribution, and he didn't die, then they will surely try again, maybe this time with more success. From what I've heard and read, there has been a smattering of renewed violence and killings in Belfast related to criminal activity, a kinda turf war, and it seems to be escalating. It's a scary time, I don't mind sayin'. T'is is why I think that Thomas whisked Aidan off to Belfast as soon as possible, even if he didn't want to go. Knowing a little bit about his brothers' reputation, Thomas probably forced Aidan to return to Belfast.'

'Forced him? How?'

'Likely by tellin', or maybe threatenin', Aidan that it was too dangerous to be close to his friends and loved ones. They could be the next target. For his and their protection, Thomas likely insisted that Aidan return to the family home.'

Maddie could only shake her head in disbelief.

'How do you know all this if you haven't spoken to him directly?'

'T'is a good question, Maddie. Aidan sent a message to me via Annie. The message was short but clear. I must never to try and contact him, nor should anyone else in this community. Aidan would never send a message like that if he wasn't worried. I have honored my best friend's request, though reluctantly, for my protection and that of my young family. My suspicion is that if Aidan has recovered his memory and he has not suffered any long-term brain dysfunction, he has chosen not to contact yeh because he wants to protect yeh from becoming another innocent victim, caught up in the nefarious underworld of tit for tat: recrimination and retribution.'

'Do you think Aidan is in danger, Michael?'

'Sadly, I do believe he is in danger. As I said, Belfast today is simmerin' with renewed violence. For the moment, he's in a bad place, and the longer he stays in Belfast, I fear, the more precarious his situation.'

The story about the O'Callaghans was not only farfetched and out of her scope of reality, it was truly terrifying. Maddie was not only afraid for Aidan, for the first time since she began her search, she was afraid for her own life. She could not ignore the physical signs of fear: tight chest, constricted breathing, ringing in her ears, and a weak voice. Her heart was pounding painfully. If Maddie had chosen to leave Ireland at that very moment, no one would have blamed her for trying to protect herself, including Aidan.

'What should I do now, Michael? Stop looking for him? Are you telling me all of this so I will go back to Canada and forget about him?' Maddie finally asked.

'I can't tell you what to do. I am merely suggestin' that you know the facts before you go any further. T'is a dangerous and potentially life threatenin' situation for you, as I am sure you now realize. The criminals on both sides of the debate have no qualms about murderin' for financial gain, or because it suits them. They killed Meghan, didn't they, a sweet, innocent young woman who adored Aidan and wanted nothin' more than to be his wife. I believe that Aidan may not have sent you a direct message to protect you. He may also think that you won't come lookin' for him. But the man did send a message to me, and I can only assume it applies to you too. Stay away for your own good,' Michael said in a tired voice.

Looking at Maddie's anguished face saddened Michael. He wished he had the power to help her and Aidan, but it would be far too risky.

'Listen, Maddie,' he continued, taking Maddie's hands to comfort the stricken woman, 'I've given you a lot to think about. I suspect your mind is spinnin' and yeh need some time to digest this information?'

Maddie nodded, 'Yes, you've given me lots to think about. I have to admit I am… feeling…scared. It hardly seems possible that Aidan, who is loving, kind and gentle, could be associated with this culture of terror.'

'Remember, t'is not his fault Maddie. He is a victim of circumstance. He was born at the wrong place and in the wrong time.'

They were both silent. The regular pub patrons were coming in in large numbers, and the seats around the bar were filling up. The bartender turned up the music. People were laughing and talking loudly. Someone yelled out to Michael, and he nodded and waved back, but didn't move from his seat.

'I have a suggestion to make,' Michael finally said with a half-smile. 'Why don't I take you to see Aidan's cottage tomorrow mornin'? T'is empty at the moment. If you are comfortable with the arrangement, you can stay there for as long as you want, or until you decide what to do next? I am sure Aidan would want you to be comfortable while stayin' in Clona'. It's quite a nice place and I'm sure yeh will like it.'

'That's a good idea, Michael.'

Maddie walked a back to the hotel, her head spinning in disbelief. Physically and emotionally drained from the lengthy conversation with Michael, she barely noticed the people scurrying about the street, umbrellas opened, trying to avoid the rain that had started falling minutes earlier. *What have I got myself into, Maddie thought, chasing after a man who was connected, though innocently, to criminals? Even Sofia would tell me to take the next flight out of Ireland and never return.*

02:01:17

Before returning to the Quality Hotel to settle in for the evening, Maddie picked up a bit of food and a bottle of wine at the nearby market. Once in her hotel room, she changed into her cozy pyjamas and warm slippers, poured herself a glass of Bordeaux, and began researching the Troubles. While she was weary from the last few hours with Michael, sleep would have to wait until she better understood the tenuous political situation in Northern Ireland, and how Aidan and his family were involved.

Maddie watched video clips, short documents, and read news reports, while jotting down notes and names so she could become familiar with the historical and political landscape. The history of Ireland, and in particular Northern Ireland, was complicated. The Troubles had lasted thirty years, and in that time period, thousands of people had died or were injured by acts of terrorism perpetrated by both sides of the political debate. Since 1998 and the Good Friday Peace Agreement, the widespread sectarian violence had ended and the Loyalists or Unionists and the Republicans or Nationalists were no longer fighting openly. The citizens could now walk freely down the streets of Belfast and elsewhere in the war-ravaged country and conduct their everyday business without the threat that some militant group would disrupt the cease-fire.

While the tenuous and fragile government system had replaced peace for guns, and the early stages of the peace accord were a war of words rather than outright acts of violence, progress was slow. The deep-rooted hatred between certain undeclared dissident paramilitary groups on both sides remained a viable threat to the peace process. A small number of sectarian killings still occurred in Northern Ireland, but they no longer made headline news in North America. Over time, sectarian violence was replaced by gang warfare, and the fight for economic supremacy and control in various illegal criminal activities such as drug and fuel smuggling. The border between the Republic of Ireland and Northern Ireland was a geographical boundary only, as the criminal element operated freely regardless of country.

As far as the O'Callaghan family's involvement, Maddie could find scant information about the brothers. She realized that the family name had turned up in her earlier search weeks before, but she had completely dismissed the connection because it seemed inconceivable that Aidan was somehow mixed up with criminals, even by association. Now, she read with keen interest anything she could find on the notorious family.

Michael's description of the family was referenced in news reports, and Thomas O'Callaghan in particular was cited as the mastermind of the modern 'Irish mafia', but few details were available. The family did not appear to be petty criminals, involved in the day to day management of illegal activities. Neither brother, Thomas nor Patrick, had spent much time in jail, even as IRA commanders, according to the web documents she found online. Whatever they were doing of a criminal nature seemed to be one step ahead of the police. By all indications, though, the men were powerful, feared, and seemingly untouchable.

While researching the nefarious world of the O'Callaghans, Maddie understood completely why Aidan wanted nothing to do with his ruthless and scheming brothers, and why he chose to keep his personal life a secret from almost everyone he met. He was probably ashamed of being connected to them, Maddie thought.

A small part of her though was angry with him for not sharing more about this life. If he had only trusted her enough to tell his story while they were together in Canada, she would be sitting by his side while he recovered from his injuries. Instead, Aidan woke up from his coma, probably frantic with worry about her, while she was desperately searching for him thousands of kilometers away. Now that she knew what really happened that fateful morning, there was no longer any doubt about Aidan's motives for not contacting her. It was clear from Michael's description of the events that he was purposely trying to protect her from the mess his brothers had caused.

After several hours of reading, Maddie stopped to seriously consider whether she should continue to venture into the dark and murky world of the Irish Mafia in pursuit of a man who didn't want to be found. It was clear from Michael's description of the O'Callaghan family, it could be dangerous—even fatal, as Michael pointed out.

Meghan's senseless death was a grim reminder that these people, whoever they are, had no qualms about murdering anyone who happened to be in their way. Maddie felt terribly isolated, sitting in her hotel room. If she persisted, and something did happen to her, how would her boys react? A week before Maddie left Canada, she sent Jean-Luc and Xavier each a long letter, explaining the reasons for the quick divorce from Dominique and her need to make some significant changes in her life. She told them her first stop was Ireland, where she wanted to explore some of her family history. They had no idea what she was really doing here. Jean-Luc, in particular, would demand she come home immediately to avoid being implicated, if he knew what she was up to.

*****

For the second night in Clonakilty, Maddie slept poorly, and woke up in the early hours of the day more fatigued then the day before. At 5 am, she finally gave up on sleep, and went into the bathroom, glancing at her tired face in the mirror. There were dark circles under her bloodshot eyes, and her face looked pale and thin. She had lost a few pounds during the last hectic weeks of moving. The stress of settling all her financial affairs before leaving Canada, packing and storing her belongings, showed on her face and figure. Aidan would not be happy to see the loss of Maddie's sexy curves, but this was a temporary condition, she thought. Once she was reunited with Aidan and their relationship could start where it had left off, Maddie was confident the weight would come back easily; gaining weight had never been an issue. For now, Maddie had more important issues to worry about.

Within a few hours, Michael sent Maddie an email with specific directions to Aidan's cottage, located only five kilometers from the hotel. Maddie followed Michael's directions exactly, driving along a twisting country road, up and down a few hills before she reached her destination.

Having only spent five days with the enigmatic Irishman, Maddie knew very little about how Aidan lived day to day. She did not know his personal habits, his favorite foods, or whether he had any hobbies or interests, other than travelling the globe as a triathlete and humanitarian aid volunteer. When Maddie pictured Aidan in his home in Clonakilty, the word 'bohemian' would pop into her mind. She expected to see a home that was a reflection of Aidan's carefree personality, and not dissimilar to his old bike: a bit dated and worn around the edges, scratched with heavy use, but lovingly maintained.

Following Michael's directions, Maddie turned left of the main road and drove up a long, narrow gravel laneway. Michael's truck was parked next to a very large, barn-like structure that looked recently built. Across from the barn stood a small, one-storey stone cottage, with smoke streaming from the blackened chimney. The cottage looked old but quaint, nestled halfway up a hill, overlooking a valley that resembled a giant checkerboard, with dark and light patches of green separated by stone fencing and vegetation. In the distance and to her right, Maddie could see an impressive, stately stone house, similar to Aidan's cottage. To her right, Maddie could see the dark blue color of the Atlantic Ocean. The view from Aidan's tiny piece of Ireland was breathtaking.

For its advanced years, which Maddie guessed to be about 150 years old, the stone cottage was in pristine condition. Though it was a dreary October morning, with grey skies and not a glimmer of sunshine, the little cottage radiated with warmth. This was not what she had expected to see as Aidan's home.

The indigenous quarry stone that clad the cottage was multi-colored, in various shades of brown, with the burnished yellow stone. Maddie had seen this stone on several older buildings in town. The front door of the cottage was painted a bright orange-red, a popular color choice in the area. There were two large windows on either side of the red front door.

When Maddie opened the heavy wooden front door, the first thing that struck her was the smell. The house had been unoccupied for several months, and with the doors and windows closed, the cottage had the distinctive aroma of a country antique store: a combination of wax, old wood, dampness, and smoke. It was a wonderful, rich smell, and reminded Maddie of the country stores she and her dad had visited during their summer holidays in the Quebec Eastern Townships.

'Good mornin', Maddie,' Michael said, standing in front of a large stone fireplace, coaxing a few small logs to burn and tinkering with the vents.

'It's taken me quite a while a get this fire going – there was no dry wood in the bin, so I had to use the damp wood outside. It will eventually catch if you give it some time.'

'It's not a problem, Michael,' Maddie replied, lingering by the front door. The house looked tiny from the outside, but it was deceivingly spacious, neat, and organized.

'Was this always a family home?' Maddie asked Michael, as she stood admiring the entire space from ceiling to floors.

'Up until Aidan started tinkerin', t'was nothing but a derelict old barn for the animals, long since abandoned,' Michael replied with pride. 'It took Aidan five years to complete the project. 'T'was was a huge undertaking, and he did all the work mostly by himself, including building all the cabinets. I would give him a hand on occasion, when the work required two people, but mostly, he toiled away on his own. He not only did all the work, he lived here throughout all the renovations. For one winter, he lived here without a solid roof, nothing but a plastic tarp between him and the punishing rain. I don't how he survived.'

Maddie walked slowly around the large room, looking at every detail of Aidan's handiwork. The main part of the space was open to a modern kitchen, dining, and living area. Off to the right was an enclosed bedroom and bathroom. On the left of the main room was another room, an office, with floor to ceiling windows that afforded a spectacular view of the valley below.

The cottage had vaulted ceilings, giving the living space a grand feel. The roof was supported by enormous, dark wooden beams that ran the entire span of the building. The foyer and fireplace hearth were tiled in natural stone, while the rest of the flooring was made up of wide planked wood. The walls were also panelled in wood. Between the living area and the office stood a honey-colored wood cabinet, filled with books, photos, and other interesting artifacts. It was an impressive piece of furniture, due to its height and span. Aside from the wall cabinet, there was very little furniture in the open space. A dark brown sofa, antique coffee table, and one overstuffed cream chair sat in the living area. A wooden dining table and four dilapidated chairs were placed next to the kitchen. The kitchen itself was very modern, with white country-style cabinets and a stark white marble counter top. A few kitchen conveniences were visible, a coffee maker and an electric kettle. There was a tiny half-fridge on one side of the kitchen sink and an electric oven with four gas burners on the other. The kitchen appliances were pristine; not a scratch or mark on them, as though they had never been used.

As if reading her mind, Michael spoke up.

'Aidan had just recently completed the kitchen before he left for Nepal. I don't think he ever used it.'

'This is beautiful, Michael. The workmanship is flawless. Aidan is equally adept at working with his hands as he is at swimming and running. I have to be honest, this was not what I was expecting to see.'

Michael laughed 'I'm not surprised, since you really don't know him yet. He is, most assuredly, a talented craftsman, and a perfectionist in his work. He demands a lot of himself. In almost everything else, though, he tends to be more carefree. This works well for him when he's on a mission. You can't go into a foreign country and expect the same standards. He doesn't, generally speaking, expect the same from others as he does from himself.'

Maddie wondered about the man she met in Mont-Tremblant, and the contrasts and similarities with the man who built and lived in this charming little cottage. Aidan's home was the natural embodiment of the man himself: uncomplicated, warm, unpretentious. It was also a testament to a part of his character that Maddie didn't know, a different side to the impetuous and carefree man who threw his belongings in a suitcase and called it packing. Here was man with good taste, extreme patience, and almost an obsessive determination to make his workmanship perfect in every way. She could hear Aidan's voice now, describing in detail, and with great pride, what he had done to transform an abandoned animal shelter into a stunning country home.

'The fire is now going pretty well. I've brought in enough wood to last a day or two. I've also turned on the gas heat in the bedroom and bathroom. You should be comfortable soon enough. There is coffee, tea, milk, cream, bread, cheese, wine, and jam in the fridge, if you are hungry. If you want anything else to eat, there is a store not far from here. You drove by it this morning on your way in?'

'Yes, I think I saw it.'

'There is a farmer's market on Fridays, down near O'Donovan's

Hotel. Colleen tells me t'is quite good, with a nice selection of vegetables and baked goods.'

'That sounds like fun. I like food markets.'

'I've turned on the cable and internet service. The instructions are on the coffee table. I can't promise t'is as fast as the service you are used to in Canada, but it works well enough, if you're patient.'

'Thank you, Michael. I am sure it will be fine for my needs. It is very kind of you to go to this trouble for me.'

'Aidan would want you to be as comfortable as possible,' Michael said as he walked towards the front door. 'I must be going now. Should you need anythin', my home is right over there…the grand old house up the valley and to the right? Colleen and I will be back around dinner. Please make your way over around 7 for a drink and some fine home cookin'.'

'That would be nice. I am looking forward to it,' Maddie replied, walking out with Michael to retrieve her suitcases in the car.

After Michael left, Maddie made herself a strong cup of coffee from the new coffee maker and continued to explore Aidan's home. She looked at his array of eclectic books, neatly stacked in the bookcase. There were a few photos of Aidan as a child, holding hands with a very large man who looked strikingly similar, and another photo with the same man when Aidan looked to be about sixteen years old. He was almost a tall as the man next to him, and they were both smiling. It was clear to Maddie that the man in the photo was Aidan's father, as the similarity between the two men was undeniable. Aidan was an exact copy of his father in almost every detail, from their hair color to their playful smile.

Maddie went into the office, which was almost bare, with the exception of a rustic looking computer table, an older model laptop computer, a well-worn black office chair coming apart at the seams, and two musical instruments, a banjo and a guitar. Maddie wondered whether Aidan had musical talent. He never mentioned his musical abilities while in Mont-Tremblant, but she knew that he loved music. It was always playing in the background when they were together.

While the furniture in the house was sparse and noticeably worn, the house construction and the finishing work were flawless. The house sparkled with fresh paint and modern conveniences. Aidan had completed all the tasks to make his house a home, with the exception of comfortable furniture, and those personal touches that come with time and someone to share it with. It appeared to Maddie that Aidan may have deliberately put on hold the last phase of this project until he found someone to share it with.

Maddie strolled into Aidan's bedroom. It was a small room, overwhelmed by a king-sized bed centered against the wood panelled wall, with a rustic night table and modern lamp on one side and a chest of drawers on the other. The bed was neatly made up with oversized fluffy pillows, a thick white duvet, and a colorful throw. The bed looked so cozy and inviting that Maddie was tempted to crawl into it and go to sleep, such was her weariness. Maddie opened a small wardrobe to look at Aidan's clothes. There was one dark suit hanging in dry cleaning plastic, a couple of pairs of pants and some shirts, several athletic jackets in various colors, and many pairs of running shoes, all neatly lined up on the floor of the wardrobe, ready for action. In the back of the wardrobe, tucked away from view, was a laundry basket. Without thinking, Maddie pulled it out and opened the lid to peer inside, almost missing the white t-shirt crumpled in a ball, resting at the bottom. Maddie scooped it up and went back to the living area.

Maddie wrapped a blanket around her shoulders and sat on the sofa next to the fireplace, clutching Aidan's t-shirt. The t-shirt was cool and slightly damp, as though it had recently been worn for a run. Maddie closed her eyes and breathed deeply. Aidan came to life for a few seconds, as his powerful, athletic smell radiated from the cotton cloth pressed against her face. Maddie silently wept with joy at Aidan's unassuming gift of himself. For a few brief moments, he was very much alive in this room, his frame nestled against her body, the soft touch of his large hands stroking Maddie's dark red hair. Sitting so close to the fireplace, the heat radiating a warm and cozy feeling, Maddie fell into a deep sleep, curled up on the sofa with her head and face buried in Aidan's t-shirt.

For the first time since Mont-Tremblant, Maddie dreamt not of swimming in a dark lake, alone and frightened, but of the sensuous Irishman. In the dream, they were naked and nestled on a sofa, Aidan's loving arms enveloping her like a duvet blanket, the moonlight pouring through the picture window. The scene was vaguely familiar.

It was snowing outside, and Maddie could see sparkling lights in the distant hills.

The romantic image of the lovers lasted but a few seconds, as another image drifted into the dreamy frame. Aidan was walking toward her with a pronounced limp and carrying a cane. His long wavy hair was gone, and there was a deep red scar just across his forehead. He was very thin. His face was gaunt and bloodless, giving him an angry and menacing appearance.

Maddie woke up in a panic and looked around the unfamiliar room. Even though the fire had almost gone out and the room was cold again, her face and back were damp with sweat. Her heart was racing. She glanced at her watch; she had been sleeping for over three hours. Maddie threw the blanket off her shoulders and ran into the bathroom, suddenly feeling sick and nauseous. She splashed icy cold water on her face several times and then sat on the toilet set trying to control her anxiety.

02:12:30

Maddie grabbed the old-fashioned door knocker and banged it twice. Within seconds, a pretty young girl with flaming red hair opened the front door. She was a mini version of her dad, Michael Bennett.

'Hello, my name is Maddie…your parents are expecting me for dinner.'

'Please come in,' the young girl replied, skipping her way to the kitchen to announce Maddie's arrival. The large stone hip-roofed house was quite old, almost as old as Aidan's cottage, but modern. The centre hall plan house appeared quite large, with a sweeping staircase to the second floor and two large rooms on either side of it. The massive dining room table on the left was set for five people.

'Hello again, Maddie,' Colleen said, as she walked into the foyer and greeted her guest, holding a tea-towel in one hand and extending the other to shake Maddie's hand. 'We were not formerly introduced. My name is Colleen. Come with me to the kitchen and I'll fix you a drink.'

They both walked into a modern and very large country kitchen, the aroma of something wonderful seeping through the oven.

'It won't be long now before we eat…Michael is out at present, but he should be back shortly. What can I get yeh' to drink? Scotch? Vodka? Beer? Red or white wine?' Colleen asked, in her hypnotizing Irish accent.

'White wine would be nice to start,' Maddie replied

Colleen Bennett was an attractive and wholesome woman, with long dark brown hair, hazel eyes framed by dark, rectangular glasses, and the most beautiful complexion Maddie had ever seen. Creamy white and nearly flawless, Colleen had the taut skin of a woman half her age. The only visible facial wrinkles were a few laugh lines around her deep-set eyes, and two sweet dimples in her full cheeks.

'How are you gettin' on, then, in Aidan's cottage? Tis lovely, isn't it? He's done a brilliant job making it a home,' Colleen said.

'He has indeed, Colleen.'

'You know, Michael gave him that cottage, but told him he would pay for all the renovations. Aidan wouldn't accept until Michael agreed to let him pay for the materials and do all the work himself. 'T'was many years to complete, but worth it,' Colleen said.

Maddie was charmed by the brunette. She had a soothing voice and a calm personality, the type of person that made you feel instantly welcomed. In her short time in Clonakilty, Maddie had met but a handful of people, but they were all helpful and very friendly. Though Maddie was too mired in worry to notice her surroundings, Colleen was the embodiment of Clonakilty's quintessential Irish characteristics: charming, good natured, and straightforward, and the very reasons why Aidan had chosen to call this his home in West Cork.

The two women continued to talk about the cottage renovations, Clonakilty, and the surrounding communities. Colleen had grown up in West Cork, and she talked about the area with authority. She was not only easy to be around, she was entertaining and a good story teller, sprinkling their conversation with Irish expressions new to the Canadian.

Michael finally arrived for dinner, just as Colleen was taking the roasted leg of lamb out of the oven. They sat in the dining room to eat the sumptuous dinner, Colleen, Michael, and their two daughters, Caoimhe and Roisin. After dinner, the young girls cleaned up the table and then excused themselves, leaving the adults alone to talk.

'That was a fine meal, Colleen. Absolutely delicious. I've never had lamb that tasted as wonderful,' Maddie said, feeling very full from two helpings of lamb, potatoes, and locally grown vegetables.

'Thank you. I enjoy cookin'.'

'….that's the best cook's secret ingredient. Love what you are doing!'

'Indeed. Would you like a glass of brandy?' Colleen asked, taking out a bottle of brandy and three glasses from the antique sideboard.

'Sure. Since I'm not driving, I can afford to indulge myself!' Maddie replied, feeling more relaxed and comfortable than she had earlier in the afternoon. The Bennetts had welcomed the Canadian stranger to their home without hesitation. They knew nothing about her, except that she was Aidan's unwavering girl and, for them, that was sufficient reason to look after the woman until Aidan returned. As long as she was in Clonakilty, they would look out for her.

As Colleen poured the dark amber brandy into the glasses, the chatter stopped and the room became silent. They had managed to avoid talking about Aidan's situation all evening.

Finally, Maddie broke the silence.

'I know you are both curious to know about my plans,' Maddie started to say. Colleen and Michael looked at each other and nodded in agreement.

'I've given this a lot of thought since Michael and I met yesterday. I am extremely thankful that you filled me in on the complex details of the O'Callaghan family,' Maddie said, looking at Michael. 'The information you provided me has been helpful, but also distressing. I knew something was wrong when Aidan didn't contact me after he left Canada. I thought of all the possible scenarios that could have prevented him from reaching out, but not the one you told me about. It's so very disturbing, and I am now, more than ever, deeply concerned about his welfare. For that reason, I've decided to go to Belfast to find him. I want to bring him back here to Clonakilty, where he will be surrounded by everything he loves and cares about: his home and his friends. After just a few hours spent in his cottage, I can see how dear this place is to him. He must come back, and the sooner the better. If there was anyone else that could do this, I would wait for him. But there isn't. The only person that can bring Aidan home is me...'

'But it's dangerous, Maddie,' Colleen interrupted.

'Yes, it could be very dangerous, but I've considered the risk to me, personally, quite low for the moment.'

'Why is that, Maddie?' Michael asked.

'Because no one from the O'Callaghan family, or their enemies, know I exist. You didn't know I existed until I showed up here. As long as I keep my distance from the family until the right time, I will be safe,' Maddie replied confidently. She failed to add that she could not predict how the O'Callaghan brothers would react at meeting Aidan's absentee girlfriend for the first time.

'Do you want me to contact Annie, Aidan's twin, to let her know you are coming? They were quite close growing up in Belfast.'

'No. I don't think it's a good idea, Michael. I have to work out a plan before I present myself to any members of the O'Callaghan family.'

'How do you think Aiden will react when he finally sees you?' Colleen asked.

'Aidan requested that you stay away, but he never specifically mentioned me, nor did he ever send me a clandestine message through you or his sister. It is possible that Aidan assumed that I would not be able to find him, as you suggested earlier, but I doubt that. He knows how resourceful I am.' Maddie took a sip of the old and silky-smooth brandy before continuing.

'In Aidan's indirect message, he could have requested that if a certain Canadian showed up in Clonakilty, you were to tell her to stay away. But that never happened, Michael. I may be over-analysing his motives, but I think that if Aidan had truly wanted me to stop looking for him, wanted me to forget about him, he would have made sure I got the message, one way or the other. He certainly has not made it easy for me to find him, and he may not even be aware of his conflicted mental state, but I am convinced that he is waiting for me to show up and take him away from his family. The sooner I can do this, the better. Based on what I read yesterday about the escalating gang warfare in Belfast, the longer I wait, the more danger he's in,' Maddie continued, thankful that she was sitting in the Bennett's' cozy house for a few hours, surrounded by warmth and love. She couldn't image what conditions Aidan might be facing at that exact moment.

'I've wasted months of valuable time. I wish I had started sooner. I am worried that Aidan has given up on me or on life.'

Both Colleen and Michael sat silently, thinking about what Maddie had just said, quietly sipping their brandy. They looked at one another with the same expression, acknowledging each other's unspoken thoughts.

'I'm not surprised at this decision, Maddie,' Michael finally said. 'I didn't think yeh' would change your mind after everything I told you. Perhaps you are right about Aidan. T'is possible that he wants you to find him. I can not speak for his motives or his silence. Are you sure that you don't want me to contact Annie, to let her know you are comin'? I don't know where he is recoverin', but I could ask her.'

'No. The fewer people who know what I am doing, the safer it will be for me and anyone else threatened by these recent events. Now that I've had a chance to spend time with you, I completely agree with

Aidan. You need to stay away from this mess, to protect your kids. I am confident I can manage on my own. I know I seem like an unlikely candidate for undercover work, given my age, my background, and my lack of experience, but I am resourceful, and Aidan knows this. I will find him, with a bit of luck and ingenuity.'

They both smiled. 'You have indeed demonstrated a good deal of both resourcefulness and ingenuity, since you found us with very little information!' Michael replied.

'When are you leavin'?' Colleen asked.

'I will leave first thing in the morning. I don't think it's wise to delay any longer. As you pointed out, Michael, there is some nasty business simmering in Belfast, and it will explode, it's only a matter of time.' Maddie took another sip of the addictive brandy, feeling the comforting effects of the alcohol. The next few days would be stressful. Tonight, she needed to relax and prepare for the journey ahead.

'Is there anythin' else we can do for you, Maddie?' Michael asked.

'Yes, as a matter of fact there is. Keep the cottage lights on and stock the bin with plenty of fire wood. I will be coming back with Aidan O'Callaghan, regardless of his condition, with or without the family's consent, even if I have to kidnap him in the process!'

They all laughed at Maddie's humour, even if it did sound overly optimistic.

02:23:59

The following morning, Maddie left Clonakilty and drove back to Dublin Airport to return the rental car, and switched to motor coach to continue her journey to Belfast. Though she was comfortable driving on the left and navigating the narrow Irish roads and highways by now, she chose to take the bus to Belfast. Travelling by bus would also give her time to think. The travel time would be anywhere from five to seven hours, depending on the traffic; plenty of time to hatch a plan to find and rescue Aidan.

Based on what Michael had told her about the O'Callaghans and their relationship with their younger brother, she reasoned that it would not be wise to simply show up at their house, if she could find it, and proclaim herself as Aidan's long-lost love. The O'Callaghans were a powerful and tight knit family that likely did not welcome strangers in their home, especially under the current climate of violent retribution. Maddie knew this, not only from what Michael had told her, but also from the limited news articles she was able to find online. One journalist described the 'notorious O'Callaghan clan' as ruthless and above the law. Thomas, in particular, was cited as a man who was 'staunchly loyal to his family and friends, and did not have boundaries when it came to protecting them'. If Maddie were to get close enough to Aidan, she would need to recruit an ally within the family, a sympathetic soul who would understand why she left her comfortable life in Canada in search of a man she only knew for five days. The ally could be Annie, Aidan's sister, or his mother Sheila.

At the Dublin Airport, Maddie boarded the nearly empty coach to Belfast. It was a short ninety-minute drive along a wide and modern highway that bridged the two largest cities on the green island. The landscape and terrain in this part of the island was almost identical to West Cork, with the exception of sheep, instead of cows, grazing the broad and hilly pastures. Soon, the coach was driving into the busy industrial city, making several turns along one-way streets and confusing roundabouts. Maddie was glad she had chosen not to drive in Belfast.

The Belfast Bus Station was a twenty-five-minute walk to the guest house on Eglantine Road, where Maddie had made a reservation the night before. Though close enough to walk, Maddie opted to take a taxi the roughly two miles to the early 19th century walk-up. Belfast had a well-deserved reputation for violence in certain areas. Since Maddie did not know anything about the city, she felt safer getting a ride than walking. As the silent taxi driver made his way down Sandy Row boulevard toward the guest house, zig-zagging along the busy street, Maddie peered out from the back seat of the cab, her eyes searching for a familiar face. No matter which way her luck ran in Belfast, she thought, Aidan would not simply pop out of a car or doorway. Nonetheless, the ever-hopeful Maddie kept her eyes on the sidewalks and cars during the eight-minute drive. There were few pedestrians out on this sunless Friday afternoon. The dreary weather did not match Maddie's optimism, though. She was one step closer to finding Aidan, hidden somewhere in this grey and gritty city.

The guest house's location was a pleasant surprise. Located in the heart of Queens' Quarter, the home of Northern Irelands' largest University, Queens University Belfast, the Victorian three storey-walk up was nestled on a tree lined street, with other historic apartments, a short twenty-minute walk from Belfast City Centre. The area catered to the thousands of students who lived close to the campus, as well as the tourists who flocked to the twenty-eight-acre Botanic Gardens, a major Belfast tourist attraction. There were plenty of restaurants, cafes, and pubs in the area, as well as shops and art galleries. It all looked pleasant enough. Maddie had no intention of visiting the numerous sites the city had to offer. She was in Northern Ireland for the sole purpose of finding Aidan. Once she found him, and if there was time, she would make a point of acting more like a tourist. For now, she planned to avoid any distractions and focus exclusively on her search.

After registering with Mrs. Kelley, the owner of the guest house, and setting up the laptop in a spacious and comfortable double room, Maddie ventured outside before darkness blanketed the city. She was conscious of the fact that some Loyalists and Republicans lived in different neighborhoods separated by 'peace walls'. For her own safety, she stayed close to the guest house until she was more comfortable with her surroundings and felt confident enough to explore other areas.

While strolling through the neighborhood, Maddie spotted a pizza parlour not far from the guest house. She was very hungry, and thirsty for a glass of red wine. As she walked toward the restaurant, she passed a newspaper box and spotted the latest headline from one of the local newspapers. In bold letters, the headline read: 'Former IRA Leader Dead at 70'. Maddie bought a copy of the paper, as well as two other competing papers, and walked into the half-empty restaurant. She ordered a large glass of Valpolchelli and a small Mediterranean pizza, and proceeded to pour through the newspapers as she waited for her meal.

The newspapers reported that a former IRA Commander had died, apparently from a massive heart attack and not murdered as some initial reports had speculated. He was, by all accounts, very popular, as hundreds turned out for his funeral at St-Patrick's Catholic Church. His life story was well documented, including his numerous arrests and imprisonment during the Troubles, his about-turn from paramilitary leader to peace activist. He appeared to be well-liked and respected, the voice of reason and a strong promoter of the political process. He was instrumental in brokering the 1998 Peace Agreement, which still held in spite of constant pressures from both sides of the historic spectrum. His sudden death both shocked and saddened the tight-knit community. Even his enemies honored his passing by paying tribute to his long-standing commitment for a unified Northern Ireland, with a minute of silence on the day he was buried.

Maddie read the newspapers' coverage twice. There was no mention of the O'Callaghans in any of the articles, with the exception of a short reference to Thomas and Patrick as having attended the funeral, along with hundreds of other well-known and high ranking 'former members' of the IRA.

After eating her thin-crust pizza, Maddie walked back to the guest house with the newspapers. She switched on her laptop as soon as she walked into the spacious guestroom, and immediately went to the local Belfast television station websites and combed through the extensive video coverage of the funeral, looking for more information and perhaps an important clue that would help her track down the O'Callaghans. Maddie dissected several YouTube videos, all covering the same subject, following different time lines, from the news that

Shamus Murphy had died, to the actual funeral procession to the cemetery. In one news segment, a female journalist was standing across the street from the church in the pouring rain, as the guests streamed out of the front doors toward black cars and limousines lined up along Donegal Road. The camera zoomed in on two men talking and walking, one with a full head of silver hair moving his arms wildly, while the other man had short hair and a cropped beard. Behind a sea of umbrellas, a tall man emerged from the shadows. He caught the attention of Maddie's keen eye. The man was walking with a cane, and, for a brief moment, raised his downcast head to face the street. The image lasted but a few seconds. Maddie replayed the video several times. She could not slow it down, nor could she zoom in, but she is sure that the man with the cane was Aidan, and that the two men ahead of him were his brothers. While the video was all too brief and the quality exceptionally grainy, the physical resemblance of the men to each other was obvious.

Confident that she found the family, Maddie looked up the address of St-Patrick's Church, and discovered the reason why this church was used for Shamus Murphy's funeral. During the Troubles, one hundred of its parishioners had died in clashes and attacks. The church's physical presence 'served as a beacon of light' for the people of Belfast, as many of the worst atrocities were committed in the parish bounds. Shamus Murphy was a long-time parishioner, and the choice of this church for a large funeral was fitting for a man who himself had served as a symbol of hope during Belfast's' darkest days. The church had just celebrated its 200th anniversary.

The church's regular religious service schedule was posted online. There was a vigil on Saturday at 7pm, and three Masses on Sunday. Perhaps, Maddie thought, the O'Callaghans were regular church goers. If she went to the Masses on Sunday, she might see them. She herself had not been in a Catholic church for years, and doubted that Aidan was a practicing Catholic, but perhaps the rest of the family were regular churchgoers. It was a stretch, she knew, but it deserved pursuing. Besides, she had nothing else to do with her time while she searched for other ways to find the whereabouts of Aidan O'Callaghan. Based on the video evidence, she was positive he was in Belfast, but where he was hiding, under the protection of his brothers, she did not know. She could start asking around, but that might raise suspicion and draw unnecessary and unwanted attention to herself. No, Maddie decided, she would find the O'Callaghans, on her own, without any outside help.

02:30:32

On Sunday morning, Maddie tucked her long, red hair in a neat bun, put on a black knit dress, and headed to St-Patrick's Catholic Church. After almost two days of waiting, she was finally doing something constructive. She had taken Michael's advice and spent Friday night and Saturday reading about modern Irish history, starting with the events that lead to the Easter Rising in 1916, all the way forward to the Peace Accord in 1998. Many hours later, she had gained some insight into the complex history of the Emerald Island, specifically around the time Aidan was born and the era of the 'Troubles'.

Maddie opted to walk the three miles to the church. She felt reasonably safe to venture on foot on a Sunday morning. She suspected that if the O'Callaghan's did attend Mass on Sunday, they would not likely be at the 8 am Mass. In her recollection, the only people who attended early Mass on Sunday mornings were seniors who couldn't tolerate the sound of crying babies, and those parishioners who just wanted to get the short service over and done with so they could enjoy the rest of the day without worrying about their religious obligations.

Maddie arrived and stood across the street next to a bus stop to watch barely a handful of parishioners, none of them familiar, stroll into the church for the 8 am service. By 8:05, Maddie was chilled and in need of coffee. There was an open coffee shop about a ten-minute walk down the road. The restaurant was empty on this damp October morning. Maddie sat near a window and killed time by reading and replying to her email messages from her son Jean-Luc. At 9:35, she headed back to the church to wait for the arrival of the 10:00 am parishioners. She was hoping the O'Callaghans would show up for this Mass, but by 10:10, nobody had arrived that she recognized from the news report. The caretaker closed the front doors as the Mass got under way. Instead of going back to the coffee shop, Maddie walked around the area and explored the side streets. The few people who were out on this brisk Sunday morning carefully scrutinized the tall redhead walking slowly down the side streets, reading signs and stopping to take notes. After decades of sectarian violence, the citizens of Belfast had learned to be wary of strangers walking slowly and acting unusually. They were vigilant about their city, never quite trusting an unfamiliar face. Maddie was oblivious to anyone's concerns and was mainly focused on how cold she felt. She chastised herself for not being dressed in warmer clothes. The dress and tights were not nearly warm enough to keep the dampness out as a deep chill ran through her body. She wrapped her wide scarf around her head and shoulders for warmth.

At 10:40, chilled to the bone and tired from waiting, Maddie made her way back to the church and stood across the street at the same empty bus stop. Within two minutes, a black car and an SUV pull up in front of the church entrance. Two men jumped out of the cars and opened the doors. From the SUV emerged a very large man, silver haired and clean-shaven, the same man from the news video. He headed toward the front doors of the church and up the two steps. An elderly woman was helped out of the sedan by a younger woman with dark hair. She turned toward the vehicle door and reached out to help someone inside. Maddie saw the cane first, and then a man slowly standing up, his height dwarfing the brunette by at least a half foot. The tall man, flanked by the two women, one of whom looked very much like him, made their way slowly into the church.

Maddie watched intently as the scene unfolded, hardly breathing. The man did resemble Aidan, but he seemed terribly frail and thin. She walked across the street and followed the rest of the parishioners into the church, her eyes fixated only on the group of men and women in front of her. Maddie needed to get a better look at the family. She walked piously to the front of the church, using the aisle on the far right, head down as if in prayer, and sat at the end of the second row in the octagon. This seat provided her with a clear view of the family in the front row and to the left of her. In spite of his altered appearance and frail condition, Maddie had no doubt that one of the men sitting not twenty feet away was Aidan.

Her pulse quickened at the sight of the beleaguered man and at her sheer luck. It had taken her only a few days to find him. Maddie's thoughts were interrupted by the rustling noise of the church choir and the organist tinkering with the organ keys.

More people began filling up the church for the 11 am Mass, and the choir began singing. There were enough distractions in the church that Maddie allowed herself a few moments to carefully study Aidan. His eyes were looking down at his feet, and his hands laid across his lap. He sat in the pew without moving, like a perfect schoolboy doing exactly as he was told for Sunday Mass. His physical appearance was alarming. The dark suit he was wearing was designed to fit a man much heavier. His wavy hair was cut very short, and what was left was peppered with an abundance of grey streaks. Aidan's disarming smile was replaced by a perpetual frown. He looked utterly miserable and sad.

Eventually, Aidan lifted his head slightly and turned in Maddie's direction. He looked at her absently-mindedly, as if she were just another parishioner, and then he looked away, his eyes having given her no sign of familiarity. A moment later, Aidan turned toward Maddie again; this time his light green eyes studied her features more intently. Dark red hair tied in a thick ponytail. Dark reading glasses framing the pretty freckled face of a middle-aged woman. The foggy haze lifted from his gaze, and a flicker of recognition lit up his serious face. Aidan's eyes widened and his expression slowly turned from bewilderment to surprise, and then concern. He looked to his right casually, to be sure no one was watching, and then he nodded to her, almost imperceptibly, 'No', pleading with troubled eyes not to acknowledge him or do anything to draw attention. Maddie nodded back with a slight movement of her head, and sat stoically in her seat, casually skimming through the missile and trying not to look obvious. They had finally connected with a furtive glance and a tilt of the head. Her stomach was doing backward somersaults.

Now what, Maddie thought. She gazed at her missile again and immediately came up with an idea. She turned toward the back of the church to see people lining up for their weekly confession. As Aidan watched, Maddie opened her knapsack, took out a pen and wrote down the guest house address on the third page of the missile. She then stood up and then walked to the back of the church, toward one of several recessed confessionals, and waited in line with others to confess their weaknesses and self-indulgences to the attending priest. Maddie had not been in a Catholic church for years, and the last time she went to confession, she was twelve years old. She was surprised that this practice still existed in the Catholic faith, and it was no longer referred to as confession, but 'reconciliation'. She glanced to her right and saw Aidan walking slowly towards her, using his cane. He stopped directly behind her. He was standing so close, she could feel his breath floating down the back of her neck. She closed her eyes for a second to feel his phantom arms around her.

Aidan looked down at Maddie's dark red hair and smelled a soft wisp of the perfume she always wore. He almost reached out to touch her waist for reassurance, when he glanced over to the family pew and saw his brother Thomas starring at him. Instead of reaching out, he forced his arms to remain rigid by his side, ram rod straight, his face showing no emotion. His heart and his head were aching simultaneously.

The confessional door opened and it was Maddie's turn to enter the cubicle. She knelt on the padded bench and spoke quietly to the priest on the other side of the screen, his face partially hidden from her view by black lattice. Maddie told the priest that she had not been to Confession in twenty years. She said nothing more. The priest made a gesture with his hands and arms, and told her to pay attention to the Mass. He gave her some instructions on prayer. The confession was over, and Maddie left, leaving the missile on the knee pad.

The two strangers crossed paths, touching each other with a tiny brush of arms. Aidan took his turn at the confessional, picked up her missile, and tucked it under his arm. He spoke to the priest briefly, waited for a response, and abruptly left the cubicle and headed toward the bathroom in the basement of the church. He navigated the wide cement stairs slowly, using the bannister for balance. He was in a hurry, but his body moved slowly. This was an ongoing struggle between the mind of a man who knows exactly what he needs to do, and a damaged body that would not cooperate. Once in the cubicle of the men's bathroom, Aidan opened the missile and tore out the page with the hand-written note. He didn't read the note. Instead, he took his cane and unscrewed the handle, rolled up the piece of the missile paper and tucked it into opening, and replaced the handle. He threw the torn missile on the floor and returned to the family pew.

No sooner had Aidan sat down, five minutes later, when the silver haired man leaned over, presumably to ask if he was okay. Aidan simply nodded his head. Maddie watched the interaction between the two men. She was struck by how much they looked alike, and was quite sure that this was Thomas, the eldest of the three brothers.

The next hour in the church tested Maddie's patience. The priest's homily was not a short, ten-minute dissertation about love and kindness, but a full-fledged rant about everyone's lack of Christian values. Maddie was desperate to leave the church and walk back to the guest house, but she knew it would be inappropriate to walk out in the middle of the service and might arouse suspicion from the family sitting to her left. She had no choice but to sit and wait, ignoring Aidan's occasional gaze and attempting to look like she was interested in the words being spoken. Staring at Aidan would not be productive under the circumstances and could erode her determination to play along with this ruse.

One hour and fifteen minutes later, Maddie quickly made her way to the front of the church to watch the O'Callaghan family drive away.

02:33:21

Maddie walked briskly back to the guest house, replaying the last ninety minutes in her head, trying to keep her mind off the bitter, cold north wind blowing in her face. She applauded herself for not overreacting on seeing Aidan for the first time in four months, and for calmly slipping him a secret note. Maddie was sure that Aidan had either taken the note or read it and destroyed it. She had watched him walk towards the back of the church with the missile tucked under his arm. Minutes later, he returned without the missile. She had done all she could under the circumstances, short of sitting beside him. The next step would be his to make, yet she was confident that he would show up, sooner or later, at the guest house.

Maddie spent the rest of the day sitting in the library at the guest house, drinking green tea and waiting patiently for a visitor. Mrs. Kelley offered her some dinner, which Maddie happily ate. Mrs. Kelly chatted about Belfast and made several suggestions for visiting interesting places in and around the area. Maddie pretended to be listening and nodding absentmindedly to Mrs. Kelley's colorful proposed itinerary for visiting Belfast.

After dinner, Maddie excused herself for the evening. She went back to her room, turned off all the lights and sat in the dark room, looking out the window, holding the white parchment envelope, watching cars and people going up and down the street. By 9 pm, fatigue began to creep in, and Maddie almost fell asleep in the big damask chair by the window, when the glare of head lights illuminated the dark room. A black Mercedes sedan, exactly the same make and model as the car Aidan had exited from St-Patrick's, stopped in front of the guest house. Maddie jumped up from the chair and ran into the bathroom to comb her hair, fix her dress, and put on some lipstick.

As she was exiting the bathroom, Mrs. Kelley knocked on the door to tell her she had a visitor waiting in the library.

Maddie headed down the single flight of stairs, taking a deep breath with every step to calm her beating heart. She did not know what to expect from Aidan, but based on their furtive glances at the church and their clandestine exchange, she was reasonably sure their first meeting would not be the romantic reunion that Maddie had fantasized about since making the decision to leave Canada. Michael Bennett's insight into the O'Callaghan family dynamics had prepared her, to some extent, that the Aidan she knew in Mont-Tremblant was not necessarily going to be the same man in Belfast. Seeing Aidan at the church had confirmed to her that he was indeed in some kind of trouble, and reluctant, or maybe terrified, to involve her in the sordid mess.

Aidan was sitting by the fireplace when Maddie walked into the library, a pained expression on his tired face, cradling a dram of whisky which Mrs. Kelley had thoughtfully given him. He was wearing an oversized black coat that hung on his shrunken frame. He looked nothing like the man she had said goodbye to months before.

'Please sit down, Maddie,' Aidan said abruptly, dispensing with small talk, his voice carrying no hint of warmth. He neither stood up or made any move to touch or embrace her.

Maddie moved to the loveseat directly across from him and sat down. Aidan was not making this easy for her. He starred at her coolly, and she felt awkward and self-conscious in her loose black dress, the delicate bracelet of hair hanging on her wrist. The site of his handiwork of love and promise seemed to throw Aidan off, and he was momentarily lost for words. He took a swig of whisky. Finally, after a prolonged silence, Aidan spoke in his typical direct style, with a touch of anger, his voice carrying a much stronger Irish accent than she had remembered.

'I don't have much time to talk so I'll get right to the point. Our relationship is over. If I had wanted yeh here, I would have reached out to yeh months ago. There's nothing for yeh here, Maddie. I want yeh to leave Belfast as soon as possible.' He did not look at Maddie, but stared at the fragile piece of cording and hair on her wrist.

Maddie was stunned. While she expected Aidan to be wary of her sudden, unannounced visit, and perhaps scold her for being so impetuous, she did not think he would dismiss her so callously. There was not a hint of love or affection in his cold voice. He told her, in plain English, that it was over, and that he had deliberately kept his whereabouts a secret from her. Horrified, she had gotten it all wrong.

She was expecting an apology for his silence, or gratitude that she had journeyed so far to find him, but she was not expecting to have a door slammed in her face so heartlessly. Maddie's body sagged into the loveseat and she was unable to string three words together.

Aidan, seeing that the Canadian was distraught, continued in a softer voice, 'I'm sorry for the grief I've caused yeh.'

Maddie looked sadly at the man sitting in front of her. He sat rigid, his face stern and a little frightening. His composure was the complete antithesis of the devil-may-care man she had known in Canada. She did not know this man.

Maddie replied, her throat dry and tight, 'I see. …direct as ever.'

Aidan shrugged his shoulders. He took another large swig of his drink.

Unsure about what to say, but not wanting to end their conversation so quickly, Maddie quickly shifted gears and asked him a question.

'All right, then, Aidan, I'll consider your request to leave, but first you must answer a few of my questions. You owe me at least that.'

'I do not have a lot of time,' Aidan replied impatiently.

Maddie frantically thought about a question that would shed light into why he was being so insensitive.

'Why are you here in Belfast and not in Clonakilty?' Maddie asked the first question that came to mind.

'I can only assume you spoke to Michael and he filled you in on my family history, so I won't get into that with yeh. The reason I am here is terribly complicated and not a pleasant story. Suffice to say that it's not safe for me to venture too far from my brothers' protection. The car accident was just the beginning of some very nasty stuff…for what's to come…there is a lot going on…I and certain family members of my family may be… they've tried before, they will likely try again. T'is not safe for yeh to be in Belfast. I do not want yeh to be implicated in this mess,' Aidan replied, twitching in his seat, his rambling and disjointed answer only adding to Maddie's concern. He was both confused and terrified.

Maddie leaned forward in her seat, put her hands on her knees and asked him another question, one she hoped would draw him out so she could be sure.

'Do you want to go back to Clonakilty?'

At the mention again of Clonakilty, Aidan's expression changed. 'Yes of course I do. I think about it often; t'is not possible, though,' he replied almost wistfully, his light green eyes betraying profound sadness. 'In any event, I didn't come here to talk about me. I came here this evening to tell yeh to leave. I have nothin' more to add.' Without any warning that the meeting was over, Aidan stood up abruptly, walked out of the room as quickly as his damaged would body would let him, and out the front door, his cane resting on the arm chair.

Maddie instantly grabbed the cane and chased after him.

'Aidan…Aidan, please stop running away from me!' Maddie cried out without thinking.

'I can hardly walk, let alone run,' he replied sarcastically, steps away from the black sedan on the road, his back facing her.

Maddie grabbed his arm and swung him around as easily as grabbing a misbehaving child. She was struck again by his frailty in the oversized coat. 'You forgot your cane…' she said, handing him the wood cane with the intricate silver handle.

'Oh, I guess I need that for support,' Aidan said, reaching for the cane.

'I think you need more than a cane for support,' Maddie shot back instinctively.

'Indeed, I do,' Aidan replied. He stood awkwardly facing Maddie, his eyes locked on hers, as if trying to decide whether to drive away or go back to the guest house with her. It was a telling moment for Maddie.

'Aidan, 'tis time to go now,' came the sound of a female voice from the open window of the vehicle.

'I am truly sorry, Maddie. I have to go now. Annie agreed to drive me here on condition that I was quick…. if I delay much longer, my brother Thomas will get suspicious and send his ghouls after me.'

Aidan got in the back seat of the sedan and the vehicle drove away. Maddie memorized the license plate number of the black Mercedes and wrote it down as soon as she got back into her room.

She starred at the license plate number for a long time. Like a video on replay loop, she reviewed those three precious minutes with Aidan over and over again. Regardless of what Aidan said he wanted her to do, she had her own ideas. She was not going to be dissuaded so easily, and she stubbornly refused to believe that he no longer cared for her. He had hesitated for a fraction of a second before getting in the car, long enough for Maddie to see a particle of hope in their relationship. She was certain that he was conflicted about involving her in the 'sordid mess', as he called it. The eyes are the windows to the soul, and Aidan's sorrowful look was evidence enough that he didn't mean everything he said.

Maddie had faced challenging situations before. The last eighteen months had been the most arduous of her life, and she was not about to turn back and quit at the first big climb on the road. She would surrender unconditionally and move on with her life, only if, and when, she was certain that there was no point in continuing to chase after a man who did not want her.

Maddie began formulating a plan for her next move, and as soon as she finished, she went to bed. For the first time in five days, sleep came easily and swiftly.

2:38:32

The next morning, Mrs. Kelley cooked a fine Irish breakfast that Maddie devoured. Her appetite had returned, and she ate everything that was put in front of her. The food, a good night's sleep, and a healthy dose of optimism fueled Maddie's self-confidence. While eating the huge breakfast, Maddie carefully replayed the events of the night before, and her next move.

While Aidan had hardly declared his undying love the night before, nor his wish to run away with her to Clonakilty, his slight hesitation before leaving the guest house gave Maddie a tenuous glimmer of hope, a tiny thread of optimism that he was conflicted about seeing her. He had only said those harsh words to protect her, she thought. He had made a good first impression on Maddie, with his callous admission that he didn't want her in Belfast and that the relationship was over, but she knew better. He had hesitated before getting into the car. For an instant, he seemed truly torn about seeing her, safety concerns or not. It was not an overt hint, but she had worked with far less. She was not ready to give up, and thus spent an hour to conceive a plan to further test Aidan's resolve.

Later that morning, Maddie walked to the local Police Service of Northern Ireland – the PSNI. She stood outside the building to watch people going in and out of the busy police station. She rehearsed her concocted story several times, unsure whether the scheme she had dreamed up would actually work. By nature, Maddie was a terrible liar, unable to hide the truth behind her honest face. But she needed to tell a convincing lie to a police officer, and this made her nervous. This was not a fictional television show and she was not a glamorous but surly detective, but this was the only way to get the information she needed.

Maddie dressed appropriately for the ruse she was about to undertake. She wore a tight-fitting light blue sweater, which not only showed off her attractive figure but also enhanced her freckled complexion, black leggings, and tall black boots. She made a point of styling her long, dark red hair to maximum effect. This outfit was chosen to turn heads and grab someone's attention.

Maddie walked into the PSNI and glanced around. She followed an overhead sign pointing to Client Services and Payment Counter. This was a large area with a long counter of constables seated at computer screens, dressed in proper police attire, answering questions and processing parking tickets. It was not busy at this hour, and most of the constables were actually talking among themselves and not working. Instead of getting a number, as instructed by the large white billboard, Maddie looked at the counter for a sympathetic constable who would easily be smitten by her charm, her pretty face and her un-Irish accent to provide her with the information she needed. She was in luck this Monday morning, as Constable Byrne, a thirty-five-year veteran of the PSNI and two months away from retirement, was sitting at the end of the enormous counter, reading his daily newspaper and ignoring both his co-workers and clients. Though he was not paying attention to the business at hand, he was not immune to an attractive face.

'Good morning,' Maddie said, smiling brightly at the portly police constable.

'Well, good morning to you,' Constable Byrne replied, putting down his newspaper and grinning broadly at the lovely woman standing in front of him. 'What can I do for you on this dreary October morning?'

'Well, I hope you can help me, as I am in a bit of a sticky situation,'

'Oh dear. Well, lets' see what I can do for you…you are not from here, are you?' he asked Maddie, noting the un-Irish accent.

'No, I am not from here. I'm a tourist from Canada, enjoying your beautiful city. I rented a car a few days ago and I was, unfortunately, involved in a fender bender.'

'A what?' the Constable asked.

'A fender bender. That's what Canadians call a minor accident when two cars collide. The damage is minimal, and the two parties involved usually work out the repair issue among themselves so as not to involve the police or the insurance companies.'

'I see. Go on wit ya.'

'Well, a woman hit my rental by accident and willingly gave me her contact information so we could settle the repairs. But sadly, I lost it, and now I need to reach her, because she was going to pay for the minor repairs. Constable Byrne,' Maddie continued, glancing at the Constable's name tag, 'I don't know if you are aware, but car rental companies will charge me a fortune for damaging their car.'

'I have heard about those companies being greedy, indeed I have. Nasty business.'

'I was hoping that…if I gave you the license plate number, you could give me her contact information so that I may call on her? I know it is unusual request, but I am quite desperate to get this fixed before I return the car next week.'

'Of course, t'is totally reasonable under the circumstances. I understand completely, dear. Let me look it up for you,' he replied, using a fatherly tone.

Maddie handed the kind police constable a slip of paper with the license plate number written on it. Maddie waited nervously for the constable to log into his computer and look for the information. Her biggest concern at that moment was whether the license plate number would be flagged as stolen or somehow connected to criminal activity, and she half expected strobe lights and sirens to go off. If so, she would need to find an excuse to remove herself from the situation quickly. Constable Byrne typed in the number in the computer, and within thirty seconds, he casually printed out the name and address of one Anne O'Brien, 350 Stanley Park, Belfast.

'There you go. Stanley Park. T'is quite the exclusive area of Belfast. Lots of money tied up in those huge homes…is this the person you were looking for?'

'Yes, I believe her name was Anne.'

'There is no phone number listed. Just a street address. Based on that address, I'm sure you will not have problems, no problems at all. I wish you good luck! However, if you run into any issues with this 'fender-bender' business, please come back and see me personally…and I'll see what I can do…' the Constable said with a flirtatious smile, winking and smiling at the woman standing across from him.

'You have been so kind. I love the Irish…you are all so friendly… thank you.'

As soon as Maddie got back to the guest house, she wasted no time in looking up the address on her computer. It was too far to walk or run from Eglantine Road. Instead, she checked out the bus route to within a kilometer of Anne O'Brien's address, put on in her running gear, and headed out the door.

*****

Maddie got off the bus near a coffee shop, about a ten-minute run to the address Constable Byrne had given her. Dressed in tights, a running jacket, and cap, and wearing dark glasses, Maddie was hoping she would not look suspicious if she was dressed as a runner in the high-end residential area, out for an afternoon jog.

Maddie looked at Google maps again to be sure she was heading in the right direction and started running down Lisburn Road toward Stanley Park. In spite of the grey skies, the cool temperatures, and the threat of rain, there were many cyclists, walkers, and joggers on the sidewalk of the busy road. Maddie ran along the sidewalk, as natural and effortless as she would be running in Outremont.

Within twelve minutes, Maddie approached Stanley Park and stopped. A large wrought-iron gate sat on cement pillars, guarding the road and blocking cars into the exclusive area. This was a private street with no access by car, at least at this end. Thankfully, there was an open gate leading to sidewalk inside the gated community.

Maddie walked through the gate and continued to run at a leisurely pace, glancing at her watch frequently and running nonchalantly, as if this tree-lined street was the usual route for the daily jogger. There were no cars on the street. All the palatial homes on the sprawling properties sat well back. This small enclave of prestigious homes, flanked by enormous trees that ran the entire length of Stanley Park, was one of the most exclusive communities Maddie had ever seen.

According to her map, the street number to Anne's home was about halfway down the road. Maddie kept a watchful eye on the straight road ahead for a black SUV or a black sedan. Her jogging cap was pulled down over her forehead to hide her face, in case Aidan happened to be out by himself, walking or driving in the area. This was one occasion where she wanted to make sure he didn't see her.

Moments later, Maddie saw the house, or rather, the estate that corresponded to the street address. She had pictured a large, modern home in an upscale neighbourhood, but this was beyond her expectations. Anne O'Brien's house was an enormous red brick three story Renaissance-style house, with contrasting white quoins and elegant pillars, and a meandering driveway that lead to the back of the house. The estate could have been the advertising poster for any exclusive property in Europe. The O'Callaghans were no petty criminals, Maddie realized with dread. The depth of their wealth, and presumably criminal activity, was vastly more than what Michael had told her, or what she expected. This was the grand estate of a wealthy family.

As she approached the house to inspect it further, Maddie noticed several surveillance cameras attached to the ornate finials that were resting on a tall, wrought iron fence that surrounded the entire property. The gate to the entrance of house was closed, and two black vehicles were parked close to the front door: a black Mercedes sedan and a black Mercedes SUV.

Just like a scene from a detective show on television, Maddie bent down on the pretense of fixing her shoe laces to get a better look at the front of the house. There were trees along the property fence shedding their fall leaves, and behind the trees stood a large, featureless man, dressed entirely in black, standing motionless between the two vehicles. Maddie listened for the sound of guard dogs, but detected none.

At that moment, she lost her nerve to proceed with the plan. This was not what she had pictured as Annie's house, or were Aidan may be recovering. This was not a house but a fortress, surrounded by heavy security and a mean-looking man standing guard. An image of the traffic accident and poor Meghan flashed through her mind. This was dangerous territory, she reminded herself.

Maddie looked down at her clothing. Given the lofty area, she was no longer convinced her jogging outfit and her story would work at getting her through the front gate, let alone into the house. She was not prepared to knock on the door and ingratiate herself to Annie O'Brien, dressed so casually. She would have to come back another day, dressed appropriately for the story she had manufactured, and with more confidence if she wanted to get past the bodyguard and speak to Annie face to face. Once she got Annie's attention, Maddie counted on the twin's natural close relationship to obtain a private and confidential meeting with the woman.

She breathed easier. She could wait another day. This was Maddie's third, nervous attempt at a clandestine operation, and she was not any more comfortable with this than she was in the church. After making the decision to abandon the plan for the day, Maddie continued running down Stanley Park until she reached Malone Road, and turned left. At Myrtlefield Park, she turned left again and doubled back to Lisburn Road. Large trees stippled the narrow street, and while the homes lacked the prestige of the neighboring street, it was still a pretty residential area that was quiet and pleasant to run through. She felt much less conspicuous running in this area. At Lisburn Road, Maddie eventually found a bus stop and waited patiently to get back to the guest house.

Later that evening, Maddie sent an email to Sofia. It was the first email to her best friend in several days. She explained that she had made significant progress with her search for Aidan and that everything was going well. She did not provide any details about where she was, and she did not tell Sofia about her visit with Aidan, her trip to the police station, and her exploration of the exclusive enclave of Belfast called Stanley Park. This information would only spark more questions from Sofia about the O'Callaghans, something she wasn't ready to share with her best friend. While Maddie trusted Sofia implicitly, she thought it wise to withhold the finer details of her search until it was safe to do so.

Maddie also sent a text message to Michael. She told him exactly what had transpired at the church and her meeting with Aidan later that evening at the guest house. She described Aidan's condition as 'alarming', but she told Michael that he was walking and talking, and he had still had his dry sense of humor, in spite of his difficulties. She did not provide Michael, either, with specific details on her scheme to present herself to the O'Callaghan family. That information would have to wait until she had insinuated herself into the tight-knit clan. At the end of the text, she told Michael she still hoped that they would return to Clonakilty soon, and not to forget to keep the cottage well stocked with dry firewood. Maddie tried to sound upbeat and positive in both her messages. In reality, though, she was worried about returning to Stanley Park, and whether she could successfully get through the front gate without incident. Her plan hinged on this one, important next step. She would deal with the consequences of an uncooperative Annie once in the home.

Finally, she sent her boys a quick note, full of tourist clichés and minor details about her travels thus far. If they only knew the truth, she thought to herself, before falling asleep.

*****

After another hearty Irish breakfast prepared by Mrs. Kelley, Maddie set out for Stanley Park. In contrast to her running attire the day before, she opted to wear something more professional that would immediately register to whomever opened the door that she meant business. Maddie boarded the same bus as she had the previous day, and got off at the same stop. She walked the 1500 meters to the O'Callaghan house in the cool rain, holding a black umbrella.

Maddie was fifty feet from the front gate of the O'Callaghan estate when it opened and a black sedan pulled out onto the street, the windshield wipers moving at high speed. The car was driven by the same featureless man who had stood guard the day before. Though the visibility was poor and the windows were foggy, Maddie recognized Aidan in the back seat, sitting next to an older woman. They were, fortunately, not looking out the window, and did not see the tall redhead standing across the street under an umbrella. The car sped away, and Maddie had just enough time to slip onto the property through the opened gate before it closed, relieved that Aidan had driven away at the exact moment she arrived. This was going well, she thought. The fates that had conspired against her months ago were now working for her.

She took two deep breaths and rang the doorbell. Moments later, a short but very stocky man opened the door. He, too, was dressed in what appeared to be the O'Callaghan staff uniform of black pants and a black jersey that fit taut across his burly chest. He seemed to be missing a neck.

'Can I help you?' the man asked Maddie, in a strong, almost unrecognizable accent that was definitely not of Irish origin.

'I would like to speak to Anne O'Brien, please,' Maddie said in a firm voice.

'For what reason?' the imposing man asked.

'She accidently rear-ended my car, and we agreed to settle the damages between us instead of going to the police,' Maddie replied with confidence, emphasising 'police in her best manufactured Irish accent. She had rehearsed this response several times that morning. Whether the accent was convincing, or the mention of police provoked a positive response, the stern and square man gestured for her to come in and wait. Her blue overcoat dripping, Maddie stood in the black and white tiled foyer for several minutes, admiring the pretty striped wallpaper and the beautiful gilded mirror. She could see beyond the foyer double doors to a massive staircase that dominated the hallway, and beyond to several open rooms on the right and left, and the white marble floor, which was covered in a stunning wool runner. The house made an immediate impression of wealth and taste. Maddie knew about the family's humble beginnings, and unlike many of the nouveau rich, this house was not ostentatious and screaming new money. This was not a grand house, but a home filled with warm furnishings and tasteful, cheery décor.

The man returned five minutes later, followed by Annie O'Brien.

Before the man in black could say anything, Maddie approached Annie.

'Hello, Mrs. O'Brien; I hope you haven't forgotten about our appointment to talk about the car damages…from the accident the other night – you remember – on Eglantine Road, around 9 pm.? As I recall, you were waitin' for your brother?'

Annie looked at Maddie, expressionless.

For a split second, Maddie was terrified that this plan was not going to work, and that she would soon find herself on a deserted road in the middle of nowhere.

Annie, though, surprised her. In a supremely cool and detached manner, she replied, 'Of course I remember. Thank you for stopping by.' She then turned her attention to the bodyguard. 'Can you ask Maureen to make us some tea? We will be in the drawing room.'

The slight woman took Maddie's arm more firmly than necessary and directed her to the large room, off the foyer. As soon as they entered, Annie closed the French doors, folded her arms across her chest, and stood perfectly straight. She was the most intimidating woman Maddie had ever met, and she did not look pleased to see the Canadian stranger in her house.

2:45:45

The women stared at one another.

'You were very convincing with that fake accent. Most people new to this country make a total mess of the Irish accent,' Annie said breaking the silence, leaning against the double doors with her arms firmly crossed.

'Thank you. I practiced quite a bit before getting here.'

'You were at the Church on Sunday. You were sitting across from us,' Annie continued. She was as direct as her brother, and wasted no time at getting straight to the point, Maddie thought, clearly a family trait.

'Yes, I was. Good observation, though I am sorry I wasn't more discreet.'

'You were discreet enough, but I know my brother very well, and I saw the strained look on his face when he recognized you. He can't hide much from his twin sister.'

Maddie put her hand out, not sure if the intimidating woman standing before her would shake it or twist it.

'My name is Maddie St-Laurent.'

'I know who you are.' She did not take Maddie's hand.

The room turned silent again. The two women continued to size each other up. Annie was shorter than Maddie, with shoulder-length brown hair and a svelte figure, bordering on thin. From the few family photos Maddie had seen at the cottage in Clonakilty, Annie looked more like her mother Sheila, while Aidan resembled his father Tom. Aidan and Annie were fraternal twins and shared little in terms of resemblance; he was tall and broad, she was small and thin, yet they had two distinct and similar physical attributes: high cheek bones and piercing, light green eyes. Annie's deep wrinkles around her mouth and forehead made her look a few years older than her twin brother, yet she was a strikingly attractive woman. Her sharp, knowing eyes had seen much in forty-four years of living in Belfast. Dressed in classic grey leggings and a white tunic, she confidently stood before Maddie, demanding attention without uttering one word.

Annie finally relented and put out her hand. 'Everyone calls me Annie. I am Aidan's twin sister, and you've come a long way to see my brother,' she said as fact rather than a question.

Maddie nodded. It was now or never. She spoke very quickly, trying to get her words out in one breath. 'I have, Annie. I met your brother in Mont-Tremblant, and shortly after we met, he disappeared. I've been looking for him for months.' Maddie opened her knapsack and pulled out the photo from the triathlon race.

Annie looked at it and snickered. 'He seems much happier in this photo then he is today, and a lot more fit.'

The housekeeper knocked on the French doors and then walked into the bright yellow room, carrying a silver tray. She placed it on the country-style coffee table and left.

'Sit down, Maddie, have some tea and let's talk,' Annie suggested.

The two women sat on a comfortable, oversized cranberry velvet sofa. The room had an enormous bay window that overlooked the vast garden, ten-foot ceilings, and dark hardwood floor. It was a bright and cheerful room, a direct contrast to the gloomy, wet weather outside.

'I gather you met Michael Bennett?' Annie asked, pouring the hot tea in a dainty floral tea cup.

'I saw him in Clonakilty a few days ago.'

'He has been a good friend to Aidan.' Annie handed the filled tea cup to Maddie. 'I have been expecting you.'

'Did Michael tell you I was coming?' Maddie asked, alarmed.

'He did not, but Aidan told me your story, after he returned from seeing you at the guest house. I could see he was emotionally drained and I insisted that he tell me what was going on. Naturally, I worry about him; he's been through a lot. He said he was sad that things had not turned out as expected.' Annie's rich accented voice was similar to her twin brother, but sharper. Her sentences tended to swing up and down, whereas Aidan's were more melodic and soothing.

'...well, not yet, anyway,' Maddie added under her breath.

Annie heard the comment and half-smiled, showing slightly more warmth toward the nervous Canadian. 'I didn't think you would stay away. Aidan described you accurately – he said you were not the type of woman who would give up easily.' Annie took a sip of the hot tea, stirring the cup delicately while staring at the redhead sitting next to her.

'How did you find us, Maddie? Did Michael tell you where to find us?'

'No, Michael didn't tell me much.' Maddie sat back in the sofa and explained how she found Michael and then Annie's addresses.

'And you found us based on that meager information?'

'Meager, yes, but one clue led to another. The hard part was getting to Clonakilty. After that, the search became easier, and I did get lucky when I arrived in Belfast.'

'How so?'

'The funeral of one of your own…the former IRA Leader?'

'Shamus Murphy? Fine man. Indeed, we were at the funeral.'

Annie watched as the talkative and innocent redhead told her story. Annie easily understood why her brother was so concerned about Maddie's safety. She had naively walking into a very precarious situation, as only Annie knew, without any real concept of the family dynamics and what she was getting into. Only love could drive a person to leave one life behind in search of another, at considerable risk, Annie thought.

Annie took another sip of her tea. 'I take it you want to return to Clonakilty with Aidan?'

'That is my goal, yes. That's why I am here talking to you. Aidan won't talk to me. We've had only one conversation, and it was completely one sided. He asked me to leave Ireland. He told me there was nothing for me here.' Maddie didn't elaborate further. His stinging admission that he kept his whereabouts a mystery for four months continued to ring in her ears. She tried not to dwell on that part of their conversation.

'And so, you should. You have presented yourself at a particularly difficulty time for this family. You said Michael didn't tell you much, but surely, he shared enough to bring you here in search of my brother? 'Annie asked.

'He told me Aidan was in trouble, that the car accident was a deliberate attempt to kill him because of something that happened in the past, but it killed his girlfriend instead. He told me Aidan was still in Belfast for his own protection, and that it was not safe to contact him or see him. Michael did not add much in the way of Aidan's past life in Belfast.'

'I see. And that didn't dissuade you to stop your search for Aidan?'

Maddie shook her head vigorously. 'No, because Aidan would come looking for me if I disappeared. I may not know that much about his life or why he is here in this mess, but I've learned a lot about the man since I arrived in Ireland, and I am convinced that he wouldn't give up looking for me. I plan on doing the same.'

'I see.' Annie took a sip of her tea. 'Perhaps you need to hear the sordid details of our family, and the 'mess', as you call it, that my brother Thomas has created, to convince you that it is not your place to be here with Aidan. I hope you will change your mind and leave here without him once you know the facts.'

'I am willing to listen to what you have to say, but I doubt you will change my mind.'

Annie looked at the eager and somewhat defiant redhead sitting next to her. She was not going to go away easily, and her resolve to help Aidan would only get stronger when she learned the truth about him. We have more in common than she could possibly imagine, Annie thought.

Annie looked up at the white marble fireplace that anchored the sitting room. Above the ornate mantle was a black and white photo of a child, dressed in tattered clothes, playing on the road with a ball, while an army vehicle drove by. Behind the child was a row of derelict and bombed out townhomes, some nothing more than shells. The area was a war zone. The photograph was jarring, disturbing, and a bleak reminder of where the O'Callaghans had come from.

'You see that photo above the fireplace? Me and my brothers grew in a house like that, not far from where that photo was taken, a tiny two up-two down row house, on a side street off the Falls Road; a poor Catholic family with few amenities. But not as poor as some.'

'And there were four of you?' Maddie asked.

Annie nodded.

'Is that your father?' Maddie asked, pointing at the bookshelf next to the fireplace, and a grainy black and white photo of a handsome man holding a two-year-old child in his arms, standing next to a petite woman.

'T'is. As you can see from the photo, he was a huge man, 6'5, 240 pounds, strong as anything. While all three of my brothers resemble

Tom in some way, only one of them inherited his kind and gentle personality.'

'Aidan?' Maddie confirmed.

Annie nodded, the aggressive tone in her voice mellowing slightly, as she shared the details of the O'Callaghan family history.

'Tom was a good man, pleasant, and he was popular in the neighborhood, you know, always helping others. He never laid a finger on any of his children, no matter what kind of trouble we got into. And there was plenty of opportunities for trouble, given the times. My two older brother, Thomas and Patrick, were a handful, always getting into mischief. This only got worse six months after Aidan and I were born in '71.'.

'That's when the Troubles began?' Maddie asked.

'More or less, and it was fuelled by a catastrophic event that permanently changed the pleasant realities of the O'Callaghan family. My father's brother Adam, along with fourteen others, died in a horrific explosion at a pub in our neighborhood. It was a senseless act of murder by the Unionists on a group of innocent Catholics who were havin' a friendly beer on a Friday night after work. My father was enraged and deeply saddened by the death of his beloved brother, but he stubbornly refused to waiver on his non-violent principals. He did not rush out to join the Provisional IRA, as so many others did, including my brother Thomas.'

'How old was Thomas when this happened?'

'Ten.'

'A ten-year-old involved with the IRA?' Maddie tried to imagine her two boys at that age, wild and out of control in the streets of Montreal.

'It's hard for you, as an outsider, to understand what it was like in the early 70s in the poor Catholic areas of Belfast. Age or gender didn't seem to matter if you were willing to stand by the cause. Thomas was also a precocious and angry lad who embraced the IRA lifestyle very quickly. He became of child of war. He could get into places that no adult could. He became a consummate spy for the IRA, and he was indirectly responsible, I am sure, for many of the successful campaigns in Belfast and other locations. By the time Thomas was seventeen, he graduated from spying to stealing, robbing, physical intimidation, and more. By this time Da had kicked him out of our tiny house. Patrick followed within two years. As you may have noticed at the church, my brother Thomas is a huge, imposing figure, certainly by Irish standards.'

'What about you and Aidan?'

'Aidan was Tom's favourite. They were so much alike, they acted more like brothers than father and son. Unlike his brothers, Aidan was a good student. He was also large and athletic for his age, beating boys much older than him in all kinds of sports. Do you know what Eleven Plus Exams are?'

'No, I don't.'

'T'is a test to determine a student's aptitude for higher learning. It is still used today, though some whiney Catholics think it's unfair because it is quite rigorous. In any event, back then, most of the kids in our neighborhood did not pass the test due to the poor quality of education in the slums of Belfast. It's hard to concentrate on school work when you are a squirmy, hungry kid, as were most of the kids in the neighborhood. But Aidan was exceptional, and he passed the test with a very high score. The Belfast Institution, an exclusive non-denominational private school, invited him to join the school on a full scholarship, primarily because they wanted him to play rugby.'

'That's an incredible accomplishment,' Maddie said, staring at the few family photos on display in the bookshelf, mesmerized by Annie's riveting story.

'Indeed, it was, but also very difficult. It makes me sad, remembering how hard it was for Aidan to make his way to school every day. He wore street clothes on the bus, so as not to attract too much unwanted attention, and would change into his uniform at school. The school promoted itself as non-denominational, but the majority of the students were from wealthy Protestant families, who all lived very far away from the Troubles, in beautiful large houses surrounded by lush gardens and privacy fences. They really had no idea what was going on in North Belfast. Aidan was most definitely a minority at the school; he was a Catholic, very poor by the schools' standards, and he lived in the 'Troubles' area of Belfast. In spite of this, Aidan made friends.' Annie smiled, thinking about her twin brother and his ability to get along with just about anyone. 'He was very popular with the boys, and especially with the girls, who fawned all over him. He could talk to anyone and had a way of making his fellow students feel comfortable, in spite of his huge size, almost 6 feet tall at thirteen, and his 'Republican-Catholic' leanings.'

'Aidan has not changed much since those days,' Maddie added. 'I saw that wonderful personality trait shine through with almost everyone he met, especially with women!'

'Indeed, he has a gift for making people feel comfortable. T'is quite extraordinary, I think,' Annie said, smiling slightly.

Annie stood up from her chair and walked over to the window. It was raining again; a slow, steady drizzle fell on the paving stones. The large house was surrounded by a grey haze, and Annie could barely make out the end of the long driveway. She turned to face Maddie, and for the first time since walking into the big home, Annie's face lost its cool detachment. There was a genuine look of sadness in her eyes, and she seemed reluctant to continue her story.

'Have you had enough of this dreary story?' Annie asked.

'No. I want to hear more.'

'Of course, you do. Well, then, as fate would have it, the school had an indoor pool, quite a luxury in those days, and once Aidan discovered swimming, he became obsessed with the sport. He continued to play rugby, and all the other sports that the school demanded of him, but his absolute first love was swimming, and here, he was exceptionally gifted. Within a year he was asked to join an elite swim team that practiced in the school pool every morning and every afternoon.'

'Aidan once explained to me why he liked water so much,' Maddie added.

'Oh? How so?' Annie asked.

'He said that the water blocked out all the noise and distractions. He said it was a safe haven. At the time, I didn't understand what that meant, but now it's clear to me.'

'How interesting. I didn't know. It makes sense, though, given the times we lived in. In any event, he pursued swimming, and he got really good at it. He was the only Catholic on team, of course, and money was an issue, but the swim club found a sponsor. Can you image it, Maddie, Aidan getting up at 5:30 every morning to rush and catch the 6 am bus, all the way to school? There, he swam for seventy-five minutes, then went to his classes. After school, he would go back to the pool and swim until 5:30, then hop on the return bus home. Sometimes the lad was so tired, he would fall asleep eating supper! Da would have to carry him to bed most nights, which got harder as Aidan grew!'

Maddie smiled, thinking about one big man carrying another. Aidan's youthful face resting in the arms of his beloved father.

'The violence, though, was never far from our doorstep. Helicopters hovering above our roof were a constant sound. There was a funeral for some innocent victim of terrorism almost every day. Though Da was adamant that he wanted no part of the IRA, they often came to the house to 'talk to him'. T'was the only time I can remember when Da was glad Thomas was on the inside. He was able to protect Da and the family from the dire consequences of non-participation in the cause.'

Maddie shook her head and could only ask 'What do you mean dire consequences?'

'T'was a very black and white situation in those days. If you weren't with them, meaning active and contributing members of the IRA, you were against them. If you didn't support the cause', you were seen as a traitor, and the unpleasant consequences were relentless; constant intimidation, kneecapping, tar and feathering, that sort of behaviour. They came to our house a few times and tried to scare us, but Da stood his ground. You dare not speak out against them either. Their mantra was 'whatever you say, say nothin'', else you suffer the consequences.'

Annie stopped talking. Her guest was visibly shaken after hearing the details of the family's problems with the IRA. 'Maddie, I can see this stuff is hard to hear, and it's upsetting, but if you want to help my brother, you need to know the facts, as unpleasant as they are.'

''I will be okay, Annie. Please go on'.

Annie moved away from the window and sat down next to Maddie on the sofa.

'Can I get you some more tea, Maddie?'

'No thank you,' she replied absentmindedly, trying to image what it was like, living in a poor, vulnerable, and dysfunctional community.

'The next bit of family business is the hardest to talk about. Even now, almost thirty years later, the events of July 13, 1987 still plague our family to this day,' Annie said. 'T'was the day our father was fatally shot dead by a Loyalist as he was walking home. My father Tom did not usually take those kinds of risks, you understand, walking alone at night, and he always reminded us to be home by 7. T'was much too dangerous to be out and about in Belfast after dark. But Father could not refuse a family in need, and on this day the O'Hara's plumbing burst, so Da went out to fix the problem. It took longer than expected, and by the time he finished, t'was past 9 pm. Mr. O'Hara urged Tom to take a cab, but he shrugged it off, saying he could not afford to spend money on taxis when his son needed it for school supplies, so the big man walked home alone through the dark and dangerous streets.'

'By this time, we were all very anxious for Da to return, so Aidan bravely ventured outside, walking in the direction of the O'Hara house, looking for him. In the distance, he could see Tom walking quickly toward our house. In an instant, two men jumped out of a moving car that had been following him and shot Tom twice, once in the chest and once in the head. Aidan ran to his defence, but it was too late. The killers sped off. Aidan has never spoken about Tom's last moments alive, though I am quite certain that it haunts him still. The men responsible for the killing were never formally convicted, of course, though their fate and that of others were sealed by my brother Thomas. This was just the impetus that Thomas needed to send him over the edge. He vowed to wipe anyone and everyone who was linked, directly or indirectly, to Tom's murder. He has spent his entire adult life inflicting revenge on the perpetrators and their families for the murder of Tom O'Callaghan. He has been good on his word, I am sad to say. T'is the reason that Aidan is here and not in Clonakilty with you, as he planned.' Annie stopped talking when she heard a soft knock on the door. The housekeeper peered in. 'Madame, I thought you would want to know that they are on their way back and should be in less than twenty minutes.'

'Thank you, Maureen, for letting me know.' Annie turned to Maddie. 'But I am getting a wee bit ahead of myself. We will get to the realities of our present situation in a moment, but for now, I will finish the story. Where was I?'

'Tom's murder,' Maddie reminded Annie.

'Aidan was crushed when Tom was murdered. Two weeks after

Da's death, though, he went back to the school and swimming, more determined than ever to make a difference in his life and that of his family. Athletics was his ticket out of Belfast and he knew it. Callously, Thomas tried to use the opportunity to persuade Aidan to join the Provos, but he refused and threw Thomas out of the house. They never saw each other again, until four months ago.'

'Aidan told me he left home when he was eighteen on a swim scholarship, so he realized his dream of getting out of Belfast and making a better life for himself.'

'Indeed, but it was short lived. He was desperately lonely in Dublin, until he met the love of his life, pretty Katie. Come to think of it, you remind me of her. She had dark curly red hair, bright hazel eyes, and a killer smile. She adored my brother.'

'Aidan told me she got pregnant and they had a son.'

'Did he tell you that she was a Protestant from county Armagh? Did he tell you that Thomas and Patrick tried to break up the relationship by threatening her Protestant family? Did he tell you that Thomas went even further and almost killed Katie and the baby?'

'What? Oh god, no. He never told me any of this. I don't believe it. What brother would do that to one of his own?'

'You don't know my brother Thomas, but you soon will. When this happened, the pressures from both families got so intense that the young couple fled to London to start a new life together, their respective swimming careers now over. For a while, the couple managed to have a normal life. Aidan worked in construction – the only real job an eighteen-year-old could get without an education. They had no money, of course, but they had each other, and their new baby boy Shane. Like everything else in Aidan's young life, his happiness was short lived. On morning in February '93, I think it was, Aidan was a hand-delivered a note, from someone sympathetic to his situation, warning him to stay away from the Liverpool underground station that morning. The message arrived only after Katie and the baby left for a doctor's appointment, heading toward the same station. Frantic, Aidan went after them, but it was too late. He never made it, as a massive explosion devastated the area, toppling a couple of old churches and destroying the underground station. T'was another deadly IRA terrorist attack.'

Maddie said, shaking her head, 'But they survived?'

'God have mercy, yes. Katie and the baby were walking away from the Station went the bomb went off, and they only suffered minor injuries in the blast, but that was enough for Aidan. He was terrified that his brother Thomas was actually targeting his young family, which wasn't true, as the bomb was not intended for Katie or the baby, but Aidan couldn't be convinced otherwise.'

'How do you know the bomb wasn't targeted at them?'

Annie paused, as she wasn't expecting this question from Maddie, and added, 'I just know, that's all. In any event, Aidan contacted Katie's father and asked him to send them to Australia, to live with relatives. Katie and Shane left a month later. The wean was only four years old. Aidan would not see him again for ten years.'

'By this point in his life, young Aidan had lost his father, his swim career, his girlfriend and his son. The disappointments were endless,' Maddie said. It did not seem possible that the man she had met in Mont-Tremblant, a loving, caring, and thoughtful person, could have endured such tragedy and still be normal.

'Indeed. But Aidan moved on. His upbringing and his father's legacy made him quite resilient, and he refused to spend the rest of his life being angry and hateful, like Thomas. That was not Tom's O'Callaghans way, nor would it be Aidan's. From that point on, he distanced himself as far as possible from his sordid past, and any association with the O'Callaghan brothers. Most people had no idea where he came from, and that was fine with him. You know about his humanitarian work, I take it?' Annie asked.

'I do. That is the one part of Aidan's tumultuous life that he was happy to share with me.'

'It is something to be proud of. Aidan has been seriously involved with this work for many years. Sheila and I would visit him from time to time in West Cork, when he wasn't volunteering in some exotic and remote country, but really, we have not seen much of him...' Annie didn't finish her sentence.

'Until the accident?' Maddie added.

'Until the accident,' Annie confirmed.

'Once again, Aidan has found himself in the middle of the sordid family business through no fault of his own.'

'Because the car accident was not an accident. It was a deliberate attempt to kill Aidan,' Maddie responded.

'…but do you know why he was a target?' Annie asked, curious to find out how much Maddie knew about the family's business dealings.

Maddie put her tea cup on the table to pour herself a fresh cup. She was stalling for time. Annie only knew her as Aidan's innocent Canadian girlfriend, whose knowledge of the O'Callaghan's story was limited to their former IRA activities. The more Maddie revealed even to Annie, the more implicated she would be in the family's illegal business activities. This is exactly why Aidan did not want her to stay in Belfast, and why he refused to contact Michael. Maddie's next step could seal her and Aidan's fate, and so she wisely chose to play dumb.

'No, I don't really.' Maddie finally answered. 'Michael said it had something to do with IRA activities from long ago. He didn't provide much in the way of detail, as I said earlier. He told me that the family still had significant enemies from their past association with the IRA, as do others from the same era, and that there is continuing warring between some groups, though this is not widely published by the media.'

Annie was skeptical listening to Maddie's explanation. Her instincts told her that the Canadian knew much about what was going on with the O'Callaghan's then she was willing to admit. It wouldn't be that hard to find out what the family was doing, if you knew where to look. In the end, it really didn't matter, Annie thought. Maddie was here and now well entrenched in the melee. She had committed herself the minute she walked in the door, and there was no turning back. First Katie, then Meghan, and now Maddie. All had unknowingly taken a chance with the family and found themselves in the unforgiving world of gang warfare. Annie would not let Aidan lose another loved one. She had one more reason to deliver on her promise to protect her family.

'T'is true. The fighting is still going on, but buried deep under the so-called Peace Accord,' Annie replied sarcastically. 'I will not get into all the finer details of the current situation because I am running out of time, but now I will tell you why Aidan was a target and why he is here.'

Annie stood up and walked to the window again, her eyes scanning the front entrance, looking for signs of traffic.

'Aidan will be back soon from physiotherapy, so I will need to make this quick...my brother Thomas has an ongoing feud with a former commander of the Ulster Volunteer Force, or UVF. His name is John Connolly. Thomas believes that John was responsible for killing our Da, and as I said earlier, he vowed to spend the rest of his life inflicting pain and torment on the little man. John Connolly, for his part, has not sat idle either.'

Annie stopped at that point, remembering the death of her late husband Fergus, another casualty of gang warfare. 'We endured this 'tit for tat' fighting for decades until ten years ago, when the feud between the two men finally stopped. T'was perhaps the general ceasefire, or perhaps because both men grew tired of the constant violence, I am not sure. In any event, I thought this nasty business was finally over, and we could stop looking over our shoulders. Until the explosion last June,' Annie continued, her voice hurried now.

'It was a calculating and precise move on the part of John Connolly, that ugly little merchant of violence. He must have been planning it for some time. The only way he could have possibly known about Aidan's' exact whereabouts was by having him and his girlfriend Meghan followed. Did Michael tell you there was a bomb in the vehicle?'

Maddie nodded.

'It was detonated by a mobile device. Those creeps were following them. The poor, innocent couple didn't stand a chance. It was gruesome. Poor Meghan. She had little knowledge of Aidan's past, and even if she did, I doubt it would not have changed how she felt about him. And Aidan? He was lucky to have survived,' Annie added, getting more agitated.

'I saw a photo of the accident. It's hard to believe anyone could survive the impact,' Maddie responded. 'Annie, is Aidan here in Belfast for his own protection?'

'Indeed, and he is recovering from his injuries under the watchful care of specialists and doctors. He has the support and more importantly, twenty-four hours a day protection, in case John Connolly decides to strike again. We all are under threat now. The last few months have been traumatic for all of us. The bodyguards, the surveillance, the stress...my children were afraid to go outside. I had to send them away. The city is teetering on the edge of lawlessness. The police, too, are a constant and unwelcome presence.'

'Are the police involved?'

'To an extent...several different police organizations from across numerous jurisdictions are involved. The accident happened in Dublin, not here, so the Gardai are still investigating. Thomas and Patrick would prefer to manage this problem with their own resources, but 'tis difficult. The police know it was no accident, and an innocent person was killed. They keep poking around asking questions and generally being meddlesome.'

'What will happen now, Annie?' Maddie asked anxiously.

'That is a very, very good question. I do not have an answer. We take it one day at a time,' Annie replied, distracted. 'I suggest you speak to Aidan first, when he comes back from his appointment, and sort things out between you. He will, of course, want you to leave immediately, but I personally think it's too late for that. Besides, his mood improved since he saw you at the church. He may be telling you to leave, but I think his heart wants you to stay...and speaking about Aidan, the car is pulling into the driveway.'

Maddie walked over to the window. The Mercedes sedan pulled up at the front of the house, and the driver, dressed in black, got out and opened the passenger door. Aidan stepped out, holding his cane, as the shorter bodyguard tried unsuccessfully to hold the umbrella over the tall man's head. Aidan looked over at the large bay window to see Maddie and Annie staring at him. He did not look thrilled to see the two women standing together.

Annie turned toward Maddie and spoke to her in a gentle, sister-like voice.

'Maddie, I can see that you are genuinely in love with my brother, and he is still in love with you, though you might need to draw him out. He is fragile and not himself at all. He has suffered many physical injuries, but his recovery is more complicated than just healing broken bones. His recovery will take time and patience. If anyone can help him recover completely, I think it is you. I agree with you – you and Aidan should go back to Clonakilty. He will recover much quicker surrounded by his friends and all that is familiar to him. To be back here in Belfast, surrounded by horrible and violent memories, is not good for him. For my part, I will take care of things so that you and

Aidan can leave Belfast.' Annie paused to watch her brother and mother make their way to the front door of the door.

'Long before you arrived, I began working on a plan to free us from this endless tyranny. You must trust my judgement on this and leave the details to me.'

After all that was said, Maddie was not sure how Annie could singlehandedly free the family from their problems. She seemed unlikely to have the power or the means to do anything but care for her mother and brother. But Maddie had travelled to Belfast to find Aidan, and she needed an ally within the O'Callaghans to ensure her safety. She decided to put her trust in Annie.

'As you wish, Annie. I will let you sort this out.'

3:05:00

Maddie and Annie stood by the window, watching Aidan and Sheila make their way inside. It was a slow process, as neither one moved very quickly. They could hear the rustling of coats in the front hallway, and finally the French doors opened. Aidan walked into the sitting room, holding his cane precariously in one hand, as if trying not to depend on it to hold him up. His face was stern and he was clearly irritated.

Annie immediately went up to her mother, who was standing next to her son, ignoring Aidan.

'Ma, I want you to meet a friend of Aidan's who has come all the way from Canada to see him. This is Maddie…?'

'St-Laurent. Maddie St-Laurent.' Maddie walked up to Aidan's mom to shake the hand of the tiny little redhead. Sheila O'Callaghan was no taller than 5 feet, her small but plump frame at odds with her tall, square-shouldered son standing next to her. Even in his frail condition, Aidan dwarfed his mother by a foot or more.

'You have come all the way from Canada? My, my…t'is a long way. Well, tank you for visitin' Aidan. He needs the company,' Sheila replied, looking up at her brooding son.

'Ma, let's go into the kitchen and have some tea, shall we,' Annie suggested. pointing in the direction of the kitchen. 'And you,' Annie said lowering her voice so Sheila couldn't hear, 'this woman cares about you very much. I strongly suggest you listen to what she has to say before you try tossin' her out.'

The French doors shut quietly behind the mother and daughter. The large room was still. Maddie did not move from the window, waiting for Aidan to initiate the conversation. The last time they spoke at the guest house, it was hurried, and Aidan had done all of the talking. This time, their conversation would be equal. Maddie had much to say to the sorrowful-looking Irishman standing before her.

'Annie is as direct as you are. It must be a family trait,' Maddie asked, bemused by Annie's bossy tone with her twin brother.

Aidan did not reply.

'I did not get a chance to ask you the other night about your injuries,' Maddie continued, trying to coax Aidan out of his somber mood. 'Annie said you were at physiotherapy this morning.'

'Indeed,' Aidan replied as he edged his body closer to the window. 'My hip broke in the accident. That's why I carry a cane. Recovery is a slow process and I'm growing impatient to walk normally. I'm growing impatient about a lot of things these days.'

They stood facing each other, an awkward and prolonged silence lingered in the large space. Instead of reaching for her, as Maddie had wished for since seeing him at the guest house, Aidan resolutely stood his ground, his long arms hanging by his side, his face pale and tired, his feet shuffling from one foot to the next, trying to ease the fatigue in his legs. He made no attempt to touch her.

Finally, he broke the uncomfortable silence, his voice edged with anger.

'You are a foolish and stubborn woman, Madeline St-Laurent. Did yeh not hear anythin' I said to yeh two nights ago?'

'I did. You asked me to leave Belfast. You said it was not safe for me here.'

'So why are you still here, then? I told you I don't want you involved in my family business.' His words came out sounding slurred and thick with pain.

'I know, but I am here now, and I am not going anywhere. You should have trusted me in Canada. If you had trusted me, things would be a whole lot different today. I would have come to Ireland immediately. I don't understand why you couldn't trust me enough to tell at least some aspects of your personal life,' Maddie replied defiantly.

'It has nothin' to do with trust, Maddie. I was prepared to tell you everythin' when the time came,' Aidan replied impatiently, shaking his head. 'Yeh shouldn't be here. I do not want yeh involved. It's too dangerous,' he repeated, this time his voice breaking from the emotional strain. 'Yeh don't know what you've gotten yourself into,' he continued. 'You're a fine, intelligent, beautiful woman who deserves to spend the rest of your life in a safe and comfortable place, and not have to look over yeh'r shoulder in constant fear that someone is after yeh. I thought this stuff was over, but I was sadly mistaken. I cannot risk losing someone I love again. Do yeh see? Yeh must go back to Canada and move on without me, I cannot bear it.'

Maddie could feel a lump in the back of her throat, pressing against her windpipe. She could hardly breath. Aidan was paralyzed with fear that something terrible would happen, and he would lose Maddie as he had Meghan, Tom, and Katie. Maddie understood his fear, and she did not dismiss it lightly. She was as scared as he was, but there was not a chance now that she was going to turn her back on him and go home.

'I know a lot more than about what's going on than you think, Aidan. I know what I've gotten myself into,' Maddie replied. 'I spoke to Michael at length, and for the last two hours Annie has filled me in about your family. I am willing to take whatever the risk to be with you. This is my life now, not tucked in some tony part of Montreal, comfortably miserable. I choose to be here…with you.'

Aidan turned away from Maddie and looked out the window.

'What can I do or say to convince you to leave?' Aidan's asked, his voice losing its strained edge and sounding familiar. This soothing voice was what she remembered from Mont-Tremblant, the same voice he used to seduce her that first afternoon when they met; the same voice he used to convince her to stay with him for five days, the same voice that acted as coach and pacer during six hours of racing. It was silky, charming, and hypnotic.

'NO,' Maddie almost shouted 'you can't convince me to leave. Your charms have worked in all kinds of wonderful ways, but not this time, Aidan O'Callaghan. I stand my ground. I am not leaving Belfast without you.'

Aidan face was expressionless. He did not seem to have the energy to do much else. They had been standing by the window for five minutes or more, and Maddie could see Aidan was physically depleted. He was leaning heavily on the cane for support.

'Let's sit down, Aidan, shall we?' Without waiting for an answer, Maddie put her arm around his thin waist and firmly guided him to the large sofa. He sat down heavily on the cushion, the weight of the world crushing his bony shoulders.

'I know you are angry that I am here, but,' Maddie started to say, but Aidan cut her off.

'I am not angry with you, Maddie. I could never be angry with yeh,' he said, seated inches from her body, their shoulders almost touching. Aidan took Maddie's hands in his and began rubbing her damp palms. He couldn't look at her, but stared at the floor. They had reached an uneasy truce for the time being. She would not leave, and he did not have the strength to send her away.

'How did you manage to find me?' He finally asked.

'It wasn't easy – that I can tell you. I almost gave up a couple of times. You certainly covered your tracks well. You could give a course on how to disappear,' Maddie said, smiling. 'When you first disappeared, I tried for two weeks to find you. I couldn't remember your last name, and there was no record of you in the race database. It was hopeless. My best friend Sofia told me you were a womanizing charlatan, and that I should forget about what happened in Mont-Tremblant. Move on, she said, and I did for a while. I kept myself busy for a few months, until one morning, about four weeks ago, I went back to the race database again. I honestly don't know why. I had been there dozens of times, looking for a clue. This time I got lucky. I found one grainy photo of you with the bib number showing, and I very nearly missed that. That photo led me to your last name, which I was able to trace to the Clonakilty Construction Company and Michael Bennett.'

Aidan could hardly believe her tenacity, but then he remembered how she was during their time together. If anyone was capable digging for a link or clue, no matter how faint, it was Maddie St-Laurent.

'You are truly a resourceful woman that can find and fix anything,' Aidan added, shaking his head.

'But you know that already, don't you?' Maddie replied.

'Indeed, I do, but I am not a bicycle, and yeh alone can not repair the damage so easily,' he replied somberly.

They sat on the sofa, holding hands for a very long time, and said nothing more. They blocked out the stress of the last few days, the noise and activity inside the house. It was enough that they were finally together. For a brief time, Aidan forgot about his aching body, his debilitating headaches, and the guilt that consumed his thoughts. At that moment in time, they were able to steal a few precious minutes alone, pretending they were safe and secure in a lovely cocoon existence, overlooking the Mont-Tremblant Ski Resort.

'You are much too thin, Maddie. 'T'is not healthy for you. Are you not eating?' Aidan asked out of the blue.

'I didn't notice I had lost weight until a couple of days ago. But I'm not the only one who looks thinner than usual,' Maddie added.

'T'is true. I haven't much reason to eat these day. Perhaps this will change.'

Their conversation drifted in and out of mundane subjects, punctuated by long moments of silence and reflection. They had yet to resolve the sticky issue of Maddie's unannounced visit and what was to come next in their fragile relationship.

'I am so sorry this happened to you, Aidan. I wish you had told me everything about your life when we met,' Maddie repeated, as she lifted her hand to stroke his dry, pale face. He did not pull away from her touch.

'I had my reasons, Maddie. You have lived your entire life in a country that has never experienced civil war. You have never lived with the constant threat of violence looming over your shoulder like a shadow. Most people are horrified when they learn the truth. They can't believe it. I didn't know yeh well enough in Mont-Tremblant to share the grim facts. I was being selfish. I thought yeh might change your mind about agreeing to come to Ireland if yeh knew the risks. That's why I avoided all aspects of my past. My plan was to get you to come to Clonakilty, and after yeh had settled in, I was going to tell yeh about my family's involvement in politics and other sordid business dealings. It would have worked out for us if it had not been for the accident. In hindsight, that was not the best decision I've ever made, though I am glad that yeh did not give up on me.'

They said nothing more. Aidan was too weary to talk, and he eventually fell asleep on the sofa, resting his head in Maddie's lap, as she gently stroked his head and hair. Maddie watched him for an hour, his eyelids flickering constantly, his head moving from side to side. His body stirred every time there was the slightest sound.

A knock on the French doors startled the couple. Aidan sat up immediately. Annie peered into the room to see the couple sitting close together on the couch.

'I am sorry to bother you. Thomas and Patrick will be here in ninety minutes.'

'I thought they were both out of town?' Aidan asked harshly.

'So did I. Word travels fast that we have a guest in our midst. I am sorry, Maddie, but it would be wise for you to change into something more formal. My brother Thomas is a stickler about dinner attire. I have a dress that will fit you.'

Maddie looked at Aidan. 'You best follow her and get dressed,' Aidan suggested.

They stood up from the sofa. Maddie could see that Aidan was unsteady and held him tightly, clinging to his frail frame so he would feel balanced and safe, just as he had done with her months ago in Mont-Tremblant. They stood like this until Aidan released Maddie's grip and kissed her on the lips. Aidan's lips were dry and passionless. It was not a kiss that promised much, and it did not send her reeling with anticipation. But it was an encouraging sign though that perhaps Aidan was slowly accepting her presence.

3:35:00

Passers-by peering into the O'Callaghan fortress from the street could see a large house in the shadows of large trees, illuminated by one low-level carriage light hanging over the front door. The driveway leading to the back of the house glistened black-slick with a recent rainfall. The rest of the property was also bathed in an eerie and somber blanket of darkness. Thomas O'Callaghan, the most senior member of the household, had peculiar ideas about his privacy, and he insisted that their house be kept under a cover of darkness so it could not be scrutinized by nosy neighbors. He did not want people to know who was coming and going inside the heavily guarded mansion.

Inside the house, though, was a complete contrast to the gloom outside. All the lights shown brightly in the hallway and staircase. The living room had an assortment of votives burning in shimmering crystal holders. There were numerous bottles of red and white lined up on the bar trolley, as well as whisky, an ice bucket, and expensive Waterford stemware. The entire first floor of the palatial home had an oddly festive feel.

Maddie walked into the large formal living room an hour after Annie told the couple the evening plans had changed, wearing a tight black dress. It was much shorter than her usual dress length, snug across her full chest and hips. Maddie had pulled up her thick dark auburn hair in a flattering knot, applied a touch of lipstick and make-up. Aidan, too, had changed into a pair of grey trousers and tailored black shirt, though this outfit did not fit him any better than the one he had on earlier. Four months previously, he would have easily filled the black shirt with his broad square shoulders and muscled torso. Instead, the shirt hung loosely, two sizes too big.

'Maddie, you look lovely, even if that dress is a bit too tight in places,' Aidan said, admiring his vivacious girlfriend as she sat down next to him on the sofa.

'I know! Your sister is much smaller than I am, and this is the largest dress she has. I think she wore it when she was pregnant,' Maddie said, not the least embarrassed that she was wearing a maternity dress.

'I doubt that,' Aidan answered without humor. 'One look at you and Thomas will be all over you like a dirty shirt. Do not be fooled by his good looks and charm. He's treacherous, slippery, and a notorious womanizer. He does not take no for an answer.'

'Oh? He sounds suspiciously like his younger brother,' Maddie shot back and kissed Aidan's dry, bony cheek.

'I'm serious, Maddie. T'is is not a laughing matter. He is not to be trusted. Please do me a favour and never be alone with him.' Aidan looked genuinely concerned so Maddie nodded her head and patted Aidan's cold hand.

'Aidan, why all the formalities of dressing for dinner? I feel like I am in an episode of Dallas,' Maddie asked, looking around the glowing living room.

'What?' Aidan responded, not understanding the connection. 'Oh, I see what you mean, about sitting down to a formal dinner? T'is my brother's convoluted idea of class and money. He does this regularly, though it's just for the family. No one, other than you, has ever stepped foot in this fortress as long as I've been here. It's pathetic,' Aidan added, shaking in his head.

As the couple sat on the sofa anxiously waiting for the head of the household to arrive, the glare of headlights flashed across the room, and two cars pulled up to the wrought iron gate just as it opened. Within two minutes, the front door opened, and in walked Thomas and Patrick, followed by their entourage of bodyguards.

Thomas strode into the brightly lit living room, his imposing and commanding frame shrinking the large space. This was the first time Maddie saw the infamous commander up close. He was a striking but somewhat flashy man of fifty-three, with shiny slick hair the color of polished silver, a rosy complexion, and nice teeth. He had few facial wrinkles or the obvious signs of a man who had spent the majority of his life living on the edge. He had evidently taken good care of himself over the years, though his girth was carrying a few extra pounds. Of the three brothers, he was by far the largest, followed by Aidan, and then Patrick, who held an uncanny resemblance to Sheila.

Thomas had all the warmth of a stalking wolf. His glacial blue eyes darted about the room, and he moved in sudden steps as though he were ready to pounce on his prey. This was a man who would never be caught unawares, always at the ready for anything or anyone to strike.

By contrast, Patrick's temperament was much more subdued. He was physically different than his older brother, shorter, with copper colored hair and facial stubble. He wore thin wire-frame oval glasses which gave him a bookish look. He was not as striking as Thomas, or as ruggedly attractive as Aidan, but there was a sophistication about him that was missing in his brothers. Michael had told Maddie that Patrick was the financial brains of the family empire, and he looked well the part. He was fashionably dressed, in a slim cut grey pin-striped suit, crisp white shirt, and dark brown, white flecked tie. He had a studious and serious demeanour.

All three men were tall, with arresting good looks, and they all shared the distinctive O'Callaghan long chiseled face and high cheek bones. Tom and Sheila O'Callaghan had produced an exceptionally handsome family.

Thomas reached out to shake Maddie's hand, keeping it a bit longer than necessary, and eyeing the sumptuous woman standing next to his brother.

'My name is Thomas O'Callaghan, and you would be?'

'Madeline St-Laurent. Pleased to meet you, Thomas.' Without hesitation, she added, 'I am Aidan's...fiancée.'

Everyone was taken aback by this spontaneous declaration, including Aidan, who shot Maddie a look, then instinctively took hold of her waist, pulling her close for protection.

Annie was the only one in the room who saw through Maddie's strategy.

'Indeed, well, this is news to me. I did not know Aidan had a fiancée. How long have you been engaged?' Thomas asked looking squarely at Aidan for a response.

'That's a good question, Thomas,' Maddie spoke up. 'Our relationship has been complicated, given the fact that I live in Canada and Aidan is...from Ireland. The accident added another layer of complication to our long-distance romance. But we are finally together now, after a brief absence, and Aidan asked me if I would agree to marry him, moments before you arrived, and I said yes, absolutely.' This was not a lie, but a variation of the truth. While Aidan had proposed to her in Mont-Tremblant, a lifetime ago, it certainly was not the subject of their stilted conversation during the afternoon.

'Well, congratulations to you both!' Thomas remarked, taking the opportunity to hug his future sister in-law, squeezing her tightly. While Maddie took no notice of Thomas' gesture, Aidan was seething internally. He knew his brother was greedy and took anything that did not belong to him. *The man has absolutely no conscience,* Aidan thought.

In his booming and commanding voice, Thomas insisted that the family celebrate this happy announcement with champagne. Within minutes, three bottles of very expensive French champagne were uncorked and poured in crystal fluted glasses.

Thomas lifted his champagne glass and said, 'To my devoted younger brother and his beautiful fiancée! Slainte!' Everyone in the room took a large swig of the champagne, except for Aidan. 'Let us wish Aidan a speedy recovery so we can have a traditional Irish Catholic O'Callaghan wedding! I am looking forward to it! I have not been to a family wedding in so long, t'will be good craic!' Thomas declared in a loud voice.

Everyone lifted their glass a second time, including Aidan, though he hardly felt like celebrating. He did not think it was possible to hate anyone as much as he hated his older brother Thomas. *The man is pure evil,* Aidan thought, while watching Thomas trying to convince his fiancée that he cared about his family. Nothing could be further from the truth. Aidan wished that the man who had caused so much grief in his family's life would disappear permanently. The sooner the better.

*****

The O'Callaghans and their guest ate a four-course meal in the grand and formal dining room. The large mahogany antique table was beautifully appointed, with fresh flowers, tall white tapers, and sparkling glasses. The large crystal chandelier created a soft glow in the room, accentuating the hand-painted, shimmering wallpaper featuring birds and vines. The total effect was mesmerizing and stunning, yet it was lost on both Aidan and Maddie, who both drank and ate sparingly. Aidan sat stoned-faced in his chair, not smiling or speaking and barely acknowledging his older brother. It was difficult to ignore Thomas. His rhetorical style of speaking commanded attention, and he monopolized the dinner conversation, seemingly controlling every aspect of the party. Maddie was hungry, but she was too nervous to relax enough to eat.

Throughout the evening, both Patrick and Thomas were interrupted several times by a black-clad body guard carrying a cell phone. He was but one of several bodyguards stationed throughout the house who were on constant alert. At one point, the two older brothers left together, but returned twenty minutes later. The wine and champagne flowed freely, but this was not enough to eradicate the tension in the room. Maddie wanted desperately to drink the vintage French red wine with her meal, but reconsidered. She needed to be alert and in full control of her mind. Alcohol would loosen her tongue, and she was fearful she might say something to offend Thomas, or worse, cause Aidan to overreact. She watched her fiancée all night, picking at his food and flinching every time Thomas opened his mouth. Compared to the fun loving and easygoing man she met in Mont-Tremblant, this version of Aidan was completely alien to her. It was clear he loathed his brother.

When speaking to Thomas, Maddie was careful to choose her words. She made a point of keeping her comments superficial. She knew that Thomas did not believe her story about having just got engaged. The former OC of the IRA was far too skeptical and wise to be fooled by a spur-of-the-moment lie. It made little sense under the circumstances, though Aidan went along with the ruse to confirm the story.

Thomas never asked either one of them any personal questions about how they met. Maddie thought this was curious behaviour, given what she knew about his relentless need for control. Michael said he was the most powerful criminal in all of the Emerald Island, north and south, yet he did not ask one question about how or where the couple met. *Unless he already knew the story,* Maddie thought. She shuddered to think what the man actually knew about her and Aiden.

Thomas was in full control of every aspect of the long evening. A natural storyteller, he loved to talk about himself and his exploits, sprinkling these anecdotes with a dry sense of humor. He spoke at length about his years in the IRA, and never tried to hide his direct involvement in terrorism campaigns. In fact, he seemed quite proud of everything he had done. Maddie was not sure if this was a scare tactic or to enlighten her to the family's involvement in a significant part of

Irish history. Thomas' stories were descriptive, comical, and tinged with dark and unflattering comments about various people and cultures. He did not shy away from voicing his strong opinions about politics and duty; *A family trait, it would seem,* thought Maddie.

Of all the family members seated at the table, Annie spoke the least throughout the evening. She appeared almost docile in front of her brothers, eclipsed by their physical presence. She tended to Sheila, her mother, making sure the matriarch was comfortable and well fed. She quietly managed the flow of food and drinks before and during dinner. Annie nodded at the right times, laughed when it was appropriate, but never gave her opinion or spoke up on any subject. The only time she participated in the dinner conversation was when Thomas mentioned the Belfast Art and Antiquities Gallery.

'So, Maddie, have your seen much of our beloved city since you've been here?' Thomas asked, taking a large swig of the French wine, barely tasting it.

'Not yet. Do you have any suggestions on what I should visit?'

'I'd like to suggest you visit the IRA Museum, but we have no such establishment here in Belfast, at least not yet,' Thomas roared, 'I dunno think it could compete with the likes of that fluffy excuse of a tourist attraction, the Titanic Museum. That's utter nonsense, that is,' Thomas added, slurring his words ever so lightly.

'If you say so, Thomas,' Annie added.

Thomas turned and looked at his sister.

'Now and again, you could visit the Belfast Art and Antiquities Gallery, of which my dear sister, here, is the proprietor and manager. Isn't that right Annie?'

'Indeed I am.'

'I dunno a thing about art and antiques, but it make's her happy and I tink it's pulling a nice profit too, isn't it,' he asked Annie.

She complied and nodded, but her sardonic expression did not escape Maddie's attention.

'And where are you staying in Belfast, Maddie?' Thomas asked, while the housekeeper began serving dessert and coffee.

'I have been staying at a guest house on Eglantine Road.'

'I take it you are staying here this evening?' Thomas asked.

Maddie looked at Aidan who answered his brother.

'She will be staying here from now on....'

Thomas did not wait for Aidan to finish his sentence. 'Well then, tomorrow my driver will take you back to the guest house to retrieve your belongings and move them here to our palatial home.' This was not a request or a suggestion, but clearly a command.

*****

Three hours after the she was introduced to the brothers O'Callaghan, Maddie and Aidan finally made their way to a large suite on the second floor. The suite was roomy and well equipped, with a king size bed, a sitting area with a full couch, and an ensuite bathroom.

'T'was Sheila's room until I moved in,' Aidan said as Maddie looked around at the impressive large space.

'Your sister is very thoughtful,' Maddie remarked, pointing to pyjamas, towel, tooth brush, and other toiletries on the sofa that Annie had left for her to use.

Aidan looked plainly uncomfortable in the room, and as exhausted as he had looked for most of the evening. Now that they were finally alone, Maddie had hoped that he would relax more, but the setting seemed to make him more agitated. While she wanted nothing more than to snuggle up next to him in the large bed, and feel his body next to her, this was not the time to be intimate. During the short time they had spent together, they had only kissed once, and it was not the kiss of lovers. Resuming any kind of intimacy seemed highly unlikely under the circumstances. To Maddie's disappointment, he clearly was not ready, either physically or emotionally, to pick up where they had left off, four months previously. Maddie was fully aware that Aidan had only agreed to have her stay with him because of his brother's nosy questions. Aidan had not been given a choice in whether she stayed or left Belfast, and he did not seem pleased about it. The decision about Maddie's future was thrust upon him, provoked by his domineering brother.

'Aidan, why don't you go and change while I make up your bed? If it's okay with you, I'd rather sleep on the sofa,' Maddie said, taking the initiative at this awkward moment to help ease his anxiety.

'That's a good idea. I do not sleep well these days, and I'm likely to keep you awake with my constant moving about.' On that note, Aidan headed into the bathroom.

Maddie changed out of the tight black dress and into the pyjamas that Annie had left for her. The suite was hot and stuffy, so she opened the window to let in some fresh air, sat on the sofa, and waited for Aidan. She could hear a car drive away, followed by the sound of murmuring voices through the opened window. It was Annie talking to Patrick, but she could not make out what they were saying.

"The fresh air feels good, Maddie. I tried opening the window before, but could not manage it,' Aidan said, as he walked back to the large bed, wearing baggy bottoms and a grey t-shirt, smelling softly of lavender.

'I think it was locked,' Maddie replied.

Aidan got into bed gingerly and lay on this side, facing his fiancée. Maddie moved to the edge of the bed and kissed him lightly on the forehead.

'Can I get you anything? Water, Advil?' She asked.

'No, I am fine, thank you,' he replied and then expectantly reached up to stroke his fiancé's face.

'You did well tonight with my brothers…not easy for a newcomer. And what were your impressions of the silver fox?'

'Is that what they call Thomas?' Maddie asked.

'Well, not to his face, but the description is apt, I think. Sly, opportunistic, sneaky.'

'Really? To me, he's more of grey wolf than a silver fox.'

'How so?' Aidan asked, sitting up, interested to hear her opinion of his brother.

'Foxes are cunning and quick, hard to catch, but the grey wolf is eminently more interesting. First of all, they are very large animals and extraordinary good hunters. They don't back down on their prey even if it's twice as large. Wolves are not afraid of anything and highly social creatures. The wolf pack operates under some well-defined rules. Does this sound familiar to you?' Maddie asked, arching her brow. 'The alpha male is the leader and his opponents cower in his presence. He always goes first. Grey wolves are highly territorial and are constantly on the lookout for prey. Finally, the grey wolf has strong family bonds – to the point that he will sacrifice himself to save his offspring.'

Aidan smiled slightly. 'I think I like the grey wolf more than I like Thomas.'

'Why?' Maddie asked, bemused.

'The grey wolf sounds like it has a conscience. My brother has not a drop of it,' Aidan replied. He continued to stare at the lovely, smiling woman sitting on the edge of the bed, stroking his bare arm gently, the woman who had left her comfortable life in Montreal in search of him. His body reacted the way it had the first time she had touched him, sprawled on the wet ground in the pouring rain, unable to move. This fetching woman, with the warm loving hands, full of genuine concern and love, had helped him then, and she was trying to help him now. He must not lose her, he told himself. He must do everything in his power to protect her, even if that means sending her back to Canada.

Aidan reached up and gently tugged her face down so he could kiss those full lips. Her lips were moist, and she tasted of honey and butter. He kissed her more forcefully, probing with his tongue. Maddie responded willingly. He kissed her soft neck and put his large hands on her full breasts, caressing them. Maddie stroked his stomach and tenderly moved her hands downward. He could feel her touching him, growing in her capable hands, and he wanted her; his exhausted and damaged body was suddenly surging with energy.

Then he stopped as quickly as he had started and pulled Maddie's hand away.

'No, I can't, I'm sorry, Maddie. I'm not ready yet,' Aidan said, and pushed her firmly away.

The room was partially dark, lit only by the outside lights, so that Aidan could not see Maddie's face flushed red with embarrassment, but he knew how upset she was at being rejected.

'T'is not your fault Maddie,' Aidan said in a strained voice. 'You are a still a beautiful and desirable woman. T'is me, you see. I am still recoverin', and I am not able to be the man I was to you once. I'm sorry. Good night,' Aidan turned over on his side and closed his eyes.

Maddie went back to the lumpy sofa, dejected and upset. Her sudden, unannounced appearance in Belfast was beginning to look like a mistake. Aidan's unpredictable actions were hurtful, even if he wasn't intentionally trying to cause her pain. Thomas was as formidable as he had been described. For the first time since arriving in Ireland, Maddie was more than frightened. She was worried about her personal safety.

*****

'When are you meeting Eammon?' Patrick asked, sitting at the kitchen counter, enjoying the tranquility of the big white kitchen, while watching the mindless movement of his sister as she put away the dinner dishes and dispensed with the numerous empty bottles of champagne and wine that were sitting on the floor.

Thomas had finally left the house around midnight, his bodyguards practically carrying the large and very drunk man to his car. They drove him to his apartment a few blocks away. Patrick was sure his brother had consumed a full bottle of champagne, two bottles of red wine, and at least six drams of Irish whiskey. It was no wonder he drank so much, Patrick thought. The recent pressures were finally getting to him.

'I'm meeting Eammon in the morning, at the Gallery,' Annie replied.

Patrick wanted to say that meeting at the Gallery was far too public, but he knew his sister would disagree with him. She always had the upper hand in any decision. She was the wisest person her knew, and he deferred to her about every business decision regarding the family. She had silently, invisibly, and patiently been overseeing the family's welfare for almost two decades, and she had never failed to be right.

'Thomas seems more stressed than usual. Do you think there is a chance that he will relent and stop the provocation and revenge tactics?'

'Not a chance,' Annie replied. 'He is incapable of walking away and letting that ugly little man have the final word. No, that would never do for Thomas O'Callaghan. He will never relent when it comes to John Connolly.'

'What do you think of Aidan's fiancée, Maddie? You spent some time with her, I take it, this afternoon?' Patrick asked.

'I did indeed. I am very impressed with the Canadian. She doesn't give up easily, and she knows what she wants. I like her, Patrick. She's good for Aidan. He seems a bit better since she showed up.'

'Now that she's here, have the plans changed at all?'

'Not a lick. The only thing that has changed is that Aidan will be safely escorted back to Clonakilty with his girlfriend, and not by a bodyguard.'

'Are you going to tell her?'

'No, of course not. That would be much too dangerous for her, Aidan, and the rest of the family. No, t'is better if she doesn't know anythin'. There is no reason at all to confide in her. She has no direct part in it. As I told you months ago, t'is a matter that can only be resolved by me and you. No one else can or should be involved.'

Patrick stared sadly at his sister. On the exterior, Annie seemed unfazed by the events to follow, her face a mask of serenity and calmness. Though he did not wish to burden his sister with his own struggles, he felt an overwhelming sense of guilt. No one was closer to Thomas O'Callaghan than him. They had been almost inseparable since their teenage years, when they were cocky and fearless para-militants with IRA, yet Patrick was about to betray his brother in the most unspeakable way. As the final details of the plan took shape, and the day was almost upon them, Patrick looked for any excuse to stay away from his older brother.

As if reading his thoughts, Annie touched her brother's hand reassuringly, and said 'Patrick, we will get through this together, as we've always done. You must trust me on this – t'is the only way.'

3:45:00

She could hear the birds chirping outside and see the sky lighting up slowly from the east window. While the guest suite was large and comfortable, the sofa Maddie slept on all night was not designed for sleeping. It was lumpy, narrow, and the fabric was making her skin itchy. Aidan spent most of the night tossing and turning in an uneasy sleep, wrestling with the bed and covers, trying to find a comfortable position. *If this is how he sleeps every night,* Maddie thought, *no wonder he looks exhausted all the time.*

Maddie laid on the sofa for a few more minutes, thinking about the night before. Since arriving in Belfast, Aidan's behaviour had been wholly unpredictable and inconsistent with the man she had met in Mont-Tremblant. One moment he was detached and harsh, and the next he was trying to be loving and attentive. His attempt at lovemaking the night before was unexpected, and his withdrawal just as surprising. Maddie was sure the physical trauma from the accident had much to do with his attitude, but she also recognized that there was a lot going on in his mind that he had yet to share with her. She tried not to dwell on being rejected. It wasn't her, he'd told her, it was him.

He will need lots of time to recover, Maddie told herself, and then they could work on their relationship.

Maddie got up from the lumpy sofa, wrapped a light shawl over her shoulders, and headed toward the kitchen. It was dark and quiet in the huge, country-style space. Everyone in the house was sleeping or hidden from view, except for the lone bodyguard, clad in black, standing motionless outside the back door.

Maddie made herself a cup of coffee and sat down at the kitchen counter. There was an iPad sitting on a stand on the counter, and it was open. It did not require a password to access the internet. She logged into her email account to see that the boys had sent her a message with a photo attached, a selfie of them celebrating Thanksgiving with Dominique. Jean-Luc was smiling in the photo, Xavier was laughing, and Dominique had his eyes closed. They seemed to be having fun. The caption read, "We miss you!'

I miss you too, she thought sadly.

Next Maddie opened Safari, and instantly, the Belfast Journal popped up, with a glaring headline from the early morning edition: ANOTHER MAN FOUND DEAD. The image of her happy and safe family instantly evaporated.

Maddie forced herself to open the link and read about the discovery of another dead body, the third in as many months. He had been shot several times and left for dead on a major city street in central Belfast, around 2 am that morning. The man's name was being withheld, pending further investigation, but he was well-known to the police as a former soldier with the UVP and a member of the notorious Connolly criminal gang, operating in various parts of the island.

The news report went on to describe, in detail, the circumstances of the previous two killings. The first man, who was savagely beaten and killed in late June, was also a member of the Connolly gang, and closely associated with the kingpin himself, John Connolly. The second man found dead was known to police as a senior member of the O'Callaghan empire, and closely linked to the 'godfather', Thomas O'Callaghan. The journalist covering the story called the string of murders vendetta killings, between two rival, powerful gangs. The news report alluded to other suspicious accidents under investigation that might be linked to the two gangs, but no further details or names were provided. Maddie opened another link to the news story and read an analysis on the recent gang-style murders. The journalist, a well known investigative reporter, discussed the consequences of these seemingly isolated gang attacks and the growing fear that they could dismantle the current peace agreement and escalate into another era of terrorism between 'the Prods and the Taigs' if not brought under some control.

Maddie felt queasy reading the news. The O'Callaghans were named in several reports, and she was sitting in the kitchen of the notorious family. The last murder happened early that morning, shortly after she had participated in a dinner party with one or both of the conspirators. Thomas and Patrick were in the throes of orchestrating this macabre undertaking, she realized, while the family was celebrating her and Aidan's engagement. No amount of anticipation or planning could have prepared her for this very real and present danger. It was disturbing, and given Aidan's fragile state, she decided not to share this with Aidan. It would likely trigger an ugly episode with his brother, worsen Aidan's already vulnerable physical condition, or force her to leave. Maddie couldn't predict what Aidan would do if he knew what had recently happened. No, she thought, the solution to their problem was to get away from this house of horrors as soon as possible and find refuge in the south, in Clonakilty. Maddie was powerless to do anything but wait patiently for Annie to follow through on her promise to take care of everything.

*****

Later that morning, after Maddie saw Aidan off to his physio appointment, she left for the guest house on Eglantine Road to retrieve her belongings, much against Aidan's wishes. He had insisted she wait until later in the day so he could accompany her, as he said it was too dangerous for her to venture out alone. Maddie dismissed Aidan's fears as overprotective and promptly asked one of the drivers to take her. *This will only take a few minutes,* Maddie thought, plenty of time to organize what little she had brought before Aidan's return.

Maddie pulled out her key to unlock the front door of the guest house, but it was already open. She stepped into the foyer and called for Mrs. Kelley, but there was no response. Although the house was quiet and there were no other guests registered, Maddie could hear the sound of crackling wood coming from the library.

She walked into the cozy room to find the fireplace aglow and Thomas' imposing frame standing by the bookcase, admiring Mrs. Kelley's extensive library. Maddie froze on the spot.

He turned to look at her.

'Hello, Maddie, 'tis a lovely room...so much to read and so little time. Why don't you sit down?' Thomas asked quietly.

Maddie ignored his request. 'Where is Mrs. Kelley?' Aidan's prophetic caution the day before about never being alone with his brother was ringing in her ears.

'I sent her out on an errand...she'll be back later in the afternoon,' Thomas replied in a cryptic voice as he pointed to the loveseat.

Maddie sat down as instructed. Thomas sat directly in front of her, in the chair next to the fireplace. This was a repeat of a few nights earlier, when Aidan was sitting in the exact spot. She was struck, once again, by the brothers' physical resemblance, in spite of the almost ten-year age gap. Thomas was even wearing the same coat that Aidan had worn.

'Thomas, why are you here and what do you want?' Maddie asked, without waiting for Thomas to initiate the conversation. Maddie was not only uncomfortable about being alone in the same room as Thomas, the man deeply frightened her. His physical size was intimidating. He had the biggest hands she had ever seen, hands that could easily crush anything, including the delicate throat of a woman. The news headline of the morning flashed in her racing mind, reminding her that Thomas O'Callaghan was a most dangerous and powerful man, who could orchestrate the murder of a rival while enjoying a good meal and fine wine with his family. In spite of her physical strength and size, Maddie was no match for his imposing frame. It would be easy for him to pin her down on the floor and take what he wanted.

'I'm here to chat with you a bit…you're a lovely lookin' woman. Maddie. I can see why my brother is so smitten by you. And to tink, you've come all this way to be with a man who you do not know at all.'

'What are you talking about, Thomas?' Maddie said, while surreptitiously glancing around the room, looking for a weapon or heavy item she could use to defend herself if it came to that. She looked at the window, but it was closed and locked. There was no way out of this room except through the French doors.

'You're not the first woman to follow Aidan home. It's happened before, ya know. Ya were just another brief romantic interlude – something to pass the time away. He has done whatever and whenever he wanted, wit no care about the consequences of his actions. I've been his brother for forty-four years. I know him very well.'

In spite of her fear, Maddie was not prepared to idly sit and listen to the twisted facts from a hypocrite like Thomas O'Callaghan. 'Get your facts right, Thomas. This sounds more like you than Aidan. You don't know your brother at all. You've been absent from his life for twenty-five years.' Maddie replied defiantly.

Thomas was not expecting Maddie to challenge him, nor was he used to defiance, especially from a woman. He stood up abruptly and placed himself directly in front of Maddie, his pants skimming her legs.

'Well, he's not the man he was in Canada, it would seem. He's damaged. Your naïve if you tink he will suddenly bounce back to normal. You're wasting your time with him,' Thomas replied, looking down at Maddie with glacial blue eyes, his gaze fixated on her ample breasts.

'I am not naïve, Thomas, and I am not wasting my time. I love him, and I will help him recover,' Maddie replied, trying to sound confident and in control. The truth was that she had never been in a situation where she felt as sexually vulnerable as she did at that moment. The man was truly a terrifying presence, standing inches from her body, his immense size blocking out the light from the window.

Thomas inched forward, his intentions now perfectly clear. Maddie frantically tried to remember what she had read about defending yourself against a sexual assault. Rape was about power, she remembered, it wasn't about sex.

Before she had time to think about her next move, Thomas grabbed her arms and pulled her up from the love seat with ease, like a rag doll, and pressed himself against her. Maddie's body went rigid with fear. She could smell the distinctive odor of whisky on his breath. He leaned down as if to kiss her, but instead he whispered in her ear. 'They say Aidan and I look alike…do we feel alike, pet?' To her horror, Maddie felt a bulge against her stomach. She tried pushing him away, but he held her firmly by the arms. She felt a nauseating sickness in her stomach and wished she could throw up all over him. Thomas began stroking Maddie's breasts, pushing harder against her, kissing her neck. She struggled to free herself, lifting a knee to kick in the groin, but he was practically squeezing the life out her.

Moments earlier, Aidan had walked silently into the house, and stood at the French doors, watching his brother Thomas grab and fondle his fiancée. For the second time in his life, he exploded with uncontrollable, seething anger against his older brother. He took two steps into the room and struck Thomas on the head with the end of the walking stick. The force of the blow split the wooden shaft in two pieces.

'You disgusting bastard!' Aidan shouted at Thomas, his face red and contorted with madness. The blow caught Thomas by surprise and he fell back into the chair, holding his bleeding head. Aidan went to swing the broken cane again, but Maddie grabbed his hand and shouted

'Stop, Aidan. Stop. Don't do this. It doesn't solve anything... as you can see I'm fine. I'm...really okay...nothing happened.'

Aidan turned toward the redhead, looking confused. He thought he was back in his old house off the Falls Road, and he and Thomas were fighting, but didn't recognize the room or the woman standing next to him. Maddie carefully but firmly took away the broken cane that was he was clutching tightly in his hand.

'What is going on here,' Mrs. Kelley said, appearing suddenly in the hallway. 'Maddie, do you want me to call the police?'

Mrs. Kelley's arrival back at the house at that moment was fortuitous. Her presence broke the tension.

'It's fine, Mrs. Kelley...we are just having a heated discussion. No need to call the police. Would you mind making us some tea?' Without waiting for a response, Maddie closed the French doors to the reading room.

Aidan regained some composure and spoke to his brother, who was still sitting on the chair, rubbing his blood-soaked head. 'When are yeh going to stop ruining my life? How many times have yeh destroyed the people I love, just because you can't find any happiness in your sad, miserable life, doesn't mean the rest of us have to suffer with yeh?' Aidan was now shouting loudly. 'Leave us alone, Thomas, or next time I will kill you with my bare hands. You know I am perfectly capable of it. Now get out of here, before the next time is now.'

Thomas cowered in the chair, caught off guard by his brother's appearance. The huge, almost indestructible man, who was larger and 30 pounds heavier than Aidan, who had spent decades as a commander with the IRA, seemed to be genuinely afraid of his younger sibling. Aidan's verbal warning was enough. Thomas stood up and walked out the front door without saying a word. They could hear the sound of screeching tires peeling away down the street, away from the Guest House.

Maddie took Aidan's arm and guided him to the loveseat, encouraging him to sit down. He was completely shaken, nodding his head back and forth and mumbling to himself.

'Aidan, it's over now. Everything is fine. Thank you for coming.'

Aidan glanced at his damaged cane, and then at his fiancée's concerned face. It took a few more minutes for him to breathe normally and shed the strain on his face.

'Oh dear, the cane is damaged…' he said, studying the snake-wood shaft of the antique walking stick. The rubber end of the cane was missing, and the wood shaft was spilt down the middle. 'Thomas' head is so bloody hard, I only just split the wood. If it had been anyone else, the cane would have been in several pieces. He's a glorified ejit, he is.'

It was reassuring to hear Aidan's dry sense of humor. It was never far from his mind even under the most stressful circumstances.

'It's just the wood part that's broken…the beautiful silver handle is still intact. I am sure you can have the shaft replaced,' Maddie replied.

'I imagine so…though perhaps this is a sign that I should be walking on my own. What do you think?' Aidan replied, his voice sounding more normal.

'Maybe it is. Where did you get it? It's quite unusual. I've never seen a walking stick with such an ornate handle. Is it old?' she asked, using a calm and soothing voice to reassure him that the incident with Thomas was now behind them.

'Patrick gave it to me. T'is from the late 1800's. You remember that Annie has an antiquities business, straight up, with a gallery and all? At least that's what Annie told me. Patrick gave me the 'walking stick' in the hospital. I don't think he knew about the secret compartment when he gave it to me.'

'A secret compartment?' Maddie asked.

'Look, I will show you.' Aidan unscrewed the silver engraved handle to show Maddie that the shaft of the handle was hollow, though now the bottom end of the wood stick was split in two. 'In the day, they used to put maps in here when they went out hiking, to keep them dry and such. It's quite ingenious, don't you think?'

'Here you go, I've brought some tea,' Mrs. Kelley said as she walked into the reading room with a large tray filled with numerous teacups, a teapot, and cookies.

'Thank you so much, Mrs. Kelley…I do apologize for the commotion a few minutes ago…'

'No need to explain, dear. I'm just glad I came back to get my umbrella.'

'Mrs. Kelley, this is Aidan... a good friend.'

'Pleased to meet you. Now that everything is under control, I must go!'

The couple sat in Mrs. Kelly's fine library for the entire afternoon. The incident with Thomas had had one obvious benefit. Whatever anger Aidan had been feeling toward his older brother, he had successfully purged, at least temporarily. Away from the O'Callaghan compound, the oppressive and constant shadowing of Thomas' platoon of bodyguards, the endless stream of people coming and going, the prison-like atmosphere, Aidan was as relaxed that afternoon as he had been in Mt-Tremblant.

'Aidan, can I ask an impertinent question?' Maddie asked, her head leaning comfortably against his shoulder.

'There is no such thing as impertinence from yeh,' Aidan replied.

'Thomas is at least 30 pounds heavier and right now, a good deal more fit than you…yet when you told him you would kill him with your bare hands, he seemed genuinely terrified. Why is that?'

Aidan flinched at the mention of his brother, and Maddie instantly regretted her question. 'I am sorry…I should not have brought it up.'

'Do not apologize. T'is a fair question, and yeh have a right to know if you are going to be my wife someday,' he said, smiling, showing his slightly crooked tooth, which seemed a little more pronounced since the accident. 'T'is not something I am proud of, but I once beat Thomas to an inch of his life. He knows full well what I am capable of, and he's reminded of it every day, when he combs that ridiculous silver head of hair.'

'Are you going to tell me what happened?' Maddie pressed.

'If you really want to know, though I am not proud of what I did. It happened after my father died. Thomas came by the house, trying to recruit me for his platoon of imbeciles.'

'Annie told me about that…'

'Did she tell you we fought?'

'No, she told me you refused to join the IRA. She said you had words and Thomas left. You never saw him after that.'

'T'is not exactly the entire story. You should know that I have a temper once in while, and on this particular occasion, I couldn't control it. I was so enraged by Thomas' cynical recruitment strategy I could not believe even he would stoop that low…using Da's death as a way to galvanize the family to commit acts of terrorism! It was calculating and hypocritical, because Thomas didn't care one bit about his father. And it was because of Thomas' involvement in the IRA that Da died. As far as I'm concerned, Thomas killed his own Da, even if he didn't pull the trigger. That day, I let him have it. I pounded the shite out of him until he couldn't open his eyes. I was wearing a school ring, and it took twenty-five stitches to close the gash on his head. My brother is the embodiment of pure evil.'

'Sometimes I wish I had killed him that day,' Aidan said with difficulty, starring at the fire and not at Maddie, 'but if I had, we wouldn't be sitting here, now would we?'

'No, we wouldn't Aidan. I would likely never have met you,' Maddie responded.

The damaged man with the broken cane didn't have an answer to that remark.

'Aidan, are you aware that you and your family have a very serious family flaw?' Maddie asked, moving the conversation away from murder and violence.

'I am sure we have many. Which one are you referring to?'

'You all have a nasty habit of leaving out extremely pertinent and essential information about yourselves and your history!'

'T'is true enough…you, of all people, should know!' Aidan replied, laughing and thinking about how little personal information he had given Maddie when they first met. 'To be fair, I don't think it's an O'Callaghan flaw. T'is more of an Irish trait…the whole truth comes out eventually, though,' Aidan added. 'Now I have a serious question for yeh. Yeh do not have to answer if yeh are not comfortable,' Aidan asked Maddie.

'Ask me. I have no secrets, none whatsoever.'

'What would you have done if I had not shown up when I did?'

'That's a good question. Thomas is scary and intimidating, and he really frightens me. I've never met a man who scares me as much as Thomas, though I don't think he would have gotten much further,' Maddie replied.

'Why?' Aidan asked, wondering how Maddie could have slipped away from his brother's clutches without a fight.

'I was prepared to hit Thomas on the head…with this…' Maddie put her hand under the loveseat and pulled out a large, heavy crystal ashtray.

'Where in God's name did yeh get an ashtray…?' Aidan asked.

'I didn't…someone else put it here. I was lucky enough to see it when I walked in the other night. It's always been there. Maybe Mrs. Kelley is a closet smoker…?'

'Well, well…resourceful as ever. I am relieved, though,' Aidan said, shaking his head and chuckling.

'It feels good to laugh again, doesn't it, Aidan…?' Maddie said, her checks aching from smiling.

'Indeed, it does. I didn't properly tell yeh, but I am truly thankful that yeh didn't give up looking for me. God knows I didn't make it easy,' Aidan said, caressing her face. 'You know, you're not exactly the same woman I met in Mont-Tremblant. You've lost something.'

'What did I lose, besides you?' Maddie asked.

'You've lost some of your tentativeness. You're more confident now, more determined to take control of the life you want. T'is a good loss, yeh understand, and I am happy to see this change.'

'You have had a lot more to do with that than you realize,' Maddie replied,

The afternoon was slipping away. They would have to go back soon to the O'Callaghan compound and remain confined indefinitely. They had had a brief respite from the tension and uncertainty at Stanley Park, and now they had no choice but to return.

'Aidan, do you remember the conversation we had just before we left Mont-Tremblant?' Maddie asked. 'You told me you were not content to stay safely at home. You asked me if I was prepared to have a 'wee' bit of adventure, embrace uncertainty and an unpredictable future. So far, you've been true to your word.'

Aidan took hold of Maddie and held her tight, whispering, 'T'is is not the kind of adventure I had in mind when I said that. I was thinkin' of less dangerous stuff, like backpacking and hiking.'

'Me too, but you can't change your past. You can only go forward, and we will do that together, regardless of the uncertainty. Anyway, things will improve. Annie promised me she would take care of everything so we could leave Belfast.'

Aidan pushed Maddie gently away, shaking his head.

'Annie? I doubt that. She has little control over the affairs of the family, and especially Thomas. She is just as much of a victim of his odious behaviour as we are. She can do nothing to help us, I am sad to say.'

Maddie did not respond to Aidan's comment about his sister. She held a different view of the composed and quiet woman who spent her days tending to her mother and her antique business. Though Maddie did not have hard evidence or proof, she felt that Annie was much more involved in the family's affairs than Aidan realized, and she was masterfully hiding her true nature, even from her twin brother. Maddie was quite confident that if Annie said she was going to resolve the family's problems, she would, by whatever means suited her.

Reluctantly, the pair left the sanctuary of Mrs. Kelley's guest house late in the afternoon and headed back to uncertainty, under the ever-present protection of two bodyguards who had been waiting outside in the cold all day.

4:00:00

As soon as Maddie and the chauffeur left for the guest house, Annie also left the confines of the O'Callaghan compound and drove alone to the Belfast Art and Antiquities Gallery. The Gallery was located two miles from the estate, in a refurbished and trendy area of the city that featured several exclusive high-end boutiques, numerous art galleries, antique shops, and sophisticated restaurants.

It was still early in the day. The Gallery would not open until 11 am, but Annie was expecting a visitor. She punched in the code to the digital alarm system, unlocked the heavy steel door, and walked into the grand space. Each time she opened the door to the Gallery, she smiled as she breathed in the distinctive smell of mud, old paper, rotting wood, varnish, and paint. For Patrick, this was the smell of money, but for Annie, it was the realization of a long-term goal of corporate and community respectability.

Six years earlier, Patrick O'Callaghan, along with his silent partner and sister Annie, began searching for a new family business venture that would be as financially lucrative as the cannabis and cocaine trade that had been the families' primary source of income for two decades, but with less risk.

In recent years, the drug trade had become increasingly unpredictable. International and local law enforcement agencies were doing a better job at seizing drug shipments and catching drug dealers and distributors. It was a constant game of shifting strategies and finding new and creative ways to get the drug haul on the street. Patrick and Annie had become weary from the constant stress of managing the family's drug conglomerate and the pressures from the police and other layers of government, trying to outfox them at every turn. Though they had never been prosecuted for drug trafficking, they were under constant surveillance. They were well known to the authorities, and it was only a matter of time before the criminal justice system would have enough concrete evidence to finally catch and prosecute the top members of the elusive and unscrupulous O'Callaghan business empire.

Gaining hard evidence and seizing the illegal goods was one tactic the police could use to catch them, but it was not nearly as effective as following the money trail. The drug trade was by and large a cash business, and for decades it was relatively easy to hide their enormous profits, usually by depositing the cash offshore private bank accounts and murky quasi-legitimate investment schemes. At one time, you could buy a house or a yacht using cash, but those types of cash deals were now nearly impossible to transact.

In recent years, governments and international bodies around the globe were enacting and enforcing new anti-money laundering legislation to combat the problem of not only the drug trade, but terrorist financing. The UK was at the forefront of these new laws, increasing their depth and reach to disrupt money-laundering activities. Young tax auditors and investigators using the latest technological platforms were monitoring all types of financial transactions, and they were doing a very good job of shutting down the various loopholes and cash conduits that criminal gangs were using to evade scrutiny. With the rise of national and international terrorism, the UK government was about to enact new, sweeping powers to investigate unexplained wealth.

As the financial manager of the families' vast wealth, it was becoming enormously complicated and difficult for Patrick to launder the huge flow of cash pouring in on a weekly basis. After years in the drug trade, it was time to reinvent the family's business activities and seek alternatives to ensure their continued wealth. A timely call from one of Patrick's university friends initiated the transformation from the distribution of illicit drugs to legitimate antiquities traders, a hugely profitable business with a strong global demand.

In the mid 1980's, Patrick was sent to Boston University to study, at the expense of the IRA. He had demonstrated his ability with numbers and financial matters in the early years of his involvement, and the organization thought it prudent to educate one of their own and prep him as a future 'business leader' within the Army.

While attending Boston University, Patrick met Amir, an international student from Egypt majoring in Archeology Studies. They became good friends and eventually roommates, and they stayed in touch long after their courses ended. On the surface, they seemed like an oddly mismatched pair: two young men from different countries and cultures, yet they had much in common. Amir was smart, unscrupulous at times, and enjoyed partying as much as Patrick. He was not the typical speckled archeologist living at remote digs, sweating it out in the hot desert sun. Amir was more like Indiana Jones than Professor Amir. He had an appetite for high risk adventures, alcohol, and women, which matched Patrick's interests perfectly.

At the start of the sub-prime mortgage fiasco in the U.S, Amir found himself unemployed, divorced and severely in debt. He reached out to Patrick for financial help, but instead of lending money to his impoverished friend, Patrick struck a business deal. He would privately fund Amir's archeology research and digs, in various parts of North Africa, in exchange for a small cut of the profits. Amir promised they could make money by selling their finds to wealthy collectors and museums.

The meticulous and well-financed archeological digs did not yield the expected results. The competition from 'illicit' digs and looters was making it difficult for Amir to compete. Frustrated with the slow progress of the business and the lack of profitability, Amir began to study how his competitors were exploiting the system. He soon learned the ins and outs of a corrupt system.

Amir thought he could do better, given his considerable expertise and the O'Callaghans money. He devised a new process that would be far more profitable than both his 'legal' digs and put his competitors out of business. Amir's strong, charismatic personality swayed Patrick and Annie, and they invested heavily in the scheme. The new venture began modestly, and the funding partners were at the mercy of one man but it paid off handsomely. Over a short period of time, the well-executed digs became extremely lucrative, allowing Amir to capture a virtual monopoly in selected areas of North Africa. The competition could not keep pace with Amir's slick methods for extricating the buried antiquities and swiftly moving them out of the country.

*****

While Patrick knew nothing about artifacts and antiquities, Annie embraced the new venture with enthusiasm by opening up the Belfast Art and Antiquities Gallery, a vast museum-quality space large enough to house many of their 'legitimate' acquisitions. By 2013, Annie had expanded the gallery to include paintings and other works of art. The art and antiquities business was so profitable, it made almost as much money as drug trafficking, and it was all deemed 'legal', though the National Crime Agency was constantly lurking about, looking for any loophole or evidence of criminality. For the first time in their adult lives, the O'Callaghans started paying taxes, something Thomas complained about constantly. The Catholic family, formerly from the slums of North Belfast, were now rich, powerful, and on the cusp of corporate respectability and community inclusion. Thomas seemed more content with the new business venture, letting his younger brother assume control, oblivious to Annie's involvement as one of the caretakers of the scheme. The O'Callaghans had settled into a life of comfort when Thomas' old adversary, John Connolly, decided it was his time to get re-acquainted after a prolonged silence, by striking a decisive blow that not only shattered the family's security, but had the potential to plunge an entire city back to the dark days of fear and senseless violence.

*****

Annie heard the soft knock at the back of the Gallery. She opened the door a fraction to see Constable Eammon MacDonald standing in the pouring rain, his coat collar pulled up high and his hat sitting low in an effort to keep the rain and wind at bay, without much success.

'T'is not an inconspicuous place to meet, Annie,' Constable MacDonald remarked, when Annie let the harried man in.

'Lurking in the dark is hardly my style, Eammon. You've know me long enough to know that. I've always operated in the open,' replied Annie, as she escorted the constable into the large semi-lit Gallery.

Eammon had never been in the Gallery before, though he knew its reputation as one of the finest in the United Kingdom. Collectors from all over Europe and North America came to Belfast specifically to buy selected pieces from Annie O'Brian. Eammon wasn't much into art and antiquities, and did not know the difference between a Pollack and a Picasso, but his eyes took in the large paintings on the wall and the numerous artifacts resting on the museum quality display cabinets of the grand space. The Gallery looked exactly like a modern museum, and Eammon was impressed. He could hardly believe his one-time lover and friend of twenty-two years was the mastermind behind this space. But then, he reminded himself often, this was Annie, *and there wasn't anything she couldn't do.*

'Let's get to the point, shall we, Eammon?' Annie said, snapping her guest back to reality and the business at hand.

'Go on then, I'm listening.'

'Everything is in place,' Annie explained, 'everyone has their instructions. By this time next week, the feud will finally be over and we can all go back to our safe and quiet lives. At least I hope so...'

'And you don't require my assistance or the assistance of the...?' Eammon's voice trailed off.

'Not directly. Me and my brother will handle John Connolly and Thomas, and your man is to follow Aidan to Dublin and then on to Clonakilty, as instructed, to ensure his safety and the safety of his fiancée.'

'His fiancée?'

'Her name is Maddie. She's Canadian. It's a long story, but yes, she will soon be part of the family.'

'Does this change anything?'

'Nothing at all, except that Aidan will not be alone.'

Eammon nodded in agreement.

'And let's be straight on this all-important detail. I have your word that once the plan is enacted, all current investigations into the O'Callaghan corporation and global business entities are to cease, including the tax audits?'

'I have assurances from all levels of government involved that you will be left alone. You have my word, Annie,' Eammon replied confidently.

Annie studied Constable MacDonald carefully. While she still cared a great deal for Eammon, she knew he would be powerless to protect her and her family in case the government had a change of heart or if the plan went terribly wrong. She and Patrick had taken steps to ensure that all traces of their past life disappeared or were buried in a Belfast cemetery. It was a long and nasty business to tie up the loose ends. This one last mission would close the book on their past, at least as far as the government and police were concerned.

'Are you sure you want to go through with this Annie? T'is your brother we are talking about – your own flesh and blood. There are other, less extreme ways to end this feud,' Eammon suggested.

'Thomas O'Callaghan and John Connolly,' Annie continued to say, without any emotion, 'will never stop hating each other. Their feud serves no purpose than to fuel each other's hatred. The people of this city are getting anxious. The murders are escalating, and while the press and the politicians are trying to reassure its citizens by saying these isolated incidents were gang-related, there is an undercurrent of fear. You know it, Eammon. The longer the feud lasts, the more anxious everyone gets. They must be stopped, or everyone in this city will begin to suffer. No, there is no other way.' Annie stopped talking for a moment, and finally added, 'Thomas stopped being my 'brother' a long time ago. He has hurt too many members of this family, especially Aidan, who has been victimised by him far too many times. No, I will take care of this problem, and I will do it on my terms.'

Eammon said nothing. He knew through a lifetime of experience he shared with the one-time IRA militant that there was no point in trying to dissuade Annie or change her mind.

4:15:00

Maddie and Aidan made every effort to stay away from Thomas after the incident at the Guest House. He too, uncharacteristically, did not spend too much time at the house, either because he feared that Aidan would come after him or because he was immersed in the chaos that had ensued after the recent murder of the UVP militant. Since the grisly discovery of the body, the vehicle traffic on Malone Park increased, and police cars could be seen outside the closed gates patrolling the street hourly.

The house became a secure fortress. The couple were not permitted to leave the premises without two bodyguards at all times. Early in the school year, Annie's two pre-teen girls were sent to a private boarding school somewhere in the United Kingdom, their whereabouts a secret to everyone except their mother. She dared not risk travelling to see them, nor could they visit her, even during the regular two-week school break in October. The tension in the house was palatable.

Maddie wanted to escape the oppressive atmosphere, at least for an hour a day, and go for a run. This, Thomas allowed, on condition that she was accompanied by one of the guards. While the guard was powerfully built, and spent hours in the gym when he wasn't guarding the O'Callaghans, he was not a runner, nor was he fit for endurance training. He had a great deal of trouble keeping up with Maddie, and she had to stop and walk several times during her daily jog so the man could catch his breath. If someone did attempt to hurt or kidnap Maddie, the guard would have been useless for protection.

In spite of the gloomy atmosphere, the bright spot was Aidan's meteoric physical recovery. He shed his cane and began taking long walks on the property, going around and around the entire perimeter of the 1.5-acre estate. At first, his pace was slow and he tired easily, but after only a few tries, he began to walk with more assuredness, picking up the tempo. He was a long way from running form – in fact, the physio therapist and doctors doubted whether Aidan would ever be able to resume running – but he made daily progress with walking. Maddie sometimes joined him outside, working on her run intervals and speed while Aidan walked. His appetite for food corresponded to his increased physical activity. He paid more attention to what he was eating, and so he could regain the weight he lost following the accident. Maddie made him protein shakes a couple of times a day, which he drank willingly. Aidan's physio therapist suggested they go swimming at the local public pool, but Thomas would not allow the couple to venture out in public.

Annie would sometimes sit by the large reading room window and watch the couple doing their exercises. She loved her brother fiercely and was happy to see that he was physically improving, thanks to the tall redhead from Canada who showed up uninvited. Annie could easily understand why Aidan adored the woman. She was gentle but firm with her brother, coaxing him to do more, making him smile, and she was always touching him affectionately. Maddie's presence in the house was beneficial in helping the family cope better with Aidan's uncharacteristic volatility. Since the accident, his personality had changed, and he was often unpredictable and moody around Annie and Sheila.

While Annie watched the couple's loving relationship take shape, Maddie was quietly struggling, worried about Aidan's mental health and his capacity to return to a normal life after the trauma of the car bomb. Like the rest of the family, she, too, saw a side to Aidan that was profoundly disturbing at times, and completely out of character from the man she met in Mont-Tremblant. He brooded around the house, silent and withdrawn. He would sometimes sit for hours, not uttering a word. Late at night, when sleep eluded him, he would skulk about, on constant alert, hypervigilant as if waiting for someone to break down their bedroom door. Maddie tried to get Aidan to take a sleeping pill, insisting that a good night's sleep would hasten his physical recovery, but he flatly refused. His stubbornness was an unfamiliar trait, and Maddie found it hard to reconcile this new attitude with the former easy-going Irishman. He was so different and alien to her at times, she often felt like she was his personal support worker and not his fiancée.

In the big house and constantly surrounded by hordes of people coming and going, intimacy between the couple was strained. Aidan was either unwilling or incapable of letting down his emotional guard in public. He would hug his fiancée and kiss her occasionally, but he would not, or could not, show real affection. Privately, he was no better. He changed his clothes in the privacy of the bathroom and slept in the big bed by himself. He told Maddie he cared about her, but he never said he loved her. It was a strange and unexpected twist in their relationship. Aidan appeared to want her and he made sure she was never far from his side, especially when Thomas was in the house. He worried like an overprotective father the minute she stepped out for a run, yet he treated her coolly when they were alone. This was more challenging than dealing with Aidan's outbursts and aggressive behavior. Maddie craved physically intimacy. She could barely keep her hands off of him, touching him often. She wanted nothing more than to lie next to him at night and feel his body heat. Yet, she dared not allow herself to reach out to him provocatively or sexually. The experience of their first night together alone in the large suite was a constant reminder that Aidan was far from recovered. When he was ready, Maddie told herself, he would reach for her.

Though she was discouraged with state of their relationship, Maddie tried to remain optimistic about their future, and waited patiently for Annie to be true to her word and let the couple leave Belfast to return to Clonakilty.

Late one night, as Aidan slept fitfully, Maddie left the bedroom suite and headed down to the kitchen to get a glass of ice water. Like Aidan, she was also suffering from sleep deprivation, and spent most nights waking every twenty minutes to the sound of Aidan's groans and movements. Halfway down the wide stair case, Maddie could hear Annie talking to someone in the kitchen, and she stopped to listen.

'You know it has to be done, Patrick. We've talked about this for months, we've discussed every possible option, every possible scenario and angle. We've no choice now.'

'I know, Annie. It doesn't make the decision any easier. He's our brother.'

'He has to go, once and for all,' Annie replied to Patrick.

Maddie's first thought on hearing this disturbing news was that the sister and brother were talking about Aidan. She froze. The realization that Annie, Aidan's beloved twin sister, was working against them, instead of helping them to escape, was impossible to fathom.

The two people in the kitchen stopped talking. Someone was opening a bottle of wine. A cabinet door was opened and closed, and someone lit a cigarette.

'Everything is in place, then, I take it?' Patrick asked.

'Yes, I met with MacDonald at the Gallery a few days ago and apprised him of the final details. He is cooperating, that I am sure, and letting us resolve the problem of Thomas and John Connolly,' Annie replied, inhaling deeply on her cigarette.

Maddie momentarily forgot where she was and also breathed deeply, relieved to hear that Annie and Patrick were talking about Thomas – not Aidan. Still, she wished she had not ventured downstairs and heard this telling piece of news. Now she was implicated, even if indirectly, into whatever was being planned for Thomas.

'I will keep working as normal until I get the signal. When do you think that will happen?' Patrick asked.

'Very soon – three days at the most.'

Maddie waited on the stairs for a long time without moving, until she finally heard the back-door close. She waited another few minutes before making her way into the kitchen. Annie was seated in her usual spot, on a stool at the large island counter, drinking a glass of red wine. She looked particularly haggard and a little drunk at this hour. Her thin face was gaunt, and the hollowness of her high cheekbones were accentuated under the glare of the kitchen lights.

'I know you were listening to our conversation Maddie,' Annie said without looking up, 'unintentionally, of course,' she added sarcastically.

'I only heard the last few sentences, Annie,' Maddie answered, taking a seat at the counter next to her.

Annie was skeptical, but remained silent.

Throughout the entire planning process, Annie had judiciously kept all the specific details to herself. She shared only what was essential to the success of the plan and as it related to both Patrick and Eammon. It was imperative to shield everyone from the facts, should something go wrong. There was some risk involved, but Annie was willing to assume all of it to permanently resolve the family's internal and external problems, and to ensure that her native country and home city would remain peaceful. Annie did not want to go to jail, but in the unlikely event that she was caught and prosecuted for what she was about to do, she had made arrangements for the long-term care of both her mother and daughters.

The two women sat in the silent kitchen, each one engrossed in their own thoughts. After what she had heard minutes before, Maddie was convinced of Annie's split personality. She had also watched the wily Irish woman carefully for an entire week. In the presence of her brother Thomas, Annie was deferential, submissive, and quiet. Around Maddie and Aidan, Annie was strong-willed, outspoken, and self-assured. Maddie believed that Aidan's twin sister was far more implicated in the family's nefarious business activities than she let on, and certainly more involved than Aidan realized. Maddie had felt something sinister brewing since she arrived, and it was not emanating from Thomas now, but from his unsuspected sister. It was time she boldly asked her future sister-in-law what was really going on.

'Annie, you are much more involved in the 'family business' than Aidan or anyone else realizes.'

Annie turned and stared at Maddie, her cool green eyes showing no emotion.

'Indeed, I am,' she finally answered. 'You're very observant, Maddie.'

'I don't have much else to do here, Annie, but watch and wait. A week ago, you said you were working on a plan. I sense that this plan is about to start. Can you tell me what's going on, and how this will impact both Aidan and myself?'

Annie took a small sip of her red wine before she continued. She thought about Aidan's fiancée and how fortunate the woman was not to have grown up in Belfast during the Troubles. She should have escaped to Canada, Annie thought, when she had the chance. Then she would not be sitting in this kitchen, plotting the end of the O'Callaghan empire.

'All you need to know is that in a few days, you and Aidan will be free to leave Belfast and return to your safe and secure life in Clonakilty. Aidan will never be bothered again by the consequences of Thomas's hatred.'

Maddie wanted to press her for more details.

'Annie, how did you get involved in all of this? You told me that during the Troubles, you looked after your mother. I thought you stayed away from the fighting.'

'T'is true, I looked after my mother when Aidan left. But there is more to the story.'

Maddie shook her head in exasperation. 'It seems there is always more to the O'Callaghans' story. Honestly, you folks have trouble telling the truth in one sitting. Why don't you confide in me now and tell me the unedited version?'

'T'is not a pleasant story, Maddie, but if you must know, I will tell you.' Annie continued, taking a sip of her wine. 'But you canna ever tell Aidan what you know. He's suffered enough. Do you understand? Do I have your word on this?' Annie said in a sharp voice.

'You do.'

'Well, then, if you must know, during the Troubles I belonged to Cumman Nam'Ban, the exclusive women's arm of the IRA. T'is not something that is common knowledge, nor am I particularly proud of that part of my life. But there it is.'

'What did you do for them – the Cumaan na'Ban?' Maddie asked, curious to find out how a slight woman like Annie was involved with the notorious para-militants. She certainly did not look like a woman who could hold or even handle a gun.

'I can see you what you're thinkin'. I do not look big enough to do anythin', but I can assure you, I was well trained. I became a bomb expert-an IRA Bomb Girl. There were many of us back in the day, pretty and innocent women who could walk anywhere around Belfast, often pushing strollers and holding fake babies to our breasts, all the time watching, spyin', reportin' back, and plantin' bombs. Sometimes big bombs that caused many deaths. Many women got caught and were jailed, and some women died in battle. I was one of the lucky ones, I guess; I was never caught. Had a few close calls, but I never spent time in jail.'

This was why Annie seemed so calm all week, Maddie thought. She was used to this type of stress.

'Don't judge me too harshly, Maddie. I grew up in the heartbeat of the Troubles, something you could never possibly image. I am not proud of what I did and who I hurt or killed, and I don't go around boasting about my involvement in the IRA like Thomas. Him, my mother, and Aidan don't know about my past, and I want to keep it that way.'

'How did you manage to stay under everyone's radar?' Maddie asked.

'That's an interesting way to put it, but yes, I stayed under the radar. T'was not as difficult as you think,' Annie continued, shaking her head. 'I went by an alias. I was disguised most of the time: wigs, clothes, that sort of thing. And you rightly pointed out that I don't look like a terrorist. This suited me just fine. I wanted to protect my mother. She had been through so much by then, I couldn't and wouldn't tell her the truth. And Thomas? Well, he was much too self-absorbed to pay attention to his quiet and devoted younger sister, and he was high up in the ranks, so he had little to do with the operations side. He and the leaders would plot and plan the attacks. We carried them out. Like a regular army.'

She stopped talking for an instant, collecting her thoughts. 'But that was then, and this is now. I've tried to bury that part of my life. I've had ten years of relative peace and calm, raising my girls, opening an antique and art gallery, becoming a respectable and contributing member of a growing and affluent 'peaceful' city. Belfast has undergone a huge change since the new millennium. We are enjoying life the way most people do, without the constant threat that someone will blow up your car or kill your children. All was well for us until four months ago, when our past actions came back to haunt us in the most painful way.'

'Aidan's accident?'

'T'was no accident, as I told you. Since then it has been tit for tat, and it will never end as long as two men, whose hatred of one another has no limits, are allowed to ruin our lives. I want my kids to grow up normally. I want you and Aidan to get married and live normally. That's all I want, and I've spent months trying to find a reasonable solution to the problem. Time is running out for me and my family. The only way to fix the problem, is to get rid of the problem.'

'Thomas? And John Connolly?'

'I will say no more. The less you know, the better. In forty-eight hours, you will be in a car and driving to Clonakilty with Aidan. You will have no connection to the events that are to follow. You will hear about it on the news feeds. More importantly, Aidan is not to know any of this. Ever. It would be unwise and probably dangerous for you to speak of this conversation with anyone, you understand?' Annie said, her voice firm and controlled.

Though it was not a direct threat, Maddie knew, without a doubt, that it would be fatal to ever cross Annie O'Brien, regardless of the reasons. The woman would go to any lengths to protect her children, her twin brother, and her mother. It was frightening to be in the same room with a person capable of terrorism, let alone the murder of a family member. Though Maddie felt nothing but revulsion toward Thomas, she did not have the ethical capacity to accept the man's assassination. Even in the heat of the moment a few days earlier, she doubted whether Aidan could have killed his own brother. In that respect, Annie was more like Thomas than her twin: hard, unemotional, and willing to go to any lengths to get the job done.

'No, I told you, I won't tell him or anyone else. You have my word,' Maddie replied nervously, and added, 'Will it truly be over in a few days, do you think, Annie?'

Annie took a drag of her cigarette. 'I hope so, but I can't say with 100% certainty. You never can, given the history of this country. Somebody, someday may come of out of the woodwork and claim vengeance. T'is possible, though I hope I am long dead by then.''

There was nothing more to say or do.

'Goodnight, Annie.'

'Goodnight, Maddie.'

After Maddie left, Annie sat in the kitchen until dawn, thinking about the dilemma that had plagued her thoughts daily: choosing between two brothers. She knew she had to do something unspeakable to protect her family. That's all that mattered. In the end, she was willing to sacrifice one brother to save the other. It was not such a difficult decision after all, Annie thought. *Aidan is good and deserves to be happy. Thomas is evil and deserves to die.*

4:28:00

Maddie was lying on the sofa, wrapped in a blanket, her eyes wide open and staring at Aidan. It was becoming a habit, waking up early every morning to watch him. It was 6 am, and still dark outside, as a gentle and cool rain quietly fell against the bedroom window. Maddie was oblivious to the weather. She had been watching Aidan on and off for several hours, as she did most nights, as he tossed and turned, talking and moaning in a fretful, unsatisfying sleep. Since her arrival ten days earlier, she under-stood completely why Aidan looked perpetually exhausted. He did not sleep well. He would drift off for an hour or two, but the majority of his sleep time was spent fighting demons in his mind.

There was a soft knock on the bedroom door. Maddie got up quietly and opened it to see Annie standing in her pyjamas, with a cup of coffee in her hands.

'You must wake Aidan and pack up your things. You're leaving as soon as possible. T'is time you returned to Clonakilty.' On that note, Annie handed Maddie the cup of coffee and closed the door. This was the day Annie promised would come.

She turned to look at Aidan, who was now partially awake and trying to sit up.

'Was that Annie? What time is it?'

'It's past 6 am,' Maddie replied.

'6 am? It feels like I have not slept at all...' replied Aidan, rubbing his face and looking exactly like he felt: tired, worn out, and looking ten years older.

'I noticed. Listen, Annie told me to pack up our things. We are leaving Belfast as soon as we can.'

'Where are we going?'

'Home. We are going back to Clonakilty.'

The tension evaporated from Aidan's face in an instant.

'Really? I can hardly believe my ears...T'is true?' Aidan asked tentatively, in the soft voice of a young boy.

'So, it seems...come, let's get you out of bed, showered, and downstairs. The sooner we get ourselves ready, the sooner we can leave this prison!'

Maddie tried to help Aidan, but he brushed her off with a wave of his hand, pulled himself out of bed, and made his way to the bathroom, practically sprinting, and shut the door.

'Okay, good, Aidan…if you need anything, I'm here,' Maddie shouted, almost laughing.

'I'll be fine on my own,' he replied above the noise of the shower.

The routine of the morning all seemed perfectly normal, as Aidan behaved more like the man she had met in Mont-Tremblant. He didn't even question why they were leaving or what had suddenly changed in the situation to allow them this freedom. While he showered, Maddie began sorting through her clothes and packing for their journey back to Clonakilty.

'Does this remind you of anything, Maddie?' Aidan called out again.

'Yes, it does seem vaguely familiar. It reminds me of …' and just as she spoke those words, the door opened, and there stood Aidan, a towel wrapped around his waist, holding on to the doorframe for support. 'Oh…'

Maddie looked at the troubled Irishman and smiled, praying the smile would mask the shock at seeing Aidan's partially naked and emaciated body. The couple had been together ten days, and during this time, Aidan had carefully avoided dressing in front of her. She knew he had lost a good deal of weight and fitness following the accident and subsequent months of rehabilitation. When Aidan did reach out and occasionally hug her, she could feel his physical frailty.

As he leaned against the door frame with nothing on but a white towel wrapped around his slight waist, he was a shadow of the man who had stood before her so confidently in Mont-Tremblant. The well-defined muscles of his upper arms were half their normal size. His broad chest muscles had atrophied over the months of inactivity, and his skin was slack. Aidan's normally thick thighs looked too small for his 6'2 frame. Gone was the perfectly proportioned and strong, athletic body that she admired. In its place stood an extremely gaunt and fragile-looking man.

It broke Maddie's heart to see him so vulnerable. If she had not understood his reluctance to be intimate before then, she clearly understood now why he had shied away from lovemaking. Maddie stood up and smiled sensuously, trying to sooth whatever apprehension he may be feeling about his physical deterioration. She loved him regardless of how he looked, and she wanted him to know it.

She moved towards him, put her arms around his delicate naked torso and kissed him on his dry lips. He hesitated momentarily before he kissed her back. He continued kissing her softly as first, and then with more urgency. Maddie reacted instantly as a powerful pulse surged through her body. Even if he didn't look or feel quite the same as he did months before, she craved his touch. *Let him lead*, she told herself, as he pressed against her, worried that he would shrink away as he had done their first night in the house. But he was hard under the flimsy cotton wrap, and this excited her more. He kissed her neck, and spoke in her ear, 'It's been so long, Maddie, I've never stopped wantin' you…I'm…' Maddie did not let him finish. She put her fingers to his mouth, and said, 'Just love me. We have time.'

He pushed her down on the bed and yanked off her underwear. He fumbled with her bra and finally gave up, pulling her breasts out and devouring them like a thirsty animal. He was moving quickly and roughly, a direct contrast to the man who had once made love to her so languidly. Aidan was impatient to have her, and Maddie let him do whatever he wanted. This was his dance and she let him lead, however awkward it felt. He needed this moment for himself, and Maddie tried not to flinch when he pierced her almost instantly. She wasn't ready for him. She was dry, and it hurt to have him on top, pinning and pushing with his bony body, thrusting himself inside her. She remained quiet as he continued his aggressive lovemaking, seemingly unaware of what he was doing.

Suddenly, Aidan stopped moving. He looked down at Maddie's flushed and stricken face and realized that his selfishness was hurting the woman he loved. He eased himself off of her and gently reached behind and undid her bra with one finger, dropping it to the floor. His hands cupped her full breasts gently, stroking their beauty. He leaned down and kissed them tenderly, the nipples becoming firm and erect with his probing lips. 'I am so sorry for hurting you,' he said quietly. 'I've thought about this moment for so long I can't control myself, even in my frail state. I want you so badly.' Maddie whispered, 'You are allowed to be selfish once in a while.' She wrapped her legs around him and pulled him close. He kissed her hard and fast again, burying his face in her thick hair, her neck, her arms. Maddie stirred with each hard, probing kiss, as he drifted down her body, searching the hollows of her stomach, her full mound, coaxing her to respond. Aidan could hear Maddie's breathing, could feel the arch her back.

They were back in a dark room in Mont-Tremblant, the sound of heavy rain beating on the bedroom window. They were alone, free, and selfish for one another. Maddie closed her eyes and let herself be taken. She could feel salty tears running into her ears.

*****

Annie was seated in her usual spot at the kitchen island, reading her iPad and writing something in a notebook, when Aidan and Maddie, carrying two suitcases, walked into the room. They were smiling lovingly towards each other. Maddie was glowing and Aidan was grinning, his face relaxed and happy. Annie had rarely seen her brother like this during the entire time he had been in Belfast.

'I know it's early, but it's important you get on the main road before the traffic delays your journey,' Annie informed the couple.

'What's the rush?' Aidan asked, putting his arm around Maddie's waist and smiling at her.

'You have an appointment with a new doctor in Cork City at 1 pm today. He and one his colleagues in Cork City will be looking after your needs from now.'

'I see. And who arranged this?' 'I did, Aidan,' Annie replied.

'Did you also arrange for us to leave? I thought we were to stay here indefinitely for our own protection,' Aidan asked in a serious voice, the blissfulness of the last hour evaporating quickly.

'Thomas and Patrick are not here to speak to you directly, so I will relay the message. They feel t'is safe now for you to leave Belfast. Apparently, there's a meeting arranged for later today that will finally resolve the recent troubles we've all been havin'.'

To Annie's and Maddie's relief, Aidan did not ask any further questions about their departure or his new doctors in Cork City. His only interest at that moment was leaving the confines of the house on Stanley Park as soon as possible and never returning. He awkwardly grabbed the suitcases and headed out to the kitchen door to the black Mercedes parked in the laneway.

'I am terribly worried about him, Maddie,' Annie said, while she and Maddie watched Aidan struggle to put the light suitcases in the trunk of the sedan. 'Sometimes I don't recognize my gentle, loving brother. He seems…'

'Unpredictable? I know, Annie. I see it too. The accident handicapped him emotionally as well as physically. Please don't worry, though. He was himself this morning when he found out we were leaving. I am sure as soon as we arrive back in Clonakilty, he will rebound quickly,' Maddie replied.

As the women watched, Aidan finally succeeded in the innocuous task of packing up the car with both suitcases. He slammed the trunk down with a resounding thump.

'I do hope so, for both your sakes.' Turning to Maddie, she continued, 'All right then. Here are the keys to the vehicle. The ownership of the vehicle is now in Aidan's name. Think of it as my engagement gift to you. Now you should leave.'

Maddie hugged her future sister-in-law tightly, wondering whether she would ever see the woman again. 'Thank you, Annie, for looking after me, but especially for looking after your brother.'

'I love him, and I want him to recover and forget about all the horrible things that have happened to him. I know he can do that with you…now listen to me carefully, Maddie,' Annie continued, looking at the sedan to ensure that Aidan was not within earshot of their conversation. 'Remember our conversation a few nights ago? I will contact you. Please do not try to contact me, Patrick or Sheila at any time. Have I made myself clear?' Annie's voice was not a request but a command, sounding eerily similar to Thomas.

'You have. Perfectly.'

Once outside, Annie hugged her twin brother one last time, and the couple got into the sedan. Maddie was driving, and Aidan sat rigidly in the passenger seat, waving to his sister as the black gates closed behind them. The couple said nothing as the vehicle slowly went down Stanley Park Road, heading toward the M1 and the national highway that would take them to Dublin and, eventually, West Cork.

4:28:57 Transition 2

After the couple left the house, Annie opened the freezer door and fished out a pack of cigarettes, hidden behind a frozen wedding cake that had been sitting on the back shelf of the freezer for fifteen years. Annie hid her nicotine habit from everyone in the family except Patrick. She promised him she would try quitting soon, after the mess was 'cleaned up'.

Sitting at the kitchen counter, the thin and haggard-looking woman lit a cigarette and inhaled deeply, thoroughly enjoying her first cigarette of the day. The tranquility of the house was exactly what she needed for the next twenty-four hours. Thomas' cronies were with him, and Annie had given her private staff the day off, including the bodyguard that was provided courtesy of her eldest brother. She had bribed the hulking figure generously to stay away from the house, and she had also given him two bottles of ultra-expensive Russian vodka. Annie was confident the burly Russian would be passed out by mid-afternoon, somewhere in the dark recesses of the gritty city, and would not impede her early evening plans.

Annie opened her lined, handwritten notebook and scratched out number 124 from the checklist-*Aidan's departure to Clonakilty*. There were several other items that she needed to complete prior to the meeting with Thomas and John Connolly later in the day.

The sequence of events for the upcoming scheme was organized to the minute, and any deviation from Annie's meticulous timetable could prove fatal to her and perhaps to Patrick. Unlike the IRA's premeditated armed attacks during the Troubles, where intelligence was not always reliable or accurate and a back-up plan was always included in case of failure, Annie's personal campaign to terminate the feud between the two most notorious criminals in modern Irish history left no room for error. If the scheme did not succeed, there would be nowhere to hide either from Thomas or John Connolly. Annie was solely responsible for orchestrating this gathering of evil, and for ensuring a final and permanent resolution to the family and to the city's ongoing struggle with Thomas and John's decades-long hatred for one another. *It was going to be bloody, nasty, and violent, just like the good old days*, Annie said to herself sarcastically.

Annie's decision to carry out this extreme mission did not come to her on a whim over a few glasses of wine. Since the car bombing in June, she had spent weeks trying to find a reasonable solution that would put an end, once and for all, to Thomas and John's marriage of violence. All the ideas she and Patrick discussed were too risky or had the potential to escalate the violence instead of eradicating it. In the end, the decision to proceed with Annie's solo mission came down to one immutable fact: no one in the O'Callaghan family was safe as long as Thomas was allowed to run the family. His rash decision-making skills over the last few years, his volatility and psychopathic behavior, and his appetite for violence and mayhem were exposing the family, and would eventually destroy them. In spite of all their efforts to normalize their lives, Thomas could not be controlled, even by his younger brother Patrick. Since John Connolly reappeared, Thomas's impulsive behaviour had only gotten worse.

Annie had spent her entire life surrounded by violence. She had lost a husband, a father, and countless friends through acts of terrorism for a cause that no longer mattered. She was weary of the constant threat to herself, but especially to her children. She desperately wanted her daughters to grow up to be normal, well-adjusted adults, generous, kind, and loving. Aidan, too, had suffered, losing so many people he loved. The blame for all of their recent woes rested squarely on Thomas O'Callaghan and John Connolly, Annie reasoned. It was time to eradicate the family, the city, and the country from a problem that would never disappear quietly on its own.

The most challenging aspect of the scheme that was about to go down was getting both Thomas and John, at the same place and at the same time, in an isolated area of the city where there was zero risk to innocent bystanders. Annie had waited several weeks for the exact moment when both parties would be ripe for a temporary cease fire: the perfect time to execute the plan. The last few days had been especially tense, and now it was time to suggest a 'truce' of sorts.

The convergence of criminals would be later that day.

The previous morning, John Connolly received a written invitation from Annie O'Brien to discuss a truce between the gangs. The handwritten message was delivered personally to him by a stunning tall brunette, who was a member of Annie's private staff.

In her invitation to John, Annie had indicated that she was prepared to pay him handsomely if he met certain conditions regarding a cease fire between the two rival families. She wanted to discuss the terms of those conditions with him personally. Annie instructed John to come to a meeting with one of his bodyguards. He was instructed not to tell anyone where he was going and what he was doing, otherwise the meeting would be cancelled. Annie's message made it clear that she was orchestrating this meeting on behalf of the rest of the O'Callaghan family, not her brothers. She was acting alone, she said in her note, and her personal goal was to find permanent solution to the ongoing feud. She reminded John that the police were putting a lot of pressures on the family, and she was quite certain he was experiencing the same level of harassment.

John agreed to the terms, because he was a greedy little monster whose curiosity about Annie's financial offer compelled him to shed his ultra-strict, paranoid security protocols and comply with her demands. He grudgingly admitted to himself that the pressures were getting out of control, and that since Annie was but a meek and mild widow, who spent her days raising her girls and looking after her aging mother, what harm could it cause if he met the woman alone?

Besides, he told himself, a financial offer was too potent to dismiss. He could never have too much money, he chuckled to himself while reading the note, and this was not only easy money, it was O'Callaghan money. He had never met Thomas's younger sister, whom he knew only through a grainy photo and the chatter among his Loyalist cronies during the heyday of the Troubles. John Connolly, like everyone else, was about to be deceived by the slender and wily woman who had recently taken a keen interest in gang warfare.

To entice Thomas to the meeting, Annie relied on Patrick. She knew full well her brother would not move an inch if his sister requested a meeting in some unsecured warehouse in a remote business park. Thomas received a text message from Patrick asking to meet at the Belfast Shipping Depot, as he had something important to share with his brother that would greatly increase the family's wealth and power. Patrick reminded Thomas that this was for his eyes only and to come with only his most trusted bodyguard, as other parties present would get nervous if Thomas showed up with a squadron of black-clad men. Patrick further emphasized that this new venture would make them rich beyond their wildest dreams and the most powerful family in the E.U., while at the same time driving another thick wedge into John Connolly's business. The smell of money, power, and retribution was just as potent as an aphrodisiac for Thomas O'Callaghan. The invitation, though, seemed impulsive and uncharacteristic of Patrick's controlled business style, but Thomas liked risky new ventures, and this one sparked his curiosity. He also trusted Patrick implicitly.

Annie lit her second cigarette of the day. She desperately wanted a dram of whisky to calm her shaking hands and pounding heart. As experienced as she was in orchestrating acts of terrorism, this situation was completely different than any other she had committed, because she personally knew the victims. She sat on the kitchen stool and chastised herself for being weak and sentimental.

4:35:00 Run

The black Mercedes sedan headed toward Cork City, followed close behind by an inconspicuous grey SUV, one of the Police Services of Northern Ireland's unmarked vehicles. Neither Maddie nor Aidan were aware they were being followed.

Tasked with doing the driving, Maddie focused her complete attention on staying on the left side of the road and avoiding a collision, oblivious to the scenery around her. Aidan was particularly tense during the trip. He sat rigid in his seat, looking straight ahead and flinching every time a car or a lorry zoomed by, the couple's short but feverish moment of intimacy earlier that morning a fading memory. Maddie knew his agitation was probably due to the lasting effects of the trauma from the car accident. Driving on the highway was a grim reminder of what had happened to him and Meghan.

The couple spoke little during their journey, which was fine for Maddie, because she needed to stay focused and alert. She drove at the posted speed limit, but they were passed frequently by drivers in excessive hurry to arrive at their destinations.

Once they arrived on the N7 toward Cork City, Maddie wanted to stop in Rathcole for a cup of coffee and something to eat, but Aidan was adamant they keep moving. He seemed particularly agitated and restless at this point in their journey. Maddie acquiesced, until Aidan was finally ready to stop, stretch his aching hip, and use the facilities.

After a short rest in Kildare, they resumed their journey to Cork City. The appointment with Dr. O'Donahue was at 1 pm at Cork University Hospital, and they arrived in the city shortly after 11:30, enough time to eat lunch before they met with the orthopaedic surgeon.

The unmarked car stayed inconspicuously behind the black Mercedes until they reached Cork City.

At 12:45, Maddie and Aidan arrived at CUH for their appointment. After checking in with the reception desk at the Orthopedic Clinic and completing the required forms and waivers, they sat in a cheery waiting room. Maddie could see that Aidan was exhausted and needed to lie down. They had been travelling since 7 am, and her fiancée was in some discomfort and stiff from the prolonged drive. Tired as he was, Aidan walked up and down the hallway restlessly, waiting to see Dr. O'Donahue.

At 1:16, they were escorted into a private cubicle for an initial assessment by an orthopedic nurse. The young woman asked Aidan several questions, all of which he answered curtly and with as little description as possible. He didn't smile, and his impatience was by now very obvious to Maddie, and to the poor young nurse who was only trying to do her job.

At exactly 1:30 the door to the cubicle opened and Dr. O'Donahue walked in, a thin man in his late fifties with snow-white hair, a pink face, and a large nose. He introduced himself with a warm smile and then did something quite extraordinary. He reached over to Aidan and stroked his arm, like a mother would do to soothe an upset child. The benevolent doctor either sensed something was wrong with the tall man from Clonakilty, or someone had told him, as he handled Aidan's agitation with genuine concern. The effect was startling and instantaneous. Aidan's demeanor swiftly changed from turmoil to peaceful, and he sat patiently listening to the doctor.

'How are you feelin' today, Aidan?'

'Right now, I am a wee bit tired. And I'm sore from the long drive,' Aidan answered.

'T'is certainly understandable, Aidan, and you should be. That fractured hip of yours is still healing,' the doctor replied, in a reassuring and heavily accented voice. 'But let's take a look at you first before we talk about your recovery. What do you say?'

'Shall I wait outside?' Maddie asked, concerned that maybe she should leave the Doctor and Aidan alone.

'Nonsense. You must stay. Now, Aidan, sit down on this excessively uncomfortable examination bed while I check your mobility.'

For twenty minutes, Dr. O'Donahue asked Aidan many questions while poking and prodding his body. He wanted to know about the severity of the pain in his hip, how much he was walking, and the level and intensity of his exercise program and physical therapy. While examining Aidan's mobility and balance, Dr. O'Donahue widened his circle of questions by asking him about his sleeping pattern, his daily habits, his nutrition, and his weight. Sprinkled among the normal examination questions, Dr. O'Donahue asked Aidan if loud noises bothered him at all, and did he mind travelling to and from the physio appointments by car. At first Maddie found the questions odd, as they had little to do with Aidan's hip injury. Soon, she realized where the doctor was heading, and his casual approach to probing the reluctant patient for information. He was looking for something more than the effects of a shattered hip, Maddie thought. Aidan's answers, though, were always short, non-descriptive and emotionless. He withheld a lot of detail that Maddie would have filled in on his behalf, but she kept quiet. Dr. O'Donahue even asked Aidan if the couple had resumed normal sexual relations, to which Aidan replied, somewhat sheepishly, more or less.

Throughout the examination, the doctor jotted down a few notes on his chart, but he spent most of his time observing Aidan's gestures, his body language, and the interaction between the couple. A nurse interrupted the appointment to say that Aidan was scheduled for an MRI, and she was to take him immediately.

'Please take Aidan. Mrs. O'Callaghan and I will wait here until he returns,' Dr. O'Donahue said, as Aidan was escorted out of the examination room to the MRI clinic in a wheelchair.

As soon as they left, the doctor turned to Maddie and spoke directly.

'Aidan's hip is healing very well. I am pleased with his progress. He still has many painful months ahead, but he is far more advanced than I was led to believe. I will know more after the MRI, but I am confident that your husband will be able to resume normal activities over time. It's says in his chart that he's quite athletic? Triathlon, I take it? This would explain his rate of recovery. I tink, with some hard work and patience, he will be able to run again, and swim. Yes, I am impressed with him. He's a good man, that Aidan O'Callaghan.'

'That's a relief. He's been through so much. He needs to know that he will be normal again,' Maddie replied wistfully. She was about to ask the doctor about Aidan's emotional and mental wellbeing, but it was not necessary.

'He will return to normal physically, I have no doubt, but mentally, I can see Aidan is struggling,' Dr. O'Donahue continued. 'Though he is trying very hard to conceal it, I see symptoms of PTSD: post-traumatic stress disorder. We often see signs of PTSD after a particularly serious injury or car accident.' The doctor looked at Maddie for a response. 'You do not seem surprised at this, Mrs. O'Callaghan?'

'No, I am not surprised, and please call me Maddie. I knew something was wrong almost the moment I saw him ten days ago. Let me explain, Dr. O'Donahue. I am not Aidan's wife. I am his fiancée, and while it's a terribly complicated and long, we were separated for a period of time due to unforeseen circumstances. I was not here when Aidan was involved in the accident. We've just recently been reunited.'

'Go on, then,' Dr. O'Donahue asked, interested to hear more.

'Aidan is…well, he's not the same man I waved goodbye to almost five months ago in Montreal. I think he is struggling with something that is far deeper than a broken hip. He's moody, irritable, angry. He hardly sleeps. He is not as affectionate as he once was, though he is trying. His behaviour is, well, unpredictable. He sometimes acts like a caged animal, restless, agitated, and … paranoid, though under the circumstances, he has good reason to feel that way.'

The doctor listened to Maddie's description of his new patient. He looked down at his desk and pointed to an orange file. 'There is little information about the accident in that file. Would you mind tellin' me happened?'

Maddie paused to think about what she should say to the new doctor, unsure whether it was wise to reveal too much. The doctor seemed trustworthy, and everything he had done over the last thirty minutes had a purpose. Her instincts told her he would be the right person to share some of Aidan's history.

'Dr. O'Donohue, there is more to this story than the car accident. I'll get right to the point, because we don't have much time before Aidan returns. Aidan was born in Belfast. He grew up during the Troubles and suffered many personal losses. He has seen a lot of things that no child or young adult should ever witness. He left the violence and trauma 25 years ago and has not set foot in that city until a few months ago. The O'Callaghan family, though, never left Belfast, and they have enemies. Almost five months ago, Aidan was the target of retribution, the innocent victim of a vendetta that started decades ago between two hateful men, one of whom is his brother. The car accident was not an accident, it was an explosion, and it was a deliberate attempt to kill Aidan and thus cause emotional injury to other members of the O'Callaghan family. It's a twisted and sick world these people live in. Instead of killing Aidan, though, these men killed his former girlfriend. He has spent the last months recovering from the accident in the very place he fled decades earlier: Belfast'.

Dr. O'Donahue sat quietly for a moment, before he took Maddie's hand thoughtfully and reassuringly, as the pretty redhead was very close to tears.

'Did Aidan share with you the details of the car accident or other troubling events from his early life in Belfast?'

'I learned the details of the accident from other people, Dr. O'Donahue, not from Aidan directly. He has not told me anything about the accident. He won't talk about it, and I have not pressured him to do so. As far as his early life in Belfast, he has only touched on the general aspects of his childhood and in broad terms. The specific details of his early, turbulent life, I learned from his twin sister and his best friend. They told me what happened to him and his family, and it's very disturbing: the senseless violence, intimidation, and blatant killings.'

'I am so sorry, Maddie. I can see how worried you are about him; you want to help him recover. It's no wonder he is suffering. The accident in itself is enough to cause PTSD, but the events that happened earlier in his life may have compounded the symptoms. I suspect, though I can't be sure, that he probably did not deal adequately with the traumatic events that impacted him as a young man. This is very common in areas of the world where there is unimaginable violence and terrorism. I also know a fair amount about the era of the Troubles. Indeed, it has touched me personally. I have witnessed first-hand the destructive forces of PTSD to the innocent victims of civil war.'

'Can a person recover completely from PTSD?' Maddie asked.

'Some do, and some don't ever fully recover. It takes an extraordinary amount of work and patience to become 'normal' again. You see, a person who has been traumatized by an event will push away all feelings associated with those memories, in the hopes that they will eventually go away. The fact that Aidan is not talking about any of this with you is one of the unmistakable signs of PTSD. You see, instead of tellin' you his horrible story and all the feelings that go with it, he is re-livin' the most grievous events in his life in his head, either through flashbacks or unwanted memories. These can be triggered by sounds and loud noises, or even by certain types of people. It depends on the person and the specific events that contributed to PTSD. Based on what you've told me, and what I have been able to observe in this short time, Aidan is anxious, emotionally numb, detached, and sleep deprived. These are all symptoms of the illness. Aidan will only recover when he is able to truly deal with those feelings of pain, fear, guilt, and shame at witnessing and losing people he cared about'

'But why would Aidan feel guilt or shame? I don't understand. None of these events were his fault.'

'In the case of the car accident, it's called survivor's guilt. The accident was meant to kill Aidan, not his girlfriend,' Dr. O'Donahue replied. 'Do you see what I mean?

'Sadly, I do. I've met so many people in the last couple of weeks, Dr. O'Donahue, who have been directly or indirectly touched by incomprehensible violence. My mind has trouble imagining what it is like to live day to day under the constant threat that someone will attack you.'

Dr. O'Donahue nodded. He did not wish to burden Maddie with his own deep and personal loss, with the events in Northern Ireland.

'Maddie, I will personally oversee Aidan's treatment to ensure that he gets all the help he needs, so that he can make a full recovery, physically and emotionally. I have something for you to read.' Dr. O'Donahue left the cubicle and returned minutes later, holding a bright blue folder.

'Aidan needs counselling as soon as possible, and with a clinical therapist who specialises in PTSD. Fortunately for you and Aidan, there is a very good therapist right here at C.U.H. I will make the arrangements today for a referral. We will tread very carefully with your fiancée and not force him to do something he doesn't want to do, as I can see he will resist any help. While I've only had a short time to read about and observe Aidan, he strikes me as someone who is more inclined to help others than to ask for help, even if he desperately needs it. Like a lot of men, he is stubbornly independent and probably thinks his mental anguish is a sign of weakness. T'is not though, I can assure you. For now, I will give these to you to read – this should help you cope better, though I tink you're doing a very good job as is. Aidan trusts you, I can see that, and he cares for you madly. You must give it time, lots of time. The healing process is very long, and progress is measured in weeks and months. Do you understand?'

'Dr. O'Donahue, patience is one of my strengths. I have all the time in the world to see this through,' Maddie answered.

When Aidan returned from the MRI, Dr. O'Donahue spent a few more minutes speaking with him privately. Maddie could not hear their conversation, but she hoped that whatever the doctor said, he would listen to his advice. Aidan was silent when they left the hospital, and he stayed that way until they were on the highway to Clonakilty.

4:45:25

The couple resumed their journey toward Clonakilty, being tailed by a grey non-descript car.

At Ballyheada, Aidan asked Maddie to take a left turn onto the R607. He suggested they take a more scenic route to Clonakilty. This highway would take them along the Atlantic Coast and the rolling farm hills of West Cork, a longer but more interesting drive. As soon as they turned off the main highway and made their way along the R607, Aidan's pensive mood disappeared, and he started talking. At each little village and roundabout, he explained where they were and who he knew in the area. He shared colorful stories about the long-time families who had lived and worked in the area. There were many farms along the route, each blessed with a stunning view of either the valley below or the Atlantic Ocean.

They stopped in Kinsale for a few minutes to walk around the popular summer tourist destination and picture-perfect harbour. It was October and well past the high tourist season, but there was still a fair number of people walking about and shopping along Market Lane.

Once back at the car, Aidan hesitated before getting into the passenger seat.

'Would you mind if I drove for a bit, Maddie?' Aidan asked.

'Are you sure you are up to it? You seemed really tired in Cork,' Maddie asked.

'Well, I was, but now I'm feelin' better. T'is the country air and smell of the sea that's energizin' me. Let me drive so you can look at the views.'

Maddie did not refuse a chance to play tourist. She sat back in the comfort of the luxurious sedan and decompressed. She realized, since arriving in Ireland, that she had lost track of the time. It suddenly dawned on her that Canadian Thanksgiving had come and gone and she hadn't called her boys. She would do that as soon as they were settled in Clonakilty.

The couple continued their leisurely journey towards Aidan's home. They drove up and down rolling hills and checker-board valleys, and soon found themselves on a magnificent coastal road that was barely wide enough for one car. Each time they encountered a vehicle driving in the opposite direction, Aidan skillfully maneuvered the sedan, either by backing up or moving forward into some tiny, almost invisible, indentation along the road, to give the on-coming vehicle enough space to pass.

Quaint farm houses dotted the lush green and tan farmland that seemed to stretch on for miles and miles. No tall buildings, cell towers, or wind turbines marred the pristine and iconic view. Where the land met the sea, the modest clay-colored cliffs dropped steeply to the water below. Along the coastal road, Maddie could see small, hidden bays and glorious wide beaches only accessible by foot. The tide was still quite far out at this time of day, and she could make out a few people walking their dogs on the hard-packed sand.

'Aidan, I had no idea the country looked like this. When I was here a few weeks ago, I didn't see much. I guess I wasn't looking in the right places.'

'Na, you had other things on your mind. Let me introduce you to West Cork, Maddie, my love, the most beautiful and friendly part of Ireland, I think, though I am a tad biased.' Aidan said, grinning mischievously, his light green eyes sparkling, instantly reassuring Maddie that Aidan could recover from his ordeal once back in his home town, surrounded by everything he cherished most in life.

They continued to follow the coastal road to Timoleague. There, they stopped to look at a Franciscan Friary, built sometime between the 13th and 14th century. The Friars, who had once lived in this simple structure, devoted themselves to the strict rules of poverty, simplicity, and chastity, 'A very dull and boring life,' Aidan added. The original stone structure was missing a roof and several walls; the entire site was filled with tombstones, Celtic crosses, and dozens of enormous ravens that claimed sanctuary in the stone crevices that remained. Though derelict, the historic landmark was charming and rich in history. Maddie enjoyed reading the inscriptions on the tombstones, some dating back as far as the 1700s.

They left Timoleague about an hour later, and continued their leisurely journey inland, towards Clonakilty, the Atlantic Ocean sparkling in the distance. About twenty minutes later, Maddie recognized where they were. They drove up a lane toward Aidan's tiny stone cottage. Michael's truck was parked in the laneway, and there was smoke streaming out of the chimney. While in Cork city, Maddie had texted Michael to alert him to their eminent arrival in Clonakilty.

As soon as Aidan parked the car, the front door of the cottage opened and Michael stepped out and sprinted toward his best friend. He grabbed the tall man and hugged him affectionately, saying something to him that Maddie could not understand at all. Aidan was visibly emotional, the tears soaking his face. The two friends had not seen each other for almost six months. They stood outside, patting each other, gesturing wildly, both talking at the same time, like two excited children sharing their recent adventures at away camp. Colleen was standing at the front door of the cottage, watching the two men, beaming at her 'boys'.

'Come, come, now, Michael, let's get out of the cold air and let Aidan rest. He's had a long journey, and no doubt he wants a pint!' Colleen yelled out to her husband.

'Indeed!' Both men replied simultaneously.

The two couples slowly made their way into the cozy cottage. The wood bin was stacked high with dry wood, as Michael had promised, and the fireplace was ablaze with a roaring fire.

Michael went to the fridge and opened two chilled Guinness beers, which he poured expertly in tall glasses, making sure to let the glasses sit while the foam settled properly, before the pint was ready for consumption. Colleen poured Maddie a glass of red wine, which she took eagerly. On the coffee table, there was a spread of cheese, olives, and artisan breads, a delectable feast for the hungry travellers.

For the next several hours, the two men talked non-stop about the recent events in Clonakilty, the construction business, and the many projects Michael was working on. Aidan interjected often, adding his comments about the various people he knew. The two men would start talking about one topic and veer off in another direction, getting easily sidetracked. Eventually, they would come back to the original topic and then move on to another completely different subject. Maddie had trouble keeping up with who was who in the village, but she was entertained for hours, listening to the friends' colorful language, embellished stories, and enormous sense of humor. Their descriptions of people, places, and events brought to life the tiny community that was more than sum of its parts. There was always a funny and light side to any topic. Serious moments lasted but a few seconds, and then someone, either Aidan or Michael, would make a comment and soon the two men would be laughing uncontrollably. They spoke fast and used Irish expressions that Maddie did not understand, but she got the general idea.

Over the course of the evening, Maddie saw a refreshing side to the troubled Irishman, one that she hoped would stay firmly in place now that they were back home in Clona, in the safety and comfort of Aidan's home, surrounded by the people he trusted.

The driver of the unmarked car had parked a safe distance from the old stone cottage, watching the evening sky slowly trickle into the valley. When it was finally dark, he took out his cell phone and sent a text message to Eammon MacDonald, telling him the package had arrived safe and sound in Clonakilty. Moments later, Eammon replied that his duties were done, and he could return to Belfast the following morning.

5:00:00

Annie had chosen dusk to execute her assiduous plan. The convergence of fading light and overlapping darkness meant that the street lights were not yet on, but it was too dark to see clearly. At this time of day, all colour faded, the edges of the metal-clad buildings lost their sharpness, the eyes had trouble focusing clearly. The large, one-storey building where the meeting would take place was tinged with a dark grey hue.

Annie had spent months roaming the stretch of highway between Belfast and Dublin, looking for the ideal place to stage her final act of lawlessness. Finally, a suitable property presented itself. It met all the criteria required to suite Annie's exacting standards, including the all-important separate access points, so that both men would show up at the rendezvous point, without seeing each other, until they were both entombed in the locked building.

Patrick had purchased the entire industrial complex, composed of ten acres of land and three buildings, using one of the family's bogus shelf companies. A paper trail leading directly to the O'Callaghans would be almost impossible to trace. Patrick offered the current leaseholders a termination offer that was too lucrative to ignore, and within a few short weeks, all the buildings were vacated. A crew of workers, paid handsomely for their discretion, arrived shortly after the last tenant left and installed equipment and signage to 'stage' the park as a 'new and bona fide' shipping warehouse space. Anyone travelling along the roads would be fooled into thinking this was a legitimate warehouse, including the two men that mattered most: Thomas O'Callaghan and John Connolly.

Annie chose the largest of the three buildings for her plan. The 10,000-square foot space had two separate doors on either side of the building, so that each man would enter at different points. The signage over the entrances were manufactured to look realistic: the lighting was configured to be dimmable using a smart phone, and the doors at both entrances had concealed locks installed that could only be accessed from the outside. Containers and pallets were purchased and installed inside the large warehouse space. While they looked like real wood pallets, they were in fact made of highly flammable cardboard. Inside one of them, Annie had placed a small explosive device that was buried deep in straw and could only be activated remotely by a cell phone, if she needed to revert to the back-up plan. The explosive device was not designed to cause a huge explosion, but to start a very hot, smoky fire.

A nineteen-foot-high steel fence was installed around the property so prospective tenants and passers-by would think the park was a secure facility. The fence, in reality, was designed to keep people in, not out, of the facility. Accessibility in and out of the park was limited to the two locked gates at both access points. Knowing a great deal about the repulsive little thug from Dublin, Annie had taken extraordinary measures to ensure that the property looked legitimate from the outside. Annie had wisely anticipated that John Connolly would send one of his men on a recon mission to scope out the park prior to his arrival, which he had done as soon as he received the invitation. The park was guarded by Annie's personal staff, who were stationed at strategic points along the fence. They had taken note of the black car with Republic of Ireland licence plate numbers cruising up and down the main road shortly after the invitation was sent.

John Connolly was given clear instructions to enter through Gate A. Unbeknownst to him, Thomas was told to drive through Gate C.

At 6:00 and 6:04 pm respectively, two dark vehicles pulled into the industrial park, at extreme ends of the property, and drove toward their rendezvous points, unaware of each another. The gates automatically closed behind them. The cars and men were now firmly trapped in the compound. There was no way out alive. Two former IRA female sharpshooters, dressed in camouflage clothing that melted into the background and each carrying a high powered semi-automatic rifle, were positioned at both ends of the park to ensure that no vehicle or person climbed in or climbed out of the locked gates. They were to remain until Annie gave the signal to leave. Both women were instructed to exit the area immediately if they saw a fire in the building.

Sickly yellow lights illuminated the doors of the metal-clad warehouse. From the highway, the business park looked perfectly normal under the dim lighting. If either Thomas or John was apprehensive about entering the property, they would show up with a platoon of bodyguards, and the mission would have to be terminated.

Thomas was the first to arrive. He stepped out of the vehicle with only his most trusted bodyguard, and headed toward Gate C. He opened the door and hurriedly walked in. Annie was relieved to see that he had followed Patrick's instructions. A few minutes later, John Connolly and his lone bodyguard walked into Gate A. He, too, had taken Annie's instructions seriously.

One kilometer away, at a safe distance from the park and out of view from the commuter traffic, Constable Eammon MacDonald sat in an unmarked police car, waiting for Annie. He was nervously smoking a cigarette, a habit he had kicked more than twenty-five years ago. *Annie's fault*, he murmured to himself, though it felt good to smoke again after all these years. His phone pinged, alerting him to a text message which he promptly forwarded to Annie.

Annie read and erased the text message, then resumed watching the events unfold on her tablet. She had placed tiny wireless surveillance cameras at specific points outside and inside the building. While the lighting was poor, she could easily see and hear John Connolly grumbling about the weather and time of day. She thought he said something about needing a drink. As soon as both men entered the building, unaware of each other's presence, their fates were sealed. The doors behind them silently locked from the outside.

This was the theatre of the macabre, and Annie was the director. She stood outside the warehouse building, dressed head to toe as a man, and watched and listened on her iPad as each man and personal bodyguard walked to the centre of the open space, surrounded by pallets and boxes. At the precise moment, Annie triggered the wireless lighting to burn brightly so that both men would see each other. She watched as they stopped in their tracks, utterly shocked to be facing one another, twenty-nine years after their feud began. In fact, Thomas and John had never met face to face before this moment. John was the first one to act, and instinctively pulled out his Glock pistol. Thomas immediately did the same with his Beretta. As if to prolong their miserable lives for a few seconds more, both men stood twenty meters apart, pointing their guns, their faces grimacing with tension and fear. There was uneasy silence, as they knew that neither would leave the space alive. Thomas was the first to break the silence, and he screamed profanities at the sweating, balding man in front of him. John reciprocated by hurling his own brand of insults, screaming Annie's name and blaming it all on her. Thomas paid no attention. The verbal savagery flew like arrows across a field. It was an obvious delay tactic, as neither man wanted to be the first to fire the fatal shot.

Annie turned the device over and only listened. She could not bring herself to watch her brother die. The verbal abuse was finally punctuated by a gunshot, by whom she did not know, followed by a maelstrom of bullets, ricocheting off the metal walls and pallets. The sound coming from the interior of the building was brutally familiar. It reminded Annie about her last and most heinous mission with the IRA. As suddenly as it started, the ricochet noise stopped. It was all over in less than sixty seconds.

Annie stood pressed against the locked door at Gate C; uncontrollable tears streamed down her face. Once again, she chastised herself for being soft. After two minutes, Annie forced herself to look at her phone, before opening the heavy steel door. Four bodies were lying on the ground. She saw a twitch of a finger from one body, a slight heave of the chest from another. She heard one last soft moan of pain from someone, and then nothing. Absolutely silence.

When Annie unlocked and opened the door, she was immediately overcome with the foul smell of blood, seared flesh, gun residue, and fecal matter. Trying not to breath too heavily, she approached the mayhem in the centre of the large space. In the light, a haze of dust floated around the dead bodies. All four men were lying in one massive pool of black blood. Annie forced herself to watch the bodies for another two minutes for signs of life, and praying that she would not have to go to Plan B. Fortunately, nothing moved. Annie cocked her Beretta instinctively and moved gingerly among the dead bodies, being extra careful not to step in the black liquid with her rubber boots.

It was a gruesome scene, even for a trained terrorist. She saw Thomas first. The big man's burnished pewter hair was perfectly coiffed, and he looked like he was sleeping. Annie scanned the rest of his body. A large, mushy crater was all that was left of Thomas's once burly chest. John Connolly appeared to have gotten the worst of the cross-fire; his face was half blown off, his chest a mess of bone and skin, and he appeared to be missing a few fingers. The two bodyguards were both each lying on their sides next to their bosses, one with the top of his head missing, while the other was clutching his abdomen. He probably died last, Annie thought, as she instinctively made the sign of the cross.

Annie retrieved the hidden surveillance cameras. Next, she opened the other pallet next to the bodies, carefully defused the small bomb, and placed in her pocket. She opened her notebook and checked her list carefully, scanning the entire space to make sure there was nothing in the area that could possibly tie her or Patrick to the scene. Confident that she had covered her tracks and that the space was sanitized to her perfect standards, Annie walked outside and around the entire building, retrieving the small cameras, and looking in both Thomas' and John's cars for a dashcam or video capture device. There were none. Even if a video image or recording existed, it would be impossible to identify Annie in her disguise. Eammon MacDonald was tasked to ensure that if a video turned up, he would take care of destroying the contents.

Satisfied that nothing more was required, Annie left the compound. She was anxious to shed her disguise and purge the smell that stuck to the back of her throat. She walked 300 meters to the front gate, unlocked it, and scooted across the street to a culvert.

In the culvert, a black gym bag lay hidden. Hastily, Annie removed the black hat, black beard, and tight spandex pants and jacket that were padded to add 30 pounds to her slight frame. The rubber boots were exchanged for a tall leather pair. All pieces of clothing went back into the gym bag, along with her lined notepad. She was now dressed in jeans, sweater, and a wool coat with a hood. She headed towards the dark woods and walked another 750 meters to a metal drum, which she had placed there the week before.

Annie threw the gym bag in the drum, added an accelerant, and threw in a match. The materials in the bag and the bag itself were highly flammable, and everything burned efficiently within minutes. While waiting, she took a few swigs from the flask of whiskey tucked into her jacket pocket. It would take considerably more alcohol to numb her body and mind from the last hour. Still, the whiskey felt like an old and reassuring hand. She needed to hold it together for a few more minutes.

Satisfied that all traces of the contents of the barrel were destroyed beyond modern forensic capabilities, Annie began the long walk to Eammon MacDonald's parked vehicle.

Fifteen minutes later, a tap on the car window woke Eammon from a light nap. He turned the car on as Annie opened the passenger door and sat down, breathing heavily. Before neither one said anything, Annie took her cell phone and sent a benign text to both her contacts at the gates. They knew what to do next.

'How was your evening?' Eammon asked after Annie put her phone away.

'Successful,' Annie replied curtly.

'I don't see any fire?'

'T'was not necessary. It all went down according to the plan.'

'Do you have the video?'

'I do, but I do not wish to see it myself…' Annie handed Eammon the iPad and a pair of earplugs. He watched the screen for two minutes, visibly shaken by the images and disturbing sound. Annie stared straight ahead, not moving or speaking and barely breathing. She closed her eyes, blocking out the last gruesome twenty minutes, and tried to image what her life would have been like if Eammon had only stayed in Belfast decades ago.

Eammon turned off the phone. 'T'is done, then.'

'It is,' was all Annie could say.

'Best we wait here for a bit until …'

'Okay,' was all she could say. She clearly didn't want to talk about the events of the last hour.

The couple sat quietly in the car and waited.

'Annie, do you ever think about us and how our lives would be different today if tings hadn't ended the way they did?' Eammon asked.

'That's funny, Eammon. I was just thinking about when we first met,' Annie replied quietly, leaning her head back and closing her weary eyes. 'I'll never forget that day. I opened the ratty shed door of our garden to find a young man staring back at me with absolute terror in his eyes. I was shaking to my core. For all my experience with the IRA, I'd never seen anyone so certain of their death until I saw your face.'

Eammon opened his pack of cigarettes, handed one to Annie, and lit both of them. The friends had not talked about their chance encounter for decades, yet it was still as fresh and clear as if it had happened yesterday.

'Well, I was young and inexperienced,' Eammon added inhaling his cigarette deeply. 'Twelve weeks of basic training in the British Army doesn't prepare you for a mob attack, in an isolated corner of Belfast, in the middle of a civil war, with no place to hide.'

Annie shook her head, remembering the horrific details of that day.

'It was truly an awful day, it was, the worst I had ever seen. I was on the street for a bit and saw the men from your platoon being dragged from the truck and ripped apart. Even today, I can't understand such human depravity. The people that did this were my neighbors, for feck's sake! How could they do such a thing to another human being? You know I'm no angel and I did some really nasty stuff, but this…this was not right, the way they handled your situation.' Annie replied, her arms waving, her eyes shining like marbles in the dark car.

'I don't know. I'm just thankful I was able to run away from it, my heart beating so hard I was sure I would collapse from sheer terror. Then I found the open door to your shed and sat in there for hours, waiting to die, sweating like a beast, jumpin' every time I heard a voice. Why didn't you report me, Annie? I was the enemy, sittin' in your backyard.' Eammon asked.

'You weren't the enemy, sitting in the dark, shaking like a train, Eammon. You were just a young boy, a beautiful young boy of nineteen, with fair skin and blond hair. I couldn't call anyone. I had just witnessed somethin' that was terribly wrong. Up until that point, I was detached, unemotional and doing my job. But then I saw what the mob did. T'was horrible and so very wrong. And besides,' Annie added softly 'I was smitten the minute I saw those soft baby-blue eyes.'

Eammon reached over, took Annie's hand, and held it quietly.

'You saved my life that day, Annie.'

'And you saved mine, Eammon. For the first time in my life I felt something besides anger and hatred. I felt love, genuine, silly, uncontrollable love. I was giddy all the time we were apart, you know, laughing to myself for no reason. And when we could steal a few hours together, it was like the war didn't exist. It was just us. You changed me, Eammon. For six months, anyway, I was happy.'

'We certainly took a few chances in the day.'

'We did indeed,' Annie said smiling. 'How did we manage it – you, a British soldier, and me, an IRA bomb girl? God, if they had ever caught us, I would have been tarred and feathered and probably dumped in some remote town, and you would have been tortured mercilessly and then shot in the back of the head.'

'T'is a damn good thing we didn't get caught!' Eammon said, smiling.

'T'is indeed.'

'I'm so sorry things didn't work out for us, Annie.'

'We tried, pet. That's all we could do. T'was not your fault you got deployed back to England on the eve of our escape to Canada. Couldn't be helped. That was our fate, I guess,' Annie remarked sadly.

'I should have tried harder to contact you, Annie. Maybe if I had, we could have tried to run away again, to Canada.'

'Eammon, remember, we promised each other that if we got separated, we were not to try and contact one another. It was far too dangerous, especially for me.'

Eammon shook his head. 'Aye, I do. I suppose you're right. Still, I think about that often, about what our life would have been like if...'

'Eammon, please don't. We can't go back. We can only go forward,' Annie said, her voice starting to give. It was too much emotional stress for the harried woman.

'I am sorry Annie, for that and for this,' Eammon said, waving the iPad. 'I know you didn't feel you had a choice in the matter and you were prepared to go through with it, but it was your brother, after all, your own flesh and blood.'

Unable to control the pain of witnessing her brother's death, Annie started sobbing, throwing Eammon thoroughly off guard. He had known Annie for over two decades, and he had never seen her shed a tear. The tears and the emotional pain were not something Annie had included in her meticulous preparation, either. Eammon took her hand and gently coerced the sobbing woman to his body, stroking her hair and patting her heaving shoulders. It felt good to have Annie in his arms again. He still loved her deeply, after all these lonely years.

'You know what they say, Annie, when one door closes, another one opens,' Eammon said, almost eagerly.

Annie allowed herself a few minutes to be comforted by her long-time friend, but then pulled away. Stoically, Annie shook off the tears and the emotional discomfort. 'Let's get out of here. I need whiskey.'

The mismatched couple headed west, as dozens of police cars and ambulances headed east toward the business park, sirens blaring and lights flashing. Someone had called 911 to report a homicide.

5:20:00

Early the following morning, Maddie woke up to the sound of birds chirping outside the bedroom window. She felt refreshed and relaxed. She and Aidan had retired around 10 pm, shortly after the Bennetts left the cottage. Both men had consumed several pints of Guinness, and Aidan went to bed very drunk. Maddie had never seen him drunk before, and she thought the whole episode was pretty amusing, especially when he tried to remove his clothes before getting into bed.

After a bit of fumbling, Maddie managed to get the big man undressed and tucked into the sheets. He mumbled something to her about wanting to make love and tried to kiss her, but as soon as his head hit the pillow, he passed out completely. Aidan succumbed to the effects of alcohol and exhaustion, and for the first time in weeks, he slept through the night without moving an inch.

Without disturbing her snoring partner, Maddie bounced out of bed, headed straight to the kitchen and made herself a strong cup of coffee. She and Colleen had polished off almost two bottles of wine over the four-hour period, and Maddie was feeling a little foggy. After popping a couple of pills to tame the headache that was fast approaching, she opened her laptop to check her emails, which she had not done in over a week. The boys had each sent a belated message wishing her a nice Thanksgiving. Sofia has also sent an email that contained nothing but question marks. She was about to reply to all her messages, but first went to her Twitter account to scan the early morning headlines and catch up on the news. She scrolled the Canadian news agencies first, then moved to Irish news. The limited characters in Twitter told the story she dreaded to hear: *mass shooting outside of Belfast.* Maddie had almost forgotten about Annie's prophetic comment earlier in the week.

Maddie opened the news story for details. Even before she read the first few sentences, she knew that one of the men found dead was Thomas O'Callaghan. He and John Connolly, a former member of the UPV and notorious gang leader, were both found shot to death inside an empty warehouse in an business park on the outskirts of Belfast.

Two other unidentified men were among the casualties. Maddie opened the video link to the news report of the mass killing. The warehouse property was sealed off with police cars and barricades. The on-camera reporter said very little information was being provided, but the speculation was the mass shooting was premeditated, based on the location and manner of their deaths. The reporter added that both men were sworn enemies and despised one another. Further details would be provided following an investigation.

Maddie immediately thought about Annie. She had no doubt that Aidan's twin was directly implicated in the violent death of her brother Thomas. Annie had been cryptic in her message to Maddie, but she had revealed enough. Maddie's thoughts turned to Aidan. She would have to share this sad news with him at some point in the day, as he would want to contact his mother and Annie, but she was reluctant to wake him. Give him a few hours, Maddie thought. Aidan's mood had changed dramatically since arriving in his home town, and Maddie did not want to bring up any subject, especially his brother, that would dampen his good humor.

While she sat reading her laptop, Aidan had quietly gotten out of bed in search of his fiancée. In spite of a throbbing headache, he was feeling lustful and wanted nothing more than to carry Maddie back to his comfortable bed. Aidan quietly approached the kitchen chair and gently put his hand on Maddie's exposed neck. She flinched ever so slightly at his touch, then placed a reassuring hand on his, all the while reading the laptop screen. He bent to kiss her neck with soft, lapping caresses. Distracted by Aidan's amorous advances, Maddie turned her head slightly to see Aidan's naked torso and his underwear hanging low on his lean hips with an pronounced bulge. Maddie ignored the laptop screen and the disturbing news, and eagerly let Aidan touch her. He moved his hands to her waist and began pulling at her t-shirt. She was naked under the flimsy cotton over-shirt, and her body felt warm and sensuous. He was going to take his time with her, Aidan thought, and enjoy their first lovemaking in his home. His kisses grew more feverish and demanding, and he was about to pull her up and take her to the bedroom when he suddenly froze. His body went completely rigid.

'Aidan, what's wrong?' Maddie asked, sitting back in the chair with naked breasts and looking at her lover's face. He was staring straight ahead at the laptop screen, his green eyes scanning the text of the news report. His surprise turned to anger.

'When were you plannin' on tellin' me this important bit of family news?' he asked harshly, all signs of affectionate gone as spontaneously as it had appeared.

'I just found out seconds before you came in. I was going to tell you...a little later,' Maddie replied. In truth, she wanted to say that she did not want Thomas O'Callaghan, dead or alive, to spoil another minute of their relationship, but refrained from saying anything more.

'I need to call Annie and my mother, to make sure they are okay,' Aidan replied curtly.

'Okay, I'll find my phone.'

The moment was lost, again.

Maddie got up from the chair to let Aidan sit. She went into the bedroom and dressed, then retrieved her cell phone from the night table and gave it to Aidan. She left him alone to make his calls, while she kept busy with making a fire, more coffee, and some breakfast.

Aidan hardly spoke to Maddie the rest of the day, nor did he eat much. He sat at the computer in his tiny office, reading the news reports regarding the quadruple homicide and talking on the phone with his mother. He finally came out of the office early in the evening and promptly went to bed. The following day, he told Maddie about the mass murder, in as much detail as he knew.

'Do they know who set them up, Aidan?' Maddie asked.

'It could have been any number of their 'associates', past and present. Who knows? I don't think anyone in law enforcement or government really cares who did it. I'm sure they are just relieved that both men are died, and this nasty feud can finally be put to rest.'

'What about the funeral? Will we go?'

Aidan shook his head vehemently. 'Annie said to stay away. There's no reason for me to attend, as the family is well represented.'

Maddie noted that Aidan did not say 'we', but 'me' in his answer, and it stung. Was he angry with her for insisting they leave Belfast and return to Clonakilty? His attitude toward Maddie was so unexpected, so cool and detached, as if he was blaming her for Thomas' murder. She didn't know what to say or do. Instead of feeling safe and secure back in Clonakilty as she had hoped, Maddie was beginning to doubt whether the location had any positive impact on Aidan's recovery. Dr. O'Donahue had told her to be patient. The information package he gave her also said that people suffering from PTSD were prone to massive mood swings. Be patient, Maddie told herself, the ship will eventually right itself with time.

5:30:00

The tiny and quaint restaurant were Maddie and Sofia chose to eat dinner was located in the town centre, tucked away in a cobblestone alley in one of the oldest buildings in Clonakilty. It was December, and the entire village, including the restaurant, was festooned with Christmas lights and decorations. Clonakilty looked like a gigantic Christmas ornament, Sofia remarked to her best friend when they drove through town. Every square inch of Pearse Street and Connolly Street was lit up with streams of multi-colored lights. It was a bright and cheerful scene, the antithesis of the somber mood that permeated the stone cottage, high on a hill overlooking the valley.

'It's so good to see you, Maddie! I can't believe I actually made it all the way to, what's this place called again...Clona?' Sofia remarked, as both women waited patiently for their wine to arrive.

'Clonakilty, but the O sounds more like an extended A. You will eventually get it right,' Maddie replied, trying to sound upbeat and positive. 'I can't believe you're here! To think you accepted my invitation, tore yourself away from the hot clime of Brazil to spend the Christmas break with me! I am so happy to finally see you after all this time. I really am. Since the boys were not able to come, I would have found the festive season very lonely without my favorite people. Thanks for making the effort. It means so much to me to have my best friend here,' Maddie added sadly.

'And when am I going to meet the elusive Irishman? The man who stole your heart and made you move so far away?' Sofia asked.

'Soon enough. I wanted to spend some time with you first, before taking you out to the cottage to meet Aidan,' Maddie replied wistfully.

'We always seem to end up eating and drinking in a restaurant, don't we Maddie?'

Maddie smiled sadly and added, 'That's so true. The universal boardroom.'

The waiter arrived with a bottle of French wine and some bread. The two women causally sipped their wine and discussed the enticing menu. Once they ordered their meals, Sofia did not waste any time getting to the point.

'Okay, Maddie, we've known each long enough to finish each other's sentences. Something is wrong, I can tell. In fact, that's why I came. To an outsider, you seem happy enough, but I know something is very wrong. You're so thin. Look at that skirt, it's hanging off your hips. What's going on now that has transformed you from full of life and deeply in love to perpetually worried?'

Maddie nodded her head. She had shared as much as she could with her best friend via email about everything that had happened since she had found Aidan in Belfast. She focused her email letters on Aidan's physical recovery, but didn't talk about his challenges with PTSD, nor about the fate of his family. There was only so much that Maddie could explain in a letter. A few weeks prior to Sofia's arrival, Maddie stopped writing and instead, called her friend and asked her to visit. Sofia had booked her flight immediately to Cork City, Ireland.

'I'm so glad you came, Sofia,' Maddie repeated, taking Sofia hands across the table. 'I've been so lonely since arriving here in October, I really needed to see a familiar face. My only friend here is Colleen, and though she visits me often at the cottage and we run together once or twice a week, she has her own family to take care of, and the construction business is also quite demanding. I can't burden her with my problems. The truth is I spend to many hours alone, even though Aidan and I share a home.'

'You told me in your emails that Aidan was recovering?' Sofia asked, watching her pale and thin friend fiddle with her napkin and stare out the restaurant window, her cheeks so hollow you could plant a tree.

'He is recovering from his physical injuries well enough,' Maddie took a sip of her wine and closed her eyes. She could feel the emotions rising in her throat. 'Mentally, though, he is not only struggling, he is suffering.'

'Suffering? What's going on, Maddie? What happened?' Sofia asked, her voice impatient with concern for her best friend.

Maddie took a deep breath, trying to put her thoughts in order so they wouldn't come out in a disjointed mess.

'Do you remember I told you about Dr. O'Donahue, Aidan's orthopedic doctor? He's been a godsend for us, helping Aidan with his physical recovery. His observations, though, have gone far beyond just the physical side of Aidan's recovery. He confirmed to me that Aidan has classic symptoms of PTSD, post-traumatic stress disorder.'

'Yes, I know what it is. Is this as a result of the car accident?' Sofia asked.

'Yes, and from other trauma that happened to him when he was a young man. You know, he grew up in Belfast, and he and his family struggled. They were caught up in the civil war, and terrible things happened'.

'Oh dear. Is he getting professional help?'

'He went once to see a doctor who specializes in PTSD at the local university hospital, but wouldn't go back again. I don't know why. He won't talk about it. In fact, he doesn't talk much about anything. Dr. O'Donahue has been trying to get him to go for counselling, but Aidan stubbornly refuses to go. You know, on some levels Aidan is doing really well. He's gained some weight, he spends a lot of time walking the beautiful green pastures around here, and sometimes he disappears for hours, usually to the beach. He spends hours hauling rocks to repair the ancient stone fence that surrounds his property. He's doing it all by hand. His fitness is slowly coming back, thanks in large part to all the manual labor he's been doing. The damaged hip is almost healed, and the limp is gone. Dr. O'Donahue is really impressed with his physically recovery.'

'But mentally, emotionally, he is not the same person I knew in Mont-Tremblant.' Maddie stopped talking and watched her best friend eat a full plate of breaded calamari, Sofia's appetite undaunted by the details of Aidan's story. Maddie could not touch her plate of prawns.

'Every day since we arrived in mid-October,' Maddie continued, 'has been a challenge. I never know what kind of day we will have; Aidan is wholly unpredictable. He is easily agitated and often starts yelling over small, simple stuff, stuff that used to make him laugh. Sometimes he walks around the house for hours, restless and impatient, as if he can't decide whether to stay or leave. As soon as his head hits the pillow at night, he has violent flashbacks and wakes up drenched in sweat. Many nights he refuses to go to bed, preferring to watch television all night than confront his memory demons. I have no idea what to do when he gets like that.'

'Oh god Maddie, are you safe?'

'Yes, I am safe. Aidan is not violent with me, but he does get very angry with himself when he struggles with a simple task, like making coffee. Usually he storms out of the cottage and finds refuge in the barn, or he walks down to the beach.'

Maddie took a sip of her wine.

'You know, Sofia, I thought coming back here would help his recovery, but it hasn't. He is reclusive, staying away from all of his long-time friends, with the exception of Michael. He refuses to go out to a pub and meet up with people he's known forever. Weekly pub visits are endemic to life this community.'

'Does he talk to you about what's going on in his head? Is he affectionate? Intimate?' Sofia asked, admiring the entrée that had just been delivered by the waiter.

'No, I told you, he doesn't talk much. The doctor also believes that talking openly and honestly about the car accident and the trauma that happened to him when he was a young boy in Belfast would be helpful in his recovery. But no, he stays silent. He doesn't talk to Michael either, though both of us try to get him to open up. There's always been two sides to Aidan, the deeply personal side and the public side, and they do not ever cross paths. It's a protection mechanism, a survival tool that he has used very effectively since he was eighteen.'

Maddie paused and looked out the window. She watched as a couple walked up and down the cobblestone laneway, wrapped in warm wool coats, hats and scarves, clinging to one another against the cold damp wind. They were laughing, and clearly enjoying the Christmas spirit that was unavoidable and contagious for everyone but the dysfunctional couple living up the road.

'Our love life is almost non-existent, which isn't to say we don't have sex. After a few pints, Aidan will loosen up enough to make love. It's usually quick and sometimes a bit rough. He just wants to get it over with. Though it may be physically satisfying, it's certainly not emotionally satisfying-at least not for me, and I doubt he's getting much out of it, either.'

Sofia rested for a moment, having devoured both the appetizers and most of the entrees. She refilled Maddie's wine glass and hers.

'Do you want to come back to Canada, Maddie, and move on

without him?'

This was a question that had circulated in Maddie's conflicted mind for a several weeks. She was expecting Sofia to ask, as she would if the situation was reversed. If Maddie was not able to help her fiancée through his troubled recovery, and their future together looking very bleak, then what good was it doing for her to stay in a relationship that was not moving forward? While Aidan never spoke about the accident that killed Meghan, Maddie often thought that she may be a hindrance to Aidan's recovery, as she was a constant reminder that he had been rash and selfish in Canada. When she spoke to Dr. O'Donahue about this issue, he reassured her that Aidan was only blaming himself and not her.

'In spite of my concerns about our relationship, I can't leave him now, Sofia,' Maddie answered. 'After everything we've been through, he needs to know that I'm here for him, as he was for me many months ago. I love him. I want to be with him when he finally breaks through this barrier of pain…if he ever does.'

''What are you going to do, Maddie?' Sofia asked.

'I can do nothing but wait patiently for Aidan to accept all that's happened to him and learn trust someone enough to talk openly about these life-defining incidents, not just what happened to him six months ago, but years ago. I am not an expert on the subject, but Dr. O'Donahue told me the PTSD started the day his father died and he buried it, tucked it away, and tried to forget. He's never shared the horrific details of that event with anyone, including his twin sister. He's certainly never shared any of those details with me or Michael, the two closest people in his life. At some point, it will all come crashing down, and my fear is that time is getting very close. Lately, he seems more distant than ever. He goes to a very dark place, locks the door, and won't let me go with him. I fear he will…'

'Don't say or think that, Maddie.'

6:05:00

Michael would not take no for an answer. He insisted that Aidan and Maddie join him and Colleen at a well-known pub in Clonakilty 'to listen to traditional Irish music the way it should be played.' Michael added emphatically to Aidan, 'T'is time, my good man, you shake off the January doldrums and put a smile on your lovely fiancée's face!'

Reluctantly, Aidan agreed to a night out at the Clonakilty Folk Pub, but with some conditions. He agreed to this rare night out on condition that he would not bring his banjo or his guitar, and that Michael would not insist that he sing. He had not played in months, he said, and he wasn't ready to perform. Maddie had asked Aidan about the banjo that was collecting dust in his office, and she asked him to play, but he always found an excuse to say no. He told her he was not in the mood. While Maddie understood his reluctance to play after months of inactivity, it was encouraging to see Aidan agree to finally step out of the confines of the stone cottage and meet a few of his long-time friends and fellow musicians at the Folk Pub.

The Clonakilty Folk Pub not only had a stellar reputation in the community as one of the finest venues for traditional and emerging Irish music, it attracted fans from all over West Cork, Cork City, and beyond. The club had an international following, as musicians from around the globe, from rock stars to balladeers, found their way to the tiny and dark pub at least once in their musical careers. The Club had been providing entertainment for over forty years. Everyone in town found themselves there once or twice a month, due to the variety of concerts and special guests.

The reputation of the pub as an authentic Irish pub certainly captivated the attention of the hordes of tourists who would show up during the summer months, craving a real Irish experience. A trip along the Wild Atlantic Way would not be complete without dropping into the Folk Pub. During the short tourist season, the music and general atmosphere of the pub shifted slightly to suit the well-meaning crowds. Regular musicians often took a break to let the younger musicians fill in and earn some college money. During the damp winter months, though, it was a different story. The pub was meeting place for the heart and soul of Irish traditional music in the area. If you could play an instrument, you joined in. No one, regardless of their musical proficiency, was refused. Each week was a little different than the previous week, which was what made the pub so popular; you never knew what you would get on any given night.

The Folk Pub was located in the heart of the town centre, in an ancient building that was as old as the town itself. The layout of the Pub was a complicated series of crammed spaces, hidden hallways, a small stage, and an outdoor area at the very back. One could enter the pub either at the back or through the front doors. The front of the pub, where the traditional musicians gathered most Monday nights, had never seen a can of paint or a good wash. Low ceilings were held up by thick, blackened beams from decades of firewood, tobacco, and peat smoke. Forgotten traditional musical instruments hung everywhere. Faded posters and playbills were pasted on the walls with dozens of yellowed autographed photos of musicians and bands who had dropped in at some point in their musical lives. The most interesting feature of the cryptic pub was the assortment of chamber pots that decorated one little cozy corner of the pub, next to the roaring fireplace. The seating was inadequate and uncomfortable and comprised of small and large bar stools, each one made of the hardest hard wood. Most people stood huddled in the tiny space no bigger than a modest living room, listening, singing, and clapping, while the musicians were crammed in one corner, oblivious to the limitations of the space, each with a pint of Guinness resting on the wobbly wooden tables. Everyone in the pub knew a song or two, and no prompting was required to break out into a roaring or poetic ballad. Whether the Clonakilty Folk Pub deserved their reputation as the epicentre of traditional Irish music in West Cork was a hotly debated topic of conversation among the neighboring communities.

Maddie was surprised to see the Pub filled to capacity late Monday night, as the two couples walked into the cramped space, moments before the musicians started to play.

As if on cue and well-rehearsed, a hush fell over the crowd when Aidan walked in. He stood awkwardly, looking around the bar in his shirt and pants that still hung loosely on his body, somewhat embarrassed by this recognition. He leaned in toward Maddie for support. Will, the wiry bartender, broke the uneasy silence and yelled out, 'Aidan, my good man, will ya have a pint?' As soon as Aidan replied, 'Indeed I will,' the tiny place erupted in applause and cheers, welcoming the beleaguered man back to his home.

For the next few minutes, a sea of familiar faces gathered around Aidan. Everyone wanted to shake his hand, pat him on the back, or touch him affectionately. One of the more senior members of the musical entourage approached him respectively to tell him he had been sorely missed these past eight months, his deep-set eyes watery with emotion. Another musician, an elderly female singer about half of Aidan's size, burst into tears when she saw him. He walked up to her and hugged the fragile, tiny bird with such care, and he almost started crying himself.

Maddie, as well as Michael and Colleen, shrunk into the background to let Aidan take centre stage and allow the regulars at the Pub to enjoy his homecoming. Maddie watched with fascination as Aidan greeted each and every person by name and asked about their families, their farms, their businesses and school work. Some people asked him if he was back permanently, and he replied he was back for a while. One man asked about his banjo and whether he would be playing, but Aidan replied kindly that he was not quite ready to resume playing. Whether out of respect for Aidan's feelings or simply because it did not matter, not one person in the pub asked him about the accident, his injuries or why he was gone for so long. What was important was that he was back in the 'community' with his family. Maddie had never witnessed anything quite like this reunion, and she was envious. Here was a man who actually made a difference in people's lives, just by being himself. He was that rare human being who was universally liked and remembered by everyone he met. *What a gift he has*, she thought. If she had been having doubts about staying with the surly and unhappy man, they vanished that evening.

6:15:00

Throughout January and February, the cold and windy weather sat in the tiny village of Clonakilty, refusing to budge an inch, and refusing to enlighten its residents with a minute of sunshine. For days it rained and rained, making every inch of the cottage property on the hill slippery and slick. The grass glistened in various shades of perennial green. The stone buildings and rock fencing were covered with a thin layer of moss and mold from the damp drizzle that fell endlessly. While shopping one morning at one of the local meat shops in the town center, Maddie commented on the cold weather to her favorite butcher. He told her that it was unusually cold and wet this winter, which prompted other shoppers to add their thoughts about the dreary weather. The entire conversation lasted over fifteen minutes, to which Maddie proclaimed to Aidan when she returned home that the Irish talk about the weather as much as Canadians do, 'And we talk about the weather all the time!' Aidan just nodded his head.

While Maddie was used to cold weather and snow, having grown up in Montreal, she found the frigid conditions in West Cork an entirely different experience, and one that she had trouble adjusting to. She wore a sweater constantly in the cottage, even though the fireplace glowed all day. Every time she stepped outside, she felt the creeping dampness. Aidan was conscious of how much the damp conditions were uncomfortable for his fiancée, so he dutifully got up early in the morning to make sure the fireplace was stoked and the gas heaters were on in the bathroom and kitchen. Aidan was used to the weather, and he and his injury hip tolerated it very well. He sometimes went out to chop firewood in nothing but a t-shirt and shorts.

Since Christmas and Sofia's short visit, Aidan's mental condition had not improved, nor had it worsened, to Maddie's relief. He was holding his own, Doctor O'Donahue said, and suggested she continue to be patient.

While Aidan flatly refused to seek clinical help for the PTSD, he did spend a lot of time talking to Dr. O'Donahue when he went for his twice monthly visit. The good doctor made a few suggestions to try and get

Aidan to resume his normal activities. He told Aidan to try cycling on a trainer to improve the strength in his legs. He calmly suggested that more sports activity would be good for him. He even went so far as to suggest that he resume swimming, as Aidan would likely be strong enough to start running by the spring. Aidan told Dr. O'Donahue that he was not going back to triathlon racing and refused to consider swimming, though there was a pool not three kilometers from the cottage that was open all day for a lane swim.

Late one afternoon in February, a miracle of sorts finally happened. The low grey stratus clouds that had been hanging over Clonakilty for weeks dissipated, and the reluctant sun finally came through. It was not a hot sun, but it was warmer than it had been. Maddie suggested to Aidan they go for a drive to Long Strand Beach. She'd heard it was a nice place to watch the sunset. If they were lucky, she told Aidan, and the fine weather cooperated, they might see an actual sunset over the Atlantic, something she had yet to witness since arriving in West Cork. Aidan casually reminded Maddie that Irish sunsets were 'underwhelming this time of year', and they would likely not see anything colorful or brilliant. She would be disappointed, he warned her, but he agreed to join her for the short ride.

Maddie used the nicer weather as an excuse to get Aidan out of the house. He had been unusually glum over the last few days, preferring to stay indoors, curled up on the sofa, staring into space, hardly moving. He had taken two steps forward since December, but now he had taken a giant step back. He hardly spoke and ate practically nothing. At night, he woke more frequently, moaning loudly or talking to someone. Maddie was sure that Aidan was arguing with someone; his arms would swing violently and his hands curled up in tight white fists. Maddie moved to the sofa on the nights when Aidan was actively fighting his demons, to avoid getting punched in the face. She kept these episodes to herself because she knew they would only upset him further if he knew.

Aidan seemed be slipping away to another dark world before her eyes. and she could not find a way to break through and help him. She re-read all the information Dr. O'Donahue had given her on PTSD. She went to blogs and chat sites, looking for support and help on how to better assist her tormented fiancée. She was frustrated with his lack of progress, not because of anything he had done, but because of her inability to fix his problem. As resourceful as she was, Aidan was not a bike that could easily be repaired with the right tools and parts. Maddie was growing weary. Her efforts to help him were useless. He seemed was more detached than ever the last few days, emotionally paralyzed and locked in a perpetual loop of reliving the most horrific moments of his life.

She would call Dr. O'Donahue first thing the next morning and arrange to see him. Perhaps he could convince Aidan to finally resume the visits at the PTSD clinic.

At 5 pm, and dressed in warm clothes, the couple set off on the N71 and   Rosscarby toward Long Strand Beach. Just past Lisavaird, they turned left on the R598, and drove along the twisting and turning narrow regional road. At Castlefreek they stopped suddenly, as a farmer was letting his cows cross the road. The cows seemed to be enjoying the warmer temperatures, as they slowly, and with great effort, made their way across, delaying the inevitable trip to the barn for the late afternoon milking. At this time of the year, cars were few and far between. In the summer, this same road would be busy with holiday travellers heading to the beaches for a day of swimming and sunbathing or watching the stars at night.

Once the road was clear, Aidan drove past Long Strand Beach and headed up the hill to a parking and viewing area. They were high on a cliff overlooking the Rosscarby Bay and Cloghna Head, a sheer drop of more 150 feet to the mint-green, swirling Atlantic below. They were alone as they sun began its descent in the western sky.

The startling and contrasting landscape took Maddie's breath away. The soft, rolling hills ended abruptly at the ocean, a sudden and dramatic end, as though a giant had taken a knife and sliced through the rock face with expert precision.

A stone wall edged the parking area, presumably to keep visitors away from the treacherous cliffs. Without a moment's hesitation, Aidan jumped over the low wall and proceeded to walk toward the edge of the cliff, through the tall, thick, light green grass that was partially flattened by the windy weather. From Maddie's perspective, it looked like Aidan was walking toward sure death, but when he turned and beckoned her to join him, she realized that the area sloped down to another, wider patch of grass and a trail that led even further out toward the precipice. Aidan knew his way around the area and confidently walked along the makeshift trail. Maddie did not like heights any more than she liked open water swimming, but she carefully stepped over the fence and followed Aidan, her stomach jumping with each step. She walked a safe distance from the cliff's edge, not venturing anywhere near the drop.

Aidan walked to the furthest point possible along the trail and then stopped to look down. He stood staring at the foaming white blue green water for a long time, not moving or saying anything. Maddie called out to him a few times as she slowly headed toward him, but he didn't hear her. The only sound he could hear was that of the white waves crashing against the dark grey rocks below. He stood looking down at the white swirl, mesmerized by the movement, shifting his feet slightly closer to the sharp edge.

'Aidan, please step back. You know I hate heights. It's making me sick just watching you standing so close to the edge,' Maddie shouted, unable to contain the terror in her voice as she watched he man she loved contemplating jumping to his death.

6:30:00

The tears streamed down her flushed cheeks; gripped with panic, her heart almost pushing itself out of her chest, terrified of what would happen next, Maddie had no choice but to inch herself closer to Aidan and try and stop him from doing the unimaginable. 'Aidan,' Maddie said softly, in a controlled voice, 'I want you to take my hand.'

Those words seemed to have jolted the tormented man from his thoughts of permanently easing the physical pain and banishing the memories of loss and destruction. He took a step back and paused, not taking his eyes off the mesmerizing ocean. It was a hypnotic and calming to watch the foaming water below. For those few moments, Aidan had wanted to immerse himself in the massive body of water and permanently block out the sounds and voices from his past. He had always gravitated toward water. It was his only constant and reliable friend when he needed a safe haven from his troubles.

Instead of jumping, Aidan stepped back from the edge and turned toward Maddie to reach for her hand. Her face was a ghostly white, she was shaking, and she pulled her hand away. He realized that she was terrified that he would push the two of them over the cliff.

'It's okay, Maddie. Don't be afraid. I am not going to jump. At least not today,' Aidan said, the corners of his mouth moving ever so casually into a wry smile. He stepped well back from the edge and put his arm around Maddie's waist to comfort her. 'T'is fine now. I'm better,' was all he said, as the two walked back in silence toward the car.

It was only when they reached the rock wall that Aidan started talking. He didn't stop talking until the sun disappeared in the western sky and they were surrounded by darkness, with only the faint stars and the tiny distant lights of the village below. Aidan had been right – the sunset was nothing memorable – but Maddie hardly noticed.

'I arrived in Dublin on time. Meghan was dutifully waiting for me at the exit. As soon as she saw me, she could see from my face that something was wrong. I guess I looked pretty bad when I arrived, you know, bloodshot eyes, pale. I was dreading seeing her, because all I could think about was you and us. I didn't want to be there. Poor Meghan; I did not have the face of a man anxious to see the love of his life and future wife. She asked a bunch of questions, patient like, but I was in no mood talk. She asked me if I was too tired to drive and I told her yes. Much too tired, I said, and much too distracted, I thought. That innocent offer to drive sealed her fate.'

'As we approached the car in the parkade, though, I remember there was somethin' not right. The doors of the vehicle were unlocked. I gave it no mind at the time, but Meghan always locked her car, it was her habit. She said she found it curious. Anyway, she threw my bag in the boot and we headed out. We were going to stop in Rathcole for tea and a bite. By this time, I had a ranging headache, and I was desperate to send yeh a text, but my bloody phone was completely dead. I was getting more frantic by the second. Meghan had thrown my bag in the back and I didn't have a cable to plug in. She could see I was annoyed, so she gave me hers. She unfastened her seat belt and handed me a cable from her pocket. If she had been wearing her seat belt, she might have survived…it's hard to say,' Aidan added sadly.

The air temperature had fallen in the last hour. Aidan stopped talking and got up from the fence to retrieve a blanket from the trunk of the car. 'Here,' he said, wrapping the wool around Maddie's shoulders. 'No sense in you catching a nasty cold on account of me, now is there?'

'The rest happened so fast, it's all a dark blur. I remember waiting patiently for enough power to send you a message. Meghan was nattering on about stuff, I don't remember exactly. Finally, I had just enough juice to send yeh a text message, but then came a horrible sound, a sound that I had not heard since I was a wean living in Belfast. It was bomb exploding under the front engine of the car. The hood to blew off instantly, shattering the windshield. Meghan immediately lost control of the vehicle, and it was propelled into the lane of an oncoming lorry. I remember seeing the lorry driver swerve his massive truck to avoid a head-on collision, but Meghan got most of the impact. Like a slow-motion video, I can still see her being thrown from the vehicle, through the shattered windshield, and again through the full windshield of the lorry. I was thrust forward and then back violently when we hit the lorry, my hip smashing against the dash, which had broken loose. I think we skidded a few more meters and flipped over. I could hear a second explosion, the gas tank I think; my ears were ringing from impact, and all I could make out were the muffled screams, shrieks, and people yelling all around me. I don't know how long I lay upside down in the vehicle, but at one point it was getting pretty hot. Someone grabbed my jacket and dragged me to safety.'

Maddie said nothing, but held Aidan's hand as he continued to share his story. He wasn't crying, but he kept his head down, looking at the ground instead of at her. It was obvious that talking about what happened was distressing and emotionally painful.

'I was sitting about twenty meters away from the wreck. I could not see much, as my eyes were swollen, but I thought I could hear anguished screams, as though someone were burning alive, but I was told later that Meghan died on impact, so I really don't know. I could clearly hear a swoosh sound coming from the firetrucks. I could see red and yellow blinking lights, and people barking orders from all directions. I finally had the courage to look over at the lorry to see the most horrific scene of my life, more horrific than anythin' I ever saw on recovery missions. The cab of the massive lorry was resting on its side. Meghan's lifeless body had pierced the lorry windshield and the jagged mess of a human body was sprawled through the opening. I can still see her mangled face, and I ask myself, why her and not me? She didn't deserve that…It should have been me. I remember someone was sitting close to me, asking me questions like. I don't remember what I said but woke up weeks later in the hospital with my hip immobilized in traction, a screeching headache, and overcome with dread that I caused Meghan's death.'

Aidan stopped talking now and finally looked up at Maddie, wrapped in warm wool and watching him intently. Maddie was prepared to sit on the stone fence all night and listen to his story. It was a fine night, the first in several weeks. The stars were blinking and not a trace of cloud streaked the night sky. The wind had stopped completely.

'T'is not the first time I've witnessed such horror, you understand,' Aidan continued. 'I've never shared this with anyone, Maddie, not my sister, or my mother or even my best friend. I tried very hard to push it all away and forget what happened, but I know that I've done a terrible disservice to myself by keeping it locked up for all these years.'

'When your Dad died?' Maddie asked quietly.

Aidan nodded his head and looked toward the dark, shimmering ocean, sparkling with the light of some distant stars. 'I went out lookin' for him that night. I could see Da in the distance, walking quickly toward our house. He didn't like to be out past 7 pm, you understand, due to the dangers lurkin' in that part of Belfast. Two men suddenly appeared out of nowhere and shot him twice. I ran as fast I could to catch them, but they scampered away in a waiting car. One of them, that little aberration John Connolly, turned around, and yelled 'That's for your brother Thomas', before he jumped into the car. The man had just shot another human being – I could not understand such depravity in a human being. My Da was doin' nothin but walkin' home. I could hear Da moaning, so I forgot about those thugs and ran back to him. He was drenched in blood from the chest down… his stomach…parts hanging out. T'was gruesome. I put my hand to stop the bleeding, but t'was no use. I felt helpless. He put his feeble hand on mine and spoke but a few words. He said, as clearly as he could, *'You are a good boy; do not let the savagery and inhumanity of Belfast change ya.'* He said, *'Get out of Belfast and make a life for yourself, and never come back. Forget this ever happened, bury it deep away, and move on.'* I was always an obedient son, and I did what my father told me to do. I buried it deep so I would never think about it. But I cannot bury any longer. It haunts me still.'

Aidan wiped his tear-streaked face and turned to look at Maddie.

'When Thomas died, I was actually glad, at least for a time, that he was dead; finally gone, never to inflict pain on anyone again. But now, months later, I just feel sorry for him. He was a victim, too. A victim of circumstance and history. I don't hate him anymore.'

'Maddie, I want to move on and get back to living, but I don't think I can do this by myself, though I've tried very hard these last few months. I think I'm ready to get some help.'

'I think you are too, Aidan. I'm so glad you shared this with me.'

They said nothing for a while; Aidan cradling Maddie in his arms as they gazed out toward the ocean.

'Maddie, I have another request for you. I don't know how you will feel about this one, though?'

'Go ahead. Ask me, Aidan. You are a hard man to refuse.'

'When I'm ready, I'd like to leave here - maybe not for ever, but for a while.'

'Do you want to go somewhere else in Ireland?'

'I like to leave Ireland entirely. I'd like us to move to Mont-Tremblant.'

'Really? I wasn't expecting this at all. You want to leave your beloved Clonakilty, your friends and your business, and move to Canada?'

'Indeed, I do, at least for a time. Clonakilty will always be here for us. T'is time we really begin our journey together. I think we should start at the very place where we met. T'is fitting, don't you think? I will try and avoid a charging deer this time!'

Maddie smiled, remembering the big and burly Irishman sprawled on the ground in the pouring rain. 'Okay. We can move to Mount-Tremblant, or anywhere else you want to go. I will follow you wherever and whenever. You know that.'

'Do you know how much I love you?' Aidan asked, kissing her cold hands.

'No, tell me again. It's been a very long time since I heard you say the nicest three words in the English language!' She replied.

'I love you. I am so fortunate that you didn't give up on me all those months ago. I don't know how or why you stuck it out, but I will never leave you again.' Aidan squeezed Maddie tightly.

His charming and melodic voice, the voice she had heard the first minute she spoke to him in Mont-Tremblant, quietly spoke in her ear: 'Are you ready for a wee bit more adventure, love? Are you ready to marry me now?'

'Indeed, I will, Aidan O'Callaghan,' Maddie answered, without hesitation.

Transition

They arrived back at the cabin early in the evening. The sun was descending behind the Versant Nord Mont-Tremblant. The vibrant sunset colors promised another glorious day in the Laurentian Mountains. Aidan and Maddie gathered their dirty knapsacks and walked to the front door of their rustic log cabin. They could hear the muted sound of Aidan's distinctive cell phone ringing. As soon as they opened the large wooden front door, the ringing stopped. They had both left their electronic devices sitting in the foyer when they left for a seven-day canoe trip to the Lake Temagami region in Northern Ontario.

Glancing at his phone, Aidan examined the screen, and counted ten missed calls from the same number. It was a not a number he recognized, though he knew it was an international exchange, somewhere in the UK, he guessed. Maddie leaned over his shoulder to look at his screen.

'Somebody really wants to talk to you, Aidan. Look at all the missed calls. Do you recognize the number?'

'Not at all. Best I call to find out what's going on.'

Aidan pressed the number, and within a few seconds, he could hear the familiar UK dial tone at the other end. After the third ring, someone picked up.

'Hey, Aidan, finally I've reached you. I was getting worried when you didn't pick up.' The voice on the other end had a strong Liverpool accent. Aidan recognized the voice instantly.

'Will...Will Brown? It's been a while, my friend!'

'Yes, it has. How are you doing? The last time we spoke, you were recovering from a nasty car accident. When was that, exactly?'

'...last year. I am fine now and have recovered, almost 100%. T'is good to hear your voice again, Will. I see yeh've been trying to reach me. Is there some urgent issue that needs my attention?'

'Have you been away the last few days? Have you not seen the news?' Will asked.

'I've been canoeing in a very remote area of Canada...and no, I've not seen the news. Hang on a second.'

He turned to Maddie and asked, 'Can you put the TV on the news channel? There is something going on we should see.'

'Canoeing, you say? I've always wanted to try that. Must find the time soon. Well then, Aidan, I diverge from the business at hand. I will keep this brief and to the point. There has been a massive earthquake in Southeast Asia. I am calling to ask you if you are fit and able enough to come with us to help with the operation. We could really use your help with this one. We are one of a handful of NGOs called in to provide search and rescue. The timing couldn't be worse, as we are seriously short-staff, and this disaster is twice as bad as Nepal.'

'Oh dear. When are you leavin'?' Aidan asked.

'Within hours. I am working on the logistics as we speak. If you agree, I'll make emergency travel arrangements for you from Canada.'

Aidan looked at Maddie as she tinkered with the television, searching the channels for the up to the minute news channel. Her dark red hair was tied in two braids, topped by a sweaty, bright pink polka dot headband. Her clothes were covered in salt stains mixed with mud, and her bare knees were scuffed and bruised from paddling for days. Since leaving Ireland, Maddie had gained back the weight she had lost, and looked healthy and fit in a dirty grey t-shirt that stretched across her ample breasts and firm hips.

She looked as beautiful at that moment as he had ever seen her, Aidan thought. No, he would never leave her again.

'I tell yeh what, Will, I will go, but only if I can bring my wife with me,' Aidan replied.

'Really? I didn't know you were married. Lots has happened since I last saw you last. We need to get caught up.' Will hesitated before accepting Aidan's conditions. For twenty-five years, Will Brown had led numerous humanitarian missions, and he knew, from experience, that bringing a loved one or partner was never a good idea. It distracted the volunteers from their duties, and their presence added a level of unnecessary risk as they were not trained to deal with the harsh and difficult environment. Aidan's request was unusual, as he knew, more than anyone on the Search and Rescue Team, the rules of engagement. This mission was particularly risky. The earthquake was located in a volatile area of a country that was struggling with economic as well as political and religious issues. It was deemed unsafe to travel by both the UK and Canadian Governments, yet the call to provide assistance could not be ignored when thousands of people were counting on aid.

Will replied, 'Well, my friend, this mission won't be easy. It's a very bad situation. It may be dangerous. The earthquake happened in, shall we say, a disputed area. There are some internal conflicts and all the rest. It's complicated. Much to my better judgement, I will agree to your conditions, but only because we can use the extra help. Your wife, is she a strong woman?'

'Indeed, she is,' replied Aidan confidently. 'Maddie can do anythin' she sets her mind to.'

CPSIA information can be obtained
at www.ICGtesting.com
Printed in the USA
LVOW07s0747050118

561939LV00001B/250/P